THE ALL-SEEING EYE

MARK MORRIS

Hellboy created by Mike Mignola

Dark Horse Books®
Milwaukie

Book design by Krystal Hennes
Cover design by Lia Ribacchi
Cover illustration by Mike Mignola
Front cover color by Dave Stewart

Published by Dark Horse Books
A division of Dark Horse Comics
10956 SE Main Street
Milwaukie, OR 97222

darkhorse.com

Library of Congress Cataloging-in-Publication Data on file.

First Dark Horse Books Edition: October 2008
ISBN 978-1-59582-142-3

Printed in the United States of America

10 9 8 7 6 5 4 3 2 1

HELLBOY ™

OTHER HELLBOY BOOKS FROM DARK HORSE BOOKS

Hellboy:

Seed of Destruction (with John Byrne)

Wake the Devil

The Chained Coffin and Others

The Right Hand of Doom

Conqueror Worm

Strange Places

The Troll Witch and Others

Darkness Calls

Hellboy: Weird Tales Vol. 1

Hellboy: Weird Tales Vol. 2

Hellboy Junior

Hellboy: Odd Jobs

Hellboy: Odder Jobs

Hellboy: Oddest Jobs

Hellboy: Emerald Hell

Hellboy II: The Golden Army

B.P.R.D.:

Hollow Earth & Other Stories

The Soul of Venice & Other Stories

Plague of Frogs

The Dead

The Black Flame

The Universal Machine

The Garden of Souls

The Art of Hellboy

The Hellboy Companion

Hellboy: The Art of the Movie

Hellboy II: The Golden Army—The Art of the Movie

 PROLOGUE

Finsbury Park tube station, London, England
Sunday, October 21st, 11:45 p.m.

"You know what Finsbury Park is backwards, don't you?" Lee said, hoping to make her smile. When she didn't respond, he said, "It's crappy-rub-sniff, innit?" and he laughed loudly, evidently encouraging her to do the same.

Jo, however, was having none of it. She had moved across to the next row of seats and was sitting with her body turned away from him, arms tightly folded beneath her plumped-up cleavage, grinding gum between her teeth. With her long blond hair and big blue eyes, she was drop-dead gorgeous, but she could be a hard-faced bitch when someone—and that someone was usually Lee—pissed her off.

"Get lost, Lee," she said without looking at him.

"Aw, c'mon, babe," he wheedled, alcohol slurring his words. "Y'know it's only because I love ya."

They were alone on the platform, waiting for a Victoria line train to Walthamstow Central. Their night out had followed what was becoming a depressingly familiar pattern: down to the pub; one drink too many; a blazing row.

The way Lee saw it, it was all Jo's fault. A few drinks and she was pushing out her chest, giving other guys the eye, peppering her conversation with lewd remarks. How was he *supposed* to react when she behaved like that? Hell, sometimes she'd even sit on other blokes' laps and plant smeary lipstick kisses on their cheeks. Then afterwards she'd claim it was all "just a bit of fun."

For her part, Jo was becoming sick of Lee's possessiveness. In her opinion there was nothing wrong with a bit of harmless flirting. Lee had been a great guy at first—funny, sexy, open minded, relaxed. But since she'd moved out of her parents' house and into his flat six months ago, he'd changed. Now she felt suffocated by him. She couldn't even smile at another guy these days without him jumping down her throat.

"If you loved me you'd trust me," she would tell him.

"I *do* love you!" he'd say.

"Yeah, sounds like it."

"I *do!* I've never felt this way about anyone before. That's why it drives me mental, seeing you with other blokes."

"I'm not *with* them, Lee," she would tut, tossing her blond hair, "I'm with you. It's not like I'm gonna shag 'em up the alley."

He'd wince and clench his teeth. "Babe, don't even *joke* about that."

"See what I mean? I can't handle this. You're stifling me. I'm a friendly person. I like talking to people."

"I don't mind you *talking* to people," he would say, "but you take it too far. You give blokes the come-on."

"Not seriously."

"Yeah, well . . . they might not see it like that."

The memory of all the times they had had this conversation, or variations on it, made her sigh. She still hadn't looked at him, was still facing the black throat of the tube tunnel. She hated tube stations late at night: the curved walls covered in tiles the color of old peoples' teeth; the echoes; the rubbish; the lingering odor of sweat and piss and vomit. It was like sitting inside a giant public toilet. It was bleak and depressing, and sometimes it was enough to make her wonder whether this was what the rest of her life would be defined by.

"I'm sorry, babe," Lee mumbled. "I *do* love ya, y'know."

She could tell by his voice that his body was now succumbing to the alcohol which had earlier filled him with fire. In ten minutes he'd be slumped against her on the train, snoring and drooling. When they got to Walthamstow she'd have to slap him awake, and as soon as they got back to the flat he'd collapse face down on the bed, and she'd untie his boots and pull off his smelly socks. Then he'd start to snore, and she'd leave him to it and sleep on the pull-out sofa. And tomorrow he'd wake up with a hangover and blunder off to work, and the whole endless cycle would start again . . .

She saw it all in a flash, and it was horrifying. It made her feel sick to her soul.

Yeah, well, I don't love you, she thought viciously in response to his words, surprising herself.

Was it the truth? Had she really fallen out of love with Lee? Staring into the tube tunnel, listening to the rumble of distant trains, she wondered whether this was the end of the line for them both.

Her thoughts were interrupted by a rustling sound coming from deep inside the tunnel. Jo stared into the blackness, folding her arms more tightly as a shiver rippled through her. Were there tiny glints of light in the darkness, close to the ground? Seconds later she leaped to her feet in revulsion.

A bristling wave of rats and mice emerged from the darkness and streamed along the base of the rail-well, as if fleeing for their lives.

"Lee!" Jo yelled, her voice bouncing off the tiled walls. "Lee!"

She was instantly and instinctively repulsed by the creatures' black, glittering eyes, their sleek little bodies, their pink, wormy tails. Even though none of the rodents showed the least interest in her, she leaped up onto her plastic chair like the maid in a *Tom and Jerry* cartoon.

"*Lee!*" she yelled again, angry now. She had no idea what she expected him to do, but she didn't see why she should have to face the flood of vile creatures alone. She turned, and was infuriated to see him dozing drunkenly, oblivious to his surroundings.

The flood of rodents continued for perhaps twenty seconds. By the time their numbers began to dwindle, Jo reckoned she must have seen dozens, if not hundreds, stream past. The experience left her with a dry mouth, a queasy stomach, and a rapidly pumping heart. Though the creatures had paid her no attention whatsoever, she shuddered with reaction. In the sudden silence she told herself she was being a wuss—and yet it still took a gargantuan effort of will to climb down from her perch.

It was only as the soles of her red slip-ons made contact with the gritty floor that it occurred to her to wonder what the rodents had been running *from*. An approaching train? Unlikely. Rats and mice weren't generally given to such behavior. Added to which, the digital display was announcing they still had another four minutes to wait before the next train was due.

So, if not a train, what then? The vile little things had been spooked by *something*. Something bigger than themselves? An animal?

Jo stared nervously into the pitch-black tunnel, suddenly remembering movies where people had been attacked by nasties on the underground. There'd been the one with the werewolf, and the one with the mutant cannibals who lived in the abandoned tube station, and the one with the giant spiders—or was that a TV show?

Licking her lips with a sandpaper tongue, she wondered whether, just this once, the two of them should head back to the surface and treat themselves to a cab.

She backed towards Lee's slumped form, keeping her eyes on the tunnel entrance the whole time, and jabbed him in the shoulder. "Lee," she hissed, "wake up."

He stirred and groaned—and at that moment a sound echoed out of the tunnel. It was a sharp scraping sound, and it caused an immediate and vivid image to leap into Jo's head. She imagined a series of metal blades—or perhaps a set of huge taloned claws—being dragged across rough brick.

Her throat seized up. She tried to speak Lee's name again, but only a rasping wheeze emerged. She shook him roughly, and then, when he did no more than offer an incoherent mumble, punched his arm as hard as she could.

"Wassup?" he muttered, scowling. "Whayadoon?"

She licked her lips, cleared her throat. "Wake up," she croaked. "Wake up, you sod. There's something in the tunnel."

Another scrape. Closer now. Pummeling her drunken boy-friend again, Jo stared into the darkness.

Could she see something in the tunnel mouth? Something moving? A shape? A shadow? Instinctively she circled Lee's body so that he was between her and the tunnel.

She saw a glint in the darkness. A gleam of light reflecting off a shiny surface. *Oh God*, she thought, *it is a knife. There's someone in the tunnel with a big sodding knife!*

But then she saw that there was not one glint of light but two. Close together. Hovering in the blackness at the mouth of the tunnel.

Eyes, she suddenly realized. *They're eyes*. Someone was stand-ing just beyond the band of light at the tunnel entrance, watching her. Jo was terrified, but adrenaline was making her angry, too. She cleared her dry throat, forced her rusty voice into use.

"Who's there? What do you want?"

There was no reply, merely the sound of what she could only imagine was something shifting in the shadows. But it wasn't the kind of sound a fleshy creature would make. This was a harsh sound. Gritty. Unyielding. Like rock on rock.

Trying to hold her voice steady, Jo said, "I know you're there. There's no point hiding."

Maybe it—whatever "it" was—didn't understand her. She gave Lee another shake. "Come on, you prat," she muttered, "we need to get out of here."

There was a sudden squealing clatter of movement from the tunnel. Jo's head jerked up. She saw the yellowish glints of light rise a meter or more into the air. Which meant they couldn't possibly be eyes, because they were now three meters from the ground.

She was still trying to work out what the "eyes" were when the thing came out of the tunnel. First, something that resembled the clawed scoop of a digger, albeit black as coal and barnacled as a sea wall, emerged from the shadows and curled around the edge of the tunnel opening. This was followed by the squealing grind of tortured rock or metal, and then the rest of the body hauled itself into the light.

Jo's mouth dropped open. Abruptly she wet herself. She was half aware of her mind frantically telling her that what she was seeing was impossible.

The thing crouching in the rail-well was crudely humanoid, albeit massive and twisted. It seemed to be composed of clusters of jagged black crystals, all of which were cemented together with rough, spiny lumps of oily rock. The thing's face was a slablike mask, its mouth a yawning, crooked hollow. Jo couldn't avert her gaze from its eyes, which were burning lumps of molten lava—pitiless and inhuman, but blazingly alive.

The monstrous figure ducked through the tunnel opening and straightened up with the crunch of shifting rock. Jo reached out and grabbed a handful of Lee's jacket. She shook it almost subconsciously, still gazing at the behemoth. *Wake up*, she mouthed. *Wake up.*

As though it could hear her silent words, the thing tilted its massive head towards her. When it lifted one vast clawed foot to step up onto the platform, Jo ran.

**British Medical Association, Tavistock Square, London, England
Monday, October 22nd, 8:16 a.m.**

The meeting of the Medical Ethics Committee was scheduled for ten thirty a.m., which gave Kirsty plenty of time. She knew Darren found it endearing that she often left home much earlier than she had to, but he was a guy who thrived on crisis management. He actually got a buzz from leaving things to the last minute.

Not Kirsty. She liked to be organized and prepared. And if that meant sacrificing some of her "quality time" at home, then so be it. Getting to work early meant she could have everything set out in the Council Chamber—briefing notes, stationery, refreshments, audio/visual equipment—by nine-fifteen at the latest. That would give her time for a coffee and a few leisurely minutes of small talk with her arriving colleagues, before catching up on paperwork left over from Friday and e-mails that had stacked up over the weekend.

She knew that if she and Darren ever took the plunge and moved in together, their different attitudes to time management, and indeed to the way they ran their lives in general, was something they would have to address. She half suspected his chaotic nature was one of the main things she found attractive about him, but how that would work long-term she wasn't sure. Her hope was that their different natures would complement one another, but her niggling worry was that they might very quickly drive each other round the bend. Much as Kirsty found Darren's recklessness exhilarating, at heart she was a list maker, a five-year-plan sort of girl. She couldn't cope with instability. She liked to know not only *where* she was going, but exactly *how* she was going to get there.

BMA House was an impressive building, beautiful even. It was neoclassical Palladian in style (its designer, Sir Edwin Lutyens, had described it as "Wrenaissance" in deference to Sir Christopher), and in the sunlight the Portland stone and red-brick façade gleamed like new.

Not only was the sun shining on this October day, but it was also unseasonably warm. Sporting large brown sunglasses, a cream cotton suit and pale-green blouse, Kirsty felt elegant, sophisticated, as she stepped from the car. All she needed was a wide-brimmed sun hat and she fancied she'd resemble one of those willowy diplomats' wives from back in the day when Britain had an empire. She could see herself surveying the Serengeti plains with a cocktail in her right hand, or strolling through the markets of New Delhi.

"Morning, Miss Reece," said Adam, the doorman, after buzzing her in. She always liked the way he tipped the brim of his cap with his forefinger—ironic but playful, as if he was acknowledging that he looked like a performing monkey but was happy to share the joke. He was a beautiful, angular man with a smoothly shaven head and a tuft of dark hair, too slight to be termed a goatee, beneath his bottom lip. At weekends he attended fetish clubs with his statuesque girlfriend, Helda.

Kirsty's feet clacked on the marble floor as she approached the Great Hall. Her first task was to collect the agenda and handouts for that morning's meeting, which she had left carefully stacked on the chairman of the Medical Ethics Committee's desk before heading off for the weekend.

The Great Hall was a magnificent room. One hundred and thirty feet in length, it had been converted into the main library in the mid-1980s. The high ceiling was supported by rows of peacock-blue marble columns, and the various committee rooms occupying the roof space were accessed by a number of elegant spiral staircases. Redolent with the delicious musk of old books, the vast room was nevertheless bright and airy. Kirsty loved it, particularly at this hour of the morning, when it was still and empty, the air languid and somehow expectant.

Halfway up the central aisle she turned left, between bookshelves so high that each was equipped with its own set of ladders and browsing platforms. She climbed the staircase at the end of the row, her feet clanging softly on the iron steps. A door at the top led into a long, plushly carpeted corridor with paneled doors on both sides. The room Kirsty wanted was just over halfway up on the right. She strolled towards it unhurriedly, unsnapping her black leather shoulder bag and delving for her keys.

There was no indication that anyone had been here before her, nothing to alert her to the foul discovery she was about to make. When she unlocked the door and entered the office, she did so with no sense of foreboding whatsoever.

For several seconds after clapping her eyes on the thing propped in the chair behind the wide oaken expanse of the chairman's desk—the desk on which were still stacked the papers she had come to collect—she could only stare in disbelief, her mind momentarily blanked by the sheer impossible awfulness of what she was seeing.

It was a naked human body. Or rather, a naked human *torso*, from which the head and limbs had been removed. Surprisingly there was no blood. The exposed meat of the ragged stumps was a dark salami-pink and relatively dry.

Before her legs gave way and she started to scream, Kirsty registered two additional details. One was that the torso was male, albeit almost hairless aside from a few wiry tufts around the blue-gray nipples, and the other was that it bore a fuzzy blue tattoo of a hovering hummingbird just above its left breast.

John Saxilby Funeral Services, Shoreditch High Street, London, England
Monday, October 22nd, 10:41 a.m.

That nice Mr. Saxilby had made a lovely job of Arthur. Lying in his coffin in his best suit, Flo couldn't remember when she had last seen him looking so well. There was a bloom to his cheeks, and a serene expression on his face. He even looked as though he'd put on a bit of weight.

In the back of her mind, however, Flo knew that none of it was real. It was all the result of carefully applied makeup and morticians' putty. But it made her feel a bit better nonetheless. It leavened the memory of her beloved Arthur's final days in the hospital. And when it came right down to it, surely that was all that mattered.

Fifty-three years she and Arthur had been married. Sitting on a chair next to her husband's coffin in the Chapel of Rest, Flo recalled her wedding as if it were yesterday. It had been a bright day, but windy. Her veil had flapped around her head as if it had a life of its own. Her dear old dad, a chubby giant of a man, had clutched her little hand in his great paw and had sobbed in the car all the way to the church.

Dad had been the local butcher, and the neighborhood kids had been scared of him with his bald head and his bloodstained apron, but he'd been as soft as a brush. Flo and her mother had always had the ability to twist him round their little fingers. And perhaps best of all, he'd adored Arthur. To Flo's delight, the two most important men in her life had got on like a house on fire.

A solitary tear wormed its way down Flo's wrinkled cheek as she pictured Arthur on that late-spring day fifty-three years before. He had half turned towards her as she'd walked down the aisle, and he had looked so proud and happy and handsome, tall and lean in his best demob suit, his black hair gleaming with oil. He had smiled at her and winked, and his apparent confidence had stilled the butterflies in her stomach. Later he had confessed, in the privacy of their hotel's honeymoon suite, that he had spent the day feeling like a rabbit in the headlights. How they had laughed as they had munched on a plate of chicken sandwiches, glad after the emotional whirlwind of the day to finally have some time alone together.

They had had their ups and downs like everyone else, but over-all theirs had been a happy life. They had never been rich or fa-mous, never done half the things they had said they were going to do, or been to half the places they had said they were going to go. But they had had a lovely home, and two children they could truly be proud of, and every night they had had food on the table. And they had laughed, and they had loved, and they had never run out of things to say to each other.

And now it was over. Arthur was gone. It was the end of a life extraordinary to no one but himself—and of course to those who had loved him.

Flo was almost surprised to find that the tears were flowing freely now. As her vision blurred she reached for the handkerchief that she'd tucked up the sleeve of her cardigan. She dried her eyes and blew her nose, hoping Mr. Saxilby wouldn't choose that mo-ment to poke his head round the door. No doubt he had witnessed grief in every shape and form over the years, but none of that meant a jot to Flo. She had always hated people seeing her upset. It made her feel weak, naked. That came from her mother. Although he had been the breadwinner, her dad had always been the blub-bering baby of the family.

"We women are the strong ones, Flo," her mother used to tell her. "Stiff upper lip of the empire we are. The real power behind the throne." Then she would tap the side of her nose and wink. "But don't go telling the fellers. Best-kept secret in England."

Flo wasn't quite the matriarch her mother had been, but she had inherited a little of her steel. Eyes dry, tears under control, she stood up and leaned forward over the coffin to give Arthur a final kiss.

Her lips were less than an inch from his unnaturally rosy cheek when he opened his eyes.

With a cry of alarm, Flo reared back, the sudden movement making her momentarily dizzy. Her first thought was that this was some involuntary reaction. Poor Arthur's muscles must be slackening

as he . . . as time passed, and the slight movement as she rested her
weight on the side of the coffin must have been enough to cause his
eyelids to spring apart like faulty shutters.

But even as she was thinking this he slowly raised his hands
and gripped both sides of the coffin. Flo watched in astonishment
as Arthur, his face slack and expressionless, struggled to sit up.

He's still alive, after all! That was her first joyous response. Almost
immediately, however, reality kicked in. Although Flo didn't know
the full procedure for preserving a body after death, she did know
enough to realize that Arthur's resurrection was an impossibility.

They drained the body of blood, didn't they? They drained it of
blood and filled the veins with formaldehyde. And hadn't she read
somewhere that they took out the brain and packed the skull cavity
with newspaper? That might have been a myth, but one thing she
was certain of was that Arthur had had a postmortem, and she had
never heard of anyone surviving one of those!

She watched in fascination as her late husband slowly sat up.
She wasn't scared, not yet anyway. What was happening was so unreal that she felt slightly detached from it. Besides, her Arthur had
never given her cause to be afraid of him, and she saw no reason
why he should start to do so now. She stepped forward, reaching
out as if to help him from the coffin (he had become awfully un-
steady on his pins over the past year or so) when the door behind
her burst open.

Flo turned. Nigel, who at twenty-one was the youngest of the
Saxilbys, was standing there, all of a fluster. His ears were red, his
eyes were wide and his lips were quivering, as if he were about to
cry. He looked at Arthur in abject horror, which Flo found a bit
insulting. As if she weren't even in the room, he turned back to the
open door behind him and shouted in a shrill and chalky voice,
"Here too, Dad!"

Arthur had now succeeded in swinging one leg clear of the
coffin and was probing uncertainly at the floor with the toe of his

gleaming right shoe. Instinctively Flo moved forward again, worried that her dead husband was about to fall flat on his face.

"*What are you doing?*" Nigel Saxilby all but screamed, making a grab for her.

Flo snapped a look at him. "I'm going to help my husband."

Nigel's neck, swelling out of the collar of his crisp white shirt, was as ruddy as his ears. "But he's dead!"

"I'm perfectly aware of that, thank you," Flo said tightly, "but I really don't see what that's got to do with anything."

Nigel goggled at her. His mouth opened and closed soundlessly. Finally he spluttered, "They've all come alive, Mrs. Jackson. The dead are walking."

Flo was not entirely sure how to respond. To be honest, she was a bit out of her depth—although, looking at Nigel, she could see she wasn't the only one.

Faced with something she didn't understand, she did what she had always done over the years—she pushed it aside. The bigger picture was not her concern, after all. Shaking her head, she said, "I don't know anything about that. All I know is that my Arthur needs me."

She half stepped towards her husband again, who had now managed to plant one foot on the floor and was attempting to lift his other leg clear of the high-sided box. Nigel, however, grabbed her wrist tightly enough to make her wince.

"How dare you! Let go of me!" she ordered.

"Sorry, Mrs. Jackson," Nigel said, looking as though he truly meant it, "but . . . he might be dangerous."

"*Dangerous?*" echoed Flo. "My Arthur?"

Nigel cast a look that was both wary and anguished towards the dead man. "Well . . . yes," he said. "I know this is all a bit mad, but . . . haven't you seen any zombie movies?"

Unable to trust herself to utter a civil reply, Flo stayed silent for a few moments. She took a deep breath and finally said primly, "I can't say I have. It's not really my sort of thing."

"They eat brains, Mrs. Jackson," Nigel said miserably.

"Who do?"

"The zombies. The dead. When they come back."

"I see," she said. "And that's what you think my Arthur's going to do, is it?"

"Well . . . he might."

She stared at him. In a quiet but imperious voice, she said, "What utter piffle. Now will you kindly let go of me."

Nigel looked down at his hand encircling her bony wrist almost with surprise. His fingers sprang apart.

"Thank you," she said, resisting the urge to rub the aching bones, then turned her back, dismissing him. She walked across to Arthur and took his flailing arm. He was still balancing on one leg, trying to drag his other from the silk-lined box in which he had been expected to remain until his cremation.

Arthur did not acknowledge Flo, but neither did he attack her, as Nigel had warned her he might. Instead the dead man simply ignored her. He seemed completely unaware of his wife's presence, of her hand on his arm. If he had some sinister motive for climbing out of his coffin, he gave no indication of what it might be. He appeared to be moving simply because, suddenly and inexplicably, he could.

Indeed, Flo couldn't help but think that her husband's actions were instinctive, almost mindless. Certainly when she looked into his glazed and slightly shriveled eyes she saw no spark of intelligence or recognition or awareness there. Arthur now appeared to be nothing more than animated meat, and the realization of this saddened her so much that she felt like weeping. There was no miracle to be found here, no dignity. On the contrary, it was awful and degrading and pointless.

Even so, she talked to her husband, coaxed him, encouraged him. "Come on, dear," she murmured. "That's it, best foot forward."

Under Nigel Saxilby's silent but horrified scrutiny, she helped Arthur clamber from his coffin and totter about the room. He did not lean on her, but she was conscious of his dead weight nonetheless, of the puppetlike heftiness of him, of his stale, slightly chemical odor.

After wandering aimlessly around the room for several minutes, Arthur—whether by accident or design—blundered out of the door and into the corridor. Flo escorted her husband as he ambled like a sleepy drunk towards the front of the building. In front of them, sunlight angled through the stained-glass windows framing the oak front door, filling the wide hallway with pools and beams of rainbow light.

"Where are we going now?" Flo said in hushed, bright tones, as though to a timid child. "Are you showing me the pretty colors?"

A door opened to the right of the front door, and then quickly closed again behind the man who emerged from it. This was Mr. Saxilby senior, portly and bespectacled, a streak of gray in the swept-back fringe of his otherwise black hair. He was wearing a maroon waistcoat over a white shirt and crisply ironed black trousers. He looked pale but composed, as he glanced first at Arthur and then at Flo.

"Oh dear," he said. "I'm most awfully sorry about this, Mrs. Jackson. It's an unprecedented event, believe me."

"I'm sure it's not your fault, Mr. Saxilby," Flo replied. She glanced back at Nigel, who was hovering behind her, and couldn't help adding, "My Arthur's not doing anyone any harm, as you can see. He just seems to want to . . . go for a little walk."

"As does the late Mr. Hayes," said Mr. Saxilby, indicating a door on the opposite side of the corridor, from behind which could clearly be heard the blundering thump of movement.

"What's making them do it, do you think?" Flo asked, but Mr. Saxilby shook his head.

"I've no idea, Mrs. Jackson."

His attempt at a reassuring smile emerged as a ghastly grimace, and in that instant Flo knew exactly what the undertaker was thinking.

He was wondering, as she was, what would happen if *all* the dead people in the world had suddenly come alive and started walking about. The police or the army would have to go out and round them all up, she supposed. But where would they put them? In prison? In hospitals?

Her mind boggled at the prospect of it. It was terrifying to consider what a world where the dead refused to lie down would be like.

"What—" she began, and then Arthur collapsed, simply fell to the floor like a dead weight. Flo cried out as he landed on his face, his head hitting the floorboards with a crack. In the room across the corridor she heard a thump as Mr. Hayes presumably hit the deck, too.

For several seconds she, Mr. Saxilby senior, and Nigel simply stood, looking down at Arthur, half expecting him to twitch back into life.

But he didn't. He just lay there, looking as dead as could be, his limbs floppy as a rag doll's, his face flat against the floorboards.

"Is he . . ." Flo began, and then found she couldn't choke the rest of the sentence past the obstruction in her throat.

"I hope so," Mr. Saxilby murmured, then realized what he had said and hastily added, "Beg your pardon, Mrs. Jackson. No offense intended."

Flo cleared her throat. "None taken," she said firmly. "What just happened . . . well, it wasn't right, was it? The dead should stay dead."

"Amen to that," Nigel said fervently.

Bartle Road, Notting Hill, London, England
Monday, October 22nd, 11:20 a.m.

"That's it, son. Get it all up. Better out than in."

Sergeant Wormley stepped back smartly as PC Firth's retching finally resulted in an almighty fountain of vomit. He glanced around to make sure he and the rookie weren't being observed by the knot of curious onlookers gathered outside the unassuming semidetached house on Bartle Road. Wormley was an old-school copper, and had always had great faith and pride in the integrity and professionalism of the London bobby. In his opinion it wouldn't do to have the city's finest looking anything other than calm and capable.

Not that he blamed the lad. First time he'd seen a bad 'un to match this he'd chucked his guts up too. Dead junkie his had been, whose remains had lain undiscovered in his filthy flat for nearly a week. The body had been bloated, the flesh black and slimy like old banana skins. Worse, though, had been the stench and the teeming maggots. Wormley had thrown up so violently he'd thought his stomach was about to turn inside out. He'd barely been able to sleep for the next week. Every time he'd closed his eyes he'd seen maggots writhing in the dead man's empty eye sockets and in the gaping cavity of his mouth.

He patted the back of the young lad, who was bent over double beside him. Having puked into the bushes which screened them, Firth was now spitting out the remainder of his regurgitated breakfast. Finally he straightened up, sniffing, his face pale and sweaty.

"Sorry about that, sarge," he said. "I feel a right numpty."

"Nothing to apologize for, son. Happens to the best of us."

"Bet it's never happened to you," Firth said ruefully.

"Oh yes it has. Man who doesn't react like you did the first time . . . well, there's something wrong with him, I reckon. Human nature, isn't it? Shows you care. *You* might think it's a sign of weakness, but *I* think it's the sign of a good copper."

"The lads'll still take the piss out of me when I get back," Firth said.

"Let 'em. That's part of the process too. Bit of ribbing, bit of humor . . . it's a release valve, isn't it? It's how we cope."

Firth took a deep breath. He was recovering now, a little color seeping back into his cheeks.

"Feeling better?"

The young PC nodded.

"Good lad," said Wormley.

"So what do you reckon about this one, sarge? Gangland killing?"

Wormley shrugged. "Could be. Though it's a bit over the top taking the arms and legs as well as the head. Usually it's just head and hands."

"Maybe the victim had tattoos or scars. Something easily identifiable."

Wormley smiled. The boy was smart. He was always asking questions, always offering ideas.

"Why dump the body in a suburban garden, though? No attempt at concealment?"

Firth frowned. "Maybe the killers panicked? Maybe they thought someone was on to them? Or maybe they wanted the body found—as a warning to others, something like that."

"All possible," Wormley said noncommittally.

"But you don't believe it?"

Wormley smiled. "Now, I didn't say that, did I?"

"I can tell by your face," Firth said, smiling back.

Wormley chuckled. "Let's just say I've got access to the bigger picture."

"So what bigger picture's that then, sarge?" Firth asked. "Or is it privileged information?"

"Maybe it *is* privileged information," Wormley said blandly, "but as far as you and I are concerned, I haven't been *told* it's privileged. Which don't mean to say you can go blabbing it to all and sundry."

Firth mimed pulling a zip across his mouth. "My lips are sealed."

Wormley nodded in the vague direction of the taped-off house, which in the past hour had become a hive of police activity. "What

THE ALL-SEEING EYE 23

if I were to tell you that headless Harry over there is not the first torso found today?"

Firth raised his eyebrows. "I'd say . . . how many we talking about here, sarge?"

"Three," Wormley said. "All different locations."

"Close by?"

"Relatively. The other two were Fleet Street and Tavistock Square."

"All north of the river then," said Firth, "and in a rough line."

Wormley said nothing. He could see that the lad was thinking it through. He wanted to see what Firth came up with before he dropped his bombshell.

"Busy public places," Firth mused, "not suburban like this. Were the other bodies out in the open, sarge?"

Wormley felt like applauding. "Good question, son. *Excellent* question. Because that's the thing, you see. The bodies *weren't* out in the open. Not like this one. They were found in unlikely places. Impossible places."

"Impossible how?"

"Secure establishments. Locked offices. The one in Tavistock Square was in the headquarters of the British Medical Association."

Firth raised his eyebrows. "And the other one?"

"Inside the premises of the *Dundee Courier*. And get this—it was a woman's body."

"A woman?" Firth blanched.

"Which makes the gangland theory a bit less likely, wouldn't you say?"

"Hmm." Again Wormley could almost see the cogs whirring in the younger man's head. Finally Firth said, "Less likely, but still not impossible."

"Not impossible, no," Wormley agreed.

Firth sighed. "So what's *your* theory, sarge? What have we got here? Gang war or serial killer?"

"What *I* think we've got," Wormley said, "is a hell of a bleedin' mystery."

"Options open, eh?" Firth said.

"Always," said Wormley.

Firth glanced over towards the cordoned-off house and fortified himself with another deep breath. "Shall we rejoin the party?" he suggested.

Wormley nodded. "Why not?"

☠ CHAPTER 1

"Damn fire-worm," muttered Hellboy, shifting in his seat.

"Still hurts, does it?" asked Liz, keeping a straight face.

The scowl he turned on her had caused lesser men to dissolve into quivering mounds of jelly, but Liz was unmoved. In fact, her lips squirmed as she fought a losing battle to keep her humor contained. If his butt hadn't been stinging so damn much, Hellboy would have relished her childlike glee. A part of him still did, despite the fact it was at the expense of his own comfort.

It was a constant weight in his big old heart that Liz, one of the few people he cared about most in the world, smiled about as much as she slept—which was hardly ever. Amazing then that her face remained remarkably unlined for a woman in her thirties. What stopped her from looking truly young, though, were her haunted eyes, and the great dark crescents beneath them. Hellboy had seen men cast admiring glances towards Liz's trim, athletic figure, only to flinch when she turned the bruised intensity of her gaze on them.

Now, however, she *was* smiling, and it transformed her. Hellboy had to employ all his willpower to stop himself smiling back. Maintaining his frown with an effort, he growled, "I'll live."

"Maybe there's some kind of cream you can use? A scorched-butt ointment?" she suggested innocently.

"You're walking a thin line, Liz," Hellboy said, though he couldn't *quite* make it sound convincing.

Liz laughed and reached up to pinch a great slab of his red cheek between her dainty thumb and forefinger. "Aw, you're so cute when your pride is wounded," she said.

"And it's getting thinner all the time," he muttered.

Liz was about the only person in the world whom he'd allow to treat him like that. Damn, she was the only person in the world who would *dare* to treat him like that.

Sitting a few seats in front of them on the private jet, working his way conscientiously through the information dossier Kate Corrigan had presented them with after last night's meeting at B.P.R.D. head-quarters in Connecticut, Abe Sapien turned around. To anyone not used to him, Abe was a startling sight. He was a humanoid amphibian of unknown origin, his skin a shimmering blue-green, albeit etched with striking markings that resembled jagged black lightning bolts. Although his face was expressionless and his large, globular eyes unset-tling, his cultured voice was full of warmth, humor, and intelligence.

"How you two doing back there?" he asked.

"Don't *you* start," grumbled Hellboy.

If Abe had had eyebrows he would have raised them. "I was only—"

"I know what you were *only* doing," Hellboy said. "You were mocking the afflicted. Hey, you try getting stung by a Sumatran fire-worm, see how *you* like it."

Shielding her mouth with her hand, Liz confided loudly to Abe, "HB's a little sensitive about his swollen butt."

"It didn't sting me on my butt!" Hellboy protested. Less con-vincingly he added, "It was my . . . lower back area."

"Burned a hole right through his shorts," Liz said breezily.

"Can we talk about something else?"

"Gladly," said Abe, and held up the dossier. "How about the particulars of our current mission?"

Hellboy groaned. "Jeez, you sure know how to kick a guy when he's down. We went through all this at the meeting!"

"Did you actually listen?" Liz asked.

" 'Course I did. Every word." His golden eyes flickered away from her almost-black ones. "Well . . . all the important ones," he amended.

Abe and Liz exchanged a knowing glance. The only time Hellboy had come alive throughout the debriefing had been right at the end, when their boss, Tom Manning, had glibly informed the three field operatives that they were to fly to London right away. The big red guy had still been smarting from a particularly bruising encounter with a Sumatran fire-worm, which had been unwittingly invoked by a bunch of college boys in Milwaukee. Eight of the thirteen amateur cabalists had been barbecued by the worm by the time Hellboy arrived, and although it had been a pretty routine stomping on his part, it had been messy and he had been knocked around pretty bad. He had arrived home wanting only three things: a big dish of paella, a hot bath, and a long sleep. But he had literally stepped off the chopper and straight into a full-blown meeting, which hadn't put him in the best of moods.

"I'm not flying anywhere right now unless it's in comfort," he had said. "No way am I getting back into one of those damn choppers. The seats *chafe*. And you can forget your Lear jets too. They're cramped and smelly and there's no tail room."

Tom Manning had sighed. "Hellboy, our helicopters are top of the line—"

"I want somewhere I can lie down," Hellboy had interrupted rudely. "And I want a bar."

"You're being a little petulant, don't you think?" Kate had said.

"You wanna see what that bastard worm did to me?" Hellboy growled at her. "Take a good look."

So he had shown her his wound, and Kate had almost passed out. Even Liz had clenched her teeth and murmured, "Yeech."

Hellboy had got his luxury jet. Liz had no idea what strings had been pulled to procure it, but half an hour later they had been climbing aboard. And now here they were, halfway over the Atlantic, flying from an American evening into an English morning.

"Well, it won't hurt to hear it again," Liz said now.

"Gimme a break," grunted Hellboy.

"Cheer up, you big lummox," said Liz. "You're going home and you're with the two people you love most in the world. Besides, it's a long flight. What else is there to do?"

"Sleep," said Hellboy. "Drink."

"If you want a drink I'll get you a drink. In fact, I'll get us all one. As for sleep, there'll be plenty of time for that later. What'll you have?"

Hellboy requested a quadruple bourbon. Abe opted for a small tequila. The bourbon smelled good, so Liz poured herself one too, though she added plenty of ice to hers.

"There," she said, handing Hellboy his glass; it looked ridiculous in his huge hand. "*Now* will you give Abe half an hour of your time?"

"Twenty minutes," Hellboy conceded grudgingly.

Abe puffed himself up and straightened his back. Leafing through the dossier, he said, "As you know, in the past eighteen hours London has been hit by a wave of odd, apparently random occurrences. Some of these are supernatural and others distinctly *not.*"

Hellboy groaned and slumped further down in his seat. "Get on with it already," he grumbled.

Liz slapped him lightly on the arm, but Abe, who was used to his friend's brusque manner, merely carried on as if he hadn't spoken.

"The most interesting thing is that even the non-supernatural occurrences do have a certain occult resonance, which suggests the events aren't random at all, but somehow interrelated. The odds are astronomical of any of it being coincidence.

"To recap, four bloodless human torsos were found yesterday in separate locations in central London. It could be we're just dealing with a psychopath. It could also be the deceased were victims of a gang war, dismembered to prevent ID. Or it could be that these are ritual killings, which would help explain the locations chosen for the placement of the bodies."

"Chosen?" said Hellboy. "You mean the bodies weren't just dumped?"

Liz concealed a smile; HB's question was proof, if any were needed, that he hadn't been listening to a word Kate had said. She wondered what expression Abe might have been wearing if his face had been less immobile. Exasperation? Smugness? Indulgence? As it was, he simply bestowed a blankly silent look on his friend, which in many ways seemed to speak volumes, before continuing.

"No," he said, "they weren't just dumped. The locations seem to have been chosen very carefully, which implies that the bodies may have been offerings—"

"Sacrifices," interrupted Hellboy.

"Exactly."

Hellboy took a gulp of his drink. "So come on," he said, "don't keep us in suspense. Tell us where the bodies were found."

"I was about to," said Abe patiently.

"You see?" said Liz. "You *are* interested."

Hellboy gave her a sidelong look. "You know me," he said. "I always like to stay informed."

Resisting the urge to scoff, Abe said smoothly, "The first body was found in a locked upstairs office in the British Medical Association building in Tavistock Square. Official history will tell you the building was designed and built for the Theosophical Society. However, dig a little deeper and it becomes clear that the building was the original headquarters of the Black Magick House of Theosophy, founded by Madame Blavatsky, one of history's most powerful practitioners of the black arts. Occultists believe that London can be divided into a magical grid, and that where certain grid lines cross there are locations of significant occult resonance."

"We're talking dark magic," Liz said. "Places where terrible things are supposed to happen because of all the bad juju seeping up from below."

"Exactly. The current BMA building was built on one such site," Abe continued, "though the members of the Theosophical Society had a different attitude towards the 'bad juju,' as Liz puts it. They believed they could harness the power and utilize it to their own ends. Whether they ever managed it remains to be seen. Certainly they didn't stick around for long."

"Thanks for the history lesson," Hellboy said, finishing his drink, "but can we move on? I'm guessing these other places are so-called crossover points too?"

Abe nodded. "The second body was found at 186 Fleet Street, in the offices of the *Dundee Courier*. Supposedly this address was once the home of the barber who inspired the story of Sweeney Todd. There's no hard evidence to support the claim, but local rumor has it that the unnamed barber murdered around a hundred and fifty people on the premises, and sold their remains to a female friend, who used the meat in the pies she sold in her pie shop."

"Nice," said Hellboy.

"The third body turned up in a flower bed in the back garden of a house in Bartle Road, Notting Hill. Again the location has a gruesome history. Although the house itself is no longer standing, this was once the setting for 10 Rillington Place, made famous by John Christie, who murdered eight women there, including his wife, and hid their rotting remains under the floorboards.

"Finally, the fourth body was found in a Masonic Hall in Great Queen Street, close to Covent Garden, which was the site of the first temple of the Golden Dawn, an occult group founded by William Wynn Westcott in 1888, and often linked to conspiracy theories involving the Freemasons, the Illuminati, the New World Order, and even the Jack the Ripper murders, which began the year that the Golden Dawn was founded."

"Though according to Kate," Liz said to Hellboy, "that was probably a coincidence."

Hellboy raised his eyebrows and rolled his eyes. He was thoughtful for a moment, and then he said, "I don't buy it."

Abe glanced at Liz. "Which part don't you buy?"

"All this occult-grid stuff. It's too pat. So a guy kills his wife and some other people in a particular house? Big deal. That just means you've got a crazy guy, not an evil house."

"There's an argument," said Abe, "that evil men are attracted to evil places. Or even that a place can warp a man's mind and push him over the edge into wickedness."

Hellboy shrugged. "Still seems to me you've just got some crank who's latched on to this grid crap and is chopping people up, thinking the nasty gods below will bestow him with superpowers."

"Stranger things have happened," said Liz.

Hellboy grunted.

"It may sound callous," said Abe, "but in some ways the deluded crank is our best-case scenario."

"Yeah, but it's small-scale stuff," said Hellboy. "Something for the cops to sort out. We didn't need to come rushing over here for this. I could at least have had a good night's sleep first."

"Aw, you're just cranky 'cause of your butt," said Liz. "You know how much you love England. You usually jump at the chance to go back."

"I'm just saying—"

"Okay, let's put the murders aside for now," said Abe, "and concentrate on the stuff that *does* fall within our jurisdiction."

He looked to Hellboy, who wafted a weary hand and said, "Go ahead. But keep it simple. This worm poison *stings*. It's giving me the mother of all headaches."

Abe nodded and said crisply, "Since yesterday morning London has been dealing with all sorts of supernatural happenings. Many people have reported seeing ghosts. A family in Willesden was forced to flee their home by a destructive force. The entity was invisible, but more than a dozen witnesses saw the place being torn apart by unseen hands. An undertaker, his staff, and an elderly widow have claimed that in a funeral parlor in Shoreditch the dead climbed from their coffins and walked. A hysterical young woman told the police that a huge creature made of black rock came out of a subway tunnel in Finsbury Park and carried off her boyfriend."

"Rock, huh?" said Hellboy, glancing at his own stone hand. "Three guesses as to who'll be handling *that* one." He rubbed his left hand over his leathery, lamp-jawed face. "You all done now?" he asked Abe. " 'Cause I really need a couple hours of shut-eye."

"Well, we *could* speculate and theorize over what we've learned," said Abe, deadpan.

"And we *could* stuff you in the bathroom and barricade the door," Hellboy replied.

"Maybe we *all* ought to get some rest," said Liz. "It sounds as if we've got a long day ahead of us."

Hellboy adjusted the mechanism that extended his seat into a makeshift bed and closed his golden eyes. "I'm already dreaming," he murmured.

☠ CHAPTER 2

Ah, Soho, thought Colin Proctor, forging his way through the cramped, narrow streets, buoyed by the warm, ever-changing tide of exotic scents emanating from the gay bars and heaving pubs, the restaurants and all-night delis. *Soho, Soho, Soho, so good they named it thrice.*

He cackled as he walked, hands thrust into the pockets of his beat-up leather coat, collar turned up against the drizzle that beaded his graying, untidy hair.

A smart young couple glanced at him with disdain as he strode by, but Proctor merely grinned at them. He knew what they would see—nicotine-stained teeth in a podgy face, a glint of the predator in his alcohol-yellowed eyes—but their evident repulsion didn't bother him. He didn't give a toss what people thought.

Even so, he couldn't help wondering what the young couple took him to be. It was a game he often played with himself. Did they imagine him to be a gangster? A pornographer? A seedy private eye? Perhaps a down-at-heel hitman or a booze-raddled artist, or merely an urban *flaneur*, on the lookout for the weird and the wonderful?

He could have been any and all of these things. This was Soho, after all. Human life was here in its abundance and its infinite variety. On these potent, heady streets the wealthy and the privileged rubbed shoulders with the needy and the dispossessed. These concertinaed buildings were home to media and city types; to tailors and craftsmen; to strippers and prostitutes; to actors, artists, and musicians; to market traders, grifters, wheelers and dealers, and entrepreneurs.

Proctor spread his arms, the drizzle forming a sheen on the brown leather of his jacket, and embraced it all.

Soho, he thought. *My Soho. Look at me, Ma—king o' the world!*

The truth was, Proctor was neither a gangster, nor a pornographer, nor a hit man. He was something far worse than any of these things.

He was a tabloid journalist.

He was forty-four years old, but he looked older. Whenever anyone pointed this out to him, usually with malicious relish, he simply laughed and told them he had had a very hard life.

He hadn't, though, not really. Or, if he had, then it was no fault but his own. Proctor's ex-wife, Tina, had told him often enough that he was great at his job but crap at life. What Tina didn't understand, however, was that her definition of "life" did not necessarily tally with her ex-husband's. Tina had frequently accused Colin of being a philanderer, a waster, a sleaze, and a drunk. But she used those terms as an insult, whereas Colin would gladly have worn them as badges of honor. He had never wanted to be staid or reliable, had always shied away from the thought of "settling down." He was a man forever drawn to the smoke and the bright lights, and he had thought that Tina *understood* that, had even thought it was one of the things—his "lust for life," to quote the great Iggy Pop—that she liked about him.

It had taken nine years and two beautiful daughters to relieve him of that notion. Tina would say that she had spent those years striving to make things work between them. Colin's opinion was that she had spent them trying to beat his square-peg philosophy into the round hole of what *her* idea of his life should be. In the end the two of them had emerged from the fray bruised and exhausted, but clutching their spoils of the struggle.

Tina, of course, had got the biggest prize, which was the girls, Chloe and Jasmine. Proctor had been resigned to losing them, but having to say goodbye and move out of the family home had been a dreadful wrench all the same. Although aware of his many failings, Colin knew that one of the accusations that could never be leveled at him was that he was a bad father. He might not have been around a lot of the time, but he was a doting dad nonetheless. He loved his daughters and he'd do anything for them. Well . . . almost anything.

"If you really loved them you'd stop this . . . this debauched life of yours!" Tina had raged at him once during one of their countless rows.

Proctor had known that in essence what she was saying was true. But his "debauched life," as she called it, was part of his nature, imprinted into his DNA. It was more than an addiction, it was a necessity, like food and drink and air. When he had tried to explain this to her, when he had said that he could no sooner give up his "debauched life" than he could shed his skin, or grow an extra head, she had curled her lip and sneered at him.

"You're pathetic," she had said. "You're a sorry excuse for a man."

"Maybe that's true, but unlike you at least I'm happy," he had retorted.

She had flown at him then, lashing out with her fists, spitting vitriol. "If I'm unhappy, then it's only because you've made me like that."

Even now, more than a year after it had become officially over between them, the arguments kept raging. They had had their latest this morning. Proctor had called Tina to tell her what he was buying Jasmine for her birthday.

"A Walkman?" she had scoffed. "She's *eight*, Colin."

"So?"

"So she's too young. What the hell do you think she's going to use it for?"

"Duh . . . listening to music?" he had said, as if she were a retard.

Curtly Tina had said, "She's not *into* music. She's still a kid. She likes riding her bike and playing with her Barbies."

"You're never too young to get into music," Colin had argued. "I'll buy her a couple of CDs to go with it."

"You will not," Tina had snapped.

"What's that supposed to mean?"

"You can't *buy* her affection, Colin. You can't stay out of her life for ninety-nine percent of the time, then lavish her with gifts for the other one percent. That's not how it works."

"You think I don't know that?" Proctor said contemptuously.

"Yes, I do. I *do* think you don't know that. You're not around all the time. *You* don't look after your girls, and kiss them good night, and listen to their problems, and dry their tears, and do all the other things a parent is supposed to do. You just do exactly as you please, and assuage your guilt every so often by buying them something expensive, as a result of which they think the light shines out of your arse."

"Oh, and that's my fault, is it?"

"Yes it is. It is your bloody fault."

"All right," he had said, "I'll move back in then, shall I?"

"Over my dead body."

He had bought Jasmine the Walkman. And he had bought her five CDs to go with it. Sod Tina. What was she going to do when Jasmine opened her present on her birthday? Take it away from her? Tell her she couldn't have it?

He shook his head. Thoughts of Tina were souring his mood, and he was damned if he was going to allow that to happen. He was a *bon viveur*, a man about town, and if he wasn't young, then at least he was free and single. He had just spent an uproarious two hours in the company of Fat Reggie Lipton, a gossip columnist from a rival rag. Reggie was a screaming queen, who didn't give a monkey's ass about world affairs. His only concern in life was to scoop the crap on the rich and famous, and the smellier and dirtier the better.

Reggie's was a clandestine world of secrets and rumors and hear-say. The things he knew! The things he claimed were true! Even if only ten percent of it turned out to be bona fide, then the world was still a far stranger place than even Proctor had ever suspected.

Stranger, but also more entertaining. Because Proctor loved trailing Reggie around the gay bars of Dean Street and Old Compton Street. Here they would pick up all the gossip from Reggie's many contacts—dancers, hairstylists, set designers, makeup artists. Bit-part players in the warped and lavish world of showbiz.

Reggie was now on his way to a select little club off Brewer Street, hot on the heels of a "scrummy" young actor who was purported to be cheating on his pregnant wife with some stunning but underage soap star. Reggie had invited Proctor along, but fun though it was to be in Reg's company, Proctor had declined. He was eager to catch up with his pals at the Nero.

The Nero was Proctor's favorite drinking den, his home from home. Established in the early sixties, it had quickly become the primary after-hours haunt of ambitious young journos like himself. Owner of the club was a brusque but warm-hearted lesbian known as Mama Lou. She favored loud checked suits and was often seen brandishing a gold-topped cane. She was well into her sixties now, but she still ran her little kingdom like a benevolent dictator. Colin had first encountered her when he had been a raw twenty-year-old back in the seventies. He had been introduced to her by his late, lamented mentor, Cyril Moon. Cyril had told Proctor that Lou tried to intimidate newcomers as a kind of initiation test, and that Colin should not allow her to give him any crap.

Sure enough, the moment Proctor had first set foot through the door, Lou had cast a contemptuous eye over him. "You're a scrawny little sod, aren't you?" she had declared. "I hope you're not going to sit in my bar all night nursing a bleedin' Babycham."

Proctor had looked back at her without flinching and had replied evenly, "I'll drink *you* under the table any time, you fat cow."

Lou had guffawed. "Oh, I *like* this one, Cyril," she had said. "He can stay."

He *had* stayed. And the next day, when Proctor went back, Lou greeted him like an old friend. She had been doing that now, several times a week, for the past twenty-five years.

The Nero was at the far end of Frith Street, near Soho Square. Despite the drizzle, Proctor felt the weight of history each time he walked these grimy, gritty pavements. Although he had never been a scholar, he loved London, and Soho in particular. He had picked up enough snippets of information over the years—most of them imparted to him in the dead, sozzled hours before dawn, but still miraculously retained in his spongelike brain—to have become quite an authority on the area.

Walking down Frith Street, he knew that John Constable, Mozart, and William Hazlitt had once resided here. He knew that Casanova and Thomas de Quincey had had lodgings on Greek Street just around the corner. He knew that nearby Broadwick Street had been the birthplace of William Blake, and that Karl Marx and his family had once lived in a couple of cramped rooms above a shop on Dean Street.

Maybe, he sometimes thought, *in years to come, people will whisper* my *name with such reverence*. Perhaps a century from now some old soak will lean across to a pissed-up young Turk in the Nero and mutter, "You know who used to drink in here, don't you? Only Colin bleedin' Proctor!"

Still dreaming his dreams, Proctor arrived at an unassuming, graffiti-daubed door squeezed between a Vietnamese takeout restaurant and a perfumed candle shop. He rapped three times, whereupon the door opened on a chain and a jaundiced eye peered out.

"Evening, Barney," he said to the owner of the eye, a tall, shaven-headed black man, whose gleaming arms resembled stockings stuffed with bowling balls.

The eye crinkled and teeth flashed in a grin. "Mr. Proctor!" Barney exclaimed, unhooking the chain and pulling the door wide. He enfolded Proctor's hand in one twice its size and shook it vigorously. "How's it hanging, my man?"

"Unfortunately, hanging is about all that it *is* doing," Proctor replied. "You know, Barn, I'm beginning to suspect that I'm losing my boyish good looks."

Barney's answering chuckle was like an earth tremor. It rumbled behind Proctor as he ascended the dingy, twisting staircase to the upper floor.

A door on the first-floor landing stood ajar. Sprawled across its entrance was a handsome young man with spiky hair, designer jeans, and a smart gray jacket. Deathly pale, he kept turning his head to one side and semi-heaving. Proctor recognized him as the current *enfant terrible* of British literary fiction, Simon something-or-other. Only twenty-two, the kid's first novel, *Claptrap*, had been nominated for the Whitbread, and the film rights snapped up by Miramax for an obscene amount of money.

"You all right, son?" Proctor inquired kindly.

"Piss off," said Simon Something.

"Fair enough," Proctor replied, and stepped over him.

Lou, resplendent in a suit of yellow-and-black tartan, greeted him in her usual exuberant manner.

"Bit quiet tonight," remarked Proctor, looking around.

"It's the week before payday, darling," Lou said. "And it's Monday. Only the die-hards like you are out tonight."

Proctor shook his head. "It's a sad indictment of my profession, Lou," he said. "All these new kids on the block, and not a single one of 'em with stamina. Where's Jeffrey Bernard when you need him, eh?"

Lou was already placing a pint of bitter and a double Scotch on the bar in front of him. She raised her own tumbler of rum—she drank it neat, like a pirate.

"Here's to him," she said.

Proctor chinked his glass against hers.

Couple of hours later he was ready to call it a night. Lou was always good company, but tonight the place was dead. Okay, so there was Simon Something and his rowdy pals in the corner, but they were very much a closed shop. None of Proctor's usual crowd were in, not even Terry Miles, who was all but a permanent fixture.

All at once he felt old and depressed. The booze sideswiped him like that sometimes. Not often, but now and again, when his defenses were down. He'd step outside himself for a moment and be appalled at what he saw. He'd wonder what the point of it all was, what the future held, and he'd see nothing but a slow and lonely decline.

Bloody Soho, he'd think then. *What a dump. What a place to live and die.*

"Excuse me? Mr. Proctor?"

Proctor turned. The young man standing behind him looked nervous, eyes darting everywhere. He was wearing a black puffer jacket and a baseball cap, the brim pulled down low. He was no street kid, however. His clothes looked new, like a disguise, and he himself looked a little soft around the edges, as if he were already too used to the good things in life.

"Who are you?" Proctor asked, and noticed how the man glanced around to ensure he wasn't being overheard.

"My name's Charles Dexter, Mr. Proctor. You *are* Colin Proctor, aren't you? The *Star* journalist?"

Despite himself, Proctor felt a puff of pride. This man, Dexter, had said *the* Star *journalist* as someone might say *the actor* or *the footballer.* It made him feel important, well known. However, he let none of that show in his face. "Yes, I am," he said, "but what is it to you?"

The man glanced around again. "Can I talk to you in confidence, Mr. Proctor?"

"Buy me a drink, son, and you can talk to me any way you like. I'll have a large Scotch—and for God's sake, get one for yourself. You look as though you need it."

The man looked slightly taken aback. "What? Oh no, I'm fine, thanks."

"Bollocks," said Proctor. "No one talks to me in here without a drink in their hand. House rules."

With a miserable look on his face, the man half raised a hand to attract Lou's attention. Proctor vacated his barstool and went to sit at a nearby table. A couple of minutes later Dexter toddled across with a Scotch for Proctor and a small glass of red wine for himself.

"Pull up a chair, son," Proctor said.

Dexter did so. He leaned forward, shoulders hunched, like an underage drinker trying to be unobtrusive.

"Now then," Proctor said, "what can I do for you?"

"I hear your paper buys stories," Dexter muttered.

Proctor took his time before replying. He took a sip of his drink, then shrugged dismissively. "That depends on the story, doesn't it?"

"This is big," said Dexter.

"Oh yeah?"

"Yes," replied Dexter. "This is *really* big."

Proctor sighed. "That's what they all say, son."

Dexter shook his head irritably. "I'm not messing you about, Mr. Proctor. I'm only here because . . ."

He trailed off. Proctor finished his sentence for him. "Because you need the money."

The kid clammed up, but the truth was written all over his face. Proctor regarded him thoughtfully for a moment. Then he said, "Look, son, I don't like bullshit and I don't see the point of pussyfooting around. Why don't you just tell me what this is about, and I'll see what I can do for you?"

"I'm not telling you anything until you promise you'll pay for my story," said Dexter quickly.

Proctor shrugged again. "In that case you're wasting my time. See you, son. Thanks for the drink."

He pushed his chair back and halfrose to his feet.

"Wait!" the kid almost yelped.

Proctor paused. "Well?"

The kid puffed out his cheeks. "Are you an honorable man, Mr. Proctor?"

Proctor laughed. "Blimey, I'm not sure how to answer that. Put it this way, son—I'll do whatever I can to get a story, and like any good journalist I'll give it a bit of a spin if I think it'll sell a few more papers. But I don't piss people about, especially not potential contacts."

"I was told you could be trusted," said Dexter, nodding.

"Bloody hell," said Proctor. "Who told you that?"

"It doesn't matter."

Proctor looked relaxed, but his mind was working furiously. He could feel his Spidey senses tingling. Instinct told him there might well *be* something here, maybe even something big, as the kid had said. Dexter clearly needed money, which usually meant he was up to his eyeballs in either drugs or debt. But at the same time he was nervous, and evidently new to all this, which made Proctor aware of not making the wrong move and causing him to bolt like a startled rabbit.

Settling back, he said, "You're right, son, it doesn't matter. All that matters is this so-called story you've got for me. What we need to do, though, is lay a few ground rules. First off, let me reassure you that a good journalist never reveals his sources—and believe me, son, I'm a bloody good journalist. Now what *I* need in order to enable us to proceed is a little hint from you of what this story of yours is about. You don't have to tell me everything; just drop me a few clues, tantalize my tastebuds. I'm sure you understand that I can't promise you anything by way of financial remuneration until I know what it is you're selling. That's not me messing you about. You'd get the same response from *any* journalist you talked to." He spread his hands, a gesture of openness. "Now, I can't be any fairer than that, can I?"

Dexter looked uncertain for a moment, and then he muttered, "Suppose not."

"So come on, son," Proctor said in his best kindly uncle voice, "give me something to think about."

Dexter swallowed, hunching even lower in his seat. For a few seconds he was silent as he struggled with his innermost thoughts. Finally he said, "I . . . work in central government. I work with a number of very senior figures, which gives me access to . . . certain information."

He glanced at Proctor from under the brim of his cap. Proctor nodded. "Sounds promising. Go on."

"I don't know if you're aware," Dexter said, "but there have been a number of . . . incidents in the city over the past twenty-four hours. *Unusual* incidents."

"The torso murders, you mean?"

Dexter flinched, as though Proctor's voice had boomed around the room. "Those, yes, but others too. Things even more unusual. Things that have been deemed . . . *supernatural.*"

He grimaced at this last word. Proctor stared at him.

"Hang on a minute," he said quietly. "I take it we're not talking silly-season stuff here? Nutters who think they've been probed by aliens? Elvis in the supermarket? That sort of crap?"

Dexter shook his head. "For the most part we're talking reliable, multiple witnesses. And we're talking about a *proliferation* of incidents. Not just a spike on a radar, but a great jagged mountain."

"Too many for it to be a coincidence, you mean?"

Dexter nodded.

Proctor raised his eyebrows, as if to show that although he wasn't impressed yet, he was cautiously prepared to be. "So how come, if these incidents are so widespread, news of them hasn't leaked out?" Almost immediately, however, he raised a hand. "Hang on. There was that kid who went missing on the underground, wasn't there? His girlfriend said they'd been attacked by a monster or something?"

Dexter nodded again. "Bits and pieces *have* leaked out, but for the most part the authorities have been able to keep things under wraps. So far, that is."

Proctor's eyebrows rose a little higher. "They're really taking it *that* seriously?"

"Yep." Dexter leaned forward. He seemed to be warming to his subject now. One thing that Proctor had found over the years was that, given a little encouragement, most people loved to show off their superior knowledge. "And I'll tell you something else. I'll tell you *just* how seriously they're taking it."

"Go on."

"They're calling in . . . outside help."

This time all Proctor had to do was give Dexter a blank look for the younger man to whisper, "B.P.R.D."

"Whoa," Proctor breathed. "You don't mean . . ."

"Yeah," said Dexter, "Hellboy."

"Holy shit," Proctor murmured.

Dexter had been right. This *was* big. So big, in fact, that there was no way the authorities would be able to keep it secret for much longer. But if Proctor could at least get the *exclusive*, then he could give the impression he was the man who had broken the story for the good of the UK public, the man who had shown courage, fortitude, and insight to unearth the subterfuge at the heart of the British government. He could pitch his story as a righteous blow for democracy and freedom. The *Star* would love that. And the punters would lap it up.

"I can get you information on the incidents reported so far," Dexter said, "and I can tell you when and where our visitors will be arriving."

"What about an itinerary?" Proctor asked.

"There isn't one. The assumption is that the B.P.R.D. will run the show when they get here. Apparently Hellboy is very independent."

Despite the booze he had consumed that evening, Proctor's mind was whirring. He presumed that Hellboy and Co. would arrive in the country surreptitiously, which meant a private airfield, almost certainly somewhere near London. If Dexter was on the level it was likely that Proctor would be the only journalist there to witness the arrival of the demonic-looking creature who, in recent decades, had become one of the most recognizable celebrities on the planet.

"How much do you want?" he asked.

"Five thousand pounds. Cash," replied Dexter.

Is that all? Proctor almost scoffed, but he kept his face straight. To Dexter's evident surprise, he proffered his hand immediately.

"Done."

"We're here, HB," Liz said.

Hellboy growled like a bad-tempered mutt as she shook him awake. The one golden eye he eventually opened was shot through with blood vessels so dark they looked black.

"How are you feeling?" she asked.

"Didn't sleep a wink," he grumbled.

"That so? Well, you sure snore a lot for an awake guy."

Hellboy scowled, cranked his seat into a sitting position and looked out of the window. He couldn't see much. A gloomy sky, a gray stretch of runway along which they were currently trundling, and, in the distance, some spiny leafless trees.

All the same, despite the uninspiring surroundings, he felt a tingle of pleasure. Whatever his mood, whatever the circumstances, there was always something special about setting down on British soil.

His lantern-jawed face gave little away, but Liz knew him well enough to detect even the most subtle change in his demeanor. "Home sweet home?" she said.

He looked at her. "Just thinking about this little place in Battersea that does the best chicken balti you've ever tasted. Take you there if we get time."

A few seats ahead of them, Abe, who was looking out of the opposite side of the plane, said, "I spy the welcoming committee."

Liz scrambled across the aisle and saw a bunch of besuited and uniformed men standing by the doors of a small, squat building beside a modest aircraft hangar. The men were waiting with grim patience, hands clasped before them. However, the darting glances that passed between them betrayed the fact that most were restless, nervous.

Liz's eye was drawn to the two people who stood out among the array of suits and uniforms. One was a young woman, pretty but studious looking, with short brown hair and spectacles. She was wearing a short skirt and an open-necked blouse despite the chill of the day, and her only concession to the weather was the B.P.R.D. jacket she wore draped loosely across her shoulders. The other person was a rangy, good-looking guy in his midthirties with tousled mousy-blond hair. He was behind the young woman, leaning against the wall of the squat, flat-roofed building, hands in pockets. He was wearing jeans, a collarless blue shirt and a rather crumpled cream jacket, and he was watching the approaching jet with a distracted half smile on his face.

The jet slowed and came to a stop opposite the group. "Time for the floor show, boys," said Liz.

Hellboy stood up, the top of his head only a foot or so beneath the curved ceiling. He shook the creases out of his duster and patted the gun holstered on the thick leather belt around his waist. Attached to the belt were various waterproof compartments stuffed with all manner of charms and talismans, technical instruments, and alternate weapons. A couple of the pouches even contained rations, in case Hellboy should ever find himself in the middle of nowhere during a mission—which, truth be told, he frequently did.

"Ready to meet and greet?" Liz teased.

"Bring it on," Hellboy said.

The pilot had already appeared from the cockpit and was opening the door. He was one of their regular flyers, an ex—air force guy of around fifty called Bud. He had grizzled gray hair cut close to his scalp, but was tougher and fitter than most men half his age. Hellboy liked him because he was straight as a die and never seemed to be phased by anything.

"How're Cheryl and the kids?" Hellboy asked him as he clomped towards the exit on his hoofed feet.

"Doing good," Bud said. "My youngest, John, just started college this fall. Can you believe it?"

Hellboy shook his head. "Where does all the time go?"

Liz was first out on the ramshackle steps that a couple of uniformed grunts had shoved up against the side of the aircraft. She took a deep breath. English air always seemed to smell greener, mulchier, more ancient than it did at home—or maybe that was just her imagination. She looked down at the upturned faces and saw the apprehension and expectation in their eyes. For the thousandth time she wondered how HB coped with it all—not with the fame, though that in itself must be a royal pain in the ass, but the *fear*, the *awe*, that those meeting him for the first time never quite failed to conceal. She wondered how many of these people would have known who *she* was if they hadn't been briefed beforehand. She guessed some of them *might* have heard of her, but she doubted they'd recognize her if she passed them in the street.

And that was just the way she liked it. If *she'd* been on the cover of *Time* magazine she'd be living on a deserted tropical island by now. She saw a ripple of reaction go through the crowd below her, heard a slight intake of breath, and knew that Abe had stepped out of the shadows behind her.

"Cheery-looking bunch, aren't they?" he murmured in her ear.

"That's the stiff upper lip you're seeing right there," she replied.

The metal creaked as Hellboy stepped from the plane and she and Abe were engulfed in his shadow. There was a collective gasp from below. Eyes boggled. A couple of the guys in suits actually took a step back.

Hellboy sighed. "Here we go again."

The three of them descended the ramshackle metal steps. The young woman in the B.P.R.D. jacket stepped forward to greet them.

"Agent Rachel Turner, London office," she said eagerly, holding out her hand. "This is a real honor, guys. Welcome to England."

She shook hands with each of them in turn. When she got to Hellboy, he said, "I remember you. You're the sambuca girl."

Agent Turner blushed. Liz looked at Hellboy and raised her eyebrows inquiringly.

"Long story," he said. "Another time."

"Or maybe never," said Agent Turner.

Hellboy chuckled.

Agent Turner introduced them to representatives from the British government, the army, the metropolitan police, the US embassy and MI5. Each of the representatives had prepared a speech of welcome. The embassy guy droned on for a good five minutes about protocol and procedure.

Liz did her best to look gracious, but was aware that just behind her Hellboy was already fidgeting. "Man, I *hate* red tape," he had muttered to her on more than one occasion, and once he had even memorably scandalized their Japanese hosts by shouting, "Enough already!" and stomping through an elaborate welcoming ceremony that had been laid on for them at Yokohama airport.

Finally it was the turn of the man in jeans to step forward. Agent Turner started to introduce him, but he said, "It's okay, Rachel,

I can do it." He shook Liz's hand, then Hellboy's big stone one, and finally Abe's webbed one. When he grimaced it was not with distaste, but with apology.

"I'm sure you've had enough of being talked at," he said, "but I just wanted to say hi. My name's Richard Varley. I'm a lecturer in Third World Studies at King's College in London. Soon as I heard about the murders I offered my services to the investigation. I . . . well, I've got a few theories of my own, which I wanted to share with you."

"Well . . . why not travel back to London with us?" Liz heard herself saying. "We can talk on the way."

Varley smiled at her. "Thanks," he said. "I'd like that. That's if Rachel doesn't mind, of course?"

Agent Turner raised her hands. "Fine by me."

All at once they became aware of a commotion to their left. One of the uniformed privates was speaking urgently into a radio mounted on his helmet. Seconds later armed soldiers, who had been strolling casually around the perimeter of the airfield, were converging rapidly on a section of chainlink fence several hundred yards away.

"What's going on?" Hellboy asked as Major Beresford, the army guy who had greeted them, approached at a semitrot.

"Probably nothing," Beresford said. "One of my men saw light reflecting off what he thought might be metal or glass. I suggest we conclude the preliminaries inside."

Hellboy shrugged. "Okay, Major. Lead the way."

This is gold dust, Proctor thought, adjusting his position. He was lying, half concealed by bushes, up against the chainlink fence bordering the private airfield. The ground was damp, and muddy water had soaked into the elbows and knees of his crumpled jacket and trousers, but Proctor didn't care. From his vantage point he had a perfect view of the front of the aircraft hangar, outside which the reception committee for Hellboy and his chums had gathered. The long lens of Proctor's camera was stuck through one of the holes in the chainlink, and he had been happily snapping away for the last twenty minutes. He had some great shots of the apprehensive-looking officials and the B.P.R.D. operatives themselves.

And what a sight *they* were! A good-looking bird whose bulky jacket couldn't conceal her trim figure, a weird-looking fish-man, and the big red demon himself. Not that Hellboy *liked* being called a demon, apparently, but bloody hell, what else were people supposed to call him?

Proctor tingled with excitement at the thought of the expression on his editor's face when he showed him these pictures later today. As far as Proctor was aware, only a handful of people even *knew* Hellboy was in the country. This location was so remote, and security so low key (nothing but a dozen or so armed squaddies, aimlessly patroling the perimeter of the airfield), that it was obvious the authorities had been confident they would encounter no intrusion from the press or from curious onlookers. Proctor had parked his car in a layby a quarter of a mile away, and had tramped across a couple of muddy fields to avoid detection, but he was now beginning to think that even these minimal attempts at secrecy had been overcautious.

He shifted position again as Hellboy and his chums turned to speak to a guy in jeans and a cream jacket, who had stepped forward to shake each of their hands. He could get some full-face shots of the freaks here if he was quick, rather than the profile shots he'd had to be content with so far. As he turned the camera slightly, he noticed one of the armed soldiers turn his head towards him. The soldier was too far away for Proctor to see his expression, but the man's sudden alertness was enough for the journalist to feel certain he'd been spotted—or at least that a flash of sunlight on his camera lens had.

Uh-oh, he thought, *time to go*. All the same, he couldn't resist rapidly squeezing off a few more shots before scrambling to his feet.

The soldier was speaking into a radio. And then there were armed, uniformed men running across the airfield towards him. Although Proctor wasn't scared for his safety (he was confident that the worst that would happen would be that he'd be questioned and his equipment confiscated), he was terrified of losing the story. Heart whacking in his chest, he burst through the bushes bordering the side of the dirt track and began to run.

The ground was slippery with mud, and he felt horribly exposed out in the open. He ran for perhaps thirty meters, slithering and almost falling a couple of times, before realizing that if he was going to have any chance of escaping his pursuers an alternative strategy was needed. Jumping from puddle to puddle to cover his tracks, he veered towards the dry stone wall on the other side of the road. He glanced behind him to satisfy himself that he was still screened by the bushes and trees opposite, and then he clambered awkwardly over the wall.

The drop on the other side surprised him a little. The field was at a lower level than the road, and he fell a good six feet into springy, boggy grass. Muddy water instantly oozed over his feet and ankles, waterlogging his shoes. Unable to keep his balance, Proctor fell to his knees. He grimaced, but forced himself to remain silent and motionless, pressing his back against the stone wall.

After a few minutes he heard shouts, and then the thump of approaching footsteps. He pressed himself even further back against the wall as the splat of booted feet seemed to sound directly above his head. He was certain that at any moment someone would peer over the wall and see him crouching in the mud. He heard shouted orders, and then the rapid-fire thud of soldiers running off up the road in both directions. There then followed a muted conversation—of which Proctor could catch only the occasional word—between what he assumed were a couple of officers. Eventually the conversation stopped, and he heard the sound of receding footsteps. He left it another five minutes and then he tentatively began to move.

He edged along the length of the wall in a semicrouch towards the corner of the field. Here the wall was bisected by a wooden fence, which seemed to be holding back a surging mass of woodland. Proctor peered over his shoulder, then bolted for the cover of the trees. He was filthy, cold, and wet, and his breath was rasping in his chest, but it would be worth it if he could reach his car and get back to London with his story.

CHAPTER 3

"So what are these theories of yours, Mr. Varley?" Abe asked.

Varley, sitting between Liz and Abe, smiled self-consciously. "Well, it's *Dr.* Varley actually. But please, call me Richard."

From the front of the Daimler, Hellboy groaned. "Don't you *ever* get tired of the info-dumping, Abe?"

Liz smiled an apology at Richard. "HB, that's rude," she said.

"Sorry," said Hellboy, and glanced at Richard in the rear-view mirror. "No offence, Dr. . . . er, Richard, I mean."

"None taken," Richard said, and laughed. Liz liked the fact that there was no hint of nervousness or uncertainty in his reaction. Too often people meeting Hellboy for the first time were too eager to please, as if afraid he would tear them limb from limb if they incurred his wrath.

"You mentioned muti murders," Abe said, "but as I understand it, *muti* is simply the Zulu term for medicine—or am I wrong?"

Richard raised his eyebrows. "I'm impressed."

"He reads a lot," Liz said dryly.

Smiling, Richard said, "You're right, of course, Abe. Muti is a catch-all term for African herbal medicine. However, there is a darker, more clandestine aspect to it. Certain sangomas, or witch doctors, have been known to mix body parts with other ingredients to increase the effect of the medicine's power. Brain matter mixed in with the muti, for example, is said to bestow knowledge or to increase intelligence, whereas breasts and genitals are thought to endow a client with greater virility."

"And how widespread are these darker practices?" asked Liz.

Richard shrugged. "No one really knows. There are reports of muti murders right across northern and southern Africa, but muti encompasses so many different rituals and beliefs that often murders which could be attributed to it are simply swept up within the general melee of lawlessness. Even in South Africa, which has a more centralized system of policing, there are no solid statistics. Muti murder estimates vary from one a month to several hundred a year. There was, however, a recent high-profile case in Grahamstown in the Eastern Cape Provinces. Nine men belonging to a Yoruban cult were convicted of a woman's murder, in which the victim had her facial skin removed with a scalpel, following which her genitalia, breasts, hands, and feet were hacked off while she was still alive. The reason they didn't kill her first is because the screams of the butchered victim are said to enhance the power of the medicine. In this case the woman's body parts were used as the ingredients for a get-rich-quick spell called *ukutwalela ubutyebi*. The men apparently smeared the woman's blood over themselves and then ate the parts they had hacked off."

"What a sweet little bedtime story," Hellboy said from the front of the car.

Grim faced, Liz asked, "And now you think one of these Yoruban cults has come to London?"

Again, Richard shrugged. "I think they've been here a long time, perhaps even years. I think they've established a whole subculture which operates beneath the law."

"Is that possible?" asked Abe. Liz and Hellboy looked at him as if they couldn't believe his naiveté. "In such a small and highly civilized country, I mean, where almost every murder becomes a national headline?"

"I think the Yoruba, if that's who they are, have become experts at covering their tracks," Richard said. "Many of their victims are illegal immigrants, children who are bought in African cities like

THE ALL-SEEING EYE   55

Kinshasa for as little as five or ten pounds and then smuggled into the country. A police inspector recently told me that out of three hundred black children from ethnic backgrounds reported missing from London schools in the first three months of this year, only two have been traced. And these are just the children who are *enrolled* in British schools. Many more slip through the net and have no official existence in this country."

In her line of work, Liz had encountered hundreds of demonic entities, had frequently come face to face with evil, and had witnessed death on a grand scale . . . and yet she had still never quite come to terms with the appalling depravity of man's inhumanity to man.

"It's what makes you strong," Hellboy had told her once when she had been weeping in his arms after a particularly harrowing mission. "Lose that and you stop being human."

"That's sickening," she said now, quietly, looking at Richard.

He nodded slowly. "It's certainly that."

"I don't know, Richard," said Abe. "These current killings don't really follow the MO I've seen in previous muti activities."

"You're right, of course," said Richard, "and that's what makes these deaths so . . . well, *intriguing*. Firstly all the victims are adults, secondly all the victims are white, and thirdly the placing of the remains has meant that the killings have become extremely high profile."

"Plus there's the occult element to consider," Abe said.

Richard looked quizzical. "I don't follow."

Abe quickly filled Richard in on the occult significance of each of the murder sites.

"Interesting," the lecturer said quietly.

"I still think we could be dealing with nothing more than a psycho here," Hellboy chipped in. "These guys, they read this stuff and think they're on Earth to do the devil's work or some such crap."

"You could be right," said Richard.

The talk turned to more general matters. As Abe questioned Richard further about his particular field of expertise, Hellboy closed his eyes and phased out the conversation. Although he was a quick healer, he was tired from the still-throbbing wounds inflicted by the fire-worm the day before, not to mention the poison his antibodies had been fighting. He rested his stone hand in his lap and decided to catch a few more z's while Abe and Richard discussed the intricacies of African tribal customs. Richard seemed like a good guy, and Hellboy had known Liz for long enough to recognize—just from the secretive little looks she had cast in the lecturer's direction and the way she had been eager for him to accompany them to London—that she thought so too. Her interest was kinda cute, and he couldn't blame her for it—Richard was good looking and intelligent, after all—but he couldn't help worrying about her all the same. Despite the tough-girl exterior, Hellboy knew that Liz was a vulnerable soul and he hated seeing her get hurt.

You better treat her right, Varley, he thought, *or you'll have me to deal with*.

Lulled by the murmur of the Daimler's engine and the drone of conversation from the back seat, he drifted into sleep . . .

Now that it appeared he'd gotten away with it, Proctor's mind was whirring again. He was no longer merely thinking about getting back to London and delivering his story before his nine p.m. deadline, he was now starting to wonder how he might make the story *even better*.

An interview, he thought. An interview with Hellboy at his hotel. How amazing would that be? First, though, he had to find out *which* hotel Hellboy and his chums were staying at. And to get that information he needed to do a certain amount of reckless driving, and trust to an even greater amount of luck.

From his vantage point at the perimeter of the airfield, Proctor had observed the various officials arrive. Some time later he had seen a chauffeur-driven Daimler with tinted windows pull in to the small car park beside the aircraft hangar. No one had emerged from that vehicle, not even the chauffeur, which had led Proctor to assume that this was the car which would take Hellboy and his colleagues to London.

Even as he was making his bedraggled and desperate escape across the fields and through the woods to the layby where he had parked his car, a plan had been churning away in the back of the journalist's mind. Almost subconsciously he sifted through the pros and cons of his scheme, and by the time he reached his scratched and battered little Astra—85k on the clock, dodgy clutch and even dodgier brakes—and sank, mud spattered and exhausted, into the driver's seat, he had pretty much decided to go for it. After all, he had thought, what had he got to lose?

His thinking was that there was no reason the Daimler wouldn't take the most obvious route to the capital. That included going up the A229, on to the M20 and from there on to the M25. All Proctor had to do, therefore, was drive like crazy and follow the same route. Eventually, if the Daimler was sticking to the speed limit, as he suspected it might, he would catch up with it. Then it was simply a case of tucking himself in behind the vehicle—though not *too* close, of course—and trailing it into London.

The main drawback of the plan was not the Astra itself—it might be a battered old wreck, whose engine rattled like dry peas in a tin, but it could really *move* —but the possibility of being pulled over by the police. However, on this particular score God turned out to be shining on him. The only cops Proctor saw were already parked behind a yellow Ferrari on the hard shoulder, gleefully giving the Ray-Ban-wearing driver a hard time. Proctor slowed down a little to cruise past them, but they didn't even look up from their notebooks.

Just over half an hour later, he struck lucky.

There it was! The Daimler! Cruising along in the slow lane at a modest sixty-five. Proctor eased off on his accelerator, then indicated left, and tucked himself nicely in, a couple of cars behind.

As the heater slowly dried his wet, filthy clothes, he smiled in satisfaction. The warm air circulating in the car might stink of the cow dung he had waded through earlier, but that no longer mattered one bit. As far as he was concerned, everything was coming up roses.

Hellboy had been to London many times, but it never failed to give him that now-familiar rush. He could almost hear the vibrant echoes of its terrible, exhilarating history reverberating through the centuries, each year merely adding another skin, another layer, to an ever-expanding past. Like a kid in a sweet shop, he pressed his face to the Daimler's tinted window, the sawn-off stumps of his horns clunking gently against the glass each time the car bumped over a patch of uneven road. In many ways the city was a mess— dirty, sprawling, congested, patched-up, a mishmash of styles and cultures—but that was also kind of what made it beautiful. It was like some impossibly old man, whose unbelievable, event-filled existence was etched into every deep groove on his gnarled and wrinkled face.

Hellboy had woken the instant they left the M25, the ever-busy motorway that encircled central London like a noose. It was as if he had a built-in sensor that informed him when the journey was about to get interesting. They approached central London from the east, bypassing Canning Town and Limehouse—once a center for shipbuilding, notorious in Victorian times for its gambling and drug dens, and a frequent haunt of Charles Dickens—and cruising through the much-renovated Isle of Dogs. Abe pointed out the glittering, rocketlike splendor of Canary Wharf, the tallest building in the UK, as it drifted by on the right, and then they were driving through Whitechapel, Jack the Ripper's old haunt, and on from there into the city.

Their hotel, the Old Bloomsbury, was a renovated Georgian townhouse, tucked away down a quiet, leafy sidestreet close to the

British Museum. After the bustle of central London, the abrupt quietude of the location was a little disorienting.

"Nice place," said Liz, a delighted grin spreading over her face as she took in the hotel's elegant façade. "*Really* nice place."

The satellite phone on Hellboy's belt started to beep and he held it to his ear.

"Yep," he said.

They all heard the tinny voice of Rachel Turner, who had been traveling in the car behind theirs all the way to London.

"This is a quiet street, but we'll be going in round the back. The car park there is surrounded by an eight-foot-high wall. We've requisitioned the hotel for as long as we need it. It'll be run by a skeleton staff, who have all signed the Official Secrets Act. Of course, your cover will be blown as soon as you hit the streets, but at least this'll give you all a chance to get a jump-start on the investigation before the paparazzi start trailing you. For now, go up to your rooms, settle in, and relax. You've got a briefing at Scotland Yard at four p.m. Your car will be waiting round the back at three thrity to pick you up."

"Got it," Hellboy said, and stuck his phone back in his belt. Glancing at the clock mounted in the walnut dashboard of the Daimler, he saw that it was two forty-five p.m.—breakfast time back home.

"Damn briefing," he muttered. "It's just dead time. What can these guys tell us that we don't already know?"

Liz shrugged. "Maybe they've got new information."

"Nah, they're just covering their asses. Then if anything happens to us they can at least claim it wasn't due to negligence on their part."

Liz knew there was a lot of truth in Hellboy's words, but she still thought it useful to get the heads-up on a situation from those directly in the firing line. Different perspectives, different insights. It was all good.

"I wonder if our luggage has arrived?" Abe mused as they pulled into the car park at the rear of the hotel.

Liz knew he was thinking of his books and music.

"Does it ever?" Hellboy snorted. "Knowing those Operations guys our stuff'll be halfway to Karachi by now."

Abe looked alarmed, the finlike ridges on his neck fluttering in agitation.

"Come on," said Liz, "let's get inside. At least if we're quick we'll have time for a proper English cup of tea."

Hellboy saw their chauffeur, Christopher, unclipping his seat belt. He guessed it was part of the guy's job to open the car doors for his clients at the end of their journey, maybe even carry their luggage for them. Personally, though, Hellboy was uncomfortable with servility, hated being treated like he was something special.

"It's okay, pal, I got it," he said, and pushed the passenger door open. He unfolded himself from the car, hooves clacking on the concrete as he swung his legs round and stood up. He was rotating his neck, shoulder muscles crackling, when he heard a car door clunk shut and a voice speak his name. He turned, tail swishing, expecting to see Agent Turner—even though the person who had spoken had sounded like a man. But Agent Turner was still sitting in her car, making a phone call, and instead what he saw was a vagrant, striding forward and pointing a camera at him.

No, not a vagrant. The guy was unshaven, his clothes crumpled and caked with mud, but the fact that he had a car, which he had parked badly just inside the car-park entrance, and a nifty-looking camera suggested that he wasn't forced to walk the streets and sleep rough.

"Hey!" Hellboy shouted as the guy snapped him, not once but several times. Throwing up his hand in the classic "no publicity" pose, he growled, "Back off, pal."

The man lowered the camera. Hellboy's anger seemed not to intimidate him in the slightest. He looked like the kind of guy who encountered threats and bluster on a daily basis.

"Might I have a few words, Hellboy?" the guy asked.

"Buzz off," Hellboy muttered.

"Please. My readers would love to know what you're doing in London."

"Who the hell are you?" asked Agent Turner, who had now spotted the man and catapulted out of her car.

"Abe Sapien, right?" the man said, ignoring her and pointing at Abe.

"Never mind him. My colleague asked who *you* were, buddy," Hellboy said.

"My name's Colin Proctor. I'm a reporter for the *Star*. I found out you were coming to London and—"

"Who told you?" asked Liz, who had followed Abe out of the car and was now standing beside him.

The man smiled—a little too smugly, Hellboy thought. He clenched his right fist, the anger rising in him.

"A good journalist never reveals his sources, Miss Sherman," he said. "By the way, may I just say that your photographs don't do you credit. You're far more beautiful in the flesh."

"Man, this guy is a piece of work," Hellboy muttered.

"Can I tell my readers that you're here to investigate the torso murders?" Proctor asked.

"You can tell 'em what you like," Hellboy said.

"In that case, can I tell them that there's more to this case than meets the eye? That there is perhaps some *supernatural* element involved? Because that's what you do, isn't it? Investigate the strange, the unexplained?"

"No comment," Hellboy said.

He began to stomp towards the hotel's back entrance. Proctor dodged around Rachel Turner, who made an ineffectual effort to restrain him, and scuttled after him.

"Are the people of London under threat, Hellboy?" he asked.

"No comment."

"Can we expect a speedy resolution to this current crisis?"

"No comment."

"Are there likely to be further victims of the torso killer, who-ever he, she, or it may be?"

"No comment."

Richard had been last out of the Daimler and was now trailing at the rear of the group. "Look, mate, why don't you give it up?" he said. "Can't you see you're not going to get anything here?"

Proctor took a photograph of Richard, then skipped nimbly out of the way as Rachel Turner made a grab for his camera.

"On the contrary," he said with a wolfish grin, "I've got more than enough, thanks."

Two hours later Hellboy was ready to kick some serious butt. The encounter with the sleazebag reporter had set his blood on a low boil, but the interminable briefing at Scotland Yard afterwards had really cranked up the heat. Tired and bored herself, Liz had found it difficult to stifle her yawns throughout the meeting. She had glanced over at Hellboy a few times, and from the look on his face had half expected to see steam jetting out of his ears.

By the time the briefing was over, Hellboy was certainly in no mood to broach any argument. When DCI Reynolds, one of the officers leading the murder investigation, suggested that the police were in overall charge of the operation and that the B.P.R.D. was answerable to the Met, Hellboy shook his head.

"We're answerable to nobody," he said. "We do this our way or not at all."

Reynolds, a brusque, broad-shouldered man with a permanent five o'clock shadow, bristled. "With all due respect, sir—"

"With all due respect," Hellboy interrupted in a louder voice, "we didn't fly all the way over here just to toe the line. We've got vast experience of this kind of crap. You don't. End of story."

There were glowers all round. Liz could almost *smell* the tes-tosterone. In the end a few calls were made and a compromise was

THE ALL-SEEING EYE   63

reached, which, although nobody seemed particularly satisfied with it, favored the B.P.R.D.

It was agreed that the Bureau would lead the investigation, but that they would involve the local authorities, and in particular the police, every step of the way. A further argument ensued when Hellboy announced that his immediate intention was to head down to the London Underground in search of the creature which had terrorized the young couple on Sunday night. Reynolds's response was that if Hellboy was doing that, he had to take two armed police officers down with him.

"No way," Hellboy protested. "I'm not playing nursemaid to nobody."

"I'm not asking you to play nursemaid," Reynolds retorted, "and frankly, *sir*, I find that remark insulting. My men are highly trained officers—"

"Who break easily," Hellboy butted in. "Unlike me."

"Highly trained officers armed with high-carbine assault rifles." Hellboy snorted.

"Kids with BB guns. If that's a demon down in those tunnels, *Chief Inspector*, then that's what those guys will look like to it."

Finally Hellboy put a call through to Tom Manning, who told him not to make a diplomatic incident out of the situation.

"It's their country, Hellboy," Manning said. "You know how territorial the Brits are. If they want to send their guys down with you, that's *their* lookout."

"Except it isn't," Hellboy said. "It's my lookout. If anything happens to those guys, I'll feel responsible."

"You'll have no reason to do so. As I say, it's their country, and—to some extent at least—we have to respect their methods and comply with their wishes."

There was a simmering silence at the other end of the line.

"Are you waiting for a direct order, Hellboy?" Manning sighed.

"Are you going to give me one?" Hellboy said.

Two minutes later he slammed down the phone and marched back up to Reynolds.

"Okay," he said, "your guys are in. But when the time comes to notify their next of kin, Chief Inspector, I hope you'll have the guts to do it yourself."

☠ CHAPTER 4

"Your friend Hellboy's a feisty fellow, isn't he?" Richard said.

Despite her liking for the young lecturer, Liz felt herself bristling. She was fiercely protective of Hellboy, would defend him to the hilt, and—good-natured banter with Abe aside—would never dream of criticizing him behind his back.

"He's my best friend," she said, perhaps a little too curtly.

Richard, who was driving, glanced at her. "Hey, listen," he said, "I didn't mean anything. I think he's a great bloke. I like a man who stands up for himself and says what he thinks."

Man. Not many people called Hellboy that without hesitating first. That was one of the things Liz liked about Richard—his easy acceptance of their weirdness. Hellboy's picture had been on enough magazine covers and TV news bulletins over the years, but when people met him they still reacted as if what they'd really been expecting was some regular guy who just donned the big red suit to fight crime. And, maybe aside from HB's old flame, Anastasia Bransfield, she had never seen anyone not flinch from that big stone hand of his before. It was an instinctive thing, like the hand had some kind of evil aura about it. But Richard had walked right up and held his hand out for Hellboy to shake. And Hellboy, perhaps taken by surprise, had shaken it.

"Sorry," Liz said, "I'm a little raw. Ignore me."

"You need some sleep," said Richard.

"Tell me about it. But I'm not going to mess my body clock up even more by conking out now. I'll sleep with the locals."

As soon as she realized what she had said, she arched an eyebrow and added, "In a manner of speaking."

Richard laughed and pushed the car through a set of changing lights. It was around six p.m. now, and already dark. London was a riot of neon and car headlights. It hurt Liz's weary eyes a little, so she closed them briefly.

"What you've got to realize about Hellboy," she said, "is that he's been in the public eye for most of his life. He's not comfortable with it, but he can't do anything about it. It's not like he can slip on a pair of shades and a baseball cap and melt into the crowd. Everywhere he goes people stare at him, and just by doing that they remind him he's different. Under the circumstances I think he's remarkably well balanced and even tempered. In fact, I'd go so far as to say that he's the sweetest guy I've ever known."

Richard nodded. "You really love him, don't you?"

"Yeah, I do," she said without hesitation. "He's the best big brother a girl could wish for."

Richard had picked Liz up from her hotel twenty minutes before. As soon as they had arrived back at the Old Bloomsbury after their briefing at Scotland Yard, Hellboy had outlined their three-pronged plan of attack for the evening. Liz was to accompany Richard, who had told them he could put them in touch with a sangoma resident in London, who might shed some light on recent events; Abe would visit the murder sites; and Hellboy himself would check out the Underground. They would rendezvous back at the hotel later and compare notes.

"So who's this guy we're going to see?" Liz asked now.

"His name's Kobus Labuschagne," said Richard. "He's a sangoma from Johannesburg in South Africa. He was forced to flee his country eight years ago after speaking out against the dark practices used by some of his peers. Because of evidence he gave to the police, his wife and two daughters were murdered and their bodies mutilated. Despite this he continues to help the police in the UK.

Three years ago the information he supplied led to the arrest of three men and two women, who were responsible for the muti murder of a four-year-old boy whose torso was found floating in the Thames close to Tower Bridge. During the trial he was under a twenty-four-hour police guard. Even today he gets threatened on a regular basis, and several times he's been attacked."

"Brave man," said Liz.

Richard smiled. "I told him that once, and he said he was just doing what was right. He's a great believer in fate. He thinks that whatever ultimately happens to him will be decided by his gods and not his fellow men. He thinks that men are just instruments of the gods, and that whatever he does will not change his fate."

"That's one way of looking at it," said Liz. "So I take it you know this guy well?"

"I wouldn't say that," said Richard. "I've met him a few times. He comes up to the college now and then to talk to the students, or to help out in an advisory capacity."

Five minutes later Richard turned into a long drive that led to a pair of enormous black iron gates topped by a row of vicious-looking spikes. Through the gates, lit up like a Christmas tree, Liz could see a glittering tower block that seemed all burnished steel and curved glass. Beyond the tower block was the Thames, black as sealskin beneath the night sky, lights sparkling and slithering on its fast-flowing surface.

"Labuschagne has an office *here?*" said Liz, goggling at the building.

"No," said Richard, "not an office—an *apartment*. What you've got here, Liz, is your archetypal, much-sought-after riverside location."

"I never realized witch doctoring was such a lucrative profession."

"I don't think it is," Richard said, bringing the car to a halt in front of the black gates.

"How does he make his money then?"

Richard shrugged. "Stock exchange? Property? Who knows?"

He got out of the car and approached an intercom located on the wall to the right of the gate. Liz saw him speak. As he walked back to the car, the gates started to slowly and soundlessly open.

A few minutes later the two of them were stepping out of the lift onto the eleventh floor of the apartment block. From the carpets to the wallpaper to the fixtures and fittings, the entire building seemed to exhale wealth and luxury, elegance and taste.

Beautiful though the place was, however, it set Liz's teeth on edge. To fit in here a woman ought to be tall and graceful; she ought to be wearing an evening dress and an ermine wrap and carrying a Chihuahua. Liz, by contrast, was dressed in combat pants and scuffed boots, and wore a battle-worn canvas jacket over a black T-shirt faded to gray from too much washing. Her hair, greasy from traveling, was scraped back into a ponytail, and instead of a Chihuahua her only accessory was a 9mm automatic holstered at her hip.

"I feel a bit underdressed," she confided to Richard as they approached Labuschagne's door.

Richard smiled at her. "You look fine. Great, in fact."

The end of the corridor was shaped like the prow of a ship. Beyond a steel handrail, a vast curved window afforded them a spectacular view of the Thames and the sparkling lights of the city beyond.

Richard rapped on the door of flat number 1101. After a brief pause it was opened by a handsomely chiseled black man in his mid-forties. He was immaculately attired in a Savile Row suit, gold cuff links, and a pink silk tie.

"Good evening, Richard," the man said in a voice that made Liz think of liquid chocolate. "Good evening, Miss . . . Sherman, isn't it?"

"Liz," she said, covering her uncertainty with a brusqueness she immediately felt she should apologize for.

"Liz," Labuschagne acknowledged with a serene smile. "Please, both of you, come in. Make yourselves at home."

He led them along a corridor into an airy, spacious living room, the design of which was modern, clean, streamlined. Abstract art in muted colors adorned teal walls; sharp-angled chrome furniture upholstered in cream fabric was arranged just so. The expansive window, unadorned by curtains, shimmered with a million points of twinkling light from across the river. The pale wooden floor was polished to the consistency of ice or glass.

Although Liz hadn't quite known *what* to expect, it certainly wasn't this. She guessed she'd been anticipating something more . . . ethnic. Earthy. Something that gave more of a clue to Labuschagne's background and culture. Oddly her own presumptions made her a little uncomfortable. If there were two kinds of people Liz hated in the world, it was bigots and zealots. Both of those were characterized by their small-mindedness, their tendency to generalize, to lump people into preconceived parameters based on such vagaries as skin color, sexual preference, religious beliefs—or even whether they had horns and cloven hooves. Liz, however, had always prided herself on taking people as she found them, judging them on their individual merits. But wasn't she now doing exactly what she hated—making assumptions based on what amounted to pretty limited information? What, deep down, had she really expected Labuschagne to be like? Had she expected him to be dressed in animal skins and a feathered headdress, to be crouched in front of a boiling cauldron and casting handfuls of bones upon the ground? Would she have been less surprised if that was what she had found? To cover her embarrassment, she gripped the sangoma's outstretched hand and gushed, "You've got a *beautiful* place here, Mr. Labuschagne."

"I'm glad you approve," Labuschagne said, smiling again, "but please, call me Kobus."

Although Liz rarely made snap decisions about anybody—experience had taught her to be wary of first impressions—she decided that she liked this man. There was a genuineness about him, and also a gentleness.

"Kobus it is," she said, returning his smile.

He leaned forward and raised his eyebrows mischievously. "I generally have a cognac around this time. Would you care to join me?"

"Why not?" Liz said.

Labuschagne waved them to a seat, then crossed to a chrome-and-glass cabinet and produced a cognac which resembled a giant crystal egg, and three enormous brandy glasses. He poured a generous measure into each glass and handed them to his guests before taking a seat opposite them, his back to the panoramic window.

Liz took a sip of her drink—and blinked as her tastebuds exploded with delight.

"I'm not usually one for cognac, but that's wonderful," she said.

"Hennessy Ellipse," Labuschagne confided, and gave a guilty shrug. "It's my greatest indulgence. Appallingly decadent, I admit, but it salves my conscience a little if I get the chance to share it with friends."

Liz took another sip, wondering how much a bottle of this stuff was. Labuschagne had named the cognac as if he expected her to know it, but she was no connoisseur. She glanced to her right, her eye caught by something on a table next to the window. Propped beside a lamp with a tall stem were a pair of photographs in a curved metal frame. One depicted a smiling woman in a headscarf, who was half bent over a wooden tub. The other was a head-and-shoulders shot of two laughing girls with their arms around each other. The girls were maybe nine and six, and the older of the two had gaps in her wide grin where her milk teeth had fallen out. Both girls had beads and ribbons meticulously threaded into their tight twists of black hair. The woman and the two girls were bronze skinned and beautiful.

Liz remembered what Richard had told her about the san-goma's wife and daughters, and her throat tightened. Her attention flicked almost guiltily back to Labuschagne. His dark eyes transfixed her own.

"My wife Reta," he said softly, "and my daughters Sakile and Kamali. Do you know what happened to them, Liz?"

She nodded. "Richard told me."

Labuschagne leaned forward, swirling the liquid in his glass. "It is because of them, and thousands like them, that the war against evil must be fought every day. We must look it in the eye, Liz, and never flinch. We must strain every sinew in our efforts to eradicate it."

"For me that's pretty much a job description," Liz said. She placed her glass carefully on the wooden floor, as if acknowledging that it was time to get down to business.

"Richard tells me you might have some leads on the torso murders?" she said.

Labuschagne nodded. "I know of certain individuals in London who have had dealings with Yoruban death cults. Some are new to this country, whereas others have been living here quietly for some time. It is possible that the recent killings are part of some long-planned invocation ritual, or even that a single individual is attempting to achieve apotheosis via a sustained campaign of sacrifi-cial murder." He shook his head, his brow furrowing slightly. "I must admit to being a little perplexed, however. From what I understand of these crimes, although the victims bear many of the hallmarks of ritualized murder, the crimes themselves seem to be . . . what's the phrase . . . a departure from the norm?"

"Because the victims are white, you mean?"

"Partly that. And also because the perpetrators seem to have made no effort to conceal their crimes. On the contrary, the victims have been placed in highly visible locations—as if the killers wish to advertise their handiwork."

Richard leaned forward. "That's what's been puzzling me too. Most of the practitioners of bad muti in this country would be here illegally, wouldn't they, Kobus?"

Labuschagne nodded. "If not the sangomas themselves, then certainly a proportion of their followers. What you have to understand, Liz, is that muti slayings are clandestine crimes. These latest killings are totally uncharacteristic."

"So if these *are* muti slayings—and at the moment that's just a theory—then for them to come into the open, there must be something big going down?" Liz said.

"I would assume so. Though I can't imagine what it might be."

"Any Yoruban festivals coming up? Ancient legends or prophesies I should know about?"

Kobus and Richard looked at each other, both pulling the same blank face.

"If you want my opinion . . ." Kobus began.

"I do," said Liz.

"I believe you should look closer to home. I believe your killers are using the muti angle as a smoke screen to mask their true intentions. I believe the bodies are offerings to some . . . unknown deity."

"Bloodless offerings," amended Liz.

Kobus pursed his lips. "In which case the blood has most likely been used in a separate ritual. Wouldn't you agree, Richard?"

"It's a reasonable theory," Richard conceded.

Reflectively, Liz said, "But even if you're right, the killers would have to have some knowledge of muti practices, wouldn't they? Which means they might still have had some contact with the people you mentioned."

"Or they could just as easily have looked the information up," Richard said.

"True. But we have to follow whatever leads we've got."

Kobus drained his glass and stood up. "Let me give you some literature. Please, finish your drinks. I won't be a moment."

He walked across the room, so light of step that his feet barely made a sound on the wooden floor.

Richard sipped his drink and watched him go. Liz watched him too, but without turning round. Instead she followed his retreating reflection in the expansive window.

When he was out of earshot, Richard said, "So what do you think?"

Liz shrugged. "I think we pursue every angle. We search methodically until we find something."

"Like policemen," said Richard.

Liz narrowed her eyes, uncertain whether he was making fun of her. "I guess so. It's part of the job."

Richard smiled. "Hellboy always makes it sound so much more exciting. I read a couple of magazine interviews with him before you arrived. He gives the impression that you guys just fly around the world punching things into submission."

Liz smiled now too, albeit ruefully. "That's wishful thinking on his part. The procedural stuff frustrates him. He's an action-oriented kind of guy."

Kobus came back into the room, carrying a clear plastic folder and a couple of books, their leather covers stiff and faded with age. Handing them to Liz, he said, "You might find these useful. One is a glossary of African spirits and deities, and is the most exhaustive text I know on the subject. The other is a history of the Yoruban people. I've marked the chapters which detail their customs and beliefs."

"Thanks," Liz said. "I'll pass these on to Abe. He's our book guy. And rest assured, he'll look after them as if they were his own children."

Kobus acknowledged this with a smile, then held out the plastic folder. "I spent most of the afternoon compiling this for you. It's a list of people in London who have been previously associated with Yoruban death cults, or involved in unscrupulous muti practices. None have criminal convictions in this country, but don't let that fool you,

Liz. Please know that each and every one of those named here has the potential to be very dangerous."

As Liz took the folder from him, the sangoma placed a hand over hers to emphasize his words. His skin was cool and dry, like a reptile's.

She raised her head and looked him in the eye. Softly she said, "Don't worry, Kobus. I can be pretty dangerous myself."

The great thing about London in October, thought Abe, was that a guy could get away with a big overcoat, a wide-brimmed hat, and a scarf without attracting so much as a second glance. Not that he was generally in the habit of covering himself up like the elephant man, but in this instance it was simply *convenient*.

For now, the B.P.R.D.'s involvement here was still a secret, not least because the British press were such a pain in the ass that it was feared their jackal-like behavior might hamper the investigation should they decide to turn Hellboy's presence into a media circus. And so far Abe's disguise had held up, and he had managed to move from place to place with impunity. He had already checked out two of the murder sites, at Russell Street and Great Queen Street, and was now on his way to the third. He hadn't found out much that he didn't already know, although in both places, hyper-attuned as he was, he had sensed the presence of rushing water close by.

Had it merely been the sinewy power of the Thames? It was possible, though Abe had had the impression that the flow of water was considerably closer to him than the nearby river. He had filed the information away in his mind, deciding that if nothing else more concrete turned up at this third location, then he would backtrack and investigate further. He was aware that London was riddled with hidden streams and tributaries, many of which flowed deep underground, and that its sewage system, cavernous and Victorian, was almost a city in itself. But even so, the notion that he was perhaps missing something important wouldn't stop niggling at him.

The offices of the *Dundee Courier* at 186 Fleet Street were cordoned off with yellow-and-black police tape. A lone uniformed PC was standing outside in the drizzle when Abe's driver eased to a halt on a double yellow line on the opposite curb.

Keeping his head bowed and his hat pulled down low, Abe climbed out of the car and hurried across the road, which was slick with rain and sheened with the shattered umber reflections of streetlights. At least the weather had driven the rubberneckers and the press away, he thought. The PC, who looked barely out of his teens, stepped forward as Abe approached.

The kid peered at Abe's proferred ID with a scowl, water dripping from the brim of his domed helmet. All at once his eyes widened. As Abe raised his head, revealing his face, the young PC gazed at him with something like awe.

"You're that amphibious bloke," he said.

Abe nodded. "I think you were expecting me?"

"Yeah we were . . . er, sir," the kid said, clearly flustered. "I'll . . . er, just tell the guv that you're here."

Abe waited patiently as the kid muttered into a radio attached to his breast pocket. When he had finished he said nervously, "The guv says he'll be down in a minute."

"Thanks," Abe replied.

The two stood facing each other, not saying anything, for several seconds. Abe was quite happy to remain silent, but the young PC looked distinctly uncomfortable, and at last he blurted, "Grotty weather, innit?"

"I like the rain," Abe said.

"Yeah, I suppose you do," the PC muttered, then reddened. "No offense, sir."

"None taken."

The PC grunted, and then, sensing movement, looked round in obvious relief. "Here's the guv now."

A lean, sallow-faced man, whose bony wrists protruded from

the cuffs of his dark jacket, unlocked the glass-fronted door of the building and pulled it open. He regarded Abe without flinching and held out a hand. "Agent Sapien, good to meet you. I'm Detective Inspector Cartwright. Come on in. Get yourself out of the rain."

Cartwright led Abe through a large open-plan office, now lit with just a couple of desk lamps, and into a short corridor at the back of the room. In the left-hand wall was an open door, through which Abe glimpsed a large communal kitchen, harshly illuminated by strip lighting, which spilled out into the corridor. Opposite the kitchen was a lift with dented stainless-steel doors. A pair of bedraggled rubber plants flanked the lift, their pots stuffed with cigarette butts.

"The woman's body was found upstairs in the editor's office," Cartwright said, pressing the lift button. "It had been dumped on the desk like a . . . bloody postal delivery."

Nodding, Abe asked, "Was the office locked?"

"No, but all outside doors leading into the building were."

"And there was no visible sign of entry?"

Cartwright spread his hands. "Same old story, Agent Sapien."

"Call me Abe," Abe said as the lift doors opened. Together he and Cartwright stepped inside.

Cartwright pressed the button for the next floor, then squatted down and pointed at a dark fleck, barely noticeable, on the smooth gray floor.

"This is the only piece of physical evidence we've found," he said.

"Blood?" asked Abe.

Cartwright nodded. "And forensic tests have confirmed it to be the victim's."

"So we know the body was carried up from ground level," Abe said. "I guess that's something. I take it no other discriminatory evidence has been found?"

Cartwright raised his eyebrows in resignation. "Well, there's plenty of physical evidence, which we're still working on. But people are in and out of here all the time. Not wishing to be defeatist, Agent . . . sorry, Abe, but I doubt we'll find anything useful."

The two of them went up to the editor's office, but there was little to see. Abe raised his head and sniffed. Just as at the previous murder sites, he could sense the nearby presence of flowing water. It was like a tugging inside him, a tingling in his skin, a stirring in his blood. He could almost taste its briny flavor on his lips, could almost plot the course of its currents and eddies in his mind's eye. It gave off a power, an energy, like a ley line or a subterranean electricity supply.

He mentioned it to Cartwright, who surprised him by saying, "That'll be the River Fleet. It runs right underneath this building."

"Really?" said Abe. "That's interesting." He told Cartwright how he had sensed the proximity of fast-flowing water at the other murder sites. Cartwright pulled a discouraging face.

"Probably just coincidence. If you're thinking the victim was brought in that way, think again."

"Oh?" said Abe. "Why do you say that?"

"It's inaccessible, that's all. Too many of the channels beneath the city are narrow and filled with water from floor to ceiling. I wouldn't be surprised if a lot of those old tunnels are blocked, or have even collapsed. They're barely maintained these days."

"And you know this for a fact?" Abe asked.

For the first time Cartwright looked exasperated. "Well, no, but it stands to reason. Believe me, Abe, subterranean rivers are not the answer to this particular locked-room mystery. The real solution is much simpler. Somehow the killers got hold of keys, that's all."

"To all three of the buildings in which bodies were found?"

Cartwright shrugged. "Why not? All it takes is a little planning and ingenuity. And these are certainly not random killings or crimes of passion. Sick though they are, a lot of attention has gone into this . . . this spree, or campaign, or whatever you want to call it."

Abe knew that, to a human, his face betrayed little of what he was feeling, that he had to convey such things as humor or compliance or understanding through words alone.

"I appreciate what you're saying, Detective Inspector," he said. "All the same, I'd like to take a look at these underground waterways, if only to set my mind at rest. I mean, what have you got to lose? I'm not a drain on your resources, plus I do have an affinity with water, which you might as well take advantage of."

He tilted his head in what he hoped was a disarming manner. Cartwright sighed.

"You do realize that that water will probably be contaminated with all sorts of disgusting bacteria?"

"I have a strong constitution," Abe replied.

Cartwright looked dubious. "It's your funeral, I suppose."

"Let's hope it doesn't come to that."

They headed back to the lift. Once inside, Cartwright pressed a button marked B.

"The river's accessible from here?" said Abe in surprise. He had assumed he might have to access the Fleet via the sewers.

"There's a manhole cover in the basement with a culvert right underneath. We checked it out this afternoon."

"Couldn't be better," Abe said.

"I'd reserve judgment until you see it, if I were you," Cartwright replied.

Stepping out of the lift into the basement, Abe was surprised not by how spacious and high ceilinged the room was, but by how much it reminded him of the cloisters of a church or monastery. Partly this was due to the central row of pillared arches, which concealed the true dimensions of the room within a series of shadowed alcoves, and gave the impression that beyond the alcoves there could be further doors or corridors. It was not difficult to imagine that there might be an entire network of catacombs snaking off from here, stretching out like roots under the city, connecting buildings in the same way that the Underground system connected train stations.

Though grand, the basement was cold and damp and evidently little used. A pair of bare bulbs, their light diffused by a coating of grime, showed where moisture had leaked through the rough stone walls in slick, glistening patches, or had mingled with bacterial spores to form fuzzy white blotches of mold. Ragged swathes of cobweb, opaque with dust, festooned the ceiling. Some old items of office furniture, spongy and sodden, lolled against the wall, along with a half-dozen lengths of warped timber and a rusted set of stepladders.

Abe saw Cartwright shiver and said, "I guess this must be where the notorious barber dismembered his victims?"

Cartwright looked offended. "That wasn't why I was shivering. It's bleedin' parky down here."

If Abe could have laughed he would have done. "I wasn't suggesting you were scared, Detective Inspector. God forbid."

Cartwright eyed Abe as if weighing him up. Then he asked, "I hope you don't mind me asking, Abe, but do you *feel* the cold?"

"Not like you do," said Abe, "but I'm aware of the temperature, yes."

Cartwright nodded, as if satisfied. "And in answer to your question," he said, "yes, this *is* where the old guy supposedly chopped up his victims, though I'm not sure exactly *where* he did it. According to the story, there was a revolving trapdoor somewhere in the ceiling, which the barber's chair was attached to. When the customer was comfortable, a catch would be released, the chair would tip over, and the poor old sod would fall twenty feet to the stone floor below. If he didn't die from the fall, he'd have his throat cut and be chopped into little bits. Apparently there was a secret tunnel, which ran from here, beneath St. Dunstan's church and the burial crypt, to the pie shop in Bell Yard. But if that's true, it was blocked off long ago."

Abe knew the story, but he couldn't deny that standing in the actual place where the dastardly deeds were purported to have occurred lent them an added *frisson*. He remembered what Kate Corrigan had said about this location possessing an occult resonance, about it calling out to bad men. What was it she had *actually* said? "Some places are steeped in wickedness." Something like that.

Well, Abe thought, if that was true then *he* couldn't sense it. No doubt there would be some within the B.P.R.D. who would. The Bureau had more than its share of psychics, sensitives, clairvoyants. He'd been with a few who had fled screaming from what had seemed to him the most innocuous of places. Hellboy had a theory that the majority of sensitives in the Bureau's employ were simply attention seekers. "There's evil here!" he would cry in imitation, adopting his flakiest voice and throwing up his hands in horror. Then he would scowl and mutter, "Yeah? Tell me about it." Cracked Liz up every time.

"Where's the manhole cover you mentioned?" Abe asked.

Cartwright pointed into the shadows where the light couldn't reach. "Just the other side of that arch." He produced a rubber-handled torch from his pocket, turned it on, and led the way.

Abe might not have been able to pick up evil vibrations, but he could hear the water calling to him loud and clear. If the Fleet proved inaccessible, as Cartwright believed, then he might have to assuage his craving with a dip in the Thames once his night's work was done.

The manhole cover was the size of a car tire, but it was thin and rusty, and lifted easily with the aid of the crowbar that Cartwright had left here earlier. The DI shone his torch into a stone channel which looked barely wide enough for a child to crawl through, along which brownish water was flowing.

"Jesus," he said, "it's even narrower than I remember it. You'll never get through there, Abe."

"I will," Abe said, removing his hat, then peeling off his scarf and coat. "I'm very flexible."

"All the same, I'm not happy. What if you get stuck? We're probably breaking all sorts of regulations even contemplating this."

Though Abe was touched by the policeman's concern, he said airily, "The channel's bound to open out eventually. And don't worry about rules and regulations. I've got special dispensation from the U.S. government. I'm fully responsible for my actions."

"Even so . . ." Cartwright murmured.

Abe turned and placed a webbed hand on the policeman's shoulder. "Detective Inspector, I'm going in whether you like it or not. This is my call."

Cartwright sighed unhappily. "Well, like I said, it's your—"

"—funeral. Yes, I know. And if the worst *does* happen, you have my permission to send a wreath spelling out the words 'I told you so.' "

Lowering himself into the culvert, his feet either side of the channel of rushing water, Abe felt the chill from the surrounding stonework settling on his skin. It was not an unpleasant sensation. Indeed, being neither claustrophobic nor afraid of the dark, there was an almost womblike comfort to be gleaned from what awaited him. He crouched down, and then slid headfirst into the water, sighing with pleasure as it swirled over and around him.

The culvert was certainly narrow. It extended through the stonework ahead, a circular tunnel barely wider than an industrial drainpipe, beyond which only blackness could be seen. Abe pushed himself forward experimentally. It was a tight fit, but he thought the flow of water and the slickness of his skin would be enough to guarantee progress . . . providing he could make himself as streamlined as possible. Lying full length in the water, he fumbled with the belt buckled around his waist. Losing it would mean having to cope without his gun, his homing beacon, his means of communication and many of the other useful accoutrements he carried about his person, but that was a sacrifice he was going to have to make.

Tugging the belt from under his stomach, he held it up. "DI Cartwright," he called, "could you arrange to have this sent to my hotel? I'll be back for it later."

"Sure," Cartwright said, his voice muffled by the water. Abe swung his arm round awkwardly in the confined space and tossed the belt up to him. He heard the clatter as Cartwright caught it.

"Thanks," he called. "Wish me luck."

Then, without waiting for a reply, he plunged his head beneath the water and propelled himself into the darkness.

Hellboy was forging through darkness, too, but the only water he had to contend with were occasional drips from the ceiling. Even so, he was cranky enough to swear each time he felt a wet splat of cold on his cheek or neck. The reason for his crankiness was that he was still unhappy about having non-B.P.R.D. operatives accompanying him on his mission. Whatever Tom Manning had said, Hellboy felt ultimately responsible for the welfare of the two guys. It was easy enough for Tom, sitting in his cozy Connecticut office, to be nonchalant about them. To Tom these guys were nothing but concessionary factors in an ongoing process of negotiation with the British authorities. He didn't have to see them as human beings.

Hellboy did, though. Oh, he had *tried* to distance himself, had done his utmost to be as businesslike as possible, but the problem was, he couldn't keep it up. Despite his fearsome exterior, he was a personable guy, and if someone treated him with friendliness and respect, then he couldn't help but respond.

And these guys *had* been, and still were, friendly and respectful. It turned out they *admired* him. Turned out they had *volunteered* for this mission just for the chance to work with him, fer Chrissakes. If they had been a couple of gung-ho morons, maybe he could have hated them a little for that. But they weren't; they were competent professionals. They listened to what he said and they took no chances. Apart from the fact that they had no real idea of what they could be facing here today—despite Hellboy's best efforts to educate them—they were perfect. Their lack of true understanding was certainly not their fault. When it came to fighting monsters, Hellboy knew no amount of preparation was ever enough. The only way to find out how you would react to the hyper-reality of encountering such a creature was to meet one head on. Which was why—if Hellboy was obligated to have any backup at all—he liked being surrounded by people he could rely on, people who had done this kind of work before. The inexperienced were unpredictable. Hellboy had seen battle-hardened army veterans freeze at the sight of their first supernatural entity; on the other hand, he had seen fresh-faced rookies barely out of high school take the appearance of some colossal, slavering swamp monster in their stride.

The two guys alongside him this evening were called Louis and Sean. Louis was a tall, broad-shouldered black man in his mid-thirties, whose easygoing, unflappable manner seemed to radiate stability and assurance. Sean, ten years younger, was sparky, alert, and receptive, but highly disciplined nonetheless. Louis, a Londoner, was married, with a five-year-old son and a nine-month-old daughter. Sean was from Aberdeen, and had a girlfriend called Lucy, who was a student at London University.

All this, and more, Hellboy had discovered in the hour or so that the three of them had spent tramping through the black, filthy tunnels of the London Underground. The only other living creatures they had seen in that time had been rats and mice, scampering away from the thin white beams of the flashlights mounted along the sights of the police officers' assault rifles. The only sounds they had heard, aside from the crunch of their own boots and the clack of Hellboy's hooves, had been the rumble of distant trains, powering through tunnels in those sections of the system that hadn't been shut down.

"D'ye mind if I ask ye a question, Hellboy?" Sean asked as they trudged through the darkness.

Hellboy shrugged. "Go ahead."

"D'ye ever get scared?"

"Not of the monsters."

"What then?" said Sean. "What scares someone like you?"

Hellboy swallowed and said, "You know what *really* scares me?"

"What?" asked Sean.

"Damn fool questions from guys who like nothing better than to poke their noses into other people's business."

He spoke in a mild rumble to show that his words should not be taken too harshly. Louis got it straight away and chuckled. "That told *you*, kid."

"Aw, man, that's a cop-out!" Sean said ruefully, but he didn't pursue the matter. He was astute enough to realize that the subject was closed.

They came to the latest of many intersections. One thing the three of them had discovered very quickly was that the tube system beneath London's streets was not as straightforward as it appeared on the standard map. As well as the wide, reasonably well-maintained tunnels that carried the trains, there was also a more intricate secondary system of access corridors, maintenance channels, and passageways leading to storage facilities where tools and equipment were kept. Additional to this were the tunnels that led nowhere—that were blocked off, or partly blocked off, or which had caved in. Some of these—the walls caked with soot, the ground inches deep in sludge—led to long-abandoned stations, known as "ghost stations," of which, they had been informed before heading down here, there were around forty scattered throughout the network.

At the intersection, Louis and Sean stepped forward to flank Hellboy's muscular form and swept their gun-mounted flashlights swiftly left and right. There wasn't much to see—more curved, soot-blackened walls; more rails; a few dark areas up ahead that might have been alcoves or side passages.

Before Hellboy had to ask, Louis was reaching into the breast pocket of his padded jacket and taking out the map they had been given at the outset of their mission. They pored over it, Louis holding one side, Hellboy pinching the other delicately between the stubby stone fingers of his right hand. Louis traced their route with a black-gloved finger.

"We're ... here," he said. "We've covered about ... what? Four miles?" He glanced at Hellboy. "So which way now, boss?"

Hellboy glowered at the map. If he was being honest, he didn't have a clue. This plan had seemed so simple at the outset. Come down here, find the monster, batter some answers out of it. It hadn't occurred to him that the Underground system encompassed some two hundred and fifty-odd miles of track. As if reading his thoughts, Sean said, "Ye reckon we'll find this beastie, Hellboy?"

Hellboy scowled. "We'll find it."

"Ye got special powers, is that it? Monster-detecting glands or something?"

Hellboy glanced at the young officer and raised one eyebrow. "You poking fun at me, kid?"

"No way!" Sean exclaimed, then gave a slight smile. "Well, a wee bit, mebbe. I just ... I don't see how we're goan find this thing, that's all."

"We know where it was last spotted," Hellboy said. "And we can guess that most of the time it sticks to unused tunnels, out-of-the-way places, otherwise ..."

"A damn train woulda hit it," said Louis.

"Yeah," said Hellboy. He glanced from left to right. "My guess is that it emerged or appeared somewhere around here, and has made its lair close by. I doubt it'll have strayed far from its place of origin."

"What makes ye think that?" Sean asked.

"Monsters are creatures of habit. Most of 'em stick to particular places—haunted lakes, blasted heaths, that kinda stuff—and terrorize the crap out of the local population."

"Until you turn up to pulverize 'em," said Sean.

"That's usually the way it goes, yeah."

"So . . ." Louis said. "Which way *do* you wanna go, boss?"

"Which way takes us away from the trains?"

"Left."

"Then we go left," Hellboy said.

Louis folded up the map and they trudged on. The dark areas set into the wall ahead *were* tunnels. The first ended in a rusty mesh grille, stretching floor to ceiling, but the second was more promising. When Louis shone his flashlight into the opening, the light revealed a passage stretching back into darkness that was both high and wide enough to accommodate even Hellboy's bulk.

"I'll go first," Hellboy said. "Stick close behind, and try to light the way ahead as much as possible. I don't want the bastard jumping out of the dark at me."

"Why? You scared?" Sean asked cheekily.

"Behave," Hellboy said.

They moved forward cautiously, alert for the slightest sound or movement. The walls glistened with damp, the water having trickled along the same cracks in the brickwork for so long that white veins of deposit had formed along the channels. The ground was thick with sludge, which caked Hellboy's hooves. As requested, Louis and Sean tried to give Hellboy as much light as possible by shining their gun-mounted flashlights through the gaps between his body and the tunnel walls on either side.

They had been moving for less than five minutes when the criss-crossing beams picked out what appeared to be a thick white worm on the ground ahead. Immediately Hellboy came to a halt, holding up his stone hand. He had seen many strange sights in his time—flying vampiric heads, giant bees with the faces of jackals, a demon that disguised itself as a camper van—and so a potential attack by giant killer worms was pretty much par for the course. He peered at the worm. It was inert, half covered in sludge, though he knew better than to assume that inactive meant harmless.

"Keep your lights trained on that thing," he murmured. "I'm gonna check it out. We don't know what it is, how fast it can move, or what it can do, so keep alert—and expect the unexpected."

He stalked forward, unconsciously bunching his fists. He fully expected the thing to rise out of the sludge and fly at him any moment. He was only a couple of meters away when he realized it wasn't a killer worm at all. The realization didn't make him any happier.

"Crap," he said.

"What is it, boss?" called Louis.

"Evidence that we're on the right track," said Hellboy. "Come take a look."

The two armed officers squelched forward, their light beams converging on the object.

"Nasty," said Sean quietly.

What Hellboy had thought was a worm was in fact a human arm. Up close they could see that the flesh was marbling as the blood coagulated inside it. The fingers, rigid and clawlike, were half buried in the mud.

Louis bent over to take a closer look at the severed limb. "Look at the way the bone's splintered at the shoulder," he said. "Looks like the poor guy's arm was twisted right out of its socket."

"Hmm," Hellboy said. He liked the way the guys were keeping it together here. Okay, so Sean was a little pale, but neither of them were freaking out, or asking dumb questions, or standing and goggling in disbelief at what their prey could do.

Louis glanced at Hellboy. "Proceed with caution?" he suggested.

Hellboy gave an abrupt nod. "You got it."

They bypassed the severed arm and moved on, a little more slowly than before. Louis and Sean tried to illuminate every meter of the tunnel as they progressed, their light beams slithering across the floor, skittering up the walls and across the ceiling. Hellboy was poised for action, his jaw set and muscles bunched, his breathing slow and regular. His tail swished from side to side and his yellow eyes were unblinking as he stalked like a gunslinger towards his own personal high noon.

Three minutes later, Louis said almost conversationally, "Whoa, guys."

Hellboy, a meter or so in front of him, said, "I see it."

"What?" Sean asked.

Louis's light beam was trained on the ground ahead—black with mud, with more blackness beyond. He shifted the beam slowly from side to side, using the light to paint in a little more definition. They saw the edge of a ragged opening, a chasm stretching from one side of the tunnel to the other.

"Jesus," breathed Sean. "Is it doon there, d'ye think?"

"Most likely place we've found so far," muttered Hellboy.

They edged forward until they were standing at the edge of the chasm. Louis and Sean pointed their beams directly into the pit, but all they could see beyond the reach of the light was blackness.

"How far down does it go, I wonder?" mused Louis.

Hellboy glanced at him. "Could be all the way into hell for all I know." He pondered a moment, then said, "I'm going in."

"Ye're goan climb doon there?" said Sean, eyes wide.

"Nah," said Hellboy. "That'd take too long. I'm gonna jump."

Louis half reached out as though to put a restraining hand on his arm, then thought better of it. Calmly, he said, "But you don't know how far down it goes."

"That's part of the fun," Hellboy said, grinning.

Still calm, Louis asked, "How far can you fall and still survive?"

Hellboy shrugged nonchalantly. "I've fallen out of airplanes in my time. Can't say it doesn't smart, but you can't do this job without picking up a few bruises."

Louis glanced at Sean, then he straightened up, planting his feet more firmly apart, adopting a combat stance. "Okay, boss," he said. "What do you want us to do?"

"Wait for me here," Hellboy said. "If I'm not back in an hour, head for the surface. If something starts to come out of the pit and it isn't me, open fire. If you give it all you've got and it keeps on coming, then run like hell. You got that?"

"We've got it," said Sean.

"Good luck, boss," said Louis.

Hellboy nodded and stepped forward, planting his hooves firmly on the edge of the pit. Peering down, he murmured, "*Arrivederci*, boys." Then he leaped into the dark.

☠ CHAPTER 5

As Abe had theorized—or at least hoped—the culvert widened out after a dozen meters or so. He had been only mildly concerned as he had wriggled through the tight brick tube surrounded by nothing but blackness and the rush of water, but he still felt relieved when he suddenly found himself with room to spread his arms, raise his head, and kick his feet. He hovered a moment in the suddenly much deeper water, blinking his eyes and getting his bearings. Behind him, through the murk, he saw a solid wall, in the center of which was the black circular hole from which he had emerged.

Upon immersion in water, Abe's body immediately and automatically began to act as a biological filtration system. Far more efficiently than most amphibians, he was able to take what he needed from the water and discard its harmful elements. Additionally he was able to assess and mostly identify the presence and volume of foreign bodies in his immediate environment. He knew that the water he was currently swimming in was from a natural source, but that it had been tainted by a degree of human and chemical effluent as it had flowed down from higher ground and found egress through the channels and conduits—some natural, some manmade—which snaked beneath the streets of London like a vast rabbit warren. Swimming in the stuff was not entirely pleasant, but neither was it unbearable, or, more importantly, hazardous to Abe's health. It was nothing, in fact, that a warm shower and a change of clothes wouldn't fix once he was done.

He allowed the water to caress his skin and ripple through his gills for a few moments, and then he kicked his feet and began to swim. For the most part he allowed the flow to carry him along; he always adored the sensation of giving himself up to the convoluted flux of streams and rivers and seas, of becoming one with the sinewy and remorseless purpose of the tides.

Abe being Abe, however, he did not allow himself to become distracted. Mindful of his mission, he was assiduous in his exploration of this new and hidden world. Meticulously he investigated each passage, each avenue, each side tunnel he came across. Sometimes a detour would lead to further detours, whereas at other times they would simply peter out, forcing him to double back. Wherever his meanderings took him, however, Abe would always—partly through instinct and partly through calculation—eventually find his way back to his main route through the city. As he swam, absorbed in his task, time became meaningless; an hour passed, then two, and still he ploughed on, searching for clues, for answers. He had an excellent sense of direction and a highly attuned ability to calculate distance, but by the time he found the sack he had only the vaguest idea where he was. Somewhere southwest of his starting point . . . he tried to picture in his mind's eye the map of central London he had studied earlier. Hammersmith, he thought, or Fulham—somewhere around that vicinity. His senses told him that he had started close to the river, then had moved away from it as he had headed west, and was now quite close to it again.

During his search he had found several black bin liners full of rubbish, one battered suitcase packed with sludge and what appeared to be reams of paper so saturated they had turned to thick pulpy blocks, and various other containers, all of which he had cursorily examined. The sack he saw now, however, set his heart beating a little faster, not least because it reminded him of the classic means of body disposal he had seen in a thousand and one gangster movies.

Sitting on the muddy bed of a particularly deep body of water within what looked as though it had once been a natural cave, the lip of the sack, secured with twine or wire, appeared to mouth at him as it shifted back and forth in the currents. Abe's limbs were aching now, but he immediately realigned his body, kicked his legs, and swam sinuously down towards it.

He grabbed the sack and tried to lift it, but could shift it no more than a few inches along the riverbed. He blinked as a black cloud of silt, disturbed by the movement of the sack, puffed up and enveloped him.

It's weighted down with something, he thought. *Rocks maybe.* He allowed the silt to settle, then began to pick at the twine securing the lip of the sack with his webbed fingers.

His hands were nimble, dextrous, and in less than a minute he had unpicked the mass of knots cinching the sack tight. Discarding the twine, he tugged the sack open . . .

. . . and reared back as a white face with staring eyes rose up out of the dark depths, mouth half open as if for a kiss.

Recovering his wits quickly, Abe pushed the bobbing head back down with the tip of one finger and tugged the sides of the sack closed over the staring face. His heart was thumping with reaction, his gills rippling agitatedly. Although he had found the evidence he had been searching for, he couldn't deny it was still a shock. He breathed deeply, allowing the cooling flow of water to calm him, and thought about what he should do.

Clearly he had to get this lot up to the surface—which meant that he had to remove whatever was weighing the sack down. If he opened the sack fully, though, he would doubtless have to cope with the grimly humorous spectacle of various body parts breaking free from inside and drifting languidly around him. In which case there was only one possible course of action. It wouldn't be pleasant, but Abe knew he was going to have to bite the bullet and get on with it. Not allowing himself to hesitate, he relaxed his grip on the top of the sack a fraction, leaving just enough room to ease his hand inside. Then, bracing himself, he delved deeper, exploring the contents of the sack.

It was like a macabre game of lucky dip. His searching fingers closed on a face, and then a smooth tube that might have been an arm or a leg, and then what was undoubtedly a foot. The jumble of limbs and heads as his hand eased its way between them rose and fell, and even seemed to squirm sluggishly, as if they still possessed a kind of feeble half-life. Abe clenched his teeth and tried to blank out his mind as he pushed his hand deeper, wincing only slightly as a probing finger found something soft and yielding. Eventually, his arm now buried in dismembered body parts up to the elbow, his fingers bumped against a rough, hard surface.

The rock was about the size of a bowling ball, and just as heavy. With a little more groping around, Abe ascertained that there were at least four of them in the sack, their combined weight effectively anchoring it beneath the water.

Tensing his muscles, he got as good a grip as he could on the rough, jagged surface of the first boulder and hauled it up and out of the sack. Body parts spun and swirled as the rock nudged them out of the way. Abe clamped his lips together as an arm somehow managed to wrap itself around his wrist like a sleepy eel. He shuddered, shaking his hand back and forth while taking care not to let go of the rock, and eventually the arm slid almost apathetically away.

He hauled the rock from the sack and dropped it on the ground, causing a slow-motion cloud of black silt to puff up around it. Now that his arm was out of the sack, Abe really didn't want to plunge it back in again. However, after only a moment's hesitation, he slid his hand back inside. The process of locating the next rock, grabbing it and yanking it through the obstacle course of heads and limbs was no easier a second time, or a third, or a fourth. At last, however, the task was done, and Abe was able to find the twine he had previously discarded and tie the sack up again. He hunkered down for a moment on the soft, silty ground, all at once feeling weak and sick. Then, hauling the sack behind him, he rose to his feet and kicked up towards the surface.

The water was a good six to eight meters deep here, and cloudy with sediment. Abe's sleek head broke the surface with barely a ripple, and immediately he was looking around, taking in his surroundings. He appeared to be in a natural cave, the rocky ceiling three meters above his head. What struck him immediately was that, although the cavern was not manmade, there was evidence that men had not only been here but that they used this place frequently.

First, there was a light source—a feeble one, admittedly, but more than enough for Abe, with his excellent eyesight, to see by. The light came from a chunky, wall-mounted lamp, not unlike a car's sidelight, that had been screwed into the rock a meter or so below the ceiling. A gray cable, affixed to the rock at intervals with U-clips, snaked out from the light and disappeared into a jagged hole in the ceiling. Also disappearing into the hole was a rusty iron ladder which was bolted to the wall. And at the bottom of the ladder, bobbing on the water, was a small green rowboat.

The yellowish light sent ripples and reflections dancing up the rocky walls in shimmering threads. Abe looked at the boat and wondered whether it was possible to use it to negotiate a subterranean course all the way from here to the murder sites. Possibly not, but the sites were certainly accessible from here for a strong swimmer; he himself was proof of that. Of course, Abe was a far stronger swimmer than any ordinary man could ever be, but in his opinion the swim was not beyond the capabilities of a fit man, providing that he wore the right equipment and stopped to rest a few times along the way.

He swam across to the iron ladder and reached up to grab the bottom rung. Looking up, he saw that the ladder ascended through the hole and into what appeared to be a circular brick-lined shaft, like a well or the flue of a chimney. He lifted the sack out of the water and dumped it in the rowboat. Even without the rocks to weigh it down, it was too heavy to drag around, not least because the coarse cloth was saturated. Abe decided that he would check out whatever was at the top of the shaft and come back for the sack later.

Hauling himself up with his right arm, he reached out with his left hand and grabbed the second rung. He pulled himself out of the water, his gills making the instant switch from water to air. As his body emerged, water streamed from his skin, leaving him dry within seconds.

Although weary, Abe had far greater stamina than a normal man. He took a couple of deep breaths, then began to climb. He felt cool air wisping down from above, and saw that at the top of the shaft was what appeared to be a metal manhole cover. He climbed the ladder to the top, then anchored his feet tightly in its rungs so that he could use both hands to push the cover upwards. Not knowing what was on the other side, his aim was to raise the metal disc as slowly and carefully as possible, so as to draw the minimum amount of attention to himself.

He positioned his hands on the underside of the cover, but before attempting to lift it he glanced back down at what was now only a tiny dark circle of water below. If the worst came to the worst, he would simply let the cover drop back into place, step off the ladder, and plunge back down the shaft.

Bracing himself, he took a deep breath and then pushed upwards. He was pleased to discover that the manhole cover was not particularly heavy, though from this angle it was still awkward to lift. He grimaced as the cover grated free of its housing, wobbling a little as it did so. As the cover rose, so did Abe's head, his keen eyes peering through the widening gap, scanning left and right to absorb as many details as possible of the unknown world above him.

He saw an empty room with gray stone walls and a low ceiling. The only light, diffuse and mustard colored, seeped in through a row of high, narrow windows, cataracted with so much grime they were almost opaque. Immediately Abe realized that he had emerged in yet another cellar. The angle of the light, trickling down from above, informed him that the ceiling of the room was at pavement level.

Satisfied there was no one down here with him, Abe lifted the manhole cover aside. He climbed out and stretched, his tired muscles cracking and popping. Looking around he saw that the room was vast yet featureless, stretching off into shadows behind him. Aside from racks of old shelving units with nothing on them, the cellar was empty.

In the far corner, adjacent to the row of windows, was a set of stone steps leading upwards. It was only when the angle of light shifted as Abe walked towards them that he realized a symbol of some kind had been daubed on the wall. It did not take a genius to ascertain that the black, crusty substance used to create the symbol was dried blood. Abe stood in front of it and weaved his head from side to side, so that the insipid light slid along its full length.

It was an eye, and a fairly simple representation of one, albeit with a small squiggle linked to the center of the bottom rim. It struck Abe that the squiggle was like a Chinese character—although it also resembled letters found in both Egyptian and Persian alphabets. Then again it might have been an obscure form of Sanskrit. Abe was reasonably knowledgeable about many of the ancient languages, and this symbol looked like and yet unlike any number of them.

It was only after noticing the first symbol that Abe glanced to his left and realized that, in fact, the wall was covered with them. Further scrutiny revealed that not only was *this* wall covered, but all four walls, the floor, and the ceiling were similarly daubed.

A thousand eyes, he thought, noting that this solved the mystery of what the drained blood of the victims had been used for. He wondered what purpose the symbols served. Perhaps they were focusing prisms for psychic power, or a pictorial form of invocation, or they might even constitute some mystical kind of surveillance system. Abe had certainly come across stranger things in his time, and if his latter theory was correct, then perhaps his arrival *hadn't* gone undetected. He would have to remain vigilant—not that he wouldn't have been anyway.

Silent as a shadow, he slipped across the room and ascended the stone steps. At the top was a door, the wood so warped that it barely fit its frame. It had either swollen or been forced into place, but by putting his shoulder against it, Abe was able to shove it open. He winced at the squealing scrape of wood, but no one came running to investigate his intrusion.

He quickly worked out that the building he had entered was an abandoned mill or factory. The rooms were vast, high ceilinged, and deserted, and the corridors and staircases had the functional angularity Abe associated with institutional edifices such as schools, hospitals, and office blocks. The worn wooden floors of the largest rooms were marked with lighter patches where machinery had once stood. The walls of these rooms were lined with rows of long windows, each of which was divided into smaller panes. The windows had evidently let in plenty of light at one time, but now they were caked with soot and grease. Many were boarded up.

Abe walked through the place with an increasing certainty that it was deserted. Even so he remained on his guard, not least because the symbol of the eye was everywhere. There was not a door, wall, floor, or ceiling that had been left untouched. The artist (or artists) was either very dedicated, or crazy, or both.

Despite the silence, Abe found it unnerving to be stared at by so many eyes. He was being foolish, he knew, but he couldn't shake off the notion that he was constantly under surveillance. As he slipped from room to room, his own eyes darted everywhere. He moved as he always did when expecting trouble—with a balletic poise, so light-footed that not even the old floorboards creaked beneath him.

On the fifth floor he found signs of occupation. In what might once have been a boardroom, beyond a row of offices which resembled a linked series of boxes constructed mostly of smoked glass, were three rolled-up sleeping bags and an equal number of grubby pillows. Beside each of the sleeping bags was a sports bag or duffel stuffed with clothes and other belongings. Half-melted candles mounted in wax-caked bottles were perched on window sills or simply stood on the floor. In one corner of the room was a camping stove, next to which stood a box full of food. Most of the food was canned, but there was also a half-finished loaf of bread and, on a shelf above, a quarter-full pint of milk, a jar of coffee, and a bag of sugar.

Aside from the eye symbol, which even in here proliferated on every surface, it all seemed so parochial. Abe took the milk down from the shelf and sniffed it. It was still fresh, which meant that whoever lived here could not have been gone long. What should he do? Fetch reinforcements? No, he didn't want to risk his quarry giving him the slip. It was a pity he had neither his gun nor his phone, but that couldn't be helped. He would simply have to be careful.

He retraced his steps to the door of the next office along the corridor. For a normal man it would have been almost pitch black, but Abe was able to make out a little definition. He tried the handle of the door, whose smoked-glass panels were surprisingly intact, and found that it opened easily. He slipped into the office, empty aside from a brittle-paged, out-of-date calendar which hung lopsidedly on the wall. Murky yellow light, which shone through the filthy windows, gave a jaundiced look to Miss October, who was happily sprawled across the gleaming hood of a red Porsche.

Abe closed the door softly, then sat in the middle of the floor, assuming the lotus position, and closed his eyes. To an observer it might have seemed as though he were meditating, or perhaps even asleep. However, he was not; he was simply entering a different state of consciousness. It was a technique he sometimes employed both to conserve his energy and stop himself becoming bored and restless. Contrary to appearances, both his mind and body were as alert as ever. Aware that he might have a long night ahead of him, Abe settled down to wait.

Hellboy landed on bones.

It wasn't a long fall. Five seconds, maybe less. He winced as he landed, the impact jarring through both hooves and meeting in a bright, brief starburst of pain in the sore but rapidly healing wound where the fire-worm had strafed him. Ruefully he rubbed the small of his back through his duster, then looked around, sniffing the air.

His senses didn't tell him much. Hellboy could see just enough to ascertain that he had landed in an earthen-walled pit, from which a tunnel led off that seemed to plunge even deeper into the earth. He reached for his belt—first, out of habit, patting the pouch which contained his gun to ensure it hadn't been dislodged by the fall—and extracted a pencil-thin flashlight. It was a fiddly thing, almost too dainty for even his left hand, but he shone it into the tunnel and around the walls.

The extra light didn't tell him much either—aside from the fact that he hadn't landed on bones at all. What had crunched beneath him had been a combination of rubble and lengths of dry timber, not that that afforded him much comfort. More than likely it simply meant that his prey scoffed its victims, bones and all (Hellboy somehow couldn't imagine a great ugly lunk of a monster delicately picking clean the skeletons of rats), or alternatively that its larder was located elsewhere. He was about to head into the downward-sloping tunnel when a voice echoed from above.

"Hellboy? You okay?"

It was Sean. He sounded concerned, but not in a nervy way. Hellboy liked the kid—and Louis too. He was glad they weren't down here with him, to get taken apart like that poor bastard whose arm they had found.

"Fine," he rumbled. "There's a tunnel here. I'm gonna check it out."

"Gotcha," Sean called. "Be careful."

"My middle name," Hellboy answered. "Catch you guys later."

Still shining the flashlight ahead, he tromped into the tunnel. It was cool, but there was no wind, and for once it smelled of nothing but earth, which made a nice change; the stench of sulfur and rotting flesh could get a little galling after a while. He let the torch play over the walls, but couldn't tell how the tunnel had been created. It could have been scooped out by the claws of a giant mole for all he knew.

Bored with the cautious approach, he yelled, "Hey! Anyone home?"

No answer, but had he heard a faint scraping in the darkness ahead? He tried again.

"If you're there, come on out where I can see you. I just want to talk."

Yeah, right. The number of Big Bads Hellboy had encountered over the years with whom he had ended up having nothing more than a cozy chat could be counted on the fingers of one hand. Hell, they could be counted on the fingers of one *elbow*.

Another scrape from the darkness, this time accompanied by a brief grating squeal. Hellboy thought of some unyielding material—stone or metal—being put under intense pressure.

The girl who had encountered the creature and lived had been in such a state of shock that she had been unable to remember anything about it except its eyes, which she had described as "burning like fire." Hellboy had heard Abe read those words and shrugged. When it came to monsters, burning eyes were a dime a dozen.

He didn't much care what the creature looked like. Or what it could do. Or how big it was. Abe and Liz always liked to be as prepared as possible, but Hellboy's approach was so straightforward that Abe had once described it, only half jokingly, as "positively Zen-like." If the beast was there, and it was mean, then Hellboy would do his utmost to batter its lights out, to hit it until it was no longer a threat. No frills. No complications. No fancy plans. His tendency to wade in annoyed the hell out of his superiors sometimes, but Hellboy suspected it was also partly what they employed him for, that they only raised a ruckus at his lack of subtlety because they felt it was expected of them.

When it came down to it, he thought the high-ups in the B.P.R.D. were simply scared of exposure, of people finding out that, for all their strategy and high tech, their job was really very simple. The man he thought of as his late father, Professor Trevor Bruttenholm, had understood that implicitly. As founder of the B.P.R.D., he was a highly educated and intelligent man, and he had had the knack of cutting through the crap, of providing the simplest and clearest of solutions to what often seemed the most convoluted of problems.

"You coming out or am I gonna have to come in there after you?" Hellboy growled, his words echoing around him.

He didn't really expect a response, and so was surprised when a voice both sludgy and gritty, and only barely discernible, came grinding out of the darkness:

"*Leave Me Be.*"

Hellboy paused—but only for a moment. "What, after taking all this trouble to come see you? Not gonna happen, buddy."

There was no reply this time, but Hellboy was sure he could hear faint, stertorous breathing from the tunnel ahead. He swung the flashlight beam, but saw nothing except more of the same—a wide passage flanked by walls of compacted earth. Just beyond the range of the flashlight the composition of the left-hand wall seemed to change from brown earth to black rock. The jagged rock seemed to bulge inwards at this point, causing the passage to narrow.

Hellboy wondered whether the creature was beyond that, lurking in the shadows. If so, it couldn't be *that* big. Jeez, he himself was not sure whether he would be able to fit through a gap *that* narrow. Not that that would be a problem, of course. If he couldn't squeeze through, he would simply punch his way through.

He strode forward, the light dancing ahead of him. He was clenching his big stone fist, making ready to widen the passageway, when the voice, louder and closer and angrier this time, boomed, "*Leave Me Be, I Say!*"

The black rock wall to his left creaked and shifted. Maybe it was just the acoustics in the tunnel, but the voice of the creature had sounded as if it were somewhere above him. Hellboy glanced up, aiming his torch in that direction. The light latched onto two fiercely glowing lumps of molten lava way up near the ceiling. For a moment Hellboy was puzzled, and then the bulging, jagged rock wall shifted again—seemed, in fact, to somehow *unfurl* itself—and all at once he understood.

The black rock wall wasn't a wall at all; it was the creature. It had been slumped against the earthen wall, looking like nothing but a huge black landslide of barnacled stone. It was bigger than Hellboy. Considerably bigger. Maybe twice as tall and twice as wide. Whereas Hellboy could stroll through this underground passage with relative ease, the ceiling still a couple of meters above his head, this creature would surely have to crawl along it, its own head scraping the ceiling, its shoulders rubbing the walls on either side.

Hellboy barely had time to take this in before what looked like the clawed scoop of a mechanical digger was swinging out of the darkness towards him. He understood, even as he flew backwards down the tunnel, that the creature had simply swatted him away as if he were no more troublesome than a fly. It was several seconds before he landed on his back on the tunnel floor. Even then he didn't stop, but skidded backwards for several more meters, his red-skinned bulk cutting a groove through the earth.

It was the curving wall which finally brought him to a halt. His head hit it with an impact that would have shattered the skull of a normal man. He clambered to his feet, scowling, his duster torn and covered in dirt.

"Now, that was just plain rude," he said, and stomped back into the fray.

As the creature turned round in the tunnel to face him, it sounded like a huge rusty machine that was slowly and tortuously coming to life. Unable to rise to its full height, it planted its massive clawed fists on the ground and glared down at him, lava eyes blazing. It looked, thought Hellboy, like some monstrous black statue to a simian god. The words that boomed from the vast and twisted outcrop of its jaw, however, no matter how full of grating fury they seemed, constituted not a threat but a plea:

"*Leave Me Be . . . I Beg You.*"

"Yeah?" Hellboy snarled. "Is that what the guy you killed said to you? Is that what he was screaming as you took him apart?"

The creature paused, perhaps trying to remember. Finally it grated:

"*I Was Lost. I Wanted Only To Talk. To Ascertain My Whereabouts. But He . . . Broke. I Did Not Expect Him To Be So Fragile.*"

The creature sounded almost wistful. Maybe not contrite, but certainly confused. Hellboy had come here spoiling for a fight, but it didn't look as though things were going to turn out as he had expected. He wasn't sure how he felt about that. He wasn't a negotiator. Abe was better at this kind of thing.

"So . . . where you from?" Hellboy said, thinking he sounded like some guy in a bar, chatting to a stranger who had just breezed into town.

The lava eyes blinked, flickered.

"*Somewhere Deep*," the creature said. "*Somewhere Dark.*"

"So why'd you come up here?"

"*I Know Not.*"

"Whaddya mean, you 'know not'? You *must* know. Did someone send you or what?"

Hellboy was not big on body language (again, that was Abe's area of expertise), but it was obvious the big rock guy was flummoxed by the question. The creature's shoulders slumped. Its head began to shake from side to side with a sound like slowly compacting granite.

"*I Was Sleeping,*" it said. "*I Have Been Sleeping For A Long Time.*"

"Okay," Hellboy said slowly. "But there must be *some* reason why you're here now. Don't tell me you've come just to sit in a pit and pull the arms off commuters?"

Again the creature shook its head confusedly from side to side. "*I Was Caught,*" it said. "*The Net Caught Me.*"

"What net?" growled Hellboy. "What the hell are you, a fish?"

"*The All-Seeing Eye,*" the creature rumbled. "*The All-Seeing Eye Begins To Open.*"

"Thanks," Hellboy said flatly. "That makes everything *much* clearer."

The creature's lava eyes seemed to dim. "*So Lost,*" it rumbled. "*So Cold.*"

Hellboy sighed. "What are we gonna do with you?"

One thing was sure. He couldn't just leave the poor guy to rot down here. He guessed that the creature had been scooped up—maybe on purpose, maybe by accident—from whatever realm it happened to inhabit and had fetched up on these dubious shores.

"Tell me about this eye," he said.

"*It Opens,*" replied the creature.

"Yeah, so you mentioned. But what *is* it exactly?"

"*It Sees All,*" the creature rumbled.

"Does it now? Pretty useful if you're looking for your car keys or the TV remote, I guess."

The joke was born of frustration more than anything. The pseudo-mystical crap was starting to piss Hellboy off.

"*I Shared Their Likeness Once Upon A Time,*" the creature said suddenly.

"Huh?" said Hellboy. "Whose likeness?"

"*The Fragile Ones,*" the creature said.

"Humans, you mean? You telling me you were once human?"

The creature inclined its head with a rumble that echoed like a subterranean earthquake.

"When was this?"

"*Before The Eye.*"

"That damn eye again," Hellboy said. "Listen, buddy, can you tell me anything that makes sense?"

"*My Memory . . . Fails Me,*" the creature said forlornly. "*We Looked Into The Eye And We Slept. The Eye Closed. And Now It Opens Once More.*"

"Bringing you with it," Hellboy said. "Okay, buddy, listen up. You sit tight. I'm gonna speak to my people, get them to come down here and talk to you. Maybe when you've told them what you know, they'll even be able to figure out a way to send you home. But you've gotta promise you won't pull any more people apart in the meantime. It's not nice for them, and what's worse for you is that if you hurt anyone else you'll make *me* angry. Got that?"

Hellboy had no idea whether the creature got it or not. It seemed to be able to handle simple questions, but too many words just seemed to bewilder it. It was like a lost child, and despite what it had done he couldn't help but feel sorry for it. Maybe it *had* been human once, but if so whatever it had got involved in, whatever process had transformed it into the creature it now was, seemed to have affected not only its body but its brain too.

Rocks in its head, Hellboy thought. Literally.

"Behave," he said.

Then he turned and walked away.

CHAPTER 6

Liz wanted to follow up some of the names on Kobus's list immediately, but Richard dissuaded her.

"Let's leave it till morning," he said. "It's not a good idea to venture into most of those neighborhoods at night."

She snorted, more derisively than she had intended. "You wouldn't be saying that if you knew some of the places I've been in my time."

"Why don't you tell me about them?" Richard said. "Over dinner."

Liz arched an eyebrow. "I have work to do, Dr. Varley."

He looked at his watch. "Come on, it's almost nine. You've been up God knows how long. Surely you're entitled to some time off?"

Sitting in the passenger seat of Richard's car, Liz rotated her head on her shoulders, grimacing at the bony crunch of her vertebrae. "True enough," she said. "But I should get back to the hotel, catch up with Hellboy and Abe."

"Just let me buy you dinner first," Richard said. "Then I'll run you back to your hotel afterwards. After all, you *do* need to eat."

She laughed. "Okay, okay, you've worn me down. Jeez, I thought you English guys were supposed to be shy, retiring types."

"Don't believe everything you read," he said.

He parked close to Embankment, and they dined on a boat permanently moored on the Thames, which had been converted into a tapas restaurant. Once the coffee and *petit fours* were out of the way, they took a turn around the deck, collars turned up against the drizzle. Less than half a mile away, the vast, glowing clock face of Big Ben resembled a numbered moon on the glittering pedestal of its tower.

"I always find it weird," Liz said, gesturing with her cigarette.

"What?"

"Seeing stuff like Big Ben and the Houses of Parliament. I mean, I've been here before, but you see that damn clock in so many movies it's like London is some giant film set."

Richard laughed. "I suppose that's how we Brits think of New York."

"Hell, it's how *I* think of New York," replied Liz. "I hardly ever go there."

She took a drag on her cigarette and watched the reflection of lights dancing on the river. She liked the young lecturer. He was laid back, intelligent, and he had a good sense of humor. During dinner they had talked mostly about their work and the current investigation.

"Nightcap?" he said to her now.

"What, here?"

"I was thinking my place. It's not far away. In fact, it's pretty much on the route back to your hotel . . . in a roundabout sort of way."

She grinned. "That's a lousy chat-up line."

Richard blushed. "It's not . . . I mean . . ."

"Relax," she said, punching his arm. "I'm kidding. Come on then, Casanova. Back to your place."

Richard's house was just south of Notting Hill, close to Holland Park tube station. The building was one of a row of similar houses, narrow and Victorian. It had a bay window, a slate roof, and a blue door.

"Here we are," he said, squeezing into a parking space. " 'Tis a humble dwelling, but mine own . . . well, a quarter of it anyway."

"You share?" said Liz.

"The house is divided into four flats. Mine's on the top floor."

They walked up the short path to the front door, the rain hissing in the long grass of the tiny, square lawn. Richard produced his key and let them into a high-ceilinged hallway with a parquet floor. The house smelled as though someone had been cooking with exotic spices. It was a nice smell, but a little cloying.

"I live at the top," Richard told her.

"Yeah," said Liz dryly, "you've already said."

"So I have," he muttered. He seemed a little ill at ease. Liz wondered whether he was hoping this might turn into a romantic assignation. If so she was going to have to let him down gently.

They started up the stairs, Richard in the lead. When he reached the top-floor landing he suddenly stopped dead. Liz glanced up and saw shock on his face.

"What is it?"

He turned to her, reaching out to the banister rail as though to steady himself. "Someone's . . ." he said, then his voice trailed off and he shook his head.

She was beside him in a couple of seconds. Now she could see the door to his flat.

A dead chicken had been hammered to it, a thick steel nail protruding from its scrawny pink neck. Its head hung down, beak open, resting on the bag of brown feathers that was its body. Its clawed feet were rigid, as though it had died while desperately trying to scrabble for a perch that wasn't there. Blackening blood formed rivulets through the feathers, turning to a half-dozen pencil-thin streams of bright red where it had run down the wooden door and pooled on the beige-patterned carpet beneath. Some of the chicken's blood had been used to finger-paint a crude symbol above the sagging body: an eye with a squiggle below that looked Arabic, or maybe Egyptian.

"I prefer mine oven ready," muttered Liz, then realized this was probably more upsetting for him than it was for her. She was used to far worse sights than this. She put a hand on his arm. "Sorry."

He licked his lips and made a valiant attempt to pull himself
together. "It's a warning," he said.

She nodded, though she didn't feel unduly concerned. If people *really* meant business, they killed you. They didn't bother warning you first.

"What does the eye symbol mean?" she asked.

"I think it means they're watching us," said Richard.

It was an odd one this, Sergeant Wormley thought as he stood in
the rain, sipping tea from a plastic cup. Odd and disturbing.

He had never known a day quite like it. He was not a supersti-
tious man, nor given to flights of fancy, but he couldn't deny there
was something about the little house behind him. Something bad.
Something he couldn't quite put his finger on.

Just thinking about the place gave him a crawly feeling up his
back. And glancing at it over his shoulder elicited a shudder that,
try as he might, he couldn't suppress. The house was well lit and
cordoned off. There were crime-team members going in and out at
regular intervals, despite the late hour. There was an uneasy-looking
PC standing guard outside to deter bolshy journalists and over-
inquisitive onlookers . . .

And yet, in spite of all the activity, the house somehow still
looked . . . *creepy*. Almost watchful.

He shook his head and told himself not to be so bloody daft.
But, despite the rain, the fact remained that at the first opportunity
he had once again chosen to come out here to drink his tea. And
he was not the only one to have been affected by the strange ambi-
ence of the place. Both yesterday and today he had noted that fellow officers and even hardened members of the forensics team had
been finding excuses to vacate the premises, even if only for short
intervals. Of course, for those working on the case, the house was a
natural rendezvous, a refuge from prying eyes, somewhere to compare notes and relay information. However, it was as if no one could

stay inside the building for long, as if there were something seeping from its walls, that not only made it impossible to think clearly, but that also affected emotions, making whoever was exposed to it anxious and tetchy.

If there *was* something—and it was a bloody ridiculous idea—then it must be a recent phenomenon. After all, the owner of the house, a "sweet and harmless" old widow (according to her neighbors) named Patricia Court, had lived here, formerly with her husband and children, and latterly alone, for nigh on forty years with no apparent problems whatsoever.

Today, though, she had flipped. And not just flipped as in allowed the stress and upset of the past couple of days to get to her, but flipped as in gone totally psycho. After finding the dismembered torso in her flower bed, she had yesterday been visited by her doctor, who had prescribed a mild sedative to help her sleep. She had spent most of the day zonked out, and then this afternoon, having spent the morning supplying the investigative team with tea and biscuits, she had once again toddled off to bed for a little nap. She had snoozed for four hours, then had got up, gone out to the garden shed, selected a large pair of shears, and walked back into the house.

PC Mike Firth had been in the kitchen at the time, washing up coffee mugs. The old lady had walked up behind him, and with no provocation whatsoever had stabbed him in the shoulder blade. The subsequent attack had been so vicious and unexpected that she had managed to slash and stab the young constable at least a dozen times before she had been very forcibly restrained. Now both she and Mike were in the hospital—Mike with a punctured lung, internal injuries, and gashes to his stomach, arms, and back, and Patricia Court with a broken right arm and three cracked ribs.

Of more concern than the old lady's physical injuries, however, was her mental state. According to reports from the hospital, she had now regressed into an almost catatonic trance, a kind of waking coma which had nothing to do with the fact that she had been slammed to the floor by three hefty PCs and a female member of the forensics team. Latest news was that she was staring into space, occasionally twitching, occasionally snarling. She had apparently also been restrained because she was considered a danger both to herself and others.

If that had been the only violent incident at the house over the past thirty-six hours, Wormley might have explained it away as a one-off, an aberration. But it had *not* been the only incident. There had been others—none, thankfully, as serious as the attack on Mike Firth, but still alarming enough to constitute a pattern, a sequence, a very real sense that something unusual and sinister was going on.

Two of the forensics team—dedicated and sensible professionals—had that morning come to blows over a minor disagreement and had had to be pulled apart. At lunchtime an experienced police constable, who had been standing at the gate monitoring the crowd of onlookers, had used his truncheon to break the nose of a neighbor who he claimed had been pestering him with questions, and had subsequently been sent home in disgrace. Plus there had been stand-up rows aplenty, people jumping down one another's throats at the slightest provocation. In fact, the wave of ill feeling had been so widespread that Wormley couldn't think of anyone who hadn't snapped at somebody else at least once that day—himself included.

He finished his tea and looked up into the night sky, watching the rain fall like silver arrows through the golden halo of the street lamps. He felt calmer out here, more clearheaded. The rain was cool and refreshing on his upturned face. All he really wanted was to go home to his wife, Alma, and his warm, cozy bed. What he *didn't* want, what he would happily never do again if it were his choice, was set foot back inside that house.

"So what's the story with the old girl?"

The voice, directly in front of him, took him unawares. Instantly Wormley was annoyed with himself. His instincts—his sixth sense—were usually good; several times in the past his alertness had got him out of potentially nasty situations. This time, though, he had had no idea that anyone was within yards of him. Put it down to the house, he thought. Clouding his thoughts. Scrambling his mind.

The man standing before him was half a head shorter than Wormley, and scruffy. He looked around fifty at first glance, though he possessed a bloated, boozy seediness that probably meant he was five, maybe ten years younger than that.

Wormley answered the man's question with one of his own. "And who might you be?"

The man smiled. A crafty smile. Smarmy. *He's either a reporter or a freeloader*, Wormley thought. The man reached into the pocket of his grubby, knee-length jacket and produced a business card, which he handed to Wormley. The card was soggy, frayed at the edges. Wormley glanced at it, clocked the man's name, Colin Proctor, and the name of his newspaper. He sighed.

"Press conference at nine a.m. tomorrow," he said. "If you're any good at your job you'll find out where."

The man's smile widened into a grin. It made him look like a chubby shark.

"Oh, but I *am* good at my job," he said. "Bloody great, in fact. That's why I'm here, to get ahead of the losers who'll all end up with exactly the same story tomorrow."

Another sigh from Wormley. "You've wasted your time then, haven't you?"

"I don't think so," said Proctor with another flash of his smarmy smile.

"*I* think so," Wormley said, "because you won't get anything from anyone here, off the record or otherwise."

"Oh, I've already got my story," Proctor said airily. "I just came to get a feel for the place, soak up the atmosphere. That's why I'm so good at what I do, Sergeant. I'm thorough, you see."

Wormley said nothing.

"Always dot the i's and cross the t's, that's me," Proctor continued. "So, this old girl . . . Patricia Court. I hear she went nutso and sliced up one of your lot."

Wormley tried not to wince. The ambulances screaming to a halt outside the house earlier had made it evident that *something* had happened, but orders had been given to those inside to remain quiet about the actual details. The gathered press had simply been told that there had been a "serious incident" and that "no further information was forthcoming at this time."

Casually Wormley said, "Oh yeah? And who told you that?"

Proctor winked. "I have my sources, Sergeant."

"I'm sure you do," Wormley said, "but if I were you, I wouldn't believe everything they tell you."

Proctor grinned again, as if he were enjoying the game. "Ah, but I have very *good* sources. I doubt there's anything you can tell me, Sergeant, that I don't already know."

"So why are you bothering to talk to me?" asked Wormley blandly.

"Well, the thing is," said Proctor, "I know *what* the old lady did, but I don't know *why* she did it. And people like a motive. It makes everything neat and tidy. And you were there, Sergeant. So I thought maybe you could shed some light. Scotch the rumors, as it were."

"And what rumors would those be?"

"*Wild* rumors, Sergeant. People round here are saying that this place is cursed. They're saying that there's something evil here, something which affects people and sends them into a murderous frenzy."

"That's what they're saying, is it?" said Wormley, deadpan.

"It is," Proctor said.

Wormley leaned forward. "Look into my eyes, Mr. Proctor. Do *I* look as though I've been driven into a murderous frenzy?"

"I'd say you're showing admirable restraint, Sergeant," Proctor said.

Wormley nodded. "I think there's only one thing that would send me into a murderous frenzy."

Proctor held up a hand. "Is it damn fool reporters and their ridiculous questions?"

"Do you know," Wormley said, "I think it is."

"Thought so," said Proctor. "But that still doesn't disguise the facts, does it, Sergeant?"

"Does it not?" said Wormley. "And which facts would those be, Mr. Proctor?"

"Well, the fact that violent crime in the vicinity of all four murder sites has spiked dramatically in the space of a single day; the fact that a middle-aged secretary in BMA House stabbed a work colleague in the face with a pair of scissors this afternoon; the fact that reports of supernatural incidents across the city have increased a hundredfold in the past thirty-six hours; the fact that several top B.P.R.D. agents, including Hellboy himself, have been secretly flown to London to conduct an as-yet undisclosed investigation."

The reporter smiled smugly and stepped back, in the manner of a man who has jabbed a tiger with a stick through the bars of its cage.

Wormley tried not to react, despite the fact that some of what Proctor had just disclosed was news to him.

"Just tell me this, Sergeant," Proctor continued, "is anyone looking at the big picture here? Or is everyone on this case as lost and scared as you?"

Almost unconsciously Wormley felt the plastic cup crumpling in his fist. Head and heart thumping, he said, "Good night, Mr. Proctor." Stiffly he turned back towards the house and lifted the yellow-and-black tape that marked the police cordon. He slipped underneath and forced his legs to move one in front of the other, up the path to the innocuous front door. As he reached for the handle, he realized his hand was trembling badly. He tried to tell himself that it was due to nothing but the cold-ness of the rain.

"So what do you think, HB? We all batting in the same ballpark here or what?"

Liz was sprawled on the sofa in Hellboy's hotel suite, boots off, a large glass of Merlot within easy reach on the mahogany coffee table beside her. Hellboy, freshly showered, was reclining on his bed, wolfing down a steak sandwich.

"How should I know?" he said. "I'm just a grunt. It's not my job to ask questions."

"Yeah, right," said Liz. "Because you've never had to use your initiative or intelligence before."

He fixed her with his golden eyes and allowed his jaw to drop slackly open, revealing the chewed meat and bread in his mouth. "Duh . . . intelligence? Wassat?" he mumbled.

She threw a cushion at him. He caught it neatly and tucked it behind his thick neck with a sigh.

"Come on, though," she said. "What's your gut instinct?"

"What's yours?" he asked.

She took a sip of her wine before replying, her brow creasing as she pondered over what she had learned that evening, both directly and after comparing notes with Hellboy when she had arrived back at the Old Bloomsbury.

It had been around midnight when a sombre and troubled Richard had dropped her off outside. Not surprisingly the two of them had foregone their proposed nightcap, the dead chicken having dampened the relaxed mood somewhat. Before getting out of the car, Liz had reached across and briefly clasped his hand. "Try not to worry," she said. "I don't think anything's going to happen. Trust me, I know. I've been threatened by experts."

He offered her a thin smile. "That's very comforting. I'll try to remember that when they're kicking down my door at four in the morning."

She felt a momentary flash of irritation, but managed to keep her teeth clamped over her instinctive, acerbic response. Reminding herself that most folks didn't face Armageddon on a weekly basis, she tried to arrange her features into a look of sympathy.

"You'll be fine," she reassured him. "Just keep your door locked and your phone close to hand—not that you'll need it."

She gave his hand a final squeeze and wished him good night. As she headed across the hotel lobby to the lift, she was hailed by the night-duty receptionist, a plump girl with dyed red hair and bad skin.

"Mr. Hellboy said to let you know he's back," she said. She looked at Liz as if she were some curious and unknown specimen. Perhaps, Liz thought, she was trying to decide what would compel such an apparently ordinary girl to keep such fearsome company.

"Thanks," Liz said, and went straight up to Hellboy's room.

He answered the door in the silk dressing gown that had been presented to him by a group of Tibetan monks after he had cleared their monastery of salt demons one time. He looked oddly sweet, she thought. Almost vulnerable.

"No Abe?" she asked.

He shook his head. "A cop dropped off some of his stuff, together with a note saying he'd gone for a swim in the sewer."

"Nice," said Liz.

They ordered some room service and spent the next twenty minutes catching up, and then Liz asked Hellboy what his gut instinct was and he bounced the question right back at her.

She had been quiet now for some moments.

"You giving me the silent treatment?" he grumbled.

"Sorry," she said, "just thinking."

"Yeah, I thought I could smell burning."

She narrowed her eyes at him and said, "Tell me what your buddy in the underground said again. That thing about the eye."

Hellboy shrugged. "It didn't make a whole lot of sense. Something about the all-seeing eye beginning to open. The usual mystical crap."

"The all-seeing eye," Liz mused. "There was an eye symbol above the bird nailed to Richard's door. That would suggest a connection, wouldn't you say?"

Hellboy shrugged and ripped the cap off another beer with his teeth. "Maybe. I guess we'll know more when our guys speak to the rock monster, or whatever he is, in the tunnels."

"You called them?"

"Well, yeah," said Hellboy, as if she were insulting his intelligence. "Rachel Turner's posted some guards, so that the big guy doesn't go walkabout. Plus, she's arranged for some people to go down there to talk to him. Communications experts. I'm not too good at that whole talking thing."

"Oh, I don't know," said Liz. "I've always found you scintillating company."

"Get outta here," he said.

She grinned, then stood up and stretched. "I'm beat. Think I'll call it a night. You gonna turn in?"

"I'll watch some TV and wait for Abe."

"You worried about him?"

"Nah. You know Abe. He's more careful than the two of us put together. All the same . . ."

"All the same, you'd like to make sure he arrives back safe and sound." She crossed the room and kissed him on the bridge of his nose. "At heart you're just a big mother hen."

"Didn't I tell you to get outta here?"

Abe opened his eyes. He had heard something. Not the distant drone of traffic this time, or the ambient sounds of the city, but something inside the building . . . the scrape-bump-scuff of movement.

He had been sitting in the same position, eyes closed, for more than two hours. But the instant he heard the sound he was rising fluidly to his feet, his mind clear and his muscles tensed and ready. His previous weariness had drained away—which didn't mean that, once his day was over, he wouldn't lay his head on the pillow of his hotel bed and be instantly, deeply asleep. Whether by design or training—and it was almost certainly some of both—Abe's body was a finely attuned machine. He might not have Hellboy's sheer brute strength, or Liz's awesome destructive capabilities, but his speed, agility, and perception were second to none.

Silently, he slipped out of the office and stood in the corridor, listening. There was definitely someone in the building. Abe estimated they were three or four floors below, but heading up towards him. He hovered a moment, wondering whether it would be best to wait here or go down and meet them halfway.

He decided on the former. His priority was to get answers to some of the many questions pertaining to the investigation, and to do that he needed to apprehend the new arrival. Without his belt he had no handcuffs, no twine, no charms, no talismans, no gun. He would therefore have to improvise with what he *did* have: clothes, sleeping bags, pillows. Slipping back down the corridor, he reentered the makeshift dormitory and stepped into the darkest of the shadows behind the half-open door.

He was motionless, his breathing so shallow it was all but silent—yet he suddenly became aware that below him the newcomer had come to a halt. Surely Abe hadn't been found out? How could the newcomer possibly have detected his presence? A few seconds later, however, Abe's suspicions were confirmed. From somewhere below came the sudden thump of rapidly retreating footsteps.

Instantly Abe was out the door and flowing down the corridor in pursuit. His quarry was at least a floor below him, which meant that he (or she) had a good twenty to thirty seconds, head start. But Abe was fast and his senses highly attuned. So unless his quarry managed to lose himself in crowds of people or a maze of streets outside the building, Abe was confident he had a good chance of making up the distance.

It was on the ground floor when he got his first look at his quarry. Abe was only a couple of flights above the newcomer when he heard the bang of the double doors on the level below and footsteps pounding across the wide expanse of wooden floor. Abe leaped down the stairs, wormed out through the doors, which were still swinging shut on rusty hinges—and suddenly there he was.

On the far side of the room was the fleeing form of a tall, skinny black man wearing a tight-fitting jacket and slightly ragged trousers a little too short for him. By contrast, his white Nikes were top of the range and looked brand new. They appeared to glow white in the gloom.

"Hey!" Abe shouted, and was delighted to see the man flinch and half turn, which caused him to stumble. Abe fixed his gaze on the oily whites of the man's frightened eyes and flowed across the floor towards him, halving the distance between them in less than four seconds.

The man clambered to his feet. But this time, instead of running, he turned and raised his arms. Then, using both hands, he formed his long fingers into the shape of an eye.

Thrashing, crackling serpents of yellow light instantly filled the space between Abe and the tall man. Abe barely had time to turn away before the light hit him with the force of a dozen electric shocks. Blinded and disoriented, he staggered and almost fell. He felt the light tearing into his mind, trying to rip away his consciousness. He fought it, momentarily aware of nothing but the need to wrest his thoughts from the force that was trying to expunge them. He felt like a drowning man fighting to keep his head above water, while tentacles coiled around his ankles beneath the surface, inexorably dragging him down.

Just as he was beginning to think he would have no choice but to succumb to the force, Abe abruptly felt it start to ebb. To his relief and astonishment, it dispersed quickly, like fog, enabling him to drag himself back into the real world. Although unscathed, his body felt sore and tender, as if he had been repeatedly stung by a school of angry jellyfish. Recovering his senses, he looked across the dusty, cavernous room.

The tall man was gone—but how long ago? Encased within the energy bubble, Abe had had no real sense of time passing. It had *seemed* like seconds, a minute at most, but it may have been longer.

Cursing loudly, he ran across the room, to a door which led into a narrow corridor, and then to a fire exit at the far end. The fire-exit door was standing ajar, creaking slightly. The cool breeze that curled in through the gap was like a balm on Abe's stinging skin.

He exited the building and found himself on the bank of the Thames. Beyond a wide tow path, the river flowed by, timeless and implacable, its surface rippling like sleek, muscled skin. Abe paused a moment, listening for signs of the fleeing man. There was nothing. He scanned the tow path in both directions, considering his options.

Which direction would *he* have gone if he had been trying to escape a pursuer? Or rather, which direction would he have gone if he *didn't* have the option of plunging into the Thames? Right towards Hammersmith Bridge and the bustle of Hammersmith itself? Or left around the outskirts of Fulham, past what looked like another half mile or so of warehouses?

Abe stood poised in the relentless London drizzle for a couple more seconds, then turned right on a hunch. Hammersmith Bridge, stretching across the river a quarter of a mile ahead, resembled the knobbly vertebrae of some vast creature. Now that he had made the decision Abe moved fast, his body cutting through the stiff headwind, spatters of rain sliding off his skin like oil. He was aware that his efforts might be futile, but urgency remained his watchword, because even if he didn't catch the man he still needed to find a phone to call Hellboy, to tell him about the factory and what he had found in the waters below.

The factories and warehouses were giving way to more residential housing, and Hammersmith Bridge was beginning to loom above him, when Abe saw movement on the path ahead. He focused his vision through the static of rain, trying to make sense of vague shapes and half-glimpsed details. It took him a couple of seconds to identify the shape of a running man, and then two more to identify the man himself. He was loping along, all gangly, sharp-angled limbs and clomping feet, his white Nikes glimmering in the gloom.

Abe wondered whether the guy had any more of that nasty eye power to dispatch in his direction. Hopefully not, judging by the brevity of the previous attack. If he could call up the power at will, then surely he would have used it to more devastating effect the first time? Abe's guess was that the power had come from elsewhere, and that the guy had been designated a limited amount, perhaps just enough to defend himself with.

The tall man looked tired, but he was almost at the bridge. Abe knew that if he could keep him in sight for the next minute or so, he would catch him. However, just at that moment, the man disappeared from view. For an instant Abe thought he had been snatched away by some arcane force. But then he realized that he had merely turned right on to a walkway that sloped upwards to meet the north end of the bridge.

The turn was so abrupt that the walkway was all but invisible until you were almost upon it. As soon as he reached it, Abe swiveled on his heel, twisting without breaking stride. The guy was a couple hundred yards ahead of him, almost at the top. Even though Abe was already running as fast as he thought he could, he dug a little deeper, looking for that extra spurt of speed.

He had no idea what time it was, but he guessed it must be around one a.m. Despite the late hour, traffic still rumbled almost incessantly over the bridge, and as Abe reached the top of the walkway and emerged onto the well-lit streets of Hammersmith, he saw that there were also still plenty of people about, many presumably heading home after a night out in the bars and restaurants of London.

What was immediately evident to Abe was that the black guy was too panicked to be thinking clearly. The only reason he was still noticeable amongst the dotted groups of people was because he was the only one running. He had crossed the road and was currently pounding past a large, grimy church on the street opposite, his lanky form slipping in and out of pools of light cast by the street lamps. He was attracting curious glances as he ran by—though the attention he received was nothing compared to the attention that was suddenly focused on Abe.

It didn't help that Abe was all but naked, having stripped down to a pair of skintight black shorts for his swim through subterranean London. Although he always hated it when people called him "the fish guy," and hated it even more when the ignorant and the bigoted referred to him as a monster, he guessed he could kind of appreciate that to the unprepared night owls of Hammersmith it must suddenly have seemed as if the Creature from the Black Lagoon had emerged from the Thames and was now running riot through their city.

Women screamed and men swore as he ran past. Many people simply scattered before him as if a tiger had appeared in their midst. A few hardy souls made halfhearted attempts to grab him, but he evaded their grasping hands easily.

Regardless of these distractions, Abe was gaining rapidly on his quarry. The guy was now staggering rather than running, his head wagging exhaustedly from side to side.

Oblivious to the traffic, the guy suddenly veered to his right, off the pavement and onto the road. A car screeched to a halt, missing him by inches. The driver gesticulated angrily, but the guy ran on, ignoring him.

Abe looked past the man, and saw immediately where he was headed. Fifty yards away was the cavernous, brightly lit entrance to Hammersmith tube station. Abe guessed that the guy's plan was to leap onto a train whose doors were about to close. It was a tactic he had probably seen successfully employed in a hundred movies. But Abe hoped that the guy would be disappointed. The odds of timing his getaway just right must be pretty slim.

Sure enough, the guy ran into the brightly lit station entrance. Abe followed, no more than thirty yards behind. He saw the guy scramble over the barrier, rousing a guard, who called indignantly after him.

The same guard reared back in shock as Abe appeared. "Sorry," Abe muttered, and vaulted over the metal barrier like an Olympic hurdler. At this hour the station was all but deserted, for which Abe was grateful. He heard the tall man clattering down the metal escalator that led to the Piccadilly line trains. Abe appeared at the top just as the guy leaped the last half-dozen steps to the bottom. The guy stumbled and almost fell, but managed to regain his balance and staggered forward, into one of the side tunnels.

Abe followed grimly, knowing that the pursuit was almost at an end. But then he heard an approaching rumble, accompanied by a distant squealing and clattering. No, he thought, surely the guy wasn't going to be *that* lucky. The train sounded as though it were mere seconds from thundering into the station.

Risking life and limb, Abe flew down the escalator and skidded into the side tunnel, bouncing off the tiled wall. Emerging onto the grime-gray platform beneath a digital display that flashed up the words ***STAND BACK***TRAIN APPROACHING***, he whipped his head left and right.

The guy was the only person on the platform—and unbelievably he was still running. In the bleaching light of the station, Abe saw the sweat glistening on his short-cropped hair, the dark wet patch on the back of his jacket, between his shoulder blades. The man was running towards the circular black mouth of the tunnel at the end of the platform. Raising his voice above the tortured squealing of the rails, Abe shouted, "Game over, my friend. There's nowhere else to go."

He felt a warm, stagnant breeze ripple over his skin, forced out of the tunnel by the approaching train. Lights appeared in the blackness. The bellowing of the train built to a crescendo.

The guy thumped to a stop and turned to look at Abe. His mouth was open and gasping, and sweat streamed down his face. He bent and put his hands on his knees. Abe walked towards him slowly, holding up his webbed hands. "I'm not—" he said.

And then, without warning, the guy jumped.

He leaped off the platform a split second before the train came screaming out of the tunnel. He was still in midair when it hit him. Although he was twenty yards away, Abe felt a warm rain of the man's blood spatter over his skin. He turned his head aside and closed his eyes briefly. Then, even as the train with its cargo of shocked passengers was still slowing down, he gave a deep sigh, turned his back, and walked tiredly away.

☠ CHAPTER 7

When Hellboy came down to breakfast, Abe and Liz were already there. They were sitting on the far side of the big, empty dining room with its crisp white tablecloths and immaculate silverware, the autumn sun shining on their window table and gleaming on Abe's pale turquoise skin. Despite turning up at the hotel at two a.m., filthy and blood spattered, Abe looked none the worse for his night's experience. After arriving back he'd taken a shower, told Hellboy his story, drunk some tea, and gone to bed.

Now here he was five hours later, filling Liz in on the details. As Hellboy came within earshot of his colleagues' table, he saw Liz screw up her face. "Euww!" she exclaimed.

"Guess he's just described the guy/train interface thing, huh?" Hellboy said.

They looked round and said their good mornings. Liz poured Hellboy some coffee, then topped up Abe's cup and her own. Hellboy pinched the handle of the little china cup between the thumb and index finger of his left hand and drained its contents in one gulp. The three of them ate fried breakfasts, and several rounds of toast and marmalade, and drank around a gallon of coffee, while discussing what they had found out so far, and their plan of attack for the day.

"Richard's meeting me at nine thirty and we're going to follow up the leads that Labuschagne gave us," Liz said. Then she spread her hands and added, "If that's okay with you, HB?"

Hellboy nodded and gave her a teasing smile. In a mock-Texan drawl, he said, "You and this Richard feller getting pretty chummy, ain'tcha, peaches?"

Liz narrowed her eyes at him. "You're not too big for a slap, you know."

Hellboy grinned and turned to Abe. "So I just called Kate. She's faxing over everything she can find on the all-seeing eye. But she suggested we might also check out the British Library, see what else we can dig up."

"And by 'we' I'm guessing you mean me?" said Abe dryly.

"Well . . . yeah," admitted Hellboy. "I was kinda hoping you might cover that. I'm going to head over to Scotland Yard with Reynolds. He called me twenty minutes ago to say they've found three more bodies . . . well, torsos. Bloodless, like last time."

"Really?" said Abe. "Where?"

"Now, see, I knew you'd ask that, so I wrote it all down and got Kate to run a check on the locations. Here's what she came up with."

He handed Abe several folded sheets of paper. Abe scanned through them quickly.

"Oh, now they're just playing with us!" he exclaimed.

Hellboy nodded.

Liz looked from one to the other. "Well?" she said. "Is one of you going to tell *me* what's going on?"

Abe brandished the sheaf of papers. "These three locations— St. George's Church, Bloomsbury; Theatre Royal, Drury Lane; St. Clement Danes Church, Strand—are virtually on our doorstep."

"Which means that not only do our enemies know we're in the country, but they know where we're staying?" said Liz.

Abe nodded.

"But I thought the first bodies were carefully placed?" said Liz. "Areas of occult significance and all that?"

"As are these," said Abe. He drew himself into a more upright position and held Kate's notes out in front of him, like a lecturer delivering an important paper.

"The Theatre Royal in Drury Lane, as well as being the oldest theater in London, also has a reputation as one of the most haunted in the world. Several murders have been committed there over the years, and interestingly, one of the earlier theater buildings to stand on the spot was designed by Sir Christopher Wren, who also designed St. Clement Danes Church in the Strand."

"And what's so special about *that* place?" asked Liz.

"Well, for one thing, it's ancient. A Christian church has stood on that particular site for over a thousand years. Secondly, Wren had Masonic and Rosicrucian connections, and was said to be conversant with the ley system. St. Clement Danes reputedly stands on a spot where at least two ley lines cross."

"And did Wren design the Bloomsbury Church, too?" said Liz.

"No," said Abe, "but one of his students, Nicholas Hawksmoor, did. *He* was known by some as the 'devil's architect.' "

Liz raised her eyebrows.

"Some people believed him to be a Satanist," continued Abe, "although Kate thinks that's probably nonsense. She says he was certainly interested in pagan symbology, though, and wove much of it into his architectural designs. Conspiracy theorists claim that his six London churches form an invisible geometry of power lines in the city, which correspond to an Egyptian hieroglyph. Others say that his churches are positioned to form a pentagram—though Kate does make the point that it was unlikely Hawksmoor actually selected the sites for his churches, which pretty much negates that theory."

"Basically, though, you're saying that all the places where bodies have been found have some kind of mystical or macabre connection?" said Liz.

Abe nodded.

"I still don't get it, though," admitted Hellboy. "I mean, London's old. *Really* old. Like you say, some sites have had buildings standing on them for a thousand years or more. So there can't be many places where something bad *hasn't* happened at some time or another."

"True," conceded Abe, "though Kate's research seems to suggest that the answer lies not in *what* has happened in those buildings, but in *why* particular events occurred in them."

"Go on," said Hellboy.

Abe flicked through the latter part of the notes again. "Kate makes the point that numerous occult texts dating back hundreds of years make reference to an ancient and malevolent source of power beneath the city of London. She speculates that the crust that contains the power source has worn thin in places, allowing the power to leak through, and that our enemies, whoever they may be, are now attempting to access it."

"And so this leakage . . . what? Attracts bad people? Or affects those who live and work on the sites, which then sometimes causes them to do bad things?" Liz asked.

"Perhaps a bit of both," said Abe, "depending on how thin the crust is in each location, and on how susceptible certain people are to its influence." He spread his webbed hands expressively. "I'll take a shot in the dark here and suggest that maybe the leakage causes the veil between various planes of existence to wear thin in places too. That could account for the increasing number of supernatural incidents across the city these past few days. It could be that our enemies are using ritual sacrifice to break the crust down, which is why its effects are becoming more widespread."

"So, bottom line is that London's a great, big, crumbling dam on the verge of collapse?" said Hellboy.

"That's about the size of it," Abe replied.

Hellboy rolled his eyes. "Great," he said. "Guess there won't be time to do much sightseeing while we're here then?"

Abe shrugged apologetically. "Guess not."

They all turned as a willowy, nervous-looking woman in a gray business suit entered the room and approached the table. Liz recognized her as the hotel's personnel manager, and noticed how she glanced from Hellboy's golden eyes to Abe's matte-black ones, like a bird confronted by a pair of snakes.

Hellboy noticed it too. Gently, he said, "Relax, lady, we don't bite."

The woman's answering smile was a flimsy, fluttering thing. "There's a Dr. Varley here to see Miss Sherman, sir. I wondered whether I should let him in?"

Hellboy winked at Liz. "Hey, Liz, looks like your date's arrived."

Liz made a point of not reacting to his comment and said, "Sure. Tell him to come through."

A minute later Richard entered, carrying a newspaper. He looked tired, as if he hadn't slept too well.

"Hey," Liz said by way of greeting. "You okay?"

He nodded. "I've had better nights, but . . . yes, I'm fine." He thrust the paper at Hellboy. "Erm . . . I thought you should see this."

Hellboy took the newspaper from Richard and unfolded it. It was a copy of that morning's *Star*. He stared at the lead story and his face crunched into a frown.

"That little creep," he muttered.

Liz and Abe leaned across to take a look. The paper's front page was dominated by a large close-up of Hellboy snarling into the camera, hand held up as though to reach out and grab the photographer by the throat. Inset photos down the left-hand side depicted Abe, Liz, and Richard Varley. The headline screamed: A MONSTER TO CATCH A MONSTER? Beneath this was a subheading: *What are we not being told?*

Hellboy slammed the paper down on the table hard enough to make the crockery rattle. "If I ever see that little bastard again . . ." he said.

Abe picked the paper up and read the story quickly, his face composed. "So our secret's out?" he said mildly. "So what? It had to happen eventually."

"It's not that," said Hellboy. "It's the tone of the piece that bugs me. It describes me as a 'surly, fanged demon, threatening bystanders with physical violence.' And it describes you as my 'cold fishy friend.' "

"Hmm," Abe said.

"What does it say about me?" asked Liz, reaching for the paper.

"I haven't *got* fangs," Hellboy grumbled. "I've *never* had fangs."

"Hey, I'm a 'dark beauty with even darker secrets,' " said Liz. She pursed her lips. "I don't know whether to be offended or flattered."

"Where did this guy get his information from? That's what I'd like to know," Hellboy said. "He even says we flew in to a secret airfield in Kent and were met by . . . what was it? Oh yeah, 'an alarming array of high-ranking government officials.' The way he tells it, it's like there's some big conspiracy going on. Like we've been smuggled into the country to start a revolution or somethin'."

"Well, we *were* flown in secretly," Abe conceded.

"Yeah, but only to avoid a media circus," said Hellboy. "Now that this guy's blown our cover, it'll make our job twice as hard."

Liz shrugged. "Like Abe says, it had to happen sooner or later. Don't sweat the small stuff, HB. This guy's nothing but a pinprick compared to what else we got to deal with, and a tiny one at that."

Abe had taken the paper back from Liz and was scanning through the rest of it. "The torso murders fill the first five pages," he told them. "Apart from the lovely young woman on page three."

"What about the other stuff?" Liz asked. "The ghosts and poltergeists and walking dead?"

"That's written up as a separate, pretty joky story on page ten. Though there's an editorial on page fourteen, again written by our friend, Colin Proctor, in which he posits a link between the murders and the so-called 'spook fest.' His theory is that our presence in the country is proof that the link exists. He says we're the 'glue that bonds these seemingly separate incidents together.' "

Liz raised an eyebrow. "You can say what you like about him, HB, but one thing he isn't is stupid."

"I guess," Hellboy said grudgingly, then he sat up straight, his neck muscles crackling. "And like you say, Liz, we got stuff we need to be dealing with. So let's deal with it."

Ten minutes later, Hellboy was squashed into the passenger seat of a car driven by DCI Reynolds. Reynolds had turned up looking mighty pleased with himself. He told Hellboy that thanks to Abe's discoveries the night before, the murder investigation was now continuing apace. The remains of the man who had thrown himself under the tube train had been scraped up and bagged and were now undergoing forensic examination in the hope of establishing his identity. He also let Hellboy know that a team of officers were currently swarming all over the factory in Hammersmith, searching for further evidence.

"You found out who the victims were yet?" Hellboy asked.

"Not yet," said Reynolds, "but now that the heads and limbs have turned up, it's only a matter of time." He rubbed his hands together. "I reckon we've got these bastards on the run."

Hellboy shrugged. "I wouldn't get too excited. We're not just dealing with one guy here, Inspector. Indications are we're up against a pretty big organization. If that's the case, then you can guarantee these people will be like roaches. Nests all over London."

"Yeah?" said Reynolds, looking disgruntled. "Well, we'll see about that, won't we?"

The metropolitan police's main mortuary was on Victoria Street. It was here where the remains of the dead—both those from last night, and those that had been discovered this morning—had been taken for forensic examination. As befitting its function, it was a grim building—flat roofed, featureless, and made of dull gray stone. Like a dirty secret, it was tucked away behind the gleaming tower block that was the public face of Scotland Yard. The inside of the place wasn't any more appealing than the outside—blank, whitewashed walls, strip lighting, and identical corridors bearing evenly spaced doors, most of which bore little gray plaques that Hellboy couldn't be bothered to read.

There weren't many people about, which meant that Hellboy's presence didn't cause much of a stir. One small, balding man in a lab coat, who was laden down with papers, abruptly halted his headlong rush along one of the building's corridors to gape at the big red guy with the stone hand and the sawn-off horns, but that was pretty much it.

The pathology labs and storage facilities were situated in the basement. There was a lift, but Hellboy and Reynolds took the stairs, Hellboy's hooves clacking on the stone steps and echoing in the square shaft of the stairwell. The lighting, with no natural light seeping through from outside, was harsher down here, and the double swing doors of each numbered path lab were more widely spaced.

"Hope you're not squeamish," Reynolds said, in a tone which suggested the opposite.

Hellboy regarded him steadily. "Nah. Some of my best friends are rotting corpses."

Reynolds didn't knock, but simply shoved open the left-hand door of lab six and strode in as if he owned the place. Hellboy followed, trying not to look like the guy's bodyguard.

The room they had entered was large, the décor clinical, composed primarily of stainless-steel surfaces and white-tiled walls. A corpse in five pieces lay on an autopsy table in the center. A chubby, bespectacled man with smears of blood on his lab coat was washing up metal implements in a vast sink in the corner, and glanced up as they entered. He blinked when he saw Hellboy, but didn't appear to be overly shocked. Across the room a woman with her back to them was washing her hands in a smaller sink. Her reddish-blond hair was scraped back and tugged into a ponytail, which swayed from side to side as she scrubbed at her fingernails with a small brush.

"You ought to try wearing gloves, Dr. Saunders," Reynolds called, smirking at Hellboy. "You'd get fewer guts under your nails."

The woman turned. She was younger than Hellboy had been expecting, with green eyes and a fine-boned face. She didn't look particularly pleased to see the policeman.

"It's the smell of latex I'm trying to get rid of," she said. "Clings for days if you don't wash your hands right away."

It was only after she had delivered the response that she turned her gaze on Hellboy. She appraised him coolly.

"You don't have to tell me who *you* are," she said. "You're bigger in the flesh than you appear in pictures. Redder too. Altogether more impressive, in fact."

"Thanks," Hellboy said, wishing he could think of some pithy response, something to make her laugh. He had never been much good at repartee, and on this occasion he found himself even more tongue tied than usual. Part of the reason was because the woman, Dr. Saunders, reminded him of someone he held very dear. Of course, the English accent helped, but it was mainly her demeanor, coupled with the sharp flash of feisty intelligence and warm humor in her sparkling green eyes, that made him think of Anastasia Bransfield.

Anastasia, archaeologist and explorer, was the love of Hellboy's life. She was one of the few people he had met who had instantly bypassed his fearsome exterior and sought out the generous soul beneath. The two of them had been an item for a while, had even traveled the world together. And then, for her benefit rather than his, Hellboy had broken it off.

She had been hurt, but she had understood. While she had been with him, she had been a target in all sorts of ways, and he wasn't prepared to watch her suffer simply because of her association with him. However much his heart tried to tell him otherwise, Hellboy knew that they were better apart.

"I doubt that this uncouth prat will introduce me," the woman was saying, "so I suppose I'd better do it myself. I'm Cassie Saunders. I'm a specialist advisor with the Forensic Science Service."

Before Hellboy could say anything, Reynolds said, "Oh, *Cassie*, is it? How come I never get the first-name treatment?"

"Because you're a sexist creep with wandering hands," said Cassie smartly.

Reynolds somehow managed to look both proud *and* indignant. "Oh yeah? And how do you know *he* isn't?"

"Woman's intuition," Cassie said, and winked at Hellboy.

Hellboy smiled, aware that if his skin hadn't already been red, he'd have been blushing. He was also aware that his smile could sometimes be mistaken for a snarl, and that there were occasions when it had reduced small children to instantaneous tears.

Cassie, however, recognized the expression for what it was and smiled back at him. "So what's so special about this case that they've flown *you* all the way over the pond? Or is that privileged information?"

Deadpan, Hellboy said, "If I told you I'd have to kill you."

Cassie laughed softly, and Hellboy grinned, pleased to get such a reaction from such an old line.

Snidely Reynolds said, "Much as I hate to break up the start of a beautiful friendship, I'm afraid we're not here to flirt, sweetheart. Any luck in identifying our stiffs?"

Cassie rolled her eyes and reached for a red cardboard folder. Flipping it open, she handed it to Reynolds. "You ought to know. I just supply the forensics; it's your job to do the rest. This report was faxed through from your mob an hour ago. I'm surprised you haven't seen it already."

Reynolds rubbed his unshaven chin. "Been out and about, haven't I? Man of action, me." He flipped through the file, which contained both Cassie's forensic reports and subsequent police findings. Eventually he said, "So they were all dossers, were they? No wonder we haven't had tearful mummies and daddies battering on our doors, worried sick about little Johnny not coming home."

"Dossers?" queried Hellboy.

"Tramps. Scroungers. Bums, as you Yanks call 'em."

"Okay," Hellboy said, disgusted by Reynolds's callousness, "I get the picture."

He held out his hand for the report and skimmed through it quickly. None of the most recent victims had yet been identified, but the four whose heads and limbs Abe had found in the weighted-down sack had now been positively ID'd. They ranged in age from late teens to midthirties. They had drifted into London from different towns and cities across the UK—Hull, Ipswich, Cardiff, and Manchester—and had last been seen alive in just as wide a variety of locations scattered throughout the city. There appeared to be nothing to link them, aside from the fact that they had been homeless and vulnerable—and were now dead and dismembered.

Hellboy stared at the details of the youngest victim, nineteen-year-old Jennifer (Jenny) Campion. She had originally hailed from Salford in Greater Manchester and had been trying to kick a three-year heroin addiction. Based on Cassie's findings, it appeared that Jenny and the rest of the victims had died as a result of massive bodily trauma and blood loss. In other words, they had been dismantled while still alive.

Trying to hide his anger at the appalling nature of the crimes, Hellboy said, "This is quick work."

"We British bobbies don't piss about, you know," said Reynolds. "Been working through the night, haven't we."

"Well, *some* of us," Cassie murmured.

Before Reynolds could retort, Hellboy said, "Nothing on the train suicide yet, though."

"There wasn't much to go on," Cassie said. "The guy was literally delivered to me in buckets. We found two fingers undamaged enough to hopefully lift prints from, plus a row of about six teeth. The rest was just soup. Speaking of which . . ." she yawned, stretched, and rotated her head on her neck, " . . . I'm famished."

Hellboy heard the click-crunch of her vertebrae—then became suddenly aware that she was staring at him intently.

"What?" he said. "Have I got something on my face?"

"I was just wondering . . ." Her cheeks reddened and she shook her head. "No, forget it. You've probably got a million and one things to do."

"What?" Hellboy said again.

Before Cassie could reply, Reynolds barked a laugh.

"I don't believe this!" he exclaimed. "Bloody hell, I've seen it all now!"

Cassie scowled. "Get lost, Reynolds, this has nothing to do with you."

"You know what she's doing, don't you?" Reynolds said, turning to Hellboy. "She's only bloody asking you out on a date!"

Hellboy scowled at the policeman. Then he and Cassie both started speaking at once.

"Not a date! Sod it, Reynolds. Why do you—" Cassie said.

"I don't think it's any—" began Hellboy.

They clammed up at the same time too. Looked at each other. Cassie was flushed with anger and embarrassment.

"Go on," Hellboy said gently, "you first." He glanced at Reynolds. "And *you* keep out of it."

Reynolds raised his hands, a sneery, amused look on his face.

Still flushing, Cassie said, "All I was going to say was, I've been stuck in here since three this morning and I really need a break. I wondered, therefore, whether you'd like to grab a spot of breakfast? With me, I mean."

"Love to," Hellboy said without hesitation.

"Oh!" She looked surprised—and pleased. "Where?"

He shrugged. "It's your city."

She nodded, looked thoughtful. "How . . . conspicuous are you allowed to be?"

"As conspicuous as I like," Hellboy said, thinking of the front page of that morning's *Star*.

"Good," she said. "In that case, there's this little place I know . . ."

If there was one thing Proctor had learned over the past twenty-odd years it was that persistence pays. A good journalist might be dogged in his pursuit of a story, but a *great* journalist (and Proctor put himself in that category) would cling on like a pit bull, refusing to be dislodged, whatever the provocation.

He had lost count of the number of times he had been threatened with violence. He had even lost count of the number of times he had had violence inflicted upon him. He had been hospitalized on six, maybe seven occasions; on one of those occasions he had almost lost an eye. Yet in spite of everything, he had never been discouraged, never been intimidated, never been frightened off. Over the years his enemies had accused him of lacking many things—integrity, tact, compassion—but one thing they had never been able to accuse him of lacking was courage.

That was why, even as his story hit the newsstands, he was fully prepared to risk Hellboy's further ire by staking out his hotel. At five a.m. he was parked outside, hoping to squeeze out one more juicy exclusive before Hellboy and his chums became public domain. The only thing Proctor had *not* revealed in that morning's exposé was where the B.P.R.D. agents were staying while in London. However, he knew it would be only a matter of time before the massed ranks of the city's newshounds sniffed out that particular snippet of information.

For now, though, Proctor had the march on his rivals, and he intended to make the most of it. Of his three targets, Liz Sherman was the first to emerge, round about nine thirty. Proctor was tempted to follow her and her companion for the simple reason that she was a tasty bit of stuff whom he'd jump at the off chance of catching in flagrante delicto. However, he resisted the temptation, deciding instead to hold out for the big red guy.

Ten minutes after Liz Sherman's departure with Richard Varley, Abe Sapien emerged wearing an overcoat, shades, and a hat, jumped into a cab, and was whisked away. And then five minutes later Hellboy himself finally clumped down the hotel steps with DCI Reynolds, one of the officers in charge of the torso-murders investigation, whom Proctor had seen arrive minutes earlier.

Reynolds was no midget, but Hellboy towered over the man. Proctor hunched down in his car as Hellboy looked around, his lantern-jawed head turning from side to side. Then, apparently satisfied, Hellboy followed Reynolds to his unmarked car and folded his massive bulk into the front passenger seat. As soon as the car eased away from the curb, Proctor was in pursuit.

They didn't go far. Just to the private car park alongside the Scotland Yard building on Victoria Street. Proctor parked on double yellows on the opposite side of the road and settled down to wait.

He waited for over half an hour, keeping a wary eye out for traffic wardens and hoping he wasn't wasting his time. He was just beginning to wonder whether Hellboy had left by a different exit when his patience was finally rewarded. He jerked upright in his seat as Hellboy appeared around the side of the building, bold as brass, fists clenched and jaw set as if defying anyone to challenge him. What made Proctor feel vindicated in his choice of Hellboy as his primary target was the fact that he now had a sexy little blond with him. Proctor saw her point at something, and next moment she and the big red demon were laughing together like young lovers.

Proctor poked the long lens of his trusty Nikon out of the driver's window and rattled off a dozen snaps.

"Beautiful," he murmured.

"This is not good," Richard said.

His hands gripped the steering wheel tightly as he drove. His eyes darted left and right. Liz sympathized with her companion to some extent; it didn't take a genius to work out that this was a *very* bad neighborhood.

All the same, she was not unduly worried. The gangs of mean-faced kids, staring with hostile blankness at them as they drove by, evoked in her not even so much as a flicker of trepidation. In fact, their mannered posturing made her chuckle.

As they passed yet another gang of kids, Richard hunched down in his seat as if he expected to die in a hail of machine-gun bullets at any moment.

"Relax," said Liz, and smirked at him. "I'll protect you."

He glanced at her, too nervous to be amused. "That's not funny." He nodded at the crumbling concrete tenements, the graffiti-scrawled walls, the rubbish-choked patches of waste ground. "This is a no-go area. Run by drug gangs and rife with gun crime. Even the police don't come here at night."

"It's not night," said Liz. "It's ten thirty in the morning. Nearly time for . . . what is it you English have? Elevenses?"

Richard didn't answer. He didn't answer because at that moment a gang of around a dozen kids leaped out from where they'd been hiding behind walls and parked vehicles ahead and started pelting Richard's car with missiles. Bottles and rocks rained down on the bodywork with a series of dull clangs and the shrill jangle of shattering glass.

"*Shit!*" Richard squealed. He stamped on the brake, then slammed the gears into reverse. The engine screeched and suddenly they were driving backward, quickly and erratically, accompanied by the harsh tang of burnt rubber.

"Watch out!" cried Liz as they missed a parked van by millimeters.

The kids—ranging in age from nine or ten to about sixteen—gave chase, still fishing missiles from their pockets. The older ones looked murderous, but some of the younger ones were laughing, as though it was all just a game to them.

Liz held on as Richard, spying a gap between the parked vehicles behind them, slued the car round in a screeching arc. He hit the brakes and the car jerked to a halt and almost stalled. Now it was side on to the charging gang of kids. Liz flinched as another rock smacked into the door just beneath the passenger window.

"Whenever you're ready," she said calmly as the fastest of the kids drew to within yards of them. Richard was hauling on the steering wheel, sweat pouring down his pale face. As the Peugeot began, laboriously slowly, to swing away from the pursuing mob, the biggest and fastest of the kids reached them. He slammed his palms flat against the passenger window, as if to thrust his hands straight through the glass and grab Liz.

She turned and regarded him steadily. He was a rangy kid, tall for his age, with swirly patterns shaved into his stubble-short hair. He would have been good looking if he hadn't been mouthing obscenities, his face twisted with hate.

"Go and play, little boy," Liz murmured, and, still looking at him, she drew on her power, albeit the barest lick of it. Even that was enough, however, to make him step back from the car, a look of shocked bewilderment on his face. Liz knew what he was seeing: the flames dancing around the tips of her fingers, the sheen of fire in her eyes. She smiled and pulled the power back down within herself. She gave him a little wave as they pulled away, the car finally picking up speed, putting distance between itself and the chasing pack.

"It's okay," Liz said several streets later, "you can slow down now."

Richard had to make an effort to ease his foot from the accelerator. When he did he pulled the car into the curb, looking warily around him. "You see?" he said in a tight voice. "What did I tell you about this place?"

Liz regarded the lecturer not without sympathy. "This isn't your world. I should never have dragged you into this," she said.

"You didn't *drag* me into it," Richard responded. "I volunteered to help, remember."

She smiled. "Even so . . . you don't deserve this crap. The B.P.R.D. will pay for any damage to your car, by the way."

"Sod the car," he said. "It's us I'm worried about."

Liz couldn't help thinking that he sounded like an anxious lover discussing a rocky relationship.

"Our physical welfare, you mean?"

"Of course," he replied. "What else?"

"You *do* know I've got certain . . . abilities, don't you?" she said.

"I know you can make fire," he said bluntly.

A little taken aback, she nodded. "Well, then."

"But that doesn't make you invincible, does it? It doesn't mean you could . . . well . . . stop a speeding bullet, say."

Again she sighed. "If you don't want to do this, Richard, I'll understand. You can drop me off here if you like—just so long as you leave me the A-Z."

He looked appalled. "*Walk* these streets? You'd be risking your life. Seriously."

She arched an eyebrow. "Believe me, this is a cakewalk compared to some of the places I've been. Go on, head home. I mean it. I'll call you later."

He huffed out a long, slow breath, hands high on the steering wheel, staring straight ahead. Concrete tenements surrounded them, some linked by high walkways. The windows were mostly black, like blind eyes. The only visible life at present was a scrawny creature, which seemed more jackal than dog, rooting in an overturned dustbin.

Liz could see he was thinking hard. She waited patiently for him to come to a decision. Clouds drifted overhead, dark and craggy as inverted mountain ranges. Their sedate motion gave the illusion that the surrounding buildings were toppling with a languor that was almost graceful.

"No," he said finally, "I'm not abandoning you. I'm not the sort of man who runs away at the first sign of trouble . . . at least, I hope not. In for a penny, in for a pound."

She grinned. "Is that an English phrase?"

"I don't know," he said. "Is it? I suppose it must be." He fished the A–Z out of the foot-well, which is where it had ended up when the kids had attacked, and opened it at the page with the turned-down corner. Studying it, he said, "We can loop round here to Salt Road, avoid this rat run completely." He handed her the A–Z, pointing at the route. "Let's get going. The sooner we get out of this dump the better."

He put the car into gear and pulled away from the curb. For the next seven or eight minutes they ran a gamut of hard and hostile stares. Gangs, comprised mostly of teenagers, were gathered everywhere—on street corners beneath vandalized lampposts; in children's playgrounds where all the equipment was wrecked; in precincts where every retail outlet had been barricaded against attack with steel shutters and wire-mesh screens.

"It's like they know we don't belong here," said Richard nervously.

"That's just paranoia," said Liz. "They've had rough lives, that's all. They've learned to treat everyone as their enemy."

They arrived at their destination without further incident. Eden House was as unprepossessing as the rest of the neighborhood buildings, a late sixties, pie-in-the-sky tower block, whose high ideals had long ago given way to neglect and disillusion. Now the place looked less like a "vertical village" and more like a prison. Even the strung-out washing flapping forlornly from the occasional rusting balcony was as gray as the patchy concrete façade.

The parking area in front of the block was home to a burnt-out car. The blackened vehicle looked brittle as charcoal, perched within a sooty strew of its own debris. The sole signs of life were a couple of kids—one a skinny redhead, the other fat with a bad crewcut—who were listlessly kicking a football back and forth in the forecourt of the adjoining tower block. The skinny kid was smoking, and even from a distance Liz could see that his fingers were brown with nicotine stains.

As they got out of the car the kids sauntered over.

"Look after your car for you, mister," the fat kid said.

"You mean if I don't pay you, you'll vandalize it," replied Richard.

The kids said nothing.

"That's extortion, you know," said Richard feebly.

"How much?" asked Liz, trying to conceal a smile, and touched Richard's arm. "Don't worry. I'll claim it back on expenses."

"Fiver," said the fat kid.

"Done," said Liz, smiling sweetly, "but if you welch on the deal I'll hunt you down and kill you. Understand?"

The fat kid blanched and nodded. Liz handed over the money, and she and Richard walked towards the building's entrance, a pair of double doors in the shadow of an ugly, squared-off porch. The reinforced glass panels inset in the doors were mosaics of glittering fragments, the pieces held in place by wire grids which ran through their centers like sandwich filling.

They were less than ten yards from the building when a quartet of shadows detached themselves from the darkness of the porch and stepped out into gloomy daylight. The four men were twenty or thereabouts, and almost identically dressed in baseball caps and puffer jackets, baggy jeans, and big white sneakers. Two of the guys were white, one black, and the cappuccino-colored skin of the fourth suggested mixed parentage.

"Where you going?" one of the white guys demanded. He was tall, and muscular as a light middleweight boxer. His stance and demeanor made it evident he was the leader of the group.

Liz regarded him evenly. "We're visiting a friend," she said, no trace of nerves in her voice.

"Yeah? What's his name?" said the other white kid. He was shaven headed, lean as a wolf, a trio of big rings in each ear, a stubble of beard on his pointed chin.

"Credo Olusanya," Liz said, and added pointedly, "not that it's any of your business."

She noted the brief glances that ricocheted between the four guys, and wondered whether they were responding to the name or to her casual bravado.

"What you want with him?" The muscular white guy again.

"Same answer as before," Liz said smartly.

The black guy, round faced and big shouldered, frowned as if he didn't understand.

"Don't get smart, bitch," said the muscle man.

"Don't call me a bitch," said Liz lightly, holding his gaze.

It was the muscle man who broke the brief standoff. Shifting his glance to Richard, he said, "You. Four-eyes. How you know Credo?"

Liz sensed Richard tense beside her. *Don't show them you're scared*, she urged him silently.

To her relief his voice was strong and clear. "We have a mutual acquaintance," he said.

The cappuccino guy snorted. Muscle man pulled a disdainful face. "A what?"

"He's a friend of a friend," Liz interpreted.

"He looks like a cop," the other white guy said, nodding at Richard.

"Well, he's not," said Liz.

"Social worker then," said the chubby guy.

"Not that either."

"You don't look like friends of Credo," said the muscle man.

"Who are you, his social secretary?" asked Liz.

The muscle man narrowed his eyes and pursed his lips, as if trying to decide whether he was being made fun of.

The other white guy said, "Why don't you get back in that car of yours before something bad happens?"

"Nothing bad is going to happen," said Liz evenly.

"I think it is," said the shaven-headed white guy.

"I *know* it isn't," said Liz.

Casually the skinhead reached into his jacket and pulled out a machete. His eyes blanked; his face tautened with viciousness. "Get out now, bitch, while you still can," he hissed.

"Oh, you boys are so tiresome," said Liz. She reached into *her* jacket and pulled out her gun. Pointing it unwaveringly between the kid's eyes, she said, "We have important business with Mr. Olusanya, and you have wasted enough of our time. Now please be sensible and get out of our way."

"You won't use that," said the muscle man, but he looked unsure.

"Yes I will," said Liz with quiet but absolute conviction.

There was a short silence, then the chubby guy said petulantly, "Knew you were a cop."

"I'm not a cop," said Liz. "And you guys are so far out of your league it's unbelievable."

Another glance ricocheted between the four of them. They stood their ground for several more seconds, and then, as if he had grown bored with the encounter, the muscle man abruptly turned away. "Let's go."

He swaggered off. His three friends paused just long enough to eyeball Liz and Richard one last time, then trailed after him. Putting the machete in his pocket, the skinhead muttered, "Your card is marked, bitch."

"Yeah," said Liz, "whatever."

She waited until the guys were out of sight before she reholstered her gun.

"My God," said Richard weakly.

Liz looked at him. He was shaking. "You okay?"

"I will be." He pressed a trembling hand to his forehead. "Would you really have shot those boys?"

She shrugged. "Wouldn't have killed them. Winged one maybe."

"You really *do* live in a different world, don't you?"

"You make me feel as though I should apologize for it."

They walked up to the entrance doors of Eden House and pushed them open. By rights they should have been locked, but the locks and bolts had been pried off long ago. Beyond the doors was a dingy hallway, the graffitied walls running with damp. The floor was strewn with discarded household refuse, and the stench of rot and stale urine hung heavy in the air. Liz reached out to a light switch on her left, then noticed that nothing but bare wires hung from the ceiling where lights had once been. She sighed and said, "You feeling fit?"

"I certainly don't want to risk the lift, if that's what you mean," replied Richard.

They trooped up the stairs, their footsteps echoing around them. Aside from that and the steady drip of water there was no other sound.

Credo Olusanya's flat was on the fourth floor. The door was standing ajar.

Liz produced her gun again. "Stay behind me," she said.

She stood on the hinge side of the door and pushed it all the way open with her foot. Beyond was a narrow hallway with a dirty blue carpet. It was featureless, as if no one lived here. She crept forward, Richard behind her; she could hear him breathing hard and fast.

To her left was a door. She pushed it open. It led into a tiny bathroom, the bath and sink layered with grime, the plug holes clogged with hair. The toilet seat was down, but the room still smelled like a sewer. Liz pulled the door closed. There was only one other—at the end of the corridor—to aim for.

She turned briefly and raised her eyebrows at Richard: *You okay?* He nodded and they moved to the second door. It had been pulled to, but it wasn't fully closed. Holding her gun in both hands, Liz again used her foot to push the door open.

Her eyes scanned the room as the door swung inwards. It wasn't until it was three quarters of the way open that she saw the body.

She knew from Richard's gasp that he had seen it a split second after she did. The room was in shadow, the thin curtains closed and admitting no more than an insipid wash of daylight. However, the violence done to the man's body was so horrific that it instantly drew the eye, like a bloodstain on a white tablecloth.

The corpse was slumped, fully clothed, in a pale gray armchair, facing them. It wore a bib of dried and crusted blood. More blood, a great deal of it, was streaked and spattered across the carpet and on the fabric of the chair itself. The victim's head and hands had been hacked off and attached to the wall like a triptych of macabre adornments. The head was in the center, the eyes staring blankly in different directions, the mouth gaping open. Something like a tent peg or a railway spike had been driven into the open mouth, through the flesh and cartilage at the base of the skull and into the masonry beyond. The hands, nailed through their centers, were positioned either side of the head, fingers pointing downwards. Blood depended in trails from the severed appendages like black streamers. Some of the blood had been used to daub the now-familiar eye symbol on the wall.

"Somehow I don't think Credo will be in the mood for a chat today," Liz murmured.

As soon as the words were out of her mouth, she wondered how Richard would take them. She was truly horrified by the sight of the dead man, and the grim humor was merely her way of dealing with it. Hellboy would have understood that, but Richard wasn't Hellboy; to him, she probably sounded flippant, callous. She turned to look at him, perhaps even to apologize—and realized it was unlikely he had even registered her comment. He was slumped against the wall behind her, taking deep, gasping breaths. She was opening her mouth to ask if he was okay when she became peripherally aware of something bright and metallic flashing out of the darkness towards her.

She recoiled instinctively, taking a step back. The metal object missed her face by inches and clattered against the wall. It was a carving knife, and it had come from the shadows to the right of the seated corpse, presumably from the corner still concealed from her view by the edge of the door frame.

She went in low and fast, gun aimed at the spot where a potential assailant's head would be. No one there—but there was an open doorway in the corner of the room, a black rectangle leading presumably to a narrow kitchen area which must run parallel with the right-hand wall of the entrance corridor, into which the attacker must have ducked. She circled round quickly to get a better angle of sight into the room. She expected to see shadowy movement, but there was nothing—and then something else flew at her from the gloom.

It was a tin, the kind that contained beans or tuna fish or fruit chunks in syrup. It shot at her head with such force that it would almost certainly have concussed her or worse if she hadn't thrown herself to one side.

Her shoulder hit the floor at the same instant the tin smashed into the wall. Liz rolled and was on her feet in an instant. Using the wall as cover, she scooted along it until she reached the open doorway leading into the kitchen. Then she stepped around the edge of the frame, pointing her gun into the room beyond.

It was dark, but not completely black. Although the kitchen was an internal room, containing no windows, enough light was leaking through the thin curtains on the far side of the main room to give its contents a shadowy definition.

What was immediately apparent to Liz was that the room was empty and there was nowhere to hide. The kitchenette contained a sink, a cooker, a fridge, a set of drawers, a wall-mounted cupboard, and that was it. She looked from left to right in bewilderment. Was she missing something here? The top kitchen drawer was open, as was the cupboard, but unless her attacker was the size of a squirrel ,there was no hiding place to be found in either of these places.

She was just beginning to lower her gun when a tin fell out of the overhead cupboard, rolled along the counter and dropped to the floor. Instantly Liz snapped her gun back up. She shook her head at her own nervousness, and was starting to relax again when the tin, which had landed on its side, gave a little shudder and flipped upright.

Liz blinked, but she had seen enough weird stuff in her life to take this in her stride. She leveled her gun at the tin and waited to see what it would do next. Without warning it suddenly flew upwards towards her head. She jerked up her gun and pulled the trigger, and the tin exploded, watery brown soup spattering in all directions.

"What's going on?" Richard shouted from the hallway, his voice thin with fear.

"I'm okay," Liz answered. "Just stay where you are and keep your head down."

The words were barely out of her mouth when several objects rose from the open drawer as if lifted by invisible hands. Liz saw knives, forks, a corkscrew, even a soup ladle. They hovered in the half-light, quivering, reminding her bizarrely of birds of prey readying themselves for the killing swoop to earth. Thinking quickly, she rammed her gun back into its holster and directed her thoughts inwards, reaching down into the ferocious and untamable inferno at her core.

She hated having to use her power in such a confined space, and especially in a building that was likely filled with people, but if she was going to survive here she didn't have much of a choice. As the items flashed through the air towards her, she unleashed the fire to meet them. The implements hurtling in her direction were reduced instantly to puddles of molten metal sizzling on the floor. More tins flew out of the overhead cupboard, and they too were transformed to spatters of metallic rain in a split second, their contents either charred to cinders or evaporated to mist.

Some instinct, primal and self-preservatory, compelled Liz to spin back round to face the main room. A lamp was flying at her, trailing its lead like a whiplashing tail. It too was incinerated, as was a portable CD player, a TV, a kettle, a suitcase, assorted crockery, and a fist-sized solid-glass paperweight. Beyond these items the carpet, wall, and curtains were burning now too, the carpet giving off a thick cloud of poisonous black smoke. Liz backed towards the door, head snapping right and left, fire still flowing out of her. It felt both glorious and terrible. As ever she experienced both a sense of delirious freedom and the utter terror of knowing she had unleashed a beast over which she had only minimal control.

A chair hurled itself towards her and became blazing spindles of matchwood. Liz stepped smartly back out of the main room, grabbing the door handle and pulling it shut as she did so. The plastic handle became toffee at her touch. She let it go before it could liquefy and fuse to her skin. Something heavy—some other item of furniture—hit the other side of the door with a shuddering thump. Liz shuddered too and, with a mighty effort, snapped the fire back in to herself. It came in a rippling gush, tingling her nerve endings, making her cry out. For an instant it seemed bigger than she was, too vast to contain.

And then it was gone. She blinked and placed one hand on top of the other. Her flesh was cool.

As always after using her gift, she felt alert, her senses temporarily heightened. She turned quickly. Richard was halfway along the corridor, pressed against the wall, gaping at her. Nimble as a cat, she padded towards him.

"Set off any alarms you can find while I call the fire brigade," she said, pulling her phone out of her belt.

His eyes were wide with fear and awe. "Then what?" he asked.

"Then we do what we can to get everyone out of here before the whole damn building goes up."

☠ CHAPTER 8

The proprietor of the Bagel Palace treated Hellboy and Cassie like
royalty. It helped that Cassie had phoned ahead to say they were
coming. Hellboy generally found that people reacted badly when
he turned up in places he wasn't expected. Sometimes they reacted
badly when he turned up in places he *was* expected, but that was
their problem.

Luigi Spineze, however, had had a half hour to get used to the
idea, and as soon as they stepped through the door, Hellboy duck-
ing his head beneath the lintel, he bustled towards them with open
arms and a wide grin. He was a jolly little beach ball of a man, his
dark bushy eyebrows and bristling moustache making up for the
fact that he had very little hair on his shiny dome of a head.

"Cassie, my lovely girl!" he exclaimed, his accent an odd combination of Cockney and his native Italian. He enfolded her in a
fatherly bear hug, then stepped back, his hands on her shoulders.
"But let me look at you! Beautiful as always! You light up my life
like a lantern!"

Cassie was laughing and shaking her head as he turned to Hellboy. "And Hellboy! What an honor! I saw your picture in the paper
this morning, but I never dreamed I would see you in the flesh!
And in my restaurant too!"

Hellboy grinned bashfully. "Yeah," he said. "Ain't life strange?"

The Bagel Palace—perhaps more of a coffee shop than a restaurant, despite what Luigi had said—was around half full. As usual,

Hellboy was aware of people staring at him. Out of the corner of his eye he had seen food fall out of one guy's gaping mouth as he had stepped through the door.

"I give you my best table!" Luigi said expansively. "Over here by the window! Come! Come!"

He began to move away. Hellboy pointed to a table on the opposite side of the room.

"Actually I'd rather sit back there in the corner," he muttered.

"But this is my best table!" Luigi reiterated.

"Yeah, it's very nice," said Hellboy. "It's just a bit . . . well . . . public."

Luigi looked crestfallen—perhaps he had been hoping that Hellboy's presence would draw the crowds—but he conceded graciously. Hellboy and Cassie sat down. The table Hellboy had chosen was sandwiched between the kitchen and the toilets, but at least it was relatively private. The two of them ordered bagels and coffee (despite the huge breakfast he had eaten that morning, Hellboy ordered six bagels to Cassie's one), and then they sat looking at each other for a moment. Hellboy tugged at his goatee a little self-consciously. "Nice place," he muttered.

Cassie let loose a burst of soft laughter.

"What?" said Hellboy. "Did I say something funny?"

She raised a hand and wafted it between them. "No, it's just . . . this is so weird."

"What is?"

"This situation. Sitting here with you. I mean . . . what do I say to you? What do I say that you could possibly find interesting?"

Hellboy shrugged. He had encountered this attitude lots of times, but that didn't mean he had ever gotten used to it. What people didn't seem to realize about him was that on first encounter he often felt just as awkward as whoever he was with.

"Everything you've said has been pretty interesting so far," he mumbled.

"But . . . I can't imagine what your life must be like. From what I've read, it sounds as though you've done some *amazing* things. I mean . . . how dull must this be to you? Sitting in a café eating bagels?"

"Believe me," said Hellboy, "when I'm doing some of the so-called amazing things you talk about, I crave stuff like this. Moments when I'm not at someone's beck and call. Moments when I'm not getting my teeth knocked in, or freezing my buns off halfway up a mountain, or lost in some stinking catacombs somewhere. This is . . . nice. More than nice." He smiled uncertainly. "I mean . . . nice place, great company, and hopefully good food. What's not to like?"

Cassie smiled shyly. Now that she wasn't having to put on a front for assholes like Reynolds she was showing her softer, more *truthful* side. Hellboy liked that. He liked people to be themselves around him, purely because it happened so rarely.

"I guess it's just . . . well, you must have met so many amazing people in your time. How can anyone . . . *normal* compete with that?"

"Most of the people I meet are jerks," Hellboy said. "Prissy government officials, know-it-all army types, psychos, megalomaniacs. I hardly ever get a chance to just meet real people and hang out." He shrugged. "I'm really not that special. Those magazines and TV shows, they always say I'm *enigmatic*, but I'm really not. Truth is, I'm not sure I even know what that means."

"It means you don't say much," said Cassie. "So people think you're deep."

Hellboy chuckled. "I don't say much because I haven't got much to say. Either that or it's because people ask me stupid questions. You know what my friend, Abe, says about me?"

"What?"

"He says I've got hidden shallows."

They both laughed.

"So . . . what *is* going on here, Hellboy?" Cassie asked a few seconds later. "People are talking about monsters and ghosts and demons. It's like the whole world's going mad. And these killings . . . is it the work of some nutter or . . ." She broke off abruptly, held her hands up. "Look, just tell me to mind my own business, okay? I don't want to put you in an awkward position. Like you say, you have enough people asking you damn stupid questions as it is."

Hellboy shook his head. "Nah, you're one of the team. You have a right to know." He started to tell her, but just then Luigi bustled up with their food, placing each plate in front of them with a flourish.

"I get your coffee!" he told them. "And if I may, Hellboy . . . a picture for my collection?"

He gestured around. Hellboy noticed that framed and signed portraits of celebrities hung on the walls. Many of the celebrities were holding up one of Luigi's bagels and grinning into the camera—though Madonna was scowling behind a pair of shades, shoulders hunched.

"Okay," he said, trying to conceal his sigh.

Luigi bustled happily away to fetch coffee and camera.

Cassie smiled sympathetically. "Sorry about that. Maybe this was a bad idea?"

"No, no, it's okay," Hellboy said. "I get this kinda thing all the time."

"And yet you don't seem comfortable with it."

"Face like mine, you think I'd get used to it, wouldn't you?" he joked. Grimacing, he continued, "Thing is, I feel like a fraud. I mean, I'm not some actor or singer. I don't have any special skills."

"From what I understand, you save the world on a regular basis," said Cassie. "That's pretty special."

"That's just biology. Genetics. I'm hard to kill, so the B.P.R.D. puts me on the front line. I'm not a master strategist. I'm not James Bond. I can just punch very, very hard is all."

"Even so, it's a damn sight more valuable than what most of this lot do." She gestured round at the walls.

"Plus I'm better looking," said Hellboy with a grin.

He submitted to the flashing eye of Luigi's camera, trying not to let his smile turn into a clench-teethed expression of anguish. Even in his left hand the bagel looked no bigger than a Polo mint, but he brandished it gamely.

When Luigi finally left, Hellboy shuddered. "Glad that's over. Give me a kraken to fight any day of the week."

They munched their bagels and drank their coffee and he told her the rest of the reason why he was here.

"So what's being done to stop it?" asked Cassie.

"Abe's gathering information and Liz is following up some leads on the muti angle."

"And you?"

"Just now I'm directing operations. That call I made in the car on the way over? That was to Agent Turner, who works for the B.P.R.D. here in London. Right now she should be negotiating with the police to organize a widespread campaign to question every vagrant in central London." He tapped his satellite phone. "Soon as we establish a link between the victims—and we will, believe me—she'll call me."

He swigged the last of his coffee and asked Luigi for a refill. Then he said, "But enough about me for now. What about you? When did you first develop an interest in poking around inside dead people?"

She smiled. "Must be in the genes. My dad's an eye surgeon, my mum's a consultant haematologist. Even my baby brother's doing medicine at Leeds University."

She took a last bite of her cream-cheese bagel. Some of the filling squidged out the side and ended up on her cheek.

"You've got cream cheese on your face," Hellboy said.

She rubbed at the wrong cheek. "Where?"

"Here." He reached out with his left hand, delicately extending a forefinger to scoop the blob of food off her face. As soon as his finger touched her skin, however, light flashed from somewhere in the vicinity of his left shoulder, harsh enough to make him blink. He turned his head, expecting to see Luigi standing there with his camera.

But it wasn't Luigi. It was Colin Proctor.

"Hey!" Hellboy shouted, and was starting to rise when the light flashed again, blinding him. He squinted and rubbed a hand across his face. Unable to see, he felt his hoof knock against something, which fell over with a clatter.

"Hellboy!" he heard Cassie say, but he didn't answer. His vision started to clear. He saw Proctor scurrying towards the door.

"Hey, you little bastard! Come back here!" he yelled.

Proctor turned briefly. "Don't think so, mate." Then he smirked and ducked out the door.

It was the smirk which did it. Hellboy felt rage rushing through him. He roared and ploughed across the restaurant. He'd tear that little creep limb from limb—or, if not, then he'd smash his camera, at least.

People screamed as Hellboy cut a swathe through them. He was not exactly oblivious to what lay in his path, but he was angry, and moving fast, and so was not as careful as he would ordinarily have been. He thumped against one table with his hip, knocking it over, scattering food and crockery. His duster, flying behind him, swept across another, tipping over a coffeepot, whose contents spilled across the lacquered surface and drooled onto the floor. In his haste to catch up with Proctor, he cracked his head on the lintel as he ducked out of the building.

"Crap!" he shouted, giving a little old lady passing by on the street outside the fright of her life.

Proctor was haring along the pavement as fast as his stubby legs would carry him. Hellboy sprinted in pursuit, hooves raising sparks from the paving slabs, duster billowing in his wake like the cape of a superhero. People screamed and leaped aside. On the opposite pavement they pointed and shouted. Hellboy was gaining on Proctor, but the journalist, sweat pouring down his face, had come to a halt beside a crappy little Astra and was ramming a key into the lock. Hellboy caught up with him just as the car began to pull away from the curb.

"No, you don't!" Hellboy shouted, and lunged forward. With his stone hand he grabbed the rust-speckled rear bumper. The car screamed, raising smoke and the stink of scorched rubber from its spinning but stationary tires. And then with a grinding screech of metal, the bumper parted from the car and the vehicle sped away. It slued into the road, narrowly missing a black cab, whose horn was a long blat of anger and alarm. Hellboy staggered backwards, the bumper still clutched in his stone hand like some bizarre weapon.

"Please drop that, sir," said a voice behind him.

Hellboy ground his teeth as Proctor's car receded into the distance, and then turned.

Two uniformed constables were standing on the pavement beside a parked panda car ten yards behind him. Both policemen looked nervous. One had his hands half raised as if to placate a cornered animal; the right hand of the other kept straying subconsciously to the handle of his truncheon.

"Hey, guys," Hellboy said, "do me a favor and follow that car, willya?"

"Which car, sir?" the officer with the raised hands asked, though Hellboy could tell by his tone of voice that the guy was merely humoring him.

"The little blue Astra. The one missing a rear bumper." He held the bumper up and instantly the two constables went for their truncheons. Hellboy supposed that if they'd had guns they'd have pulled them on him.

He rolled his eyes. "Take it easy, guys. I'm the wronged party here. Look, I'll put this down if it makes you happier."

He bent and carefully placed the bumper on the pavement. Then he said, "So are you gonna help me or not?"

"Could you tell us *why* you caused damage to the car, sir?" asked the second policeman.

Hellboy sighed. "I was trying to stop the driver from getting away. No chance of that now."

"And exactly *why* were you trying to stop him getting away, sir?"

Hellboy closed his eyes briefly. "Because he's been hounding me ever since I arrived here."

"Hounding you in what way, sir?" asked the second policeman.

"He's a journalist," said Hellboy. "He's been following me around, taking pictures."

The two policemen exchanged a glance. "There's no law against taking pictures, sir," said the first officer blandly.

"We have a policy in this country, sir—freedom of the press," added the second.

"*Oh, fer Chrissakes!*" exploded Hellboy. "That little bastard is compromising the integrity of my mission here and you stand there spouting crap about freedom of the press. You guys are priceless, you know that?"

He turned away, but the first policeman said, "Where do you think you're going, sir?"

"To finish my breakfast," Hellboy said, "or is there a law against that as well?"

"I think you should accompany us to the station, sir," the second policeman said.

Hellboy turned back. "What?" he said quietly.

The officer looked nervous, but doggedly continued, "Regardless of your status here, sir, I really think you should come with us. We wouldn't be doing our job if we just let you go. There are certain charges you may have to answer at the station."

"Charges?" Hellboy repeated. "Like what?"

"Causing an affray," said the first policeman.

"Criminal damage," said the second.

"So you're arresting me?" said Hellboy.

"We're just pursuing our inquiries, sir," said the first policeman.

"Just doing our jobs," added the second.

Hellboy expelled a long, deep breath. "Aw, great," he muttered.

When Richard and Liz arrived at Labuschagne's apartment block the gates were already open. Parked close to the entrance of the building were two police cars and a blue riot van with grilles over the windows. The back doors of the van were open and Liz could see two rows of men, bulky in padded jackets, sitting facing each other. Standing beside one of the cars, Abe was talking to a rangy man in a gray suit. Although he was not wearing a uniform, the rangy man looked every inch a police officer. Kind of like Clint Eastwood in *Dirty Harry*, thought Liz, but with shorter hair.

A uniformed constable stepped into their path and raised a hand as they drove up to the gates. Liz showed him her B.P.R.D. pass and he allowed them through.

Richard parked on the far side of the riot van. Although on the drive over he had heard Liz making the call requesting that a backup team rendezvous with them at Labuschagne's residence, the physical reality of the police presence still seemed to daunt him somewhat.

"You can stay in the car if you like," Liz said softly.

Richard shook his head. "No, I don't want to sit here like a lemon." He glanced at the glittering tower block, which was at the opposite end of the luxury scale to the one in which Credo Olusanya had lived and died. "I might not come inside with you this time, though, if that's okay?"

Liz smiled. "I doubt you'd be allowed in anyway, what with being a civilian and all."

They got out of the car and walked over to Abe and the rangy man.

"Hey, Abe!" Liz called. "Where's Hellboy?"

If Abe had been able to raise an eyebrow she felt sure he would have done. "Would you believe, in police custody?"

"You mean he's been arrested?"

Abe nodded.

"What the hell for?"

Abe looked pointedly at the rangy man, who grimaced with embarrassment. "It's a misunderstanding, that's all. It's being sorted as we speak."

Abe introduced the rangy man as Detective Inspector Cartwright. He shook hands with Liz and Richard, and asked, "So what's the situation here, Agent Sherman?"

Liz liked him immediately. She liked him because he didn't seem to mind that she was the one calling the shots. Most British cops seemed resistant to the idea of being ordered about by an American girl, but there was no challenge in Cartwright's voice, no resentment, no cynicism. His body language indicated that he was prepared to trust her judgment and defer to her greater experience.

Of course, she told herself, she might be reading him completely wrong. After all, she had instinctively liked Labuschagne, and he had sent her into a trap.

She quickly filled Abe and Cartwright in on the events of that morning.

"And you're certain that this man, Labuschagne, was behind the attack?" said Abe.

Liz nodded. "It's got to be him. He was the only one who knew we were going to see Olusanya this morning."

Abe turned to Richard, who was pulling a face. "You don't seem so sure, Dr. Varley?"

He flashed Liz a look of apology and said, "Well . . . I'm not, to be honest. I mean, what Liz says makes perfect sense, but . . . I *know* Kobus. Or at least I think I do. He's a good man, and a brave one.

He's always spoken out against the more unscrupulous practitioners of muti, and he's taken a lot of flak for it over the years."

"A smokescreen," said Liz dismissively.

"But his wife and children were killed . . . brutally murdered."

Liz looked at him sympathetically. "I'm sorry, Richard, but that changes nothing. Like I said before, you don't live in my world. You really have no idea how ruthless some people can be."

Richard looked unhappy, but he continued to shake his head. "I still don't believe it," he said, "and I won't until someone proves otherwise."

Cartwright had listened to the exchange patiently, but now he turned to Liz. "So what's the plan, Agent Sherman?"

"We go in," Liz said simply. "Me, Abe, maybe a couple of your guys. But Abe and I take the lead. We don't know what Labuschagne's capable of."

"He's just one man," said Cartwright. "Surely four armed officers will be sufficient to deal with him?"

"He's a sangoma," said Liz. "And if he's tapping into the energy unleashed by the sacrifices, then literally anything could happen."

Cartwright rubbed a hand over his face. "To be frank with you, Agent Sherman, all of this is a bit outside my comfort zone."

Liz smiled. "Don't worry, that's why Abe and I are here." She glanced towards the riot van. "Okay, let's get going. Can you handpick a couple of men for us, Detective Inspector? We need guys who stay cool in a crisis, who think quickly and take orders without question."

Two minutes later they were good to go. A besuited guy with too much gel in his hair was hovering by the main doors to let them in. Liz guessed he was from whichever firm of glorified landlords owned this place. He was clearly unhappy about the unwanted attention the building was attracting, but he would just have to lump it.

"I'll need the master key to get into apartment 1101," she told him.

He shook his head firmly. "I can't just hand it over. I'll have to come up there with you and let you in."

"No way," Liz said. "This is a B.P.R.D. operation and you're a civilian. If anything happens to you, we'll be the ones to get our asses kicked."

Gel guy pulled a petulant face. "Then I'll have to call my superiors," he said.

"You do that," answered Liz, and held her hand out. "In the meantime just give me the key. By which I mean, not the whole bunch, just the one I need. I don't want anything to slow me down up there."

Gel guy still looked uncertain. Liz sighed. "Unless, of course, you want to be busted for obstructing a police inquiry, or whatever the hell it's called over here."

His resistance crumbled. Suddenly he looked like a little kid who had been ordered to hand over his dinner money by the school bullies. His voice quivering, he said, "I want it to be noted that I do this under protest."

"Whatever," replied Liz, and took the key off him.

"I promise we'll be as discreet as possible," Abe said as he followed Liz into the building.

Gel guy stared at him, aghast. Clearly he hadn't expected the strange fish-man to talk.

Once inside, Liz and one of the riot cops took the lift while Abe and the other cop took the stairs. All was quiet, just as it had been the previous afternoon. The four of them congregated on the landing outside Labuschagne's door, but no one said anything; they each knew what was required of them. Despite their protective clothing and heavy-duty weapons, the cops' role was simply to hang back and allow the B.P.R.D. agents to enter Labuschagne's apartment alone. They would only come running if either Liz or Abe called for them, or if Labuschagne somehow eluded the two agents. If all went well, the cops wouldn't have to do anything at all. If it *didn't* go well, then Liz had instructed them in no uncertain terms how they should respond.

"He gets past us, you take him down," she had said. "Labuschagne might *look* like an unarmed civilian in a snazzy suit, but in his case appearances are deceptive. So you take him down, and you take him down *fast*. You understand me? Hesitate and you're dead."

The two men had nodded grimly, their faces showing not a flicker of emotion. Liz was satisfied. Cartwright had chosen well. She only hoped they wouldn't have cause to find out *how* well.

She held up the key and they all nodded. Then slowly and deliberately she fitted it into the lock. She turned it and pushed the door, stepping out of the line of fire as she did so. When nothing happened, she and Abe went in.

They found Labuschagne in his elegant and understated living room. He was dead. In contrast to the pale, muted tones of the décor, his blood was a vulgar shout of color. Most of it was pooled beneath his body on the polished wooden floor. He had been stripped not only of his clothes, but his skin as well. His raw, oozing remains were twisted into a position of frozen agony. His lipless mouth yawned in a dying scream. Liz noted with contained fury that the frame containing the photographs of his wife and daughters had been dashed against something, perhaps the corner of the table on which it had been standing. The remnants, including the mangled photographs themselves, were scattered across the floor. Shards of glass had been selected from the shattered pieces and rammed into Labuschagne's eyes. His flayed skin, like a bundle of bloodied rags, had been dumped almost casually on a chair. On the largest section of blank wall, in the sangoma's blood, was the sign of the eye.

Abe surveyed the dreadful scene with what to the uninitiated would have seemed like dispassion. Then he crossed to Liz and placed a hand on her shoulder.

Trying to keep her voice steady, she said, "I was wrong about him, wasn't I? He *was* on our side, just like Richard said. I feel awful now for doubting him."

Abe's voice was soft. "No, Liz, you were right all along. When you first met Labuschagne you instinctively believed he was a good man. It was our enemy who made you doubt your instincts, and that's who you should blame."

"Our enemy," repeated Liz and swiped angry tears from her face. "Who *is* our enemy, Abe?"

Abe shook his head. "I don't know," he said, "but he'll show his hand soon enough. You can bet on that."

☠ CHAPTER 9

"Screw it," Hellboy said.

DCI Reynolds snorted. "Oh, very mature. What's that supposed to mean?"

Hellboy glared at him. "It means screw it. It means I don't want a lift back to my hotel. It means I'm not a government resource and I'm sick of being treated like one. It means I'm gonna go off and do my own thing and no one's gonna stop me."

Reynolds weathered the storm with equanimity. When Hellboy had done yelling, he said with spiteful amusement, "Your date really didn't go well, did it?"

Fully aware that the policeman was trying to wind him up, but still unable to prevent himself rising to the bait at least a little, Hellboy said, "It was going fine until your guys decided to try and get their faces on TV."

"Are you suggesting, Hellboy," said Reynolds mildly, "that the officers in question arrested you simply because they were seeking self-aggrandizement?"

"Damn right I am," Hellboy said.

"I'll have you know that's a very serious allegation," Reynolds said. "Tantamount to slander, in fact."

"So sue me."

Reynolds laughed. He was clearly enjoying this. "But surely, Hellboy, you can't *deny* that you were acting in a manner liable to cause a breach of the peace? We have dozens of witnesses who claim they saw you running along the street, shouting, making threats, pushing people out of the way ..."

"I didn't push anybody," Hellboy protested.

"Furthermore, you surely can't deny that you caused criminal damage to a motor vehicle belonging to one Colin Proctor of ... hmm, on second thoughts, maybe giving you Mr. Proctor's address wouldn't be such a good idea. After all, we don't want to add assault or malicious wounding to your litany of misdemeanors, do we?"

Reynolds was grinning widely now. Hellboy narrowed his eyes.

"You really don't like us being here, muscling in on your territory, do you?" he said.

Reynolds shrugged as if the matter was neither here nor there. "It's not as though I've got anything against you *personally*, Hellboy. It's just that as far as I'm concerned, you're doing nothing but muddying the waters of this investigation. I mean, you haven't exactly covered yourself in glory so far, have you?"

If he had been in an argumentative mood, Hellboy might have pointed out that he and his friends had actually been instrumental in opening the investigation out in all sorts of new and interesting directions. But he couldn't be bothered. Standing up, he said, "You know what? I'm not in the mood for this."

"So what are you going to do?" Reynolds asked. "Walk out of here? Take a stroll through the streets of London?"

"Yeah, why not?" said Hellboy.

"I think you might find it difficult to blend into the crowd," Reynolds said.

Hellboy shrugged his massive shoulders. "Thanks to your wonderful press, I don't think that's an issue anymore. Might as well show my face. Say hi to the locals."

Reynolds shook his head, wafted a hand dismissively. "It's your life."

"Yeah," said Hellboy, "it is."

As soon as he exited the station, descended the steps, and began striding along the street, Hellboy felt the steel band of stress that was clamped around his thoughts easing a little. It might have been a typically murky day in London, but the cool, damp breeze felt good on his skin. He looked around, trying to get his bearings. Luigi's place had been tucked away in a little side street close to Covent Garden, and the police station he had been taken to for questioning was just off Piccadilly. That meant to get back to his hotel he needed to head north up Shaftesbury Avenue and then on to Charing Cross Road.

But did he *want* to head back to his hotel? He had half a mind to jump in a cab and go visit his pal Father Simon Finch at his vicarage in the beautiful Cotswolds village of Winograd Heath. He often went there when he wanted solace from dealing with the endless stream of demonic manifestations and supernatural visitations that seemed to define his existence. He went there to find peace, equilibrium; to breathe good, clean air and remind himself how sweet and simple and downright idyllic an ordinary, uneventful life could be. He also went there to remind himself exactly what he was fighting *for*, because sometimes it was hard to keep track of that; hard to remember what, ultimately, was the point of his endless daily struggle.

Yeah, the thought of hailing a cab now, of dozing in the back while the miles unspooled behind him, of leaving all the crapola behind . . .

Unrealistic, of course. He was needed here. As if to underline the thought, the beeper on his belt went off. He unclipped his satellite phone from its pouch and put it to his ear. "Yeah?"

Liz's voice was tinny. "HB, it's me. I've been trying to call you."

"Yeah, sorry. Been kinda busy," Hellboy said.

"Getting arrested—I heard. So where are you now?"

"Heading back to the hotel, I guess. I've just been released back into the community. What's happening with you?"

She told him about Credo Olusanya and Kobus Labuschagne.

"Sounds like you guys have been getting all the fun jobs," he said.

"Yeah, it's been a riot. Listen, we're meeting for lunch. Abe's got some stuff to tell us about these eye people. You up for that?"

"Sure," he said. "Where?"

He heard her voice change, become slightly hesitant. "Please say if you think this is a bad idea, but we thought . . . well, you know the Three Cups just off Great Russell Street, don't you?"

He was silent for a moment. The Three Cups. He hadn't been back there since the summer of '79. It was where he had met Anastasia.

"HB?" Liz said.

"Still here."

"You *do* think it's a bad idea, don't you? Listen, we'll meet somewhere else. I just thought . . . since it's a place you know—"

"The Three Cups is fine," he said.

"You're sure?"

"Sure I'm sure. Why shouldn't I be? That place holds nothing but good memories for me."

He arranged to see her there in a half hour, then resumed his walk. On this quiet street, it was weird to think of all the stuff going down in London, weirder still to think that somewhere beneath these cracked pavements and patchy roads was a bubbling volcano of malign energy—a volcano which, if they didn't prevent it, might well erupt and engulf the entire city.

It was hard to believe all of that when birds were singing away, and cars were hooting their horns at each other, and people were just getting on with their daily business. But then again, that was always the way, wasn't it? When it came to stuff that couldn't be seen or properly understood, people tended to turn a blind eye to it until it was right in their faces. They denied and denied until they could deny it no longer.

Hellboy himself was a case in point. He had been famous since the late fifties, and yet the majority of people never *actually* seemed to believe in him until they saw him in the flesh. Even now, even though he'd been on the front page of that morning's newspaper, he was aware of people staring at him in wonder as he passed by. Some pointed; some shouted; some grinned and whooped. Someone even yelled, "Freak," but Hellboy refused to favor *that* particular individual with the satisfaction of a response. Wherever you went in the world there was always at least one idiot.

As he turned from the relative quiet of Down Street onto the main route through Piccadilly, Hellboy caught the eye of a little kid who was walking towards him along the sidewalk, clutching his mom's hand. He saw the little kid's eyes turn to saucers and he winked.

"Hey, little buddy, how ya doin'?" he said.

The kid said nothing. He was struck dumb with awe. The kid's mother stared up at Hellboy with a nervousness he was familiar with and asked, "Excuse me . . . Hellboy?"

She used the name shyly, deferentially. In his gentlest voice, Hellboy said, "Yeah?"

"Er . . . I hope you don't mind," said the woman, "but Dale here is a big fan of yours."

"Really?" Hellboy said, surprised.

"Oh yeah. Ever since he saw your photo in a magazine, he's been obsessed. Got pictures of you plastered all over his wall."

Hellboy looked down at the kid, who was gazing at him like he was Father Christmas. "Well, how about that," he said, touched.

"And we wondered . . . that is, *I* wondered . . . would you mind if I took a photo of you and Dale together? It would really make his day."

"Sure," Hellboy said. "How do you want us?"

"Could he maybe sit on your knee?"

"Would he be happy to do that?"

"Oh yeah." She turned to her son, bent down so that her face was level with his. "Dale, would you like a photo with Hellboy?"

The kid nodded slowly. The look on his face suggested that all his dreams had come true.

Without hesitation Hellboy sat cross-legged on the pavement. He was attracting quite a crowd now, but he studiously ignored the rubberneckers. He patted his left knee. "Hey, little buddy, you wanna take a seat?"

Dale nodded again, moved across to Hellboy, and perched on the vast red boulder of his knee. Hellboy put his hand gently on the kid's shoulder (he could have held the kid's head in his hand like an apple) and then Dale's mom produced a little instamatic from her bag and began snapping away.

Next moment Hellboy heard a bunch of young, excited voices calling his name. He half turned and saw a crocodile of nursery kids on the opposite side of the road, shouting and waving. He waved back, eliciting squeals of delight. The kids surrounded the nursery assistant and Hellboy heard them imploring her to let *them* have their photo taken too.

"You see what you've started?" Hellboy said softly to Dale, ruffling the kid's hair.

Dale smiled at him. Hellboy beckoned to the nursery assistant. "Bring them over if you want."

Pretty soon he had kids scrambling all over him. They rapped on the sawn-off flats of his horns; they clambered up onto his shoulders. People grinned and took photos. Dale's mom and the nursery assistant struck up a conversation, like neighbors meeting in a playground. Traffic slowed as car, bus, and van drivers leaned out of the windows of their vehicles to stare and laugh at what was going on.

Eventually a car pulled up to the curb beside him. It was a car Hellboy recognized, one he had sat in earlier that day. The passenger window slid down and Cassie Saunders leaned across. She was grinning too.

"I can see you're busy," she called, "but I just wondered whether you needed a lift?"

"Daddy, you're here!" Jasmine screamed, running up and flinging her arms round him.

Proctor laughed. "Well, of course I'm here. You didn't think I'd miss your birthday, did you?"

"Do you like my new rollerblades?" she asked, tilting her feet back and forth so that he could view them from all angles.

"Very smart," he said. "Did Mummy buy you those?"

"Yep. And this new top. Look, there's sparkly bits round the collar."

"Wow," said Proctor, and handed over the large white plastic bag he was carrying. "Here's my present, sweetheart. Happy birthday."

Jasmine took the bag from him, eyes shining. Her friends crowded round as she put it down on the wooden floor of the school hall and lifted out the box inside. The present was wrapped in pink Barbie paper, which prompted one of her friends—earrings, lipstick, eye shadow; no doubt destined to become the class bitch, Proctor thought—to make a gagging noise. However, hers was the only dissenting voice. Jasmine looked up and asked, "Can I open it now?"

" 'Course you can," he told her.

A little anxiously she asked, "You are staying for the *whole* party, aren't you, Daddy?"

"As long as you promise me a bit of cake," he said, winking.

Jasmine ripped the paper off her present, her friends crowding round to see. "Oh, wow, a Walkman!" she exclaimed.

To Proctor's satisfaction, his gift met with a universal chorus of approval:

"*Amazing!*"

"You are *so* lucky!"

"I wish *I* had a Walkman."

He was still basking in the glory when a voice behind him said, "Well, well. Look what the cat dragged in."

He turned. Tina was all glammed up.

"Hello, Tina," he said, "you look lovely."

Sotto voce, she replied, "You look like shit—as usual."

"How gratifying that you're making the effort to be nice for the sake of our daughter's birthday," he said with a smile. "I'm touched."

She ignored the barb. "I suppose it was Jasmine who told you we'd be here?"

Before their exchange could escalate into a quiet war of bitterness, Jasmine burst from her circle of friends and held up her present. "Look, Mum!" she cried. "Look what Dad bought me! And some CDs too! Isn't it fantastic!"

Tina tried, for Jasmine's sake, to share her daughter's enthusiasm, but her face seemed unfamiliar with the muscles required. "It's lovely, Jas. Have you said thank you?"

Jasmine placed the now-opened box carefully on the floor, then flew at Proctor again with enough force to knock the wind out of him. "Thank you, Daddy! It's a brilliant present! And you're a brilliant dad!"

Proctor flashed his ex-wife a point-scoring smirk. She flared her nostrils at him before stalking away.

As Jasmine had told him on the phone last week, hers was to be a rollerblading party. This basically involved Jasmine and her friends whizzing round and round the school gymnasium all afternoon, to the accompaniment of blaring music provided by a DJ in a silly hat. Tina had been able to hire the gymnasium because it was half-term. Proctor had previously promised his daughters that sometime this week, while they were off school, he would take them shopping on Oxford Street, and then to a proper West End show. However, this Hellboy story had gobbled up his time, and would no doubt continue to do so for the foreseeable future. His only hope was that the girls had forgotten his rash promise.

No such luck.

The first thing his eldest daughter, Chloe, said to him when she saw him was: "So what show are you taking us to, Dad?"

Proctor put his arm around Chloe's shoulders. She was a snub-nosed ten-year-old, with long, dark, glossy hair. It was already abundantly clear—to him at least—that she was going to be a heartbreaker.

"Not sure, sweetheart," he said. "I'm still working on it. With it being half-term, tickets are a bit hard to come by."

"But I thought you knew people? I thought you said it would be no problem?"

"I *do* know people. And I *will* get tickets, I promise. It's just . . . it might not be this week."

Chloe looked disappointed. "We *can* still go shopping, though, can't we?"

Crossing his fingers, Proctor said, " 'Course we can."

"When?"

"I'll give your mum a ring about it," he said glibly, "sort something out."

He spent most of the next hour standing aimlessly on the sidelines and raising a hand in response to Jasmine's excited waves each time she sped by. There were plenty of other parents there—some helping out, some filming the event for posterity on their chunky camcorders—but none of them spoke to him. Proctor could only assume they'd been prewarned about his wicked ways by Tina. He wondered what Hellboy was doing now, and whether he was missing anything by being here. In truth, he was itching to get back to his story. He already had the angle. He would be asking how, when Hellboy had been brought into the country at the British taxpayer's expense, he had the time to sit around, chatting up women. He would report how

Hellboy had reacted violently when asked this very question. As evidence, the article would feature photos of Proctor's damaged car. So clear was the story in his mind that Proctor could actually see how it would look on the page—the layout, the positioning and size of the photographs . . .

It was Chloe who snapped him from his reverie. She gripped his arm and pointed. "Dad, what's that?"

Proctor blinked, tried to focus. Chloe appeared to be pointing at the opposite wall of the gymnasium. But for some reason he couldn't see it properly; there was a haze in front of his eyes. He blinked again . . . and then he realized that Chloe was pointing *at* the haze. It was there in the room with them, hovering a meter or so beneath the high ceiling. It was like and yet unlike smoke, a grayish, pearly iridescence. Proctor found himself having to adjust and readjust his eyes to keep it fixed in his vision. It seemed almost to be not quite there, not quite real, like a ghostly image clumsily overlaid onto film.

Chloe repeated her question. There was no fear in her voice, only curiosity. "What is it?"

Proctor glanced around, searching for a rational explanation. Was someone smoking? Or cooking maybe? Maybe someone had burned the sausages intended for the party tea afterwards? Other people were looking at the haze now, some of them pointing at it or filming it, many pulling their faces into uncomprehending expressions. Even a few of the rollerbladers had stopped to peer at the grayish cloud above their heads.

There was a sudden sound. A crackling and tearing, audible even over the pounding music. It sounded like a bad scratch on an old vinyl record—or the hugely amplified noise of someone ripping apart a gristly bit of chicken.

This thought had barely entered Proctor's head when the "haze" split open. It split horizontally, revealing a thin and jagged black gash, edged with purplish-blue light.

Some people gasped, as though witnessing a particularly fine firework display. A few of the younger girls let out squeals of surprise. Some of the rollerbladers, distracted by the phenomenon, either slowed right down to look up at it or carried on going and crashed into fellow rollerbladers and fell over.

The gash widened. Most people simply stood and stared at it in wonder, waiting to see what would happen next. Proctor, however, noticed that one or two of the adults, and even a few of the children, were starting to back away warily. Considering the events of the last couple of days, he thought this latter group probably had the right idea. To him, the widening slash of darkness looked too much like a slowly opening mouth.

"I think we should get out!" he yelled suddenly. "Everybody! Get out of here!"

No one moved. It was unlikely that most of them had even heard him above the thumping music. He turned to Chloe, who was still standing next to him, and said, "Find your mum and get out of here. Now."

"What is that thing?" Chloe asked. She looked almost as though she were in a trance.

"I don't know, but it's not good. Just do as I say."

He began to move forward. Chloe grabbed his arm. "What are you going to do?"

"I'm going to get Jasmine. See you outside."

Chloe nodded—and at that moment several people screamed. Proctor's head snapped back round. In a hideous parody of childbirth, something was pushing itself out of the dark slit above him. It was a patchy, hairy, spindly thing, with a domed cranium and a jagged, skull-like face. Proctor felt a cold shudder, a shudder of primal terror, go all the way through his body. He suddenly wished that Hellboy were here to deal with this. And then he saw Jasmine, who had been backing slowly and awkwardly away on her new rollerblades, trip over the outstretched legs of another fallen child and crash to the floor.

That got him moving. Feeling shaky and uncoordinated, he plunged towards his daughter. The thing coming out of the slit was thrashing and shuddering now in its efforts to tear itself free. All at once it let out a hideous, ratcheting screech, which was immediately echoed by the screams of the people below.

Proctor reached Jasmine and bent down to scoop her up. She was crying, though whether that was because she was terrified of the thing pushing its way into the world, or because she had whacked her elbows on the floor when she had fallen, he wasn't sure.

The thing screeched again. The sound corkscrewed its way through Proctor's body with such force that it seemed to make his bones vibrate. Gritting his teeth, he slid one arm around Jasmine's waist, the other beneath her knees and picked her up.

As he straightened, a massive shadow fell over him. He looked up. The thing had succeeded in freeing one of its spindly, multi-jointed limbs, and was now unfurling it, to reveal a vast and ragged wing. It was the wing that was casting its shadow over Proctor and Jasmine. He scrambled to his feet just as the thing tore itself fully from the slit.

It took to the air, flapping around the gymnasium. Now that it was out, Proctor could see that it was huge, maybe eight feet tall, with an equally wide wingspan. It was horrible to look at, a nightmarish combination of spider, ba, and monkey. As it swooped towards him, screeching, Proctor hunched over, Jasmine clutched protectively to his chest.

The claws of the thing raked his back, slashing open his leather jacket. Proctor dropped to his knees and hunched over further, to make himself and his terrified daughter as small a target as possible. He braced himself for a second attack, but the creature swooped away, evidently distracted by the commotion at the exit doors. Insensible with terror, most of the forty or fifty people in the gymnasium were now tearing and scrabbling at the doors in an effort to get out—though incredibly a couple of the dads were still pointing their camcorders at the thing. Children were screaming and shouting and crying. Proctor saw one hefty father shove a little girl aside with such force that she rebounded from the wall and was trampled underfoot.

From the corner of his eye, Proctor saw the DJ in the silly hat jump down from the stage and start to run across the gymnasium. He was a portly man, his belly bouncing beneath his tight T-shirt as his feet thumped the floor. The thing hovering above the mass of panicking humanity suddenly spotted him. It changed direction and swooped down, like a hawk diving for its prey, landing with unexpected grace and accuracy right in his path.

The DJ skidded to a halt, his mouth dropping open in his red face. The thing appraised him with apparent curiosity, cocking its head to one side, its movements jerky, like a bird's. With the creature temporarily motionless, Proctor absorbed further details. He noted its dusty blue-black skin; the knobbly bone formations across its shoulders and down its back; the black hair, wispy as cobweb, which covered its body in clumps and patches; the long, twisting talons which curved from the ends of its fingers.

Suddenly, shockingly, the creature sprang forward, slashing at the DJ. The man's T-shirt parted like wet paper, as did the flesh beneath. Proctor saw a gush of bright red innards and then the portly man collapsed backwards, a dead weight, into an already-widening pool of his own blood.

Proctor covered Jasmine's eyes and, protecting her body as best he could, began to run towards the now-open double doors. He couldn't see Chloe or Tina, and could only assume (could only *hope*) that they had managed to get out.

He was almost there, almost within reach of what he hoped would be safety, when the shadow fell over him again. The ratcheting screech of the creature was hideously close this time. Utterly terrified, Proctor ran like a soldier under fire, head tucked in low.

He crushed Jasmine to him, shielding her. She and Chloe were the only people he cared about more than himself. He focused on the open door. In ten steps he would be there. He felt burning, stabbing pains in both sides of his rib cage. Stitch, he thought. But the pain increased, until it felt as if he were being stabbed by knives, and suddenly he became aware that the pain was accompanied by wetness, and a sense of tugging.

He felt his feet leaving the floor. In agony, he turned his head. To his horror he realized that the creature had dug its talons into him and was lifting him up. He kicked and screamed, but it was no use. He was like a vole in an eagle's grip.

The creature turned in the air, swinging him round. The agony of its claws embedded in his flesh was unbelievable. Proctor could feel his own blood—far too much of it—running down his sides like hot water. He could barely see, barely think, with the pain, but he suddenly realized what the creature was doing. It was heading back towards the black, jagged rent that had opened up in midair—and it was taking him with it! The horror of that was almost overwhelming. Frantically Proctor tried again to struggle free of the talons buried deep into the meat between his ribs.

It was no use. Struggling merely cranked up his agony to such a degree that he could neither move nor scream. It was only his terror of what was about to happen that kept him from passing out.

He felt something squirm in his arms and remembered that he was still clutching Jasmine to his chest. All at once there was something even worse than the prospect of seeing what was on the other side of that horrible slash of darkness, and that was the thought of his daughter having to see it too.

"Run . . . find . . . Mum . . ." he barely managed to whisper into her soft blond curls, and then he opened his arms and let her go. She clung to him for a moment and then she tumbled to the floor.

The last thing Proctor saw before the unknown darkness rushed to meet him was his youngest daughter's upturned, tearstained face. And the last thing he heard, distorted and echoing and finally spiraling into nothing, was her anguished scream of "*Daddy!*"

☠ CHAPTER 10

The Three Cups had barely changed. It still reminded Hellboy of an old coaching inn from a Hammer horror movie. It was all dark wood and minimal lighting. The low ceiling was inset with raddled beams. The floor, coated with a fine layer of sawdust, creaked like the deck of a ship beneath his weight.

The barman, Martin, hadn't changed either—although, on second glance, Hellboy realized there was *something* different about him. He was halfway to the bar before he twigged what it was.

"Hey, Mart!" he called. "You've shaved off the face furniture."

Subconsciously Martin touched his upper lip, where once had dwelt a rather luxuriant moustache.

"I was warned you'd be coming," he growled. "Your friends are in the back."

"What?" said Hellboy, grinning. "No tearful reunion? No welcome-back hug?"

"Just be thankful you're not barred," said Martin. "Every time you come in here, stuff gets broken."

Hellboy glanced at Cassie, who was standing beside him. "He loves me really," he said. "What'll you have?"

"White wine spritzer, please."

"And I'll have a pint of Wobbly Bob. And a big bowl of that prawn curry if you still do it, with poppadums and pilau rice."

They carried their drinks through to the row of booths at the back of the pub. Cassie noted that most people blanched or gaped as Hellboy clumped past, and realized what a fearsome sight he must seem, emerging unexpectedly from the gloom and the swirling clouds of cigarette smoke.

His colleagues were tucked away in a booth, out of sight. Cassie recognized the graceful and rather beautiful Abe Sapien from magazine articles she had read. She guessed that the pretty girl who managed to look both hard and fragile at the same time was the camera-shy Liz Sherman. She had no idea who the rather studious-looking man with the spectacles was.

"Hey, HB," said the girl, before appraising Cassie coolly. "Hi."

Cassie said hi back, and then Hellboy stepped in and made the introductions. He was bumbling and awkward. It was clear that social etiquette did not come naturally to him. Rather than diminishing him, however, Cassie found his self-consciousness irresistibly endearing.

Those who hadn't already ordered food did so, and then they got down to business.

"Abe's got the lowdown on the All-Seeing Eye," said Liz.

"You mean he beat Kate to it?" Hellboy replied, raising his eyebrows. "I'm impressed."

"Kate didn't have the British Library archives at her disposal," Abe said, "though to tell the truth I was almost ready to quit when I chanced upon a little-known text entitled *The One True Way* by Maximus Leith."

"Not *the* Maximus Leith?" said Hellboy.

Abe's expression didn't alter. "I know you've never heard of him, Hellboy. How gullible do you think I am?"

"On a scale of one to ten?" Hellboy said, which earned him a punch from Liz.

"Quit it, HB. Let Abe speak," she said.

Hellboy rubbed his arm as though Liz's punch had hurt. Abe gave a short nod in her direction. "Thanks, Liz."

"My pleasure."

"Now," Abe continued, "Leith was basically a nobody, a minor nineteenth-century occultist who drifted from one organization to another, forever seeking the one true path. However, he couldn't find fulfilment in any of the existing organizations, so in 1895 he decided to establish his own. This he called the All-Seeing Eye. They held regular weekly meetings above a Chinese laundry in Limehouse. As far as I can tell the group never numbered more than a dozen or so members, and their influence on occult society, even at the time, was pretty much negligible."

"Sound like a fearsome bunch," said Hellboy. "I'd be quaking in my boots if I were wearing any."

"The All-Seeing Eye appear to have been active for only a short period at the end of the nineteenth century and the beginning of the twentieth," Abe continued. "Leith's pamphlet was published in 1902, and I can't find any mention of the organization after that date. I *did* find a reference to Leith, though, in a copy of *the London Times* dated December, 1902. It seems he mysteriously disappeared, leaving all his worldly possessions behind."

"And presumably his organization couldn't carry on without him?" Liz said.

"Seems not," said Abe.

"Did Leith's pamphlet give you any insight into the beliefs and activities of the group?" asked Richard.

Abe nodded. "The All-Seeing Eye's core belief was that the Devil was not a physical being, but a wave of destructive energy at the center of the earth. They claimed that this energy had the capability to corrode the barrier between dimensions and to corrupt men's minds, giving them an overwhelming urge to inflict pain on their fellow human beings, even to kill."

Liz sat up straight in her chair. "Well, that pretty much ties in with all the stuff we already know."

"Right," said Abe. "And what's even more interesting is that

Leith talks about the 'Lock of London' and also about the' Devil's Eye.' Listen to this."

He took a photocopied sheet of paper from the buttoned-down pocket of his leather flying jacket, unfolded it carefully. and read: " 'Certain knowledge has been presented to me, and that knowledge is this: that there are establishments within the city which have been configured in such a way so as to formulate a locking mechanism of gargantuan proportions. Said establishments are but tumblers in this great lock, this Lock of London, and each plays its own part in keeping closed the Eye of the Devil. But it occurs to me: what of the man who discovers the key to this lock? What power shall be granted to him who holds the devil in thrall? I asked this question of my confederate, a most learned man whom I shall not name, while in his cups, and at first he would offer me no answer. But I persevered and finally he did. "The blood shall have it," he told me, "but beware, for he who falls into the Devil's Eye shall be his forever." And that is all he said.' "

Abe refolded the piece of paper and put it back in his pocket.

"A dam, a lock. I guess it amounts to pretty much the same thing," said Hellboy.

" 'The blood shall have it.' That obviously refers to sacrifice," Richard said.

"Almost sounds too easy, though, doesn't it?" said Liz. "I mean, if blood being spilled is all it takes to pick this lock, why hasn't it been done before?"

"Perhaps because it's too dangerous, hence the warning," said Abe. "Or maybe it's just that no one worked out before that London itself was the lock. It's a pretty audacious notion, you've got to admit."

" 'He who falls into the Devil's Eye shall be his forever,' " mused Liz. "Why 'fall,' do you think? Why not 'look' or 'stare'?"

Abe shrugged. "It could be metaphorical. Or it could be that the source of the energy, the Eye, is underground, maybe at the bottom of a pit or something."

Cassie had been following this exchange silently, and with growing alarm. This was so far out of her comfort zone. However ,in a game attempt to contribute to the conversation, she said, "So do you think Leith and his followers fell into this Eye, despite the warning?"

Before Abe could answer, Richard said, "Maybe they didn't see it as a warning. Maybe Leith interpreted it to mean that by opening the Eye, the devil's power would be his to control?"

"Maybe," Hellboy shrugged. "Not sure how much further all of this gets us, though." He pondered a moment, then asked, "Who was the last person to look at that pamphlet before you, Abe? Because whoever it was—"

"I already thought of that," said Abe, "and the answer is no one. According to lending records, no one has looked at the pamphlet since the day it was bequeathed to the library."

"Bequeathed?" said Cassie. "By whom?"

"By Maximus Leith's landlady. As soon as it became apparent that he wasn't coming back, she donated all his books—of which there were many—to the library."

"Did you *see* the rest of his books?" asked Liz.

"I saw a list. Standard occult texts for the most part. I didn't have time to examine them closely because you, Liz, called me away."

There was no rancor in his voice, no tone of accusation; he was merely stating a fact. Their food arrived and they began to eat. Hellboy swallowed a mouthful of curry, then said, "So unless they've been hiding themselves away for the last eighty-odd years, it looks as if someone's started up Leith's organization again. Only this time with an added ingredient."

"Muti magic," said Liz.

Hellboy nodded. "Right. And now they're trying to open this damn Eye up again."

Even as he was propounding his theory, however, he was frowning, as if he didn't quite believe it.

"Problem?" said Liz.

Hellboy shook his head. "Aw, I dunno. I guess it's just that it still seems all messed up to me. I mean, why complicate things with this muti stuff? It doesn't make sense."

"You're the expert in this area, Richard," said Abe. "What's your opinion?"

Richard looked thoughtful. He toyed with his fork a moment. "I think there are a couple of possibilities," he said eventually. "One could be that the muti angle is a smoke screen, to throw the police off track. And the other could be that a group of muti practitioners are simply utilising the magic they know in an attempt to open the Eye."

"I guess," said Hellboy. Then he nodded more decisively. "Yeah, that makes sense."

He was about to say more when their chat was interrupted by a commotion from the bar area. A woman was shouting, her voice shrill with fear.

"What the hell—" Hellboy said, half turning.

"Aw, it's just people arguing, HB," said Liz. "The British do that when they've had too much to drink. It's an old custom."

Hellboy arched an eyebrow at her. Cassie said, "The woman's talking about something outside."

"I'm gonna check it out," Hellboy said.

"I'll come with you," said Abe.

"Yeah, me too, I guess," sighed Liz, putting her fork down. "Look after my lasagna for me, would you, Richard? I'll be back in a minute."

The three of them trooped through to the bar, Hellboy in the lead. It was immediately evident whose voice they had heard. The woman in question was propped against the bar, sipping a brandy. Martin and another man were attending to her solicitously.

What surprised Hellboy—though he didn't know why it should—was that the woman was young and well dressed. She looked as if she had just come from a business meeting, or was on her way to one.

"What's the problem here?" Hellboy asked.

The woman turned to see who had spoken—and almost passed out. She gave a screech and her whole body jerked, causing brandy to slop from her glass and over the bar.

Hellboy raised his hands. "Hey, lady, take it easy."

She continued to goggle at him. Then she raised a trembling hand and all but poked him in the chest.

"You're that . . . that Hellboy person," she said.

Hellboy grinned. "You know, it's funny. People are always mistaking me for that guy. I think it's the goatee."

Liz tutted and pushed herself in front of Hellboy. "Are you all right?" she asked.

"Ask me again after another few of these," the woman said, holding up her glass. She redirected her pointing finger towards the door. "There's something out there."

"What sort of something?" Hellboy asked.

"I don't know. It opened up right in front of me."

"What did?" asked Abe.

"A kind of crack in the air. One second it wasn't there, and the next it was. And then it started to open, like a . . . like an eye or something. And that's when I ran."

"An eye?" Hellboy glanced at his companions, and then the three of them were racing for the door. Hellboy barreled out of the pub—and instantly someone ran smack into the side of him. It was a black man in spectacles and a blue suit, carrying a briefcase. Hellboy was unaffected by the collision, but the man went "oof" and bounced backwards as if he had hit a wall. His spectacles and briefcase went flying.

"Sorry," said Hellboy and bent to pick him up. The man was sitting on his backside, blinking and open mouthed, head lolling like someone in a cartoon who has been hit with a mallet. Liz retrieved the man's spectacles and Abe picked up his briefcase. Another few people ran past—a young couple, hand in hand; a mother and her two preschool-age children—all of whom seemed too preoccupied to give Hellboy and Abe more than a startled passing glance.

"You all right, buddy?" Hellboy asked, lifting the man up and setting him on his feet. The man swayed a moment, and then puffed out a big breath and seemed to come to. He squinted at Hellboy.

"You *are* him, aren't you?"

Hellboy looked momentarily stumped, unsure how to respond. Liz handed the man his spectacles and said, "He's Hellboy, yes."

"Have you come to sort this out?" the man asked, gesturing vaguely behind him.

"If I can," Hellboy said.

"Well, if *you* can't . . ." the man trailed off, shaking his head, as if to say: *then we're all doomed.*

Hellboy patted him on the shoulder and ran in the direction from which the man had come. More people ran past him coming the other way, most of them double-taking in midstride. Hellboy was almost at the end of Great Russell Street, Abe and Liz in tow, when he heard people screaming and shouting, sounds of panic and fear. He put on an extra spurt of speed, his hooves clacking against the paving stones, and turned right into the mad bustle of Tottenham Court Road.

The first thing he saw, beyond a crowd of horrified and fascinated rubberneckers, was a yellow car being eaten by a giant black mouth. The mouth was hovering in the air, perhaps eight feet above the ground, and the front of the car was tilted up into it, its back wheels barely touching the road. There was someone in the car—a woman. She was battering on the rear window, trying to break it with her shoe, her face twisted in panic. The bodywork of the car was buckled, like a can that was slowly being compressed. This was evidently why the woman couldn't get out through either of the back doors.

The glass of the rear window was chipped and cracked where the woman had hit it. However, despite what had clearly been a prolonged attack, the window had remained intact, and exhaustion and panic were now weakening her blows. Four uniformed police officers were hovering around the tail end of the car, trying to placate and reassure the woman with soothing words and hand gestures. For some reason, instead of trying to break the window and haul the woman out, they were hanging back, as if reluctant to get too close. Hellboy could only imagine that they were fearful of being sucked into the maw themselves, but that didn't stop him from being appalled at their willingness to stand by and watch the woman be consumed. Some people in the crowd were baying at the officers to do something, to rescue the woman, but their words were having no effect. Others were weeping, or covering their faces, unable to watch. Most, however, were simply gaping blank faced at the spectacle, too shocked to register any emotion at all.

Hellboy began to push his way through the crush of onlookers. "Pardon me," he muttered, "pardon me." People shuffled aside to let him through. Most gaped at him, but some were too dazed by the impossible drama unraveling before them to even register his presence. As he got closer to the jagged black fissure, he realized that there was a gap of around twenty feet between those people in the front row and the back of the yellow car. He thought this was odd, until he reached the front row himself and saw what was holding the cops at bay.

Some sort of blue, frothy slime was leaking from the bottom of the black crack and drooling onto the road. Where the blue slime fell, the road was blistering, splitting, steaming, as though subjected to the most intense acid. Hellboy could see a shoe in the slowly spreading pool that had melted like plastic on a hot plate. He could see a bird too, a once-fat London pigeon that was now nothing but a heap of charred bones and sizzling innards.

"How many steps to the car, do you think?" he asked Liz, who had appeared beside him.

"You're not going to walk *through* that?" she said.

"I'm not gonna stand by and watch someone die."

Liz looked around, searching for inspiration. One of the back tires of the car, which was touching the slime, swelled and popped, running like black treacle.

"Oh, hell," she said, and ripped off her canvas jacket. "If you're going to try and get across there, at least have *something* between that stuff and your feet."

"You can have mine too," said Abe, peeling off his flying jacket.

When they saw what he was planning, various onlookers began to offer *their* coats and jackets too. One of the police officers even unbuttoned his tunic and handed it to Hellboy with a slightly shamefaced, "Here you go, mate."

Within a minute Hellboy was laden down with donated garments. He gave some to Liz and Abe, and kept some for himself. He strewed items on the ground in front of him as he walked towards the car, creating a makeshift carpet of denim, leather, cotton, and man-made fibers. As soon as the jackets and coats touched the blue slime they began to smolder and warp and melt. Where Hellboy's hooves pressed down, the layers of material burned even more rapidly. Each of his footsteps was accompanied by a hiss, like the application of a hot iron on a damp shirt, and a curl of smoke around his hooves. Hellboy was halfway to the car when he ran out of garments. He half turned towards Liz, and she threw him a fresh bundle without having to be asked. A few of the flimsier items fluttered to the ground, but Hellboy caught the majority of them cleanly, and once again began to drape them on the ground before him.

In this way, aided by Liz and Abe, he reached the car in less than a minute. He gestured for the woman to move back and then he punched the glass out with his stone hand. As the safety glass shattered into tiny fragments, the crowd cheered and clapped. "Come on," Hellboy instructed. "I'll catch you." Without hesitation the woman scrambled out of the back window and fell into his outstretched arms.

The applause intensified. Hellboy ignored it. He carried the woman back towards where Abe, Liz, and the four police officers were standing, gritting his teeth against the burning pain on the undersides of his hooves, where the blue corrosive stuff had seeped up through the rapidly disintegrating layers of clothing.

Abe and one of the police officers moved as close to the edge of the still-spreading pool of slime as they could, holding out their arms to take the woman from Hellboy's grasp. They were lifting her clear when what looked like a fleshy length of pinky-red tubing came snaking out of the jagged black crack behind Hellboy. It ranged about blindly for a moment, slapping against the metal bodywork of the yellow car. Then slowly, with whatever senses it possessed, it seemed first to become aware of Hellboy, and then to fasten on him. It rose into the air, all twenty or thirty feet of it, its featureless blob of a "head" weaving from side to side like that of a king cobra. And then, with a high and hideous squealing sound, it struck out.

"*Hellboy!*" screamed Liz, her voice merging with the battle cry of the creature, but he was already spinning round.

Even so, he barely had a chance to react before the tubular thing was corkscrewing around his torso, tightening its grip with each slithering revolution.

"*Dammit!*" Hellboy shouted, and began to wrestle with the creature, trying to grab its "head," tearing at it with his stone hand. It responded by lifting him into the air. The crowd gasped as he was lifted thirty feet, forty, and then higher still.

The creature, which was still coiling, seemingly endlessly, out of the black fissure, suddenly flexed its body and cracked like a whip. Its "head" end, which was coiled around Hellboy, snapped forward, smashing him face first into the side of a building.

Yells of panic and dismay rose from the crowd, and there was a wavelike ripple through the sea of bodies as they tried to scramble back from the sudden tumble of broken glass and shattered masonry.

"*Son of a bitch!*" yelled Hellboy. That had *hurt*. The stubs of his horns were throbbing and his nose was a fiery starburst of pain. With renewed fury he dug the fingers of his stone hand into the pinky-red hide of the creature and *tore*. However, the thing's flesh was as tough as fortified rubber, and at first nothing happened. Hellboy gritted his teeth and dug his fingers in deeper, and suddenly the creature's skin ripped a little. A milky-white ichor, sticky and hot, came trickling out. Hellboy roared in triumph and clawed savagely at the tear. The wound widened, and all at once the milky stuff was *gushing* out, coating Hellboy's hand. It smelled disgusting, worse than the rotting whale blubber he had smelled once in Iceland and had hoped never to smell again. Even so, he continued to work at the wound, widening it, ripping off chunks of flesh with his bare hands.

The thing screamed and began to thrash more wildly. Hellboy was whipped back and forth in the air. It was like being on the world's most vomit-inducing fairground ride.

He smashed into the wall of a building again—his left shoulder this time. More glass broke; more rubble fell.

He felt something tightening around his ankle and looked down. Another of the pinky-red serpents, or tentacles, or whatever the hell they were, had emerged from the fissure and was coiling over his still-smoking hoof and up his leg. For an instant, before his temporarily steadying vision once again became a careering blur as he was whipped through the air, he glimpsed a *third* tentacle emerging from the crack.

Great, he thought. One was bad enough. How many more of these damn things were there?

Suddenly he heard the boom of a gunshot. Clasped by the weaving tentacle many feet above the ground, he twisted his head, trying to focus his vision on the antlike crowd below.

There! Abe and Liz standing with their arms outstretched, weapons drawn. There was another boom and as the whistling screech of the creature suddenly intensified, Hellboy felt the crushing grip around his ankle loosen. Looking down, he saw that one of his friends—and he'd guess it was Abe; he was the best shot of the three of them—had succeeded in cutting the tentacle that had hold of his foot clean in half. The lower section appeared to be in its death throes. It was thrashing from side to side, ichor spraying in all directions, spattering across the fronts of buildings and over the crowd below. Meanwhile the severed top half of the creature unspooled lifelessly from Hellboy's leg and fell to the ground like a dead snake, landing with a thump in the blue slime.

"*Ha!*" he shouted, and renewed his attack on the creature's flesh, trying to injure it still further. It screamed and smashed him against the wall again. Hellboy swore and spat out blood that was trickling down the back of his throat, but he didn't let up. He got the fingers of his stone hand deep into the gushing wound he had created, grasped a flap of skin the size of a large rump steak and pulled upwards with all his might. The flap of skin stretched and then gave, tearing clean off and pulling a sizable lump of flesh with it. There were stringy white things attached to the flesh, veins or tendons maybe. The creature bellowed in pain, the whistling screech it made so loud that windows shattered and people on the ground below clapped their hands over their ears.

Hellboy's ears were ringing too, and he was covered in ichor. As soon as he felt the thing's grip around him slacken, he dropped the chunk of flesh he was holding and reached for his gun, which had previously been inaccessible. Slipping his hand beneath the loosening red coil of the creature's body, he dragged the weapon from its holster. The weight of the revolver, a big-bored, .50-caliber thing that had been especially made for him, felt good in his palm. With no thought for his own safety, he placed the muzzle of the gun against the injured part of the creature—the part that was wrapped, albeit more loosely now, around his waist—and pulled the trigger.

The gun roared, the pink tentacle came apart, and Hellboy fell.

His body turned over once as he plummeted towards the ground. It was not the first time he had fallen from a great height, and he tried to relax, knowing that if he braced himself the pain when he hit would be worse.

He landed on his back, not on the sizzling slime-covered road, but on the buckled roof of the half-consumed yellow car. The car was tilted at a forty-five degree angle, and the full force of Hellboy's quarter-ton weight slamming down on it had the same effect as someone karate-chopping a similarly angled piece of wood. With a screeching crunch of metal, the car broke in two, the back end, with Hellboy on top of it, crashing onto the ground. The impact rattled Hellboy's bones and caused his teeth to clash together. Damn, he was gonna be sore in the morning. But for now he had work to do.

He allowed himself a couple of seconds to catch his breath, and then he propped himself up on one elbow. The fissure, the crack, the rift, the mouth, the eye—whatever the hell that thing that had opened up in the center of London actually *was*—was directly behind him now, mere inches, in fact, from the little ponytail at the back of his head. As he had fallen, Hellboy had managed to keep hold of his gun (he *always* kept hold of his gun), and he twisted round with it now in his hand, the tortured metal of the wrecked car creaking in protest as he shifted his weight on its roof. He pointed his weapon directly into the impenetrable blackness of the fissure and he began to blast away, firing slugs into God only knew where.

Eventually he stopped. "Let that be a lesson to you," he growled. This close to the fissure he could feel the strange sucking pull of it, could feel its icy chill, not on his skin but deep inside him, where the nightmares, if he should ever have any, would reside.

He didn't know whether shooting the "eye" had made the slightest bit of difference, but at least the corrosive blue slime had stopped trickling out of it, and at least the third tentacle—the only one that he or his friends hadn't blasted to bits—had disappeared back to where it had come from. The other two tentacles were lying like shattered drainpipes on the ground. The slime wasn't affecting them, as it affected everything else on this side of the fissure, but maybe something else was—the London air or the daylight, perhaps—because already the tentacles were turning the dull gray of old cement. They were withering too, becoming as brittle as autumn leaves. If the present rate of decay was maintained, Hellboy doubted there would be anything left in an hour or two.

Aching pretty much all over, and coated with the creature's life fluid, which was now drying to a foul-smelling gum on his skin, Hellboy clambered off the roof of the car and lowered himself to the ground. He picked his way carefully back to where Abe and Liz were standing across the carpet of coats and jackets, treading on the areas where the layers of material were so thick that the blue slime hadn't yet burned all the way through to the surface.

So intent was he on not adding to his already considerable physical woes that he didn't realize he was receiving what amounted to a hero's homecoming until he was almost back on safe ground. Suddenly he tuned in to the noise, and looked up to see that everyone was clapping and cheering and grinning at him. There were whistles and whoops of delight. Liz stepped forward.

"Despite what the papers say, I think they love you," she said.

CHAPTER 11

As he worked his way through the jubilant crowd, wincing at the congratulatory back slaps raining in on his bruised and battered body, Hellboy's phone started to ring. He fished it from the pouch on his belt and held it to his ear.

"Hellboy, it's Rachel Turner," said the voice on the other end of the line.

"Hey, Rachel," Hellboy said, "what's up?"

She sounded under strain, but in control. She informed him that reports were coming in of fissures opening up in midair all over London.

"Yeah, we've just encountered one firsthand," Hellboy said. He told her what had happened at Tottenham Court Road.

"Jeez," she said. "We're getting reports of creatures coming through in other places too—all different kinds from the sounds of it." She hesitated a moment, as if trying to gather herself. "So what do we do about it, Hellboy? This is your call."

"Just do exactly what you'd do if I weren't here," Hellboy said soothingly. "Evacuate the areas where the cracks have appeared, and have them monitored constantly by armed personnel. Get everyone in on this, Rachel. Call the government, the secret service, the army, and the police. Make them realize that this is an emergency—no, more than that: make them realize that this could be the *direst* emergency this country has ever faced. We need everyone working together. We need a unanimous promise that a

coordinated containment operation will be implemented immediately. You got that?"

"Yes, sir," Rachel said, responding to the authority in his voice.

"Okay, good," Hellboy said. "As for me, I'll be on the front line
with Abe and Liz—which means I'll need a comprehensive list of
locations where the fissures have opened up, plus details of exactly
what kinds of creatures have emerged from each of them."

"I'll have that information faxed to your hotel as soon as possible."

"Great," Hellboy said. He was still walking through the crowd,
Abe and Liz in tow, phone clamped to his ear. "Once we know
exactly what we're up against, we'll prioritize the threats and deal
with them as best we can. The three of us will split into two operating units with military backup—Abe and Liz in one and me in the
other."

"I'll organize that for you," Rachel said.

"But one thing you gotta make the army guys realize, Rachel,
is that this is a B.P.R.D.-led operation. Some of the things that
have emerged from those fissures are *bound* to be impervious to
conventional firepower. So I don't want people getting all gung ho
and taking unnecessary risks. I want the casualty rate to be as low
as possible. Understood?"

"Yes, sir," Rachel said.

Hellboy was pretty much through the crowd now. He length-
ened his stride. "By the way," he said, "what *is* the casualty rate so
far? Do we have any numbers?"

"Hang on," said Rachel, "I'll check." She was back thirty seconds later. "We've got twenty-seven confirmed fatalities to date,"
she said, "but there are . . . things loose all over the place, Hellboy.
It's going to go higher, no matter how fast we move on this."

"I know it," said Hellboy grimly. "Just do your best, okay?"

"Will do," she said, and let out a breath. "Can I just ask—do we
know what these fissures are exactly?"

"They're cracks in the dam," Hellboy said. "We gotta plug 'em for now, but we've also gotta figure a way of sealing the whole thing up for good. Otherwise . . ."

"The entire structure will collapse and we'll be swept away in the torrent?" guessed Rachel.

"You got it," Hellboy said quietly.

He heard her swallow. In a slightly shaky voice she said, "Before you go there's just one more thing. We think we've got a lead on the torso killings. Our guys have tracked down a vagrant who claims to have information on one of the murdered men."

"Is he on the level?" Hellboy asked.

"I think so—as much as you can tell anyway. He asked to speak to you, but I guess you're a bit busy just now."

Hellboy thought about it. "Can you get him to the hotel in the next half hour?"

"Sure, if you think it's worth it?"

"Do it," said Hellboy. "If there's even the slightest chance of finding out who's behind all this or where they're hiding, then we gotta take it. Okay, well, if that's everything . . . ?"

"It is," said Rachel.

"Then you better go and make those calls," Hellboy said. "Catch you later."

As soon as he cut the connection, Abe and Liz started to ask questions, but Hellboy held up a hand. "Just give me one more minute, guys."

He called directory inquiries and got the number for the Three Cups. Then he called the pub and asked to speak to Cassie. Abe and Liz waited patiently while he briefly explained to her what was happening and told her to sit tight.

"I'll come for you when I can, okay?" he said. He listened to her response and grinned. "Yeah, you too. Stay safe."

On the walk back to the hotel he filled Abe and Liz in on his conversation with Rachel Turner and their plans to combat the threat.

"It worries me that we're still not getting to the real heart of the problem, though," said Liz. "We're only tackling the symptoms, not the cause."

"It's all we can do for now," said Hellboy. "Damage limitation."

"Yeah, I know," she sighed, "but still . . ."

"Maybe this homeless guy can lead us to our enemy," said Abe.

The homeless guy was called Duggie. He was waiting nervously in the hotel foyer with a B.P.R.D. agent when they arrived. Duggie was tall and scrawny, with bad teeth and a bird's nest of filthy-looking hair. One of his eyelids was red and swollen, as if it was infected.

To the disapproval of the snooty hotel manager, Mr. Trenchard, Hellboy ordered a pot each of tea and coffee and then, accompanied by Liz and Abe, led Duggie into the hotel bar.

"Okay, feller," he said, "so what's your story?"

Duggie looked nervous. He huddled into his threadbare tweed coat, retracting his head, turtlelike, as if he expected the ceiling to come crashing down at any moment.

When he finally spoke, they were all surprised at how soft and cultured his voice was.

"I had a friend," he said. "Michael. He disappeared a few days ago. It's not like him to just go off. Michael's a man of habit."

"Where did you last see this friend of yours?" Hellboy asked.

"It was at the homeless persons' refuge on Sire Street, near King's Cross Station. We slept there on Sunday night, but when I woke up on Monday morning, Michael had gone. Him and three others."

Liz looked at Hellboy and raised her eyebrows. He, however, seemed unimpressed.

"Maybe he just upped and left early," he said, "and maybe the others did too."

Duggie shook his head vigorously. "I've told you, he wouldn't have done that. Michael wouldn't just go off without telling me.

Mr. and Mrs. Hipkiss, who run the refuge, claimed that Michael had left early in the morning without saying where he was going, but I don't believe them. What I think is that they drugged the food to make us all sleep, and then Michael and the others were taken. And I think the ones last night were taken too."

This made them all sit up and take notice.

"Last night?" repeated Abe.

Duggie nodded. "I woke up feeling groggy again this morning, just like the last time, to find that exactly the same thing had happened. Four people gone. No one's ever suspicious because . . . well, because most of the people who stay at the refuge come and go as they please. Sometimes they move on to different towns. Sometimes they just leave without saying anything and you never see them again."

"So four people go missing from the refuge on Sunday night, and the bodies of four homeless people are found on Monday morning," said Liz. "Last night four more people go missing, and this morning more bodies are found." She turned to Hellboy and Abe. "Now is it just me or is that a hell of a coincidence?"

"Only three bodies were found this morning," Abe said.

"Which probably just means there's one still to be discovered," said Liz.

The drinks arrived. Abe poured coffee for Hellboy, Liz, and Duggie, and tea for himself. He offered a biscuit to Duggie, who took one and looked at the rest hungrily.

"Take them all," said Liz, then watched as he scooped them up in two handfuls and dropped them into his pockets.

"Do you know the names of any of the people who disappeared at the same time as your friend?" Hellboy asked.

Duggie nodded. "Yes, there was a man called Big Ronnie . . . er, Ronnie Marsden. And there was a girl . . . Jenny something."

"Not Jenny Campion?" said Hellboy quietly. "Young? About nineteen?"

"That's her," Duggie said. "You know her?"

Hellboy shook his head. "She was one of the murder victims. I remember her name from the forensics report."

"Ah," said Liz quietly. She placed a hand on Duggie's arm. "I'm afraid you know what this means, Duggie?"

Duggie nodded. "Michael's dead, isn't he?"

"It looks that way," said Liz. "I'm really sorry."

Duggie swallowed, rubbed a hand rapidly back and forth across his mouth, making his stubble rasp. Resignedly he said, "It's okay. I knew he was dead. Deep down I knew he wouldn't have just gone without saying anything."

"Did you tell the police what you've told us?" Abe asked.

Duggie snorted. "Do you think they'd have believed me, or cared? They think people like me and Michael are animals. They think we'd slit each other's throats for a crust of bread."

"The question is, do *we* go to the police?" pondered Abe.

Hellboy pulled a face. "I say we deal with this one ourselves."

"I agree," said Liz. "This is *our* area. From what Abe found out last night, we know that this group who call themselves the All-Seeing Eye committed these murders, and we know too, from the attack on Abe in the factory, and from the one on Richard and me at Olusanya's apartment, that they've got at least *some* measure of occult power."

"My guess would be they're tapping directly into the energy source beneath the city," said Abe, "which means they have access to the energy's point of focus, wherever that may be."

"A lodestone?" said Liz.

"Exactly."

Hellboy shook his head angrily. "Jeez, why don't these idiots ever realize how stupid they're being by messing with this stuff? Can't they see they're just like kids playing with fire?"

"But kids never realize how dangerous fire is until they get burned," said Liz quietly.

THE ALL-SEEING EYE 203

Both Hellboy and Abe looked at her. There was a beat of silence. Then Hellboy said, "Okay. So we know these Eye guys have been to the refuge twice. Reckon they'll chance a third visit?"

Abe looked thoughtful. "Possibly. But if I had to bet on when, I'd say sooner rather than later. Maybe even tonight."

"Because, now that the Eye is opening, they'll want to provide it with more victims, to speed up the process?" said Liz.

"Partly that, and partly because they might feel that the net is closing in on them. They know that we're looking for them, plus they'll be aware that the full remains of the first set of victims have now been found, which means it's only a matter of time before the victims are identified and traced to the refuge. They might feel, therefore, that this is the last time they can take a gamble on visiting the place."

"Or maybe they've already decided it's a gamble not worth taking," said Hellboy. "Maybe they'll go someplace else."

"Maybe," mused Abe, "but you said, didn't you, Duggie, that you thought the food was drugged? Which means that the people who run the refuge . . . what did you say their name was again?"

"Hipkiss," Duggie said.

"Hipkiss, right. So maybe the kidnappers have got a deal going with Mr. and Mrs. Hipkiss. Maybe the Hipkisses are even Eye members themselves."

"There are still plenty of homeless people on the streets," said Liz. "The kidnappers could just pick some up from there."

"They could," agreed Abe, "except for the fact that what they've caused to happen today might actually work against them. By tonight London will be in a state of emergency. The streets will be in virtual lockdown, swarming with soldiers and cops."

"Hmm," said Hellboy. "It's all good reasoning, Abe. Still a lot of ifs, buts, and maybes, though."

The ridges on Abe's neck rippled gently—Liz recognized it as a sign of amusement. "Aren't there always?"

"So what are we gonna do?" asked Liz. "Stake out the place?" She and Abe both looked to Hellboy.

"What time is lights out at this refuge place?" he asked Duggie.

"Ten," Duggie said.

Hellboy nodded. "Then we spend the rest of the day cleaning up the streets and we meet at the refuge at nine thirty. I'm guessing these guys have a vehicle of some sort to transport the victims—in which case, I'll call Rachel Turner and tell her we need a car."

Thoughtfully Liz said, "I'm thinking it would be a good idea if we had an inside man—or woman—on this job. How easy would it be for you to get me a bed for the night, Duggie?"

Duggie shrugged. "It's first come, first served. I'm usually there about five."

"Then that's when I'll be there too," said Liz. "That's if it's okay with you, HB?"

Hellboy chewed the idea over for a moment, then he nodded. "Makes sense to me. It'll give you a chance to look the place over, check out all the exits and entrances."

"My thoughts exactly," said Liz. "I'll wear a big coat and smuggle my phone in, let you know if I find anything useful."

"Take your gun too," said Abe.

"Goes without saying. Hey, you don't get searched on the way in, do you, Duggie?"

Duggie shook his head. "The Hipkisses are very laid back."

"That's settled then," said Hellboy. "Now all we need is the info from Rachel, and we can get rollin'."

Right on cue, the hotel's personnel manager, the same woman who had appeared at breakfast that morning to inform them that Richard had arrived, entered the coffee lounge and came over to their table.

"There's a fax coming through for you, Mr. Hellboy," she said. All three B.P.R.D. operatives jumped instantly to their feet, followed, a few seconds later, by a hesitant Duggie.

"Time to go," remarked Abe.

"No rest for the wicked," added Hellboy, an expectant gleam in his eye.

Cassie felt a little overwhelmed by it all. This was definitely the strangest day of her life. It was as if meeting Hellboy had tipped reality on its head. She was usually so practical, but her thoughts were currently in a whirl, her emotions all over the place.

Even so, she put her empty glass down on the table, having come to a decision.

"Another drink?" asked Richard, who was sitting opposite her.

Cassie shook her head. "I'm not staying here," she told him.

He looked taken aback. "But Hellboy said to sit tight, didn't he? He said it wasn't safe out there."

"I don't care," Cassie said. "My car's parked just round the corner on Bedford Square, and I only live in Camden. No offense, Richard, but if I've got to be stuck anywhere, I'd rather be stuck at home than in some smoky pub."

"But you might not *make* it home," Richard said. "I mean, I don't want to scare you, but—"

"That's a risk I'm prepared to take."

He raised his eyebrows. "Well . . . it's your decision, I suppose . . ."

"Yes it is," she said. "So what are *you* going to do?"

He looked around. The pub was packed now, largely with people who had either witnessed the incident in Tottenham Court Road or who had fled from it, and were now attempting to steady their nerves with a drink or two.

"Stay here, I suppose," he said. "Wait for news."

"You could be waiting all night."

He shrugged. "There are worse places to be."

Cassie thought of how unbearable this poky little pub would become six or seven hours from now if the all clear failed to materialize. It would be hot, and so smoky you would barely be able to

breathe. And it would be full of drunken people with frayed nerves
. . . she shuddered at the prospect.

"You sure I can't drop you off somewhere?" she asked.

"No thanks. I'll take my chances here."

"Okay, well . . . nice to meet you." She took his hand and
shook it.

Richard's eyes looked big and dark behind his spectacles. "Good
luck," he said quietly. "I hope we meet again."

She left him there, perched on a stool by the bar, and shouldered her way through the crowd. Oddly it was almost like a party
atmosphere in the pub, people standing with drinks, chatting ex-
citedly about Hellboy's exploits. Cassie had pieced together what
had happened from various eyewitness reports even before Hellboy
himself had called to let her know what was going on. She had
been mightily relieved to hear his voice. According to what some
people had said, he had been smashed up pretty bad.

She liked Hellboy. She'd heard of him before she met him, of
course, and like most people had always found him a fascinating
character. She had only seen him on TV a couple of times, and
on those occasions had thought how ill at ease he looked with a
camera pointing into his face. The impression he had always left
her with was of a brooding, taciturn man, who valued his privacy,
and whose friendship and respect you probably had to work hard
to earn.

There was undoubtedly something attractive about that, if only
in the sense that it made you want to get under his skin and find
out what made him tick. When he had turned up that morning
with that creep, Reynolds, Cassie had been shocked, thrilled, fearful, and excited all at the same time, but she had somehow managed
to rise above it, to just be herself and speak to him as an equal.

And he'd liked that, she could tell. She suspected he got tired
of the fact that people found it hard to be "normal" around him; in
fact, he had said as much during their disrupted breakfast together.

The thing that had most surprised Cassie about him—apart from his sheer physical presence; in the flesh he was massive and impressive and far redder than she'd expected—was how gentle and shy and diffident he was, and how easy to relate to.

She pushed open the door and stepped outside. After the dingy fug of the pub, the day seemed incredibly cool and fresh and bright, and she paused for a moment, breathing deeply, attempting to clear her head. After what Hellboy had told her, and from the snippets she had heard in the pub, Cassie had half expected to find London in chaos. She had been bracing herself for the sight of wrecked cars and buildings, and bodies lying in the streets, but at first everything seemed reassuringly normal.

The impression did not last long.

She had taken no more than a couple of steps when she heard a police siren. Almost instantly that was overlaid by another, further away. Attuning her ears, it suddenly occurred to her that the city was *full* of sirens, though most were so faint that they were barely audible. And yet, despite them, it was actually quieter on the streets than it usually was. There was not the underlying rumble of traffic that she was accustomed to. Uneasily she looked to her left, and realized that the cars further down the road had, in fact, been abandoned by their drivers. She was wondering whether *all* the roads in the city would be choked by discarded vehicles when, drifting on the breeze, she heard a voice, amplified and distorted by a megaphone.

"This is a state of emergency," the voice said. "For your own safety, the government of Great Britain is advising all citizens to clear the streets of London. We suggest that you enter the nearest accessible building and remain there until further notice. Once you have found a safe place, please stay calm and await further advice. The British government would like to reassure everyone that it is using all available resources to bring the current situation under control. Thank you for your cooperation."

There was a pause and then the message began again. Cassie shuddered. There was something horribly unreal about all this. She hunched her shoulders and hurried along the street, half expecting a patrol car or a military vehicle to come screeching round the corner, and for its inhabitants to arrest her for breaking some just-imposed curfew, or to surround her with weapons drawn.

She was relieved, therefore, when she turned on to Adeline Place, which led up towards Bedford Square, to find that other people *were* still out on the streets, after all. A small knot of them, two men and three women, were huddled on the steps of a townhouse that had been converted into the premises of a consulting agency upmarket enough to have a gold engraved plaque bearing its name mounted beside its glossily black front door.

The people were conversing in hushed voices, as though to raise them any higher might bring some terrible retribution down on them all. As she walked past, Cassie caught the eye of one of the women and nodded a greeting. The woman offered Cassie a tight, cautious smile in response.

Further along the same street, at the intersection with Bedford Avenue, a man in a gray anorak was talking to a uniformed police officer, who was leaning against his parked panda car. The policeman had his arms folded and looked relaxed—so much so that Cassie decided to brazen it out and stroll past as if this were a normal day.

"Excuse me, miss," the police officer said, breaking off from his conversation with the man in the anorak.

Cassie sighed inwardly, but smiled sweetly at the policeman. "Yes, officer?"

"Are you aware that a state of emergency has been declared? We're advising people to stay indoors."

"I just heard the announcement," Cassie said truthfully. "That's why I'm on my way back to my car."

"Where *is* your car, miss, if you don't mind me asking?" the policeman said.

"Literally at the end of this road. Just the other side of Bedford Square."

"And where are you heading?"

"Camden," Cassie said. "Mandela Street."

"If you'll just wait a moment, miss, I'll check that it's safe for you to proceed."

Cassie waited while the officer reached into his car and unhooked the radio from its housing. He made several inquiries and received tinny, static-filled responses, which Cassie couldn't make out. Finally he leaned back into the car and placed the radio back in its bracket beneath the dashboard.

"That's fine, miss. But stick to the most direct route and go straight home. And once you're there, stay there."

"Will I get arrested if I don't?" Cassie asked cheekily.

She meant the question as a joke, but the policeman didn't seem to find it funny. "I'm offering this advice for your own safety, miss."

"Thank you, officer. I appreciate your concern," Cassie said, suitably chastened.

The policeman wished her a safe journey and she continued on her way. Thirty seconds later Bedford Square came into sight, and her car parked on a meter on the far side of it. Cassie looked left to right, unnerved by the quiet, by the faint but persistent sirens, by the megaphone message, snatches of which she could still hear when the breeze was drifting in her direction.

She crossed to her car, unlocked it, and got in. Only when she had closed and locked the door did she realize she had been holding her breath. She released it slowly, and wondered whether she would see Hellboy again. She hoped so, but both times they'd met up today they had been interrupted before getting to the stage where they might have exchanged addresses or phone numbers. She knew he was staying at the Old Bloomsbury, and he knew where she worked, so hopefully they would manage to hook up. Although now that the shit had well and truly hit the fan, she guessed that his time in the UK would be at a premium.

The rap of knuckles on the driver's-side window made her jump out of her skin. Heart pounding, she turned to see the man in the gray anorak smiling and waving apologetically. He was a nondescript little man—around fifty, with watery eyes, a scrubby moustache, and thinning hair the color of dust. Cassie wound down her window.

"Hello?" she said.

"Sorry to startle you, miss," said the man, "but I couldn't help overhearing you telling the officer you were going to Camden?"

His voice was weedy and nasal, to match his appearance. "That's right," said Cassie.

"In that case, and I know this is a terrible imposition, but is there any chance at all that you could give me a lift? I live on Bayham Street, y'see, and my wife will be worried about me, I know she will."

Can't you ring her? Cassie thought, and immediately felt ashamed of herself.

Although under normal circumstances she would never have countenanced giving a lift to a stranger, she couldn't abandon the poor guy in the middle of the city. Forcing a smile, she said, "Sure, hop in."

He smiled ingratiatingly, hunching his shoulders like a vulture, then scuttled around to the passenger door and pulled it open. He eased himself into the seat beside Cassie.

"I really am most grateful," he said.

"No problem," said Cassie, and reached for the ignition key.

As she did so, the man took a syringe from his overcoat pocket, stuck it in her arm, and depressed the plunger.

It happened so quickly that Cassie couldn't even begin to react. It wasn't until the man had pulled the syringe out of her arm and dropped it back into his pocket that she turned to him, startled.

"What did you—" she began, but then the world blurred and receded from her. Cassie was vaguely aware of her body slipping sideways and of being unable to do a thing about it. The last thing she saw before cloying darkness closed over her was the man's grinning, skull-like face.

CHAPTER 12

"I oughta get a clothing allowance," Hellboy growled, brushing at the spatters of gloopy black ichor on his duster. Even so, he was grinning as he emerged from the Electric Cinema on Portobello Road.

"Is it dead?" asked a young and very nervous soldier, peering around Hellboy and into the gloom of the entrance foyer.

"As a doornail," Hellboy said, "though that doesn't mean some of the pieces aren't still twitching."

It was almost six p.m. and dusk was descending on London's unnaturally quiet streets. Assigned to an army unit comprised of four jeeps and two dozen armed soldiers, Hellboy had spent the last few hours on a monster-fighting tour of London. In Covent Garden he had done battle with a big hairy insect thing that had a face like a steel bear trap and more legs than he could count; close to the Sadler's Wells theater in Islington he had had a gargantuan scrap with a trio of savage little green bastards who looked like turtles crossed with scorpions; on a Kilburn housing estate he had fought something that resembled a giant pulsating mass of purple porridge from which—through blowholes in its lumpy hide—extended sinewy tendrils tipped by viciously snapping beaks.

His body had taken a hell of a beating. He had been stung and stabbed and bitten, as well as battered to kingdom come and back, but there was no denying that he was in his element. Despite a few hairy moments, he had emerged from each encounter victorious. He was covered in blood (thankfully very little of his own), or what passed for blood amongst the varied collection of other-dimensional creatures he had engaged in combat, and he stank like an abattoir.

Someone tossed him a towel and he used it to wipe his hands and face, and to remove as much of the gunk from his coat as he could.

"Right," he said, "what's next on the list?"

Captain Kneale, who was in charge of the troops accompanying Hellboy, unrolled a large map of London on the bonnet of one of the jeeps, in what had now become something of a post-battle ritual. The map was marked by red circles where the various emergent creatures had been spotted. Wherever possible, the army or police were destroying the creatures, or at the very least keeping them contained until either Hellboy or his colleagues could arrive to deal with them. Each time a creature was destroyed the red circle denoting it was overlaid with a black cross. So far around half the circles had been crossed out, though the extermination—referred to by the British military as Operation Hellfire —had not been achieved without casualties. Official figures currently stood at fifty-one civilians, seventeen army personnel, and six police officers dead, with many more injured, some seriously.

Kneale jabbed a finger at the map. "Goldhawk Road's our next port of call, just south of here."

"What we got there?" Hellboy asked.

"Wilkins?" Kneale barked at a private who was holding an open dossier in his hands.

"Snakelike creature, sir. Black, segmented, approximately fifteen feet long. According to eyewitness reports, it has four heads and a pincer on its tail. And it spits a sort of green fire, sir."

Hellboy grinned in anticipation. "What are we waiting for?"

The troops began to climb back into their jeeps. Hellboy was walking towards his when his attention was caught by something on the opposite side of the street. A bank of TVs which had been left on in the window of a locked-up electrical-goods shop were all showing the same image. Next to the BBC News logo, a headline in white on a red banner across the top of the screen proclaimed LONDON IN CRISIS. Beneath this was grainy camcorder footage of a man trying to protect a little girl from a winged monstrosity that was flapping above them.

It was the man who had attracted Hellboy's attention. Hellboy had taken one look at his stricken face, and even given the distance and the mediocre quality of the picture, had recognized him instantly. He watched grimly as Colin Proctor was picked up by the winged creature and borne like a mouse in an eagle's talons towards a vertical black fissure that seemed to hang impossibly in midair. He watched Proctor release the child he was holding a split second before the fissure swallowed him. It was only when the picture cut back to a somber-faced newsreader that Hellboy realized Captain Kneale was standing at his shoulder, looking at him quizzically.

"I knew that guy," Hellboy muttered by way of explanation.

Kneale's face rearranged itself into an expression of sympathy. "Friend of yours?"

Hellboy grunted. "I wouldn't say that. In fact, the guy was a pain in the butt, to tell you the truth. Even so, nobody deserves to die like that. And that little girl saw the whole thing." His face seemed to tighten. "Come on, we got work to do."

He stalked back across the road and climbed into the passenger side of his assigned jeep. His driver turned on the engine in readiness to move out when Lance-Corporal Jeffers, the communications officer, opened the passenger door of a jeep further up the queue and stuck out his head, which was enclosed by a pair of headphones.

"Sir!"

Kneale paused in the act of stepping up into his own jeep. "Yes, Jeffers, what is it?"

"Phone call for Hellboy, sir. It's been relayed from his hotel. Apparently it's urgent."

"I got it," Hellboy said, climbing out and walking across.

Jeffers removed his headphones and handed them to Hellboy. Hellboy had to adjust the headband to its fullest extent to get them over his head, and even then it was a tight fit.

"Hellboy," he said into the attached microphone.

"I'll make this very simple," said a clipped, arrogant voice. "Either you and your colleagues cease this investigation and leave the country tonight or your new lady friend, Cassie Saunders, dies."

Hellboy blinked. This he hadn't been expecting. "Who the hell is this?" he snarled.

"Don't be tiresome," said the voice. "Do you honestly expect me to answer that? I have said all that I intend to say. Goodbye."

"Hey, wait!" Hellboy shouted. "How do I know you're not bluffing?"

There was an exaggerated sigh from the other end of the line, followed by a brief pause. Then a small, scared voice said, "Hellboy? Is that you?"

"Cassie!" Hellboy shouted. "Where are you?"

"I don't know. I'm—"

The line went dead.

Hellboy glared at Jeffers, who quailed before his anger. "What happened?" he roared.

"The caller must have put the phone down, sir," Jeffers replied.

"Can you trace it?"

"I'm afraid not. As I say it was relayed from the hotel and—"

"Damn!" Hellboy yelled. He punched the side of the jeep, denting it. "Damn! Damn! Damn!"

Jeffers and the driver looked at him in alarm. There was silence from the other jeeps too. Even Kneale seemed reticent to speak in the face of Hellboy's wrath.

Hellboy turned away briefly, breathing hard, trying to bring his fury under control. After a few seconds he turned back, stalked towards his assigned jeep, and climbed in.

"Let's go," he muttered.

• • •

An hour earlier, Liz had arrived at the King's Cross refuge with Duggie, wearing a long shabby overcoat and balaclava. The clothes had been procured from a charity shop on Euston Road, though only after Liz had persuaded the cowering staff inside to open up by showing them her B.P.R.D. ID card. She had told them she needed the clothes for a top-secret mission, and had had to fend off questions about when things would be back to normal.

"Hellboy *will* sort this out, though, won't he?" one of the girls asked her desperately.

"He'll do his damnedest," said Liz. "Now, don't forget to lock up after me."

She met Duggie outside the entrance to an eerily deserted King's Cross station, having walked the mile or so from Regent's Park, where she had said goodbye to Abe. Even over that short distance she had been stopped and questioned three times by police patrols, but after a quick flash of her ID she had been allowed to proceed. Despite the occasionally abrasive relationship which she, Hellboy, and Abe had had with the British authorities, Liz had to admit that their handling of the current situation had been swift and thorough. London had been locked down with commendable efficiency, its transport services suspended, its streets cleared. It was weird seeing the city so deserted, and weirder still to think that every building she passed was packed with people, despite outward appearances. Hotels, cafés, pubs, restaurants, theaters, department stores, office blocks ... all were currently refuges for London's displaced population. No doubt some had made it home, but many more had simply sought sanctuary where they could, and were now waiting, tense and silent, for the all clear, just like their parents and grandparents must have done decades before during the Nazi bombing raids.

The windows of many buildings had been blinded—some with steel shutters, some with curtains, some merely with sheets of paper—

to conceal the inhabitants from view. Those buildings whose frontages were almost *all* glass—department stores, restaurants, coffee shops—often had interior barricades of stacked furniture and boxes to provide an extra layer of protection. Now and then Liz saw wide, fearful eyes peeping out at her. Sometimes she heard noises—muffled sounds of movement; even, in one instance, voices raised in furious argument. But for the most part there was silence. And with no one left on the traffic-choked streets to obstruct the progress of emergency vehicles, even the overlapping blare of sirens had been stilled.

Liz didn't see Duggie until he detached himself from the gloomy corner created by the station entrance and the WHSmith store which jutted out to the right of it. It was almost five p.m., but already the graininess of approaching dusk was in the air, and shadows were blooming and darkening in the city's numerous nooks and crannies.

"Hey, Duggie," Liz said, "how you doin'?"

Duggie's eyes flickered around. He clearly felt exposed and vulnerable out in the open. "Okay," he said, "but I don't like this. It's weird."

"Isn't it?" said Liz. "How far's the refuge from here?"

"A couple of streets away. Less than five minutes' walk."

"In that case . . ." Liz opened the white plastic bag which contained her purchases and pulled out the coat and balaclava. The coat was big and baggy and came down past her knees. She dragged the balaclava over her head, tugging strands of hair out from the sides to cover as much of her face as she could. She considered rubbing some dirt on her face as well, to further reduce the risk of being recognized, but then decided that that was overdoing things. Although Duggie was unshaven and had an overall look of bedded-in grime, he didn't have streaks of dirt on his face like some kid playing a Victorian street urchin in a school play.

Hoping that merely keeping a low profile would be enough, she followed Duggie to the refuge. It was an unprepossessing red brick building tucked away down a grubby back street. It was hard to tell what the building's function might originally have been. It could perhaps have been the premises of a small manufacturing company, or even a modest school. As Duggie knocked on the door, Liz hunched over, keeping her chin tucked into her chest. She was not as famous as Hellboy, but it was still possible she *might* be recognized, particularly if their enemies had been keeping tabs on them.

The door was opened by a thin man with black-rimmed spectacles and a blond beard. His long hair was pulled back in a ponytail. He was wearing a light gray sweatshirt with a faded Oxford University logo on it, and baggy, frayed jeans.

"Hey, Duggie," he said, as if he were genuinely delighted to see him.

Duggie nodded with rather less enthusiasm. His voice little more than a mumble, he said, "Can me and my friend come in?"

"Well, sure," said the man. "We're not turning anyone away today. But I'm afraid all the beds are taken. With what's been going on outside, the last of them were snapped up by three this afternoon. We'll be turning the dining hall into an extra dormitory after supper, though. You're welcome to stay there, if you don't mind sleeping on the floor."

"No, that'll be okay," Duggie said, and slipped inside.

Liz shuffled after him, still hunched over. A hand was thrust into her vision. She looked down at it.

"Hi there," said the voice of the man above her head, "and who might you be? I don't think we've seen you before."

"Annie," Liz muttered, hoping her attempt at an English accent was not too much of a giveaway.

"Annie?" said the man. "Annie what?"

Liz shrugged.

Ahead of her she heard Duggie say, "Her name's Annie Davis. She doesn't say much. She's shy."

"Is that so?" said the man. "She a friend of yours, Duggie?"

Liz guessed that Duggie must have nodded, because after a pause the man asked, "How come she hasn't come around here before?"

There was a longer pause this time. Then Duggie said, "She had somewhere, but the landlord kicked her out."

Liz hoped that Duggie's explanation didn't sound as flimsy to the man as it did to her. Apparently not, because he said, "Oh, that's too bad. Well, you're welcome here, Annie. We might not be able to promise you a bed on this occasion, but at least you'll get supper and a roof over your head."

Liz nodded and shuffled after Duggie. However, the man was not yet finished with her.

"My name's Alex Hipkiss, by the way. I run this place with my wife, Jess. You'll be meeting her soon enough."

When Liz failed to respond, he said, "So tell me what's going on out there, Duggie? I've heard all sorts of stories—from wild animals to terrorists to monsters. What have *you* seen?"

Liz raised her head a fraction and chanced a peek at Duggie. He shrugged, looking uncomfortable. "Nothing."

"Nothing?" said Alex disbelievingly. "Are you telling me that none of the rumors are true?"

"Don't know about that," Duggie mumbled. "I just haven't seen anything, that's all."

"Hmm," said Alex, and turned to Liz, who instantly cast her eyes downwards once more. "What about you, Annie? Have *you* seen anything?"

Liz gave a brief shake of the head.

"Well, I don't know," said Alex good-humoredly, "maybe everyone's making a big fuss for no reason, eh? Maybe it's just mass hysteria. What do you think, Duggie?"

Duggie shrugged.

Alex sighed, evidently exasperated that his attempts to strike up a conversation were proving unsuccessful. The tone of his voice changed, became more businesslike. "Well, you know where everything is, Duggie. Perhaps you'd like to show Annie round? Supper will be at seven thirty, as always."

Liz spent the next couple of hours getting to know the place, and trying to keep as low a profile as possible. There were three floors to the building, though Duggie told her that the top floor, which apparently consisted of two sizable attic rooms, was never used. The ground floor housed administration offices, a kitchen, a dining room, male and female toilets, and a medical room, all of which, aside from the dining room and toilets, were generally kept locked. On the second floor was a pair of dormitories (one for men, one for women), two bathrooms (ditto), a shower room, and a games room.

Looking around, what immediately struck Liz was that the refuge was dying on its feet. The blankets on the beds were rough and full of holes, the toilets stank, the taps dripped, and the walls of the shower room were running with condensation and thick with mold. Indeed, the facilities throughout were minimal. The games room contained nothing but a rickety table-tennis table, a few secondhand board games, and an ancient black-and-white TV, which was attached to the wall by brackets and a chain.

Huddled next to Duggie in the dining room, waiting for supper to arrive, Liz asked how long the refuge had been up and running.

"About six years, I think," Duggie said.

"And how is it funded?"

He shrugged, a gesture which Liz had come to recognize as an autonomic response to virtually every question he was asked, even those to which he knew the answer.

"I think the Hipkisses sunk a lot of their own money into the place when they set it up," he said, "but I think they find it hard to keep it going. I suppose they rely on charitable donations and the occasional pissy government handout." He gave her a sidelong look. "Why do you ask?"

"I'm just trying to work out their part in all this," Liz murmured. "Either they're philanthropists, who have no idea what's going on under their noses, in which case one of the staff—and most likely one of the kitchen staff—is in league with the Eye. Or they're so desperate for funds that they're accepting payment in return for turning a blind eye to kidnapping and murder. Or they're in it up to their hippie hairdos, which probably means they've been working towards this day for years, and set this place up purely to provide the Eye with victims when the time came."

Duggie looked shocked. "You really believe they've been planning this for as long as that?"

"I'm keeping my options open," said Liz, "but it's not beyond the realm of possibility. Believe me, Duggie, plans of this kind are frequently set in motion decades, sometimes millennia, before." She nudged him. "Here comes the food."

Liz kept her head down as the food was served, but watched the servers closely. As well as Alex and Jess Hipkiss, both of whom seemed infinitely cheerful, there was a hefty, sweating woman with pasty skin and stringy hair and a tough-looking man with grizzled, close-cropped hair and fuzzy blue tattoos on his sinewy arms.

The food consisted of two dollops of fish pie with a potato-and-grilled-cheese topping, and a spoonful of mixed vegetables which had been bleached almost colorless by overboiling. As each portion of food was slopped unceremoniously onto a resident's plate, the recipient attacked it without preamble. Liz noted that almost all the residents ate ravenously, hunched over their plates and shoveling food into their mouths, as if they expected their meals to be snatched away at any moment.

It was the tough-looking man who served Liz. She kept her head down and muttered, "Cheers," but he didn't respond.

Liz was concerned that her and Duggie's reluctance to eat would be noted, perhaps even commented upon, but she needn't have worried. As soon as everyone had been served, the hefty woman and the tough-looking man exited the dining room, pushing trolleys stacked with now-empty serving dishes. Alex and Jess Hipkiss hung around to chat to residents, but they were on the far

side of the room, laughing with a big guy in beat-up biker's leath-
ers and a bandanna, whom they seemed to know well. All the same,
Liz kept a forkful of food ready, just in case, and even put it in her
mouth at one point when Alex glanced in her direction. As soon as
he had turned away, she took it out again.

Eventually the old man on her left tapped her arm. "You gonna
eat that, darlin'?"

"Er . . . no," said Liz.

"Pass it over here then."

She hesitated a moment. If the food was drugged, she wouldn't
want to be responsible for providing the old guy with a double
dose of whatever it had been laced with. Then again, if the worst
that had happened on the previous occasions was that people had
woken up the next morning feeling groggy, she guessed the dos-
age couldn't have been *too* high. And what couldn't be denied was
that swapping plates with the old man would prevent her having to
answer awkward questions as to why she hadn't eaten her meal. She
pushed her plate across to him.

"Share it," she said in the closest thing to an English accent she
could muster. "I'm sure some of the others will want some too."

As the old man shared out her portion of food with his immediate neighbors, she glanced at the clock on the wall. Almost
eight thirty. If all was well, Hellboy and Abe would be moving into
position soon. It reassured her to think of them outside, watching
over the place, but she couldn't help feeling a little anxious about
the overall situation. She hoped the three of them had made the
right decision in staking out the refuge. She had the sense that time
was running out, and knew that an error of judgment at this stage
could result in the loss of countless lives.

"How can you be so freakin' calm?" Hellboy asked.

He and Abe were sitting in a darkened car across the road from
the refuge. They had been here for over an hour now and Hellboy

was ready to explode. Since receiving the phone call from Cassie's kidnapper, he had felt torn apart with rage, anxiety, and guilt. The creatures he had battled since the call had been no match for his blistering fury, and even Abe had been subjected to the sharp edge of his tongue on several occasions.

Not that Abe minded. He understood Hellboy's anguish. He sympathized with his desire to be *doing* something, rather than just sitting around, waiting. Even though Hellboy knew their current course of action (or *in*action) was their best shot at tracking the Eye members to their lair and recovering Cassie, it didn't help. Hellboy was a doer, and sometimes, for him, the logical choice was also the most excruciating.

His latest outburst had come after he had said, for approximately the tenth time, "This is pointless. We should be in there, breaking heads."

Abe had known he was just letting off steam. Hellboy was to the point and often hotheaded, but one thing he was not was reckless, particularly when lives were at stake. Even so, Abe felt duty bound to give a variation on his standard reply:

"Our target is the big fish, not the minnows. You know that. Be patient and the minnows will lead us to the main catch. Disturb the water now, and the minnows will scatter."

Hellboy glared at him. "Is that some kind of amphibian philosophy?"

"No," said Abe mildly, "it's just an observation."

It was at this point that Hellboy asked Abe how he could be so calm.

Abe said, "It's just my way of staying focused. If I get angry or upset, I make mistakes. And in our job, if we make mistakes, people die."

Hellboy was silent for a moment, glowering at the closed door across the street, which stood in a cone of light from the lamp affixed to the wall above. Slowly his brow unknitted and he sighed.

"Yeah, you're right, buddy. I'm sorry."

"No problem," said Abe.

"It's just . . ." Hellboy's face contorted with anguish ". . . if Cassie hadn't met me this morning she'd be home now, watching TV or eating dinner or listening to some music. Instead of which, she's . . ." He waved his hand to indicate he had no idea where she was or what was happening to her, but that he was sure it was nothing good. "Why do these creeps have to go after my friends all the time?" he said. "If they want a fight, *I'll* give them one."

"But that's the point, isn't it?" said Abe. "They *don't* want a fight. They go after your friends in the hope you'll go away. They do it because they're scared of you—which means they're vulnerable."

"If I ever get my hands on them, they'll be scared, all right," Hellboy said.

Abe nodded. "Aggression is good—but it needs to be channeled positively."

"What are you, my guru?"

The fins on Abe's neck undulated in what might have been the equivalent of a smirk. "Frequently, yes."

They lapsed into silence again, watching the door, waiting for something to happen.

"Wonder what Liz is doing now," Hellboy said eventually.

"Probably wishing she were sitting here, sharing the merry banter," said Abe.

Hellboy grunted.

Liz, in fact, was hot and uncomfortable, and desperate to rid herself of the overcoat and balaclava. The coat was an encumbrance, but the balaclava was worse. It was itching like hell, and the trapped heat was giving her a headache. Lying on a makeshift bed of lumpy matting, surrounded by the snores, grunts, and coughs of fellow residents, the air thick with the smell of unwashed bodies, she felt as if she were suffocating.

She consoled herself with the thought that it surely wouldn't be much longer now before *something* happened—if it was going to at all. She had no way of telling the time, but she guessed it must be somewhere around eleven. If all had gone to plan, Hellboy and Abe would be outside now, keeping watch. Liz's job was simply to make sure that nothing occurred here which might result in their prey giving them the slip. She had already ascertained that the only likely entry and exit point from the building was the street door. There *was* a back door, but it led into a small yard which had no vehicular access and was surrounded by high walls on all sides. There was little chance that the Eye members would choose to enter or leave that way—particularly if they were transporting heavily drugged kidnap victims.

One thing Liz hadn't been able to check was the kitchen, and that worried her. She kept thinking about how the Eye had infiltrated the buildings in which they had planted the bodies—from below, via the city's ancient sewage system—and wondering whether they would do the same here. Maybe the building had a cellar, and maybe it was accessible from the kitchen. She had asked Duggie about it, and he had told her that he was pretty sure the building *didn't* have a cellar. He also said he had been in the kitchen several times (as a frequent and nonviolent resident, he occasionally helped set the tables for dinner) and that there were no doors or trapdoors in there which might lead down to one.

But what if he was wrong? What if the cellar entrance was hidden? What if the Eye managed to slip in, unseen and unheard, and snatch away their victims from right under Liz's nose?

In fact, what if they were here *right now?* What if they had already *been?* Liz went cold at the thought. She had reasoned that if the Eye were going to turn up, they would leave it until midnight at least, or maybe even the early hours, to be sure that the place was at its quietest.

But they might not. They might risk coming earlier—particularly if they were desperate to push ahead with their plan, and were worried about the police making the connection between the victims and the refuge. Since lights out, Liz had been straining for the slightest sound from outside the room, but unless any intruders started clomping about like a herd of elephants, she doubted she would hear much through the thick material of the balaclava and the surrounding chorus of sleep sounds.

She finally decided, therefore, that for the sake of her sanity she was going to have to make a move *now*. She couldn't wait any longer and risk missing all the action. If she was spotted outside the room she'd just say she was going to the toilet. That might not wash, of course—if the food *had* been drugged, the Hipkisses would question why she wasn't zonked out like everyone else—but she'd try it and see what happened. Judging by the evidence, she was inclined to believe that a drug of some kind had indeed been used. Despite the cacophony of snorts and snuffles and groans from all around her, she was pretty sure that everyone in the room except for her and Duggie was asleep.

She could tell he wasn't by the tension in his body. He was lying on his back, hands meshed together over his flat belly. Now and again he would clear his throat nervously; it was the kind of sound only a conscious person would make. She rolled over and put her mouth close to his ear.

"Duggie," she whispered, "I'm going to check things out."

His face was a pale blurred oval in the darkness. "Do you want me to come with you?"

"No, you wait here. You've risked enough just by getting me in. If the kidnappers turn up, I'm planning on following them, in which case I may not see you again."

"Okay, well . . . good luck."

"Thanks, buddy. You too."

She rose from the floor, stifled by the clothes she was wearing. Carefully she picked her way across to the door, stepping over and around sleeping bodies in the grainy darkness. No one raised their head to look at her, or ask where she was going. Even when she accidentally stepped on someone's leg they did nothing more than grunt and turn over.

At the door she turned back for a last look at Duggie. But in the darkness it was impossible to identify his individual form among the lumpy mass of sleeping humanity. She raised a hand regardless, then opened the door a crack and peered out. The dimly lit corridor was deserted, though from the main office down near the entrance she could hear a murmur of voices.

She slipped out of the room and closed the door quietly behind her. Her instinct was to move quickly, and to keep to what few shadows there were, but if someone stepped out of the office and saw her sneaking about, or came down the stairs to the left of the kitchen at the opposite end of the corridor, their suspicions would be instantly aroused.

Mindful of this, she moved like a lost old woman, shuffling along and making no attempt at concealment. Even so, she had a definite plan in mind. First she wanted to check out the kitchen. If the door to the room was still locked, then all well and good. Then she wanted to recce the dormitories upstairs. She had no idea whether the Eye would take their victims from there or from the closer and more convenient dining room, but with the dining room only in use today because of the unusually large influx of residents, she thought it more likely the Eye would stick to their tried-and-tested plan and access the less heavily populated dormitories.

Of course, Liz was aware that if she were found upstairs she would have little chance of bluffing it out, but that was a risk she would have to take. Hopefully she'd be able to subdue any opposition without attracting unwarranted attention, but just in case . . .

She slipped across to the female toilet on the opposite side of the corridor and pushed the door open. Beyond was a grotty, smelly little room, its taps, cracked sink, and toilet bowl coated with a grime-encrusted layer of lime scale that no amount of scrubbing with disinfectant would ever shift. The wall tiles had long faded from gleaming white to a dull ivory-yellow, and the grout between them was black with damp and dirt.

Liz closed the door behind her and reached beneath her coat for the satellite phone in the pouch on her waist. Like Hellboy and Abe, she rarely had her phone switched on, for the simple reason that she didn't want to forget about it and have the damn thing go off at inappropriate times. Of course, their tendency to go incommunicado drove Tom Manning crazy, but he wasn't the one who frequently had to sneak about in the most inhospitable of environments, facing off against supervillains with magical powers and big bad nasties from hellish realms.

She turned the phone on now, and fast-dialed Hellboy. He answered immediately, as if he had been waiting for her call.

"What's happening?" he said.

"Nothing so far. Just thought I'd let you know where I'm at." Quickly she filled him in on what she had learned, and of her intentions. "So where are you and Abe?"

"Sitting right outside, staring at a closed door. It's a thrilling pastime. You should try it."

She smiled at his dry humor, but she could hear the frustration in his voice. "Hang in there, big guy. If I find out anything more I'll call you."

She expected him to say okay and end the call, but he hesitated. Before she could ask him what was wrong, he said, "It won't change how we do things, but I guess you should know—they've got Cassie."

"Damn," Liz said quietly. "I'm sorry, HB. What happened?"

Briefly he told her about the phone call.

"Okay," said Liz, "well, I guess that makes it doubly important that we get these bastards. Talk to you later."

She put her phone away, listened for a moment, then opened the door of the toilet. The corridor was still deserted. She could hear nothing but the same murmur of voices she had heard before and the occasional extra-loud snort or groan from behind the door of the dining room. She walked boldly up the corridor towards the kitchen door, thinking that if anyone challenged her now she would claim she was hungry. She reached the door and tried it. It was still locked. Good. She put her ear to it and listened for a moment. Silence. Okay, now to check on the dormitories upstairs.

She ascended to the second floor, gritting her teeth at each creak of the wooden staircase. She reached the top and was making her way along the corridor towards the dormitories when a door beyond them—the door that led into the games room—abruptly opened and the tough-looking guy who had served her supper stepped out.

Liz could only assume that he had heard the stairs creaking and had come out to investigate. He was holding a copy of the *Racing Post* and from the expression on his face it was clear that he had expected to see someone he knew. This again supported the notion that the food had been drugged. Otherwise, why would the guy have been so surprised to encounter a resident?

"What the hell are you doing here?" he said, his expression changing from shock to aggression.

Liz thought quickly. She allowed her head to droop and shambled towards the man, weaving from side to side, as if she was indeed heavily drugged and fighting desperately to keep awake.

"Oi," the man said, "where do you think you're going?"

He marched up to Liz and grabbed her roughly by the shoulders. She felt his strong thumbs digging into the muscle below her shoulder bones, but she forced her face to remain slack. She mumbled incoherently, and rolled her head loosely forward as if she were finding it too heavy to keep upright.

"You what?" the man said aggressively. "Speak up, you daft bitch, I can't hear you."

He leaned towards her in an attempt to make sense of her words, whereupon she suddenly leaped forward, butting him in the face with the top of her head.

She heard his nose crunch, and then the grip on her shoulders weakened and he was staggering backwards. She looked up, to see blood pouring down his face, his eyes rolling in their sockets. Trying not to be hampered by the heavy overcoat and balaclava, she danced forward like a boxer and followed up her initial attack. She had nothing like Hellboy's punching power, but she was fit and quick. She punched the man once, twice, three times in the face before he could even think about reacting.

His legs buckled under him, and he hit the wooden floor with a thump that she hoped hadn't been heard downstairs. As he was gurgling blood, his hands groping feebly at the floor in an attempt to push himself upright, she whipped her automatic out from under her coat and pointed it at his face.

"Don't make a noise and don't try to get up," she said. "That way we'll both be happy."

She wasn't sure if he was conscious enough to register what she had said. Certainly he kept trying to lever himself up, and managed to get into a semi-sitting position before she stepped forward and kicked his arms out from under him again.

"I *said* stay down," she muttered. "Do you understand?"

His body became still and his eyes began to blink rapidly. He focused on her with difficulty and then gave a slight nod.

"Good," said Liz, and waved her gun in his face, like a mother showing a baby a rattle. "Now, don't forget, I'm the one with the weapon here."

Quickly she pulled off the balaclava, her hair crackling with static as it rose up, then tumbled down around her shoulders again. Next she shrugged off the overcoat, which she used to wind rapidly around the man's feet. Grabbing the thick wad of material fully in her left hand and partially in her right, while still pointing the gun at the man's prone body, she lifted his feet and dragged him over to the door of the women's dormitory.

He was heavy, and if the floor had been carpeted instead of laid with old wooden planks worn smooth as glass by decades of passing feet, she doubted she would have been able to move him at all. Once she got going, however, his semiconscious body slid along easily, his arms even rising involuntarily above his head to trail behind him. She backed to the door, opened it awkwardly with the hand that was holding the gun, and dragged him inside.

The sound of two dozen women breathing in sleep was like the soughing of the tide. Not a single one woke, or even stirred, when Liz entered the room, dragging the man behind her.

She knew that to maintain her advantage she had to move swiftly and decisively. There was nothing to be gained in fumbling about in the dark—and so, taking a calculated risk, she reached out and switched on the room's main light.

The bulb dangling from the center of the ceiling was not particularly bright, but it was bare, and the light seemed momentarily harsh in contrast to the darkness that had preceded it. The semiconscious man groaned and screwed up his eyes, even half raised an arm to shield them. The blood on his face looked startlingly red in the sudden light.

In comparison to the man, the sleeping women barely reacted at all. A few grunted or half moaned; a couple turned over. The most significant response came from a youngish woman with masses of tangled hair, who screwed up her face and dragged a sheet over her head.

With a silent apology Liz crossed to the nearest bed and peeled the top blanket away from its sleeping inhabitant. The blanket was made of thin, coarse material that looked as though it would rip easily. Keeping a wary eye on the man still lying on his back, dripping blood onto the floor, Liz tucked her gun back into its holster and quickly tore the blanket into strips.

When she was done, she twisted the strips into tight corkscrews to strengthen them, then bound the man hand and foot. Once he was incapacitated, she wiped the blood carefully away from around his nostrils and mouth, checked to make sure he could breathe okay through his broken nose, and then gagged him. She dragged his body to the far end of the dormitory and rolled it under the furthest bed from the door, out of sight. The man was all but fully conscious now and staring at her with undisguised hatred.

Liz reached into a pouch on her belt and withdrew a small brown bottle. Extending her arm, holding the bottle directly under the man's nose, she pulled out the rubber stopper. He continued to glare at her for a few seconds, and then his eyes rolled back in his head and his eyelids closed.

"That's right," Liz said, "you have a nice little sleep." She patted his face and left the room, switching the light off behind her. She noticed there were spots of blood on the wooden floor of the corridor. Using one of the remaining strips of blanket material, she wiped them up.

Gun out, making no attempt at pretense whatsoever now, she checked out the games room and the men's dormitory. The games room was empty, and the dormitory contained only its sleeping inhabitants. That done, she moved to the head of the stairs and listened, but all remained quiet below.

She sat down on the upper landing, her back against the wall. All she could do now was wait, and right here was pretty much the best place to do it. From this position, she would hear if anyone entered the building downstairs, be it via the main door or through the kitchen at the back. She would also hear if anyone started to ascend the staircase, and so would have plenty of time to find a hiding place.

She felt happier now, more in control of the situation. Now no one could sneak into the building without her knowing it, or take her by surprise. She briefly considered calling Hellboy again, then discarded the idea. It was best to stay quiet, she thought, and to keep her hands free of everything but her gun, in case something unexpected happened.

She didn't know how long she had been waiting before she heard sounds of activity downstairs. She guessed it was well over an hour, maybe even close to two. Although she had been too tense to feel tired, Liz had sensed her mind beginning to drift a couple of times during the waiting period. Whenever that happened, or whenever her limbs or back began to stiffen up, she got to her feet and walked up and down a little bit, in the hope that if the Hipkisses heard her downstairs they would assume it was the guy whose nose she had broken. She wished she had something to eat. She'd had nothing since her half-finished meal in the Three Cups at lunch-time. Her stomach was rumbling so loudly she felt sure it could be heard throughout the building.

Eventually, just as she was beginning to wonder what she would do if the members of the Eye *didn't* show up, the quiet was broken by three stealthy taps on the main door downstairs. Instantly Liz was on her feet and all but leaning over the banister to listen. She heard an internal door open, footsteps on the wooden floor in the lower corridor, and then the sound of bolts being slid back. Liz felt the faintest kiss of cool air on her skin as the main door was pulled open and a breeze passed through the building. There was an exchange of low voices, the words too muffled for her to make out. Then more footsteps as the new arrivals, two or three of them maybe, entered the building.

The main door was closed with a slight thump. Still Liz tried to make out what the men—she was sure they were men—were saying. However, she could discern nothing of the conversation, apart from the fact that one of the speakers was Alex Hipkiss, and that another had a deep, rumbling voice, and seemed to be speaking with a foreign accent.

After a brief conversation the men started walking along the corridor. However, because of the slight distortion of sound as it echoed up the stairwell, Liz didn't realize they were ascending the stairs until she heard one of the lower steps creak.

Immediately she crossed silently to the men's dormitory, having decided that this would be the most likely room that the abductors would enter. She slipped inside, paused for no more than a second to allow her eyes to adjust to the sudden darkness, and then moved along the central aisle between the beds to the far end. When she reached the final bed on her right, in which a bewhiskered old man was lying on his back and snoring gently, she dropped onto her stomach and rolled underneath.

Sure enough, a few seconds later the door opened and a spill of light entered the room. Liz lay motionless, gun at the ready, and peered through the low tunnel created by the even row of beds. Three pairs of feet followed the light into the room, casting thin black shadows before them. There was a pause, then a low guttural voice in an accent that Liz recognized broadly as African, said urgently, "Don't switch on the light."

"It's quite safe," replied Alex Hipkiss, sounding so cool and self-assured that he seemed like a different man to the amiable hippie she had met earlier. "They won't wake up."

"And even if they did . . ." said the third man, whose voice was richer and more cultured than his companion's, yet with a twang of that same African accent. He then said something in a language which Liz didn't understand, but which made the two Africans laugh.

"Very amusing, I'm sure," Hipkiss said, sounding peeved at being excluded from the conversation, "but you can put that away. I'm not cleaning up your mess."

One of the men sighed. Then the African with the more cultured voice said, "Despite what you say, Mr. Hipkiss, let's do as Solomzi suggests and keep the light off. There's no point taking unnecessary risks, and we can see well enough with the light from the corridor."

The door was opened wider, presumably to spread a little more illumination, and the men moved further into the room.

"So who do we take, Mr. Hipkiss?" the third man asked.

Liz saw Hipkiss's feet swivel in one direction, then another, and assumed he was pointing out potential victims.

"This one's strong enough . . . that one too . . . and him . . . and . . . him . . ."

"All men?" the third man said, his voice gently mocking.

"What's the difference?" said Hipkiss coldly.

The guttural man laughed and muttered something, which made him laugh all the more.

"I think your friend has got his priorities wrong," Hipkiss said in the same cold voice. "This isn't about individual gratification."

"Males may endure longer, but the female reaction is more intense," said the third man. "The muti is therefore purer."

"You'll have to forgive my skepticism," said Hipkiss dryly, "but by all means, take a couple of the women if you want to. It amounts to the same thing in the end."

One of the men walked over to a bed halfway down Liz's row and stood beside it. Although Liz could only see him from his knees down, she got the impression he was well dressed, in suit trousers and polished black leather shoes. He stood there a while, and Liz wondered what he was doing. Finally, in his guttural voice, he said, "This one is ready. Help me with him."

"I hope you haven't given him too much of that stuff," Hipkiss said. "We do need him awake for the final ceremony."

"I know what I am doing," said the guttural-voiced man indignantly.

Although she could only see their feet, and hear the sounds that they were making, Liz knew that Hipkiss and the two Africans were lifting the drugged man from the bed. From what they had said, she gathered that he had been given some kind of supplementary drug, one that would presumably ensure he remained unconscious until they had transported him to wherever the "final ceremony" was due to take place.

The drugged man was carried from the room and down the stairs. Liz assumed that they would load him into whatever mode of transport they had brought with them and then return for the next victim. Again, she thought about calling Hellboy, but decided that the risk was too great. Hopefully he and Abe were currently observing what was going on, keeping a low profile and biding their time. Everything now depended on their not being discovered, on being able to tail the Eye members without making them suspicious. From the way the men had been talking, the "final ceremony" would be taking place soon. If she, Hellboy, and Abe were not there to stop it, there was every likelihood that the ensuing maelstrom would do untold damage before they could even *begin* to regroup.

Something else to think about was *how* they were going to tail the Eye members through the all-but-deserted streets without being spotted, but she guessed they would have to deal with that when the time came. That question, of course, led to another: how had the Eye members managed to get here in the first place without attracting the attention of the police and military patrols dotted about the city?

Before she had time to ponder on the puzzle, the men were back and prepping another of the sleeping residents for the journey ahead. This time, as they exited, they pulled the dormitory door closed behind them, consigning the room once again to darkness. Liz took this as a sign that they had finished, and that they would next move across to the women's dormitory to repeat the process. Hoping she wasn't wrong, she slid from under the bed and ran silently up the aisle to the door. She pressed her ear against it, listening for sounds of the men coming back. After a couple of minutes she heard the creak of their feet on the stairs. As a precaution she ran across to the nearest bed and slid beneath it. Holding her breath, listening hard, she heard the low rumble of the men's voices, and then the click of a door opening on the opposite side of the corridor.

She hadn't been wrong. They were entering the women's dormitory. She slid back out from under the bed and pressed herself against the door once again. She hoped they wouldn't find the unconscious man under the bed at the far end of the room. If they did the game would be up. Her heart pounded as she waited, half expecting to hear an exclamation of surprise from the men. However, after a minute or two she heard them come quietly back out of the room and start to make their way down the stairs. From the slow way they were moving it was clear they were carrying another body.

A few minutes later they were back for their fourth, and presumably final, victim. As they began to descend the stairs, Liz knew this was where the tricky part would begin. Somehow she had to keep close enough to the men without being spotted to make it outside in time to join Hellboy and Abe before they set off in pursuit of whatever vehicle the men were driving.

From here on in, therefore, it was going to be down to precise judgment and a huge amount of luck. She waited until she was sure the men were at the bend on the stairs, and thus no longer in sight of the upper landing, and then she eased the dormitory door open and slipped out. Now she could hear the men below. They had reached the bottom of the stairs and were moving along the corridor towards the front door. Hoping that the clomp of their footsteps would mask the sound of her descent, she crept down the stairs, keeping to the inner side of each step to reduce the creak of the old wood. When she was halfway down she dropped to her haunches and peered around the handrail at the point where it curved back on itself and descended to the floor below. The two Africans, carrying the unconscious, blanket-shrouded body of a woman, were almost at the front door, Alex Hipkiss hovering behind them. Liz could see that both Africans were tall with close-cropped hair, one lean and hollow cheeked, the other bulkier and broad shouldered. The lean man's skin was so dark that it seemed to gleam like plastic. Both were wearing suits and ties, which made them look like businessmen, or hospital consultants.

For Liz, the next couple of minutes would largely rely on how long Alex Hipkiss hung about in the corridor after the men had gone. If he stood in the open doorway and watched them leave, her chances of joining Hellboy and Abe would be zilch. If, however, he closed the door after them and went straight back into the office, then she would have a chance.

Muscles thrumming, poised for action, she waited to see what he would do. She saw the men carry the woman outside, Hipkiss follow them as far as the door, his left hand reaching out to encircle the inner handle.

Close the door and go, Liz urged him. *Just close the door and go.* As if obeying her silent command, he pushed the door closed behind the men and began to slide the bolts back into place. However, he did it, in Liz's eyes, agonizingly slowly. She clenched her teeth, imagining the two men loading the body into their van or truck, and then hauling ass out of there while she remained stuck at the top of the stairs, missing out on the action.

At last Hipkiss completed his door-locking routine and turned round. Suddenly aware that her eagerness was making her reckless, Liz shrank back, slowly releasing the long, frustrated breath she had been holding in her lungs. She counted to three, then chanced another peek into the hallway below. She caught the barest glimpse of Hipkiss disappearing into the office to the left of the main door.

It was now or never. She was going to have to go for it. She wasn't frightened of Hipkiss or his wife—she felt more than capable of dealing with them—but she *was* frightened of being delayed, or of the Eye being alerted to her presence. Lithe and silent as a cat, she ran down the stairs, which barely creaked beneath her weight.

She was reaching out to undo the first of the heavy bolts on the main door when Hipkiss re-emerged from the office.

He stared at her in astonishment, an empty coffee mug in his hand. Then his expression stiffened and a coldness came into his eyes. He threw the mug at her head to distract her and darted back towards the office door.

Liz was too quick for him. She dodged the mug easily, which shattered against the wall behind her, brought up her gun, and started running forward all in the same movement. Hipkiss had got the door half closed when Liz smashed into it, booted foot first. The force of her momentum caused the door to fly open and Hipkiss to stagger backwards. His face creased with pain as his back slammed into the edge of a desk hard enough to make a pile of books fall over and avalanche onto the floor in a slithering heap.

Liz jabbed the muzzle of the gun none too gently against his forehead, leaving a round red mark.

"Sit down!" she hissed. "Sit down and don't move!"

"You won't shoot me," he said, his voice cracked but defiant. Even so, his legs folded and he plumped onto his backside, sliding down the edge of the desk.

"Don't tempt me, Hipkiss," Liz said. "The stakes are way too high to take any bullshit from you."

She looked around quickly to locate the telephone. She had no doubt that this was what Hipkiss had been trying to reach. She spotted it on a desk equally as large as the one Hipkiss had collided with, tucked into the alcove of the curtained bay window. She moved across to it, her gun still trained unerringly on the center of Hipkiss's forehead. Another quick glance around confirmed that it was the only phone in the room. With one savage tug, Liz ripped the connecting wires out of the wall. The socket sparked and fizzed briefly, then fell silent.

"You won't stop us," Hipkiss said with a smirk that Liz knew would have made Hellboy want to rip the guy's head off.

"Shut up, you pathetic little creep," snapped Liz.

From outside she heard the rumble of an engine and then the unmistakable sound of a vehicle moving away.

"Damn," she muttered.

Hipkiss sniggered. "Told you, didn't I? You're too late."

Liz tried not to let her disappointment show on her face. "*I* personally might not be at Eye Central to kick some ass, but my friends Hellboy and Abe will be," she said. "And believe me, Hellboy kicks ass a damn sight harder than I do."

The words were barely out of Liz's mouth when something hit her from behind. It was so unexpected that it wasn't until she was falling that she was even aware it had happened at all. She put up her hands instinctively and felt them slap the wooden floor a split second before her face would have. The gun was jarred out of her grasp and went skidding across the floor, but already she was feeling too dizzy and sick to retrieve it.

She lay there a few moments, certain her skull had been cleaved in two. She was vaguely aware of Hipkiss scrambling to his feet, scuttling across the room to pick up her gun. She was aware too of her assailant moving into the room behind her and across to the desk. She heard Hipkiss say, "She's disconnected the phone," but his voice was muzzy, like bad radio reception.

The new arrival, Hipkiss's wife, Jess, swore and asked, "Who is she?"

Hipkiss snorted. "Don't you recognize her?"

"No."

"She's Hellboy's friend. B.P.R.D."

Jess Hipkiss sounded panicky. "Then they're onto us."

"Much good will it do them," Hipkiss said. Then he gave an exasperated sigh. "Will you relax, Jess. Everything's under control."

Liz had no idea whether Jess was reassured by her husband's words, but she still sounded nervous when she asked, "What are you going to do with her?"

"Shoot her," Hipkiss replied.

"Not here?" said Jess.

"Why not?"

"Can't you take her out in the backyard and do it there? You can leave her to rot with the rubbish."

Hipkiss laughed. "Poor Jess. Squeamish as ever. How are you going to cope when the Eye opens?"

"I'll cope," Jess said angrily, "and I'll do whatever I have to. You know I will, Alex. Don't make fun of me."

"My poor Jess," he repeated, and laughed again. Then his voice hardened and Liz felt a foot in the ribs. "You. On your feet."

Throughout the exchange between the Hipkisses, Liz had been trying to pull her scrambled thoughts together. Her head still pounded like a bastard, and she didn't have Hellboy's capacity for healing, but she could take the physical knocks a damn sight better than most people. Even so, she didn't think she was yet mentally capable of defending herself by channeling the fire inside her. In her present state, the result might well be akin to when she had first discovered and inadvertently unleashed her power at the age of eleven. That day thirty-two people had died, including her entire family. Liz knew she would rather have her own life ended by a bullet than run the risk of burning down the building and spending the rest of her days with yet more innocent lives on her already overburdened conscience.

Pretending to be more woozy than she was, she pushed herself onto all fours and then rose, shaky legged, to her feet.

"Look at her," Hipkiss laughed. "She's like Bambi."

"Just take her outside and do it, Alex," Jess said tightly. "Then we can leave here and never come back."

Still swaying on her feet, and keeping her expression slack, Liz slowly raised a hand and touched the back of her head. There was a cut there, but it was not as bad as she'd feared. She gaped at her blood-speckled fingers, mouth open and eyelids drooping, then held them out to Jess. "Look," she said.

Jess grimaced distastefully. Liz noticed she was still holding the saucepan she must have used to whack her with.

"Move," Alex said, jabbing Liz in the back with her own gun.

"Where-we-going?" Liz slurred.

"Magical mystery tour," Alex said. "Just walk."

Liz stumbled ahead of him, thinking furiously. If Hipkiss was going to take her into the back yard, then they'd have to go through the kitchen, which meant he would have to unlock the door. If she could convince him that she was no sort of threat, she might be able to jump him while he was fumbling with the lock. With this in mind, she staggered against the door frame as she was exiting the office and half slid down it, then made a big show of trying to haul herself back to her feet.

"Get up," he snapped at her.

"My legs . . ." she sniggered drunkenly. "Feel a bit . . . funny . . ."

"Get up or I'll shoot you now," he said.

"Okay, okay," she mumbled, "don't get y'knickers in a . . . thing . . ."

She hauled herself back to her feet, hand over hand on the door frame, like a novice skater trying to remain upright on the ice. Then she swayed out of the door and stumbled off down the corridor, Hipkiss prodding the gun into her back to keep her moving.

They were passing the door of the dining room when it was suddenly plucked open and what appeared to be a flapping shape with legs emerged. It took Liz a second to realize the shape was Duggie with a brown blanket in his outstretched arms. The homeless man hurled himself recklessly at Hipkiss, throwing the blanket over his head. Before Hipkiss could react, Liz spun round and wrenched his gun arm upwards. Whether by accident or design, Hipkiss's finger jerked on the trigger and a gunshot that sounded like a small explosion echoed through the building. The bullet hit the ceiling, and plaster and debris rained down on them. Still holding Hipkiss's wrist in one hand, Liz grabbed his throat through the

THE ALL-SEEING EYE 243

blanket with the other and slammed him backwards, his head hitting the wall with a resounding *clonk*. She smashed his hand against the wall several times, until he dropped the gun. Then she shoved him so hard that he went down in a heap, the blanket still tangled around his upper body. She picked up the gun and pointed it at him just as he succeeded in tearing the blanket from his head.

His face was red and his spectacles were hanging askew. He straightened them with trembling hands, glaring at Duggie as if outraged at the homeless man's intervention.

"Thanks, Duggie," Liz said. "I owe you one."

"No problem," Duggie replied, looking almost embarrassed.

Liz turned to Hipkiss. "Not very good at this, are you?"

"Get stuffed," Hipkiss said, sounding like a petulant schoolboy.

Liz laughed. "Oh, *now* I'm hurt. Back on your feet, dumbass."

She marched him at gunpoint back to the office, Duggie bringing up the rear. Inside, they found Jess Hipkiss sitting behind her desk, hands gripping the arms of her chair as if her life depended on it. She was trembling and her face was deathly pale. When she saw her husband, her face crumpled.

"What's the matter with you?" he snapped, as if she were letting him down.

"I thought . . ." Her voice was barely audible. She looked at Liz and tried to appear defiant. "What's going to happen to us?"

Liz stared at her without expression. "That depends on you."

Jess swallowed, licked her lips. "What do you mean?"

"I need you to give me some information," Liz said, "and if you cooperate, I'll simply hand you over to the police and you'll be tried as an accomplice to murder . . ."

She let it hang there. She could see that Jess wanted to know—but was too terrified to ask—what would happen if they *didn't* cooperate.

Before Jess could say anything, however, Hipkiss snarled, "We're not going to tell you anything!"

"Aren't you?" said Liz lightly.

"There's nothing you can do to hurt us," Hipkiss said. "We've already won."

"I'm not sure Jess agrees with that. Do you, Jess?" said Liz.

Jess was shaking and swallowing and sweating. She looked to be coming apart in front of Liz's eyes. Liz wondered how the young woman had ever become involved with Hipkiss and his poisonous, warped view of the world.

Jess's mouth opened, but before she could speak, Hipkiss said, "Don't say anything, Jess. You don't have to tell them *anything*."

Liz sighed and handed the gun to Duggie. "I'm going to tie him up," she said. "If he tries anything, shoot him."

"Okay," Duggie said.

Liz tied Hipkiss up using more of the strips of material from the torn blanket. When she was done she stood up, took her gun back from Duggie, and pointed it at Jess.

"Come with me," she said coldly.

Jess looked stricken, terrified. "Where?" she asked in barely more than a whisper.

"Don't question me!" Liz shouted suddenly. "Just come! Now!"

Her anger had the desired effect. Jess Hipkiss leaped to her feet and circled the desk.

"Please don't hurt me," she said.

"That's a good one, coming from somebody who supplied victims to a group of torturers and murderers," Liz replied.

"I didn't . . . that is . . . I wasn't the one who . . ."

"Just move," Liz said.

She directed Jess Hipkiss up the stairs and into the games room, where she ordered her to sit in one of the ratty old chairs. Jess was shaking in fear, her face white.

"You're really not cut out for this, Jess, are you?" Liz said.

Almost weeping, Jess said, "What do you want?"

"I want an address. I want to know where the final ceremony will take place."

Jess shook her head. Tears were squeezing themselves from her eyes, running down her cheeks.

"I can't . . ." she said, "I can't . . ."

"Yes you can," replied Liz.

Jess gave an almighty sniff and tilted her trembling chin up in a final show of defiance.

"I won't," she said, the tears wet on her face.

Liz slipped her gun into her holster. She let the fire come, let it fill her eyes and her open mouth with cool yellow flames.

Jess's eyes widened and she began to make inarticulate whimpering sounds, too terrified to scream.

Liz held up her right hand. It was gloved in flame. She moved it to and fro in front of Jess's face.

"You will," she said almost gently.

☠ CHAPTER 13

The question that had occurred to Liz, of how to tail a vehicle through a deserted city, was one that Hellboy, Abe, and their driver, Tony Mancini, had discussed at length. Hellboy was in favor of simply ambushing the Eye members when they emerged from the refuge and beating the truth out of them, but Abe unclipped a pouch on his belt and produced what looked like a bundle of small bleached bones bound together with colored twine and a glass vial of reddish-brown powder.

"What the hell's that?" Hellboy asked.

"It's a Venezuelan gulu charm," said Abe. "It won't make us invisible to them, but they'll have to work really hard to notice us."

He got out of the car and slipped across to the vehicle that the two Eye members had arrived in. Hellboy watched silently as he poured powder onto his hand and blew it across both wing mirrors, and then walked all the way round the vehicle, tapping the metal bodywork with the bones in a ritualistic pattern, muttering as he did so.

"That should do it," he said, getting back into the car a couple of minutes later.

"Okay," conceded Hellboy, "but I still say if these guys *do* spot us, we run them off the road and beat the crap out of them."

An ambulance. That was how the Eye guys had made it through the streets without being stopped and questioned—somehow they had managed to procure an ambulance. They had even had the temerity to drive it through the city at speed, lights flashing and siren wailing.

"Whoever these guys are, they're not dumb," Hellboy had noted with reluctant admiration. "I mean, who the hell is going to stop an ambulance on a mission of mercy?"

Indeed, Hellboy and Abe had themselves almost been taken in by the ambulance stunt. When the vehicle initially turned up, announcing its arrival from several streets away, Abe very nearly blew their cover by getting out of the car to greet it, assuming that something had gone wrong inside the refuge, that maybe Liz had been rumbled and was now hurt. It had been the more experienced Hellboy who had struck a note of caution, placing a hand on Abe's arm even as he had been reaching for the door handle.

"Hang on," he had said quietly.

Abe had turned to him. "What's wrong?"

"Things may not be as straightforward as they seem," Hellboy said.

Seconds later the driver's door and the passenger door had opened and the two men had emerged.

Hellboy looked at Abe, his golden eyes shining in the gloom. "How many paramedics do *you* know who wear suits and ties?" he had said.

The three agents sat tight as the two men went into the refuge. Then they watched as the men loaded their victims into the ambulance one by one. Once the fourth victim was aboard, the men slammed the back doors shut and climbed into the driver's cab.

"Here we go," Hellboy said as the ambulance's engine turned over and its headlights came on. Tony Mancini twisted the ignition key of the black Rover 3500 that the Brits had provided them with, and they eased out, headlights off, in pursuit of their quarry.

At first everything ran smoothly. The Eye guys in the ambulance did not seem to realize that they were being tailed, and Mancini drove with skill and precision, tucking neatly in behind the leading vehicle, matching its speed, its occasional sudden turns, its progress through lights and intersections. They headed north, up through Camden, passing Holloway Prison on their left. It was when they came to Holloway Road that things began to unravel.

The only army checkpoint they had encountered until now had waved them through without any problems. Hellboy and Abe had been a little tense, wondering whether only the ambulance would be allowed to proceed, but either the army guys must have assumed the two vehicles were on the same mission, or they had spotted Hellboy in the back seat of the Rover.

Unfortunately the B.P.R.D. agents did not have the same luck with the next patrol. This one, comprised of police officers, was positioned at the junction between Parkhurst Road and Holloway Road. This time the ambulance was waved through, but a police officer pointed to a space between a police van and a patrol car, indicating that the Rover should pull over.

"Idiot," Hellboy muttered. "Just ignore him."

Mancini nodded and maintained his speed. Angrily the policeman stepped forward, raising a hand, forcing Mancini to swerve and miss him by millimeters.

"What are you doing, you moron!" Hellboy yelled at the officer, though his window was up and there was no way the man could hear him. Turning to Abe, he muttered, "Jeez, don't these guys *have* brains? Isn't it obvious we're trailing the damn ambulance for a *reason?*"

Abe turned and looked through the back windscreen. "Oh, great, now they're following us," he said wearily.

Sure enough, two officers, including the one they had almost mown down, had run across to the patrol car parked by the curb and leaped in. The car was peeling out into the road now. Almost immediately it began to flash its lights at their rear bumper, its siren blaring.

"Hey, let's stop!" Hellboy said brightly. "Then we can tell those halfwit cops they've just wrecked our last slim chance of saving their city."

Abruptly the ambulance put on a spurt of speed, drawing away from the Rover.

"Either we've been spotted or they think the cops are after them," Mancini said calmly.

"Just keep with them, Tony," said Abe.

Mancini nodded. "Do my best."

The next few minutes were like a scene from one of the seventies cop-show reruns—*Starsky and Hutch* or *The Streets of San Francisco*—Hellboy liked to watch late at night with popcorn on the rare occasions when he got to relax back home in his quarters at B.P.R.D. HQ in Connecticut. There were plenty of hairpin bends taken at high speed, plenty of near misses and squealing brakes and gouts of rubbery smoke kicking up from scorched tires.

Despite the very real risk of losing their quarry, Hellboy found himself enjoying the ride. He leaned forward as they skidded round corners, felt a rush of excitement each time they swerved around an unexpected obstacle.

Abe, by contrast, who was more vulnerable to physical injury than his friend, was pressed back into his seat, clinging on for dear life. His skin had turned a pale and slightly sickly blue, and the ruff of fins around his neck fluttered in alarm.

On a straight stretch of road, Hellboy leaned forward to speak to Mancini.

"Fun as this is, Tony, there's no way these bastards will go back to their HQ if they know they're being followed—which means that we're gonna have to catch 'em. Think you can force 'em to stop without anyone getting killed?"

"I'll try," Mancini muttered, eyes fixed on the road.

He put his foot down, coaxing a little more speed from the car. Abe hunched up his shoulders and closed his eyes, bracing himself for the collision, as the Rover roared right up to the ambulance's rear bumper, its white double doors filling the windscreen.

Just as the two bumpers seemed destined to touch, the Rover peeled off to the right, looking for a space wide enough to overtake. A split second later Abe was gasping, thrown to his left, as Mancini swerved back in to avoid a traffic light mounted on a concrete island.

Behind them the patrol car was still flashing its lights, its siren screaming like some enraged animal.

Mancini tried again, putting on another spurt of speed, easing the Rover again to the right. The patrol car behind them aped their actions. Clearly the police driver believed they were trying to escape by overhauling the ambulance, perhaps intending to use it as a buffer between themselves and the pursuit vehicle.

The road they were on now was lined by tall Victorian houses. It had once been a residential area, but the buildings had long ago been converted into offices. There were cars parked on either curb, but no further obstacles immediately ahead. The Rover's engine began to scream as Mancini coaxed yet more revs out of it. The car pulled out wider to overtake the ambulance, its nose edging along the ambulance's flank, the hot metal of the two vehicles no more than a millimeter or two apart.

Hellboy wound down his window, and Abe half expected him to reach out and dig his fingers into the side of the ambulance as they eased past, perhaps in a crazy attempt to slow it down by sheer brute strength. Before he could ask him what he was planning, however, the ambulance sashayed sideways, its solid back end clipping the passenger side of the Rover.

Inside the car, the bang of impact sounded like a small explosion. The car skidded and slued sideways as Mancini hauled on the steering wheel, trying desperately to bring the vehicle under control. However, instead of stabilizing, it went into a screeching spin, its speed and momentum sending it careering towards the cars parked on the opposite curb. Mancini tried to prevent an impact by stamping on the brakes, but this simply locked the wheels, exacerbating the problem.

Abe was hurled sideways as the Rover crunched side on into the front wing of a parked BMW. He was only prevented from landing in Hellboy's lap by his seat belt, which clamped across his chest with bruising force. He was vaguely aware of Mancini also being thrown sideways and banging his head on something, and of the ambulance veering wildly for a moment, before regaining its equilibrium and streaking away up the road. Then his senses were overwhelmed by the screech of tortured metal and the stink of burnt rubber. By the time it stopped, so abruptly that it was like jerking awake from a bad dream, Abe's ears were ringing and his brain felt as if it had been rattled loose in his skull.

"You okay?" Hellboy's voice seemed to echo up from the blanketing silence of an incredibly deep well.

Abe opened his mouth, his jaw aching from clenching his teeth so tightly, and instantly his ears popped.

Sound and clarity rushed back in. He heard a hissing like escaping steam, groans from the front seat, the siren of the police car whooping, as if in triumph, then falling silent.

He looked around, and for a moment was disoriented. Everything looked different, back to front somehow. Then he realized that the Rover must have spun all the way round in a circle, and had come to rest facing back in the direction it had come. The police car was now parked nose to nose with them. He saw the policemen get out, placing their peaked caps on their heads and pulling the brims firmly down, as if to cement their authority.

"Dammit," Hellboy muttered, and reached out to open his own door. However, it was buckled with impact, jammed in the frame. With a snarl, he pistoned out his stone right hand and the door not only flew open, but was knocked clean off its hinges. The two policemen stopped and gaped as the door shot out into the road, pirouetted for a moment, then toppled over with a resounding clank.

As soon as Hellboy unfolded himself from the back seat and rose to his full height, the officers' faces changed from grim intent to childlike shock. Through the cracked front windscreen, Abe saw them blanch, saw one of them take an involuntary step back. He unclipped his own seat belt, scrambled across the back seat, wincing at the pain of his injuries, and climbed out through the frame of buckled metal where the door had been.

"Thank you *so* much," Hellboy said heavily. "Do you morons realize what you've done?"

Evidently stung by the insult, the officer who had taken a step back now stepped forward again.

"With all due respect, sir, we were just doing our job," he said.

"Your job," Hellboy muttered. "Well, thanks to you guys, you won't *have* a job tomorrow. And do you know why?"

The two policemen looked at each other. The one who hadn't spoken shook his head.

"You won't have a job because you won't have a city. This time tomorrow there'll be nothing left of London but a big smoking hole in the ground. So congratulations, gents. Nice work. Now get out of my sight before I *really* lose my temper."

Liz knew that ringing Hellboy was a risk, but a calculated one. Like her, he hardly ever had his phone on when he was working. He'd only turn it on when he wanted to *make* a call, was specifically *waiting* for a call, or if he wanted to check his messages. However, she also knew he'd have been worried by her nonappearance after the Eye guys exited the refuge, and that he would call to check on her the first chance he got. She was not surprised, therefore, when she punched in his number and got his automated answering service.

"Hi, HB, it's me. Just calling to let you know I'm okay, and on my way to meet you at the house in Ranskill Gardens. I had a little trouble at the refuge, but it was nothing I couldn't handle. Turned out the Hipkisses, who run the refuge, are Eye members. Surprise, surprise, huh? I managed to persuade Mrs. Hipkiss to give me the Ranskill Gardens address. Plus she lent me her car and a London A-Z. Isn't that nice? If all's gone to plan at your end, I guess you must be nearly at the house now—that's if you're not there already. Call me if you get a chance. See you guys later."

She dropped the phone on the passenger seat and concentrated on where she was going. She didn't expect Hellboy to call her back anytime soon, and so was surprised when the phone bleeped three minutes later.

She picked it up. "Yeah?"

"Liz, it's me."

"Hellboy. What's happening?"

"We lost 'em," he said tersely. "But you know where they're heading for, right?"

"44 Ranskill Gardens, Crouch End," Liz said. "That's where the final ceremony will take place."

"How sure are you of that?"

"Put it this way—Jess Hipkiss wasn't lying when she gave me the address. I was very persuasive."

"I'm sure you were," Hellboy said. "So where are you now?"

"Driving up Camden Road. I've just come through the army checkpoint. They stopped me, but I showed them my pass. One of the army guys told me the ambulance had gone through ten minutes before."

"You should be with us in a few minutes then," Hellboy said. "We're on Holloway Road, not far from the Royal Northern Hospital. Can you pick us up?"

"Sure. What happened to your car?"

"It got kinda totaled. Long story."

"Are you guys okay?"

"Yeah, we're fine."

From the background Liz faintly heard Abe say, "Speak for yourself," which made her smile, despite the situation. Hellboy went on as if Abe hadn't spoken.

"Our driver's gone to the hospital with a concussion, but he'll be okay. See you in a few minutes."

"Not if I see you first," Liz said.

Even though the ambulance had given Hellboy and Abe the slip, it cheered Liz to think that the three of them would be together for what might turn out to be the grand finale. Sure enough, a few minutes after talking to Hellboy she came across a mangled car on the road, and her two friends standing on the pavement a little way beyond it. Solemnly Hellboy raised a thumb in the traditional hitcher's manner.

Liz eased to a stop beside them and wound down her window. Adopting a southern-belle accent, she asked, "Where you fine-lookin' boys headed?"

"Apocalypse Central," Hellboy said.

"Well, fancy that. That's where I'm headed too. Hop in."

Hellboy climbed in beside her, pushing the seat in the little Metro as far back as it would go to give himself some legroom. Liz noted how gingerly Abe moved as he eased himself into the seat behind her.

"How you doin', Abe?" she asked.

"I've been better," Abe said, "but it's nothing terminal."

They drove on, Hellboy navigating. "So what did you do with the couple at the refuge?" he asked.

"Tied them up, called the cops and left Duggie standing over them with instructions to bash them over the head if they tried to escape. They won't phone ahead and warn the Eye we're coming, if that's what you're worried about."

"*They* might not, but thanks to the cops, the guys in the ambulance now know we're onto them," Hellboy said.

From the back seat, Abe said, "But they only know we know about the refuge, and they must have guessed we'd make that link sooner or later. From what we know now, tonight's visit was clearly going to be their last. They must have decided it was worth taking the risk."

"Won't they worry that we've found out about Ranskill Gardens from the Hipkisses, though?" Liz asked.

"Why should they? As far as they're concerned, we were waiting outside the building for them. There's nothing to make them suspect any of us were inside."

"Even so, they might consider it a possibility that we were—or even that we went back there after we'd lost the ambulance and made the Hipkisses tell us where the HQ is."

"Liz is right," said Hellboy. "If they've got any sense they'll vamoose and set up elsewhere, just to be on the safe side."

Abe was silent for a moment. Then he said, "Maybe . . . but what choice do we have? It's not as if we've got a whole bunch of leads we could be following up. And besides, we're only ten minutes behind the ambulance. They might not have *time* to go anywhere else."

"Plus there's a chance they've already put everything in place for the ceremony," mused Liz. "Charms and stuff, I mean. Stuff they can't redo easily."

"And the house itself might be significant," Abe pointed out. "This campaign has been characterized by occult placement, remember, so locations are important to them."

"In which case, they'll be on their guard," said Hellboy. "Which means that we should be too."

"When are we not?"

Ranskill Gardens was situated in the very heart of Crouch End, in a poorly lit, tree-lined street of what must once have been rather grand Victorian homes. Now the street looked a little shabby, a little bedraggled. A number of the expansive front gardens were overgrown, or uncared for, or strewn with litter, or had simply been concreted over to provide extra parking spaces. Around half the houses had evidently been purchased by landlords or housing corporations and converted into flats. Many of the buildings were in dire need of repair. Looking around as they cruised almost silently into the street, Hellboy saw paint peeling from doors and windowsills, roofs missing slates, drainpipes sagging from walls, stonework blotched with mold. Dotted here and there were houses which were just as grand and well maintained as they must have been in their heyday, but these buildings were few and far between, and stood out like occasional healthy teeth in a mouthful of rotted and broken ones.

Number 44 was even darker than most of its neighbors. Not a single light burned behind its tall, curtained windows. In fact, if the house had not been one of a row, a casual observer might not have known it was there at all. The building lurked behind a pair of huge, twisted trees, which flanked the central gravel path that led to the front door. The hooded streetlamps lining the pavement cast a limp, foglike sheen, which masked the building rather than illuminating it, seeming to drive it even further back into the blackness that enshrouded it.

Liz brought the car to a halt a little way up the road and turned off the engine. Instantly the silence rushed in. If Liz hadn't been so pragmatic she might have described it as an expectant silence, a silence that was waiting for something to happen.

"There's no sign of the ambulance," Hellboy observed.

Abe shrugged. "I'd have been surprised if there had been. They're not going to advertise their whereabouts, are they?"

"I guess," Hellboy said.

"Okay, so how do we approach this?" Liz asked. "Split up or stick together? Go in with all guns blazing or adopt the cautious approach?"

"We stay together and keep it low-key for now," Hellboy said. "Let's find out what's happening in there before we start busting heads."

Abe and Liz nodded. "Around the back?" queried Abe.

"Around the back," Hellboy confirmed.

"Right, then. Let's go and save the world," said Liz.

☠ Chapter 14

The worst thing was the sense of helplessness, of vulnerability. Being trussed and gagged and blindfolded, and knowing that if her captors decided to torture or kill her she would be unable to do a thing about it, had sent Cassie into a cold, shaking panic on several occasions. Each time it had happened her imagination had gone into overdrive, and her craving to move—to run and scream and whirl her arms about—had been so overwhelming that she had begun to hyperventilate; had even, a couple of times, almost passed out.

Whenever the panic came, she had felt her mind dividing into two distinct parts. One part—the part that threatened to overwhelm her—was like a hysterical child, almost insensible with escalating terror. The other part, the part which desperately attempted to rein the child in, was the adult side—calm, rational, practical. It was this part which clung to the hope that even now people were missing her and looking for her, and which told the child that it had to remain calm and patient, and eventually—inevitably—release or rescue would come.

But where would it come *from?* Who even *knew* she was missing?

Hellboy, she thought. Hellboy knew. And Hellboy would come.

She tried to cling to this thought as the hours passed. Tried to cling to it even as the voice of the child grew louder, insisting that Hellboy didn't know or care where she was, that he had far more important things to do than run around looking for her.

She wondered how long she had been here. It seemed like hours since she had regained consciousness. And how long had she been unconscious before that? Twenty minutes? Ten hours? Three days?

And where was she? Still in London? Still in *England?*

All she knew of her surroundings was that they were quiet and cold. And pitch black, of course, because of the blindfold.

What else? She knew that it smelled musty, dank, which might mean that she was belowground, in a cellar perhaps. And she knew that she had woken up tied to a hard wooden chair, and that she was dreadfully thirsty.

And was she hungry too? She supposed she was, in a way. Well, maybe not *hungry* exactly—she was too scared to be hungry—but her stomach was certainly growling through lack of food.

What else? As time went on it was becoming increasingly hard to think beyond her fear and her physical discomfort. Because she had been sitting in the same position for so long—her arms pinioned and trussed behind her, her ankles tied to the legs of the chair—her back was aching, her hands were numb, and her muscles were bunching and cramping. The pain, in fact, was becoming so intolerable that Cassie kept having to fight down bouts of panic caused purely by her inability to stand and stretch, to relieve the grinding throb in her back, the persistent clenching spasms in her arms and legs.

Oh God, how long would this go on for? How long would it be before something *happened?* Although Cassie was dreading what her captors might be planning to do to her, there was a part of her that thought the worst thing of all would simply be to be left here to die slowly in a dark agony of cramped limbs and gnawing hunger.

When it finally came, however, the sound of footsteps somewhere above her head offered her no relief at all. Her head jerked up as a new fear gripped her, and she started to shake once again, her guts turning to water.

The footsteps were muffled, measured, ominous. They moved in a diagonal across the ceiling. And then, shockingly close, a door somewhere to her left clunked and creaked, making her jump.

And suddenly Cassie could hear breathing, the rustle of fabric, the faint sounds of movement. *There was someone in the room with her!* She whimpered, shook with terror, tried vainly to shrink into herself, as the footsteps came slowly across the room towards her.

Getting in was easy. At the back of the house was a conservatory, its glass panels speckled with green mold. The door leading in to it was flimsy. Hellboy simply leaned on it until the lock gave way with a soft crunch.

He went in first, and the others followed. All three had their weapons drawn. The conservatory was full of squashy, lived-in furniture. Well-thumbed magazines about gardening and home improvement were stacked on a small side table. There was a bookcase; a selection of pottery frogs on one windowsill; a cushion in the shape of a cat. It all seemed very ordinary, homely even. Liz hoped they hadn't been sent on a wild goose chase, hoped Jess Hipkiss's fear, which Liz would have sworn was genuine, hadn't been an act, after all.

The door from the conservatory into the kitchen was unlocked. Again, Hellboy went in first. The kitchen was spacious, but unremarkable. There were a couple of rinsed-out milk bottles on the draining board, an up-to-date calendar on the wall with nothing marked on it. A red zero on the display panel of the dishwasher showed that the machine had been switched on earlier and had now completed its cycle. Liz opened a cupboard and saw breakfast cereal—Special K, Weetabix, Cheerios.

Abe glided across to Hellboy, silent as a fish through water, and pointed at a solid-looking door tucked into an alcove in the far right-hand corner of the room.

"I see it," Hellboy whispered. He too could be remarkably quiet when required.

"Should we check it out?" whispered Liz, moving across to join them.

Hellboy considered for a moment. "Let's cover the rest of this floor first, then come back."

They moved into the long, tiled hallway, where a Victorian grandfather clock sonorously ticked away the seconds. There were framed batiks on the walls, original stained glass in the front door through which the insipid light from outside glowed dimly. The tasseled shades around the ceiling lights looked as though they might have been purchased in a Turkish bazaar. A long, high bookcase was stuffed full of paperbacks.

There was nothing to suggest that the house was the center of operations for a group of murderous occultists. On the contrary, it seemed like a friendly house; it possessed an aura of Bohemian academe. Liz could imagine a middle-aged university professor and his wife living here. She could imagine such a couple bringing up a family within these walls, children who had now grown up and moved on, perhaps to university, perhaps to start families for themselves.

Again she wondered whether they had been outwitted, outmaneuvered. She would almost have welcomed an attack by Eye acolytes, because then at least they would have known they were in the right place.

The next room they entered was the sitting room. More big, squashy furniture—the sofa had some sort of throw with an ethnicky print draped over it. In the far corner was a tall wooden sideboard bearing a music system and a shelf of CDs, with another shelf of ornaments above it. In the alcove beside the fireplace was a Victorian washstand with a black marble top. Candles and decorative glassware were arranged on the mantelpiece. The bay windows were curtained floor to ceiling by red velvet drapes.

Hellboy produced his torch from his belt and shone it around. Even the extra light failed to reveal anything untoward. Liz was looking at one of the paintings on the walls—a smeary abstract of reds and blues—when, as if he'd been reading her thoughts, Abe said, "There is *something* unusual."

Liz turned to him. "Oh?"

"There are no photographs. In a house like this there are usually photographs. Children. Grandchildren. Weddings. Graduation ceremonies." He shrugged. "It's just an observation."

Hellboy nodded, his tail weaving lazily behind him like a snake. "Don't think it's a convictable offense, but yeah, you're right, buddy. It *is* a little odd."

He wandered over to the sideboard, the beam of the torch shrinking to a bright circle of light. He peered at the CDs, not quite sure what he was looking for. Demonic chanting perhaps? The Lord's Prayer read backwards? But all he saw was Dvořák and Mendelssohn and Strauss. Nothing unusual; nothing sinister.

He turned, about to suggest they try the door in the corner of the kitchen. But as his torch beam swept round, Liz gasped.

Before Hellboy could ask her what was wrong, she had collapsed. For no discernible reason her legs simply buckled beneath her and she dropped to her knees, throwing up her hands as if to defend herself against a swarm of stinging insects. She grunted and cried out as she twisted and turned, uttering short, sharp sounds of pain and distress.

"What the hell—" Hellboy said, and took a step towards her. Then, on the far side of the room, he saw the same thing happen to Abe.

Elementals, he thought, as the amphibian crumpled, writhing, to the ground. He had seen this kind of thing a couple of times before. It was a psychic bombardment, usually laid as a trap, and it apparently felt as though you were being mercilessly pummeled by invisible assailants. There was no way to defend yourself and no way to fight against it. All you could do, if possible, was vacate the area, put yourself out of attack range.

Hellboy moved forward, with the intention of scooping up his friends and carrying them from the room. But he had taken no more than a step when he felt the first blow on his shoulder. It was hard and sharp, like being whacked with a steel cudgel. Almost immediately it was followed by a second blow, to the back of his head, and then a third, in the small of his back.

Within seconds the bludgeoning assault escalated, and suddenly what felt like vicious blows were raining on Hellboy from all angles, smashing into his ribs and shins, battering down on his head and shoulders. He grunted, instinctively sweeping his arms from side to side, even clenching his fists and punching at thin air. But there was nothing to fight against. And meanwhile the stinging blows continued, seeking out every vulnerable, exposed spot on his body, never letting up for an instant.

Liz and Abe were crumpled heaps on the ground now, both battered into unconsciousness with savage, rapid efficiency. Hellboy was made of sterner stuff, but with no means of defense even he felt himself gradually succumbing to the tumultuous attack. He tottered back and forth like a boxer on the ropes, his hooves stamping the ground. He bellowed in fury, as if that alone would be enough to overcome the pain, or even drive it away.

Little by little, however, he felt consciousness seeping away, his defensive resources breaking down. His thoughts began to fragment, his muscles to weaken. He howled like an animal as his legs gave way and he crashed to the ground. With nothing to fight against, he simply began to hit out at whatever was closest to hand. A footstool was smashed to firewood; a door was ripped from the sideboard in the corner; the expensive music system was destroyed with a single devastating punch.

But none of it made any difference. The physical and mental bombardment continued as remorselessly as ever. Hellboy felt himself dwindling, becoming detached from his beleaguered body. He felt reality narrowing, darkness bleeding in from all sides. He fought to the bitter end, clinging tenaciously to the ever-crumbling cliff of consciousness.

But eventually, inevitably, the cliff gave way, and Hellboy tumbled into darkness . . .

He was chained. That was the first thing he realized when consciousness returned. Even before he opened his eyes he was flexing his aching muscles, trying to break free, but the chains were too plentiful and too heavy duty even for him.

He had been chained before. He had been chained on many occasions, in fact. However, he couldn't honestly say he had ever gotten used to it—on the contrary, it never failed to royally piss him off. It was undignified was what it was. In the movies it was always the giant apes and the dinosaurs which got chained. But Hellboy wasn't an ape. He wasn't a savage, mindless beast.

Grouchy as all hell and spoiling for a fight, he opened his eyes. He was in some sort of cavern or chamber, a vast amphitheater, composed entirely of rock. It was hard to tell whether the chamber had been naturally formed or whether it was a man-made structure, hewn from the earth. Not that it mattered. The only important thing was whether he could get away, whether he could stop the world from turning to crap, and whether his friends were okay.

The last of these questions was answered almost immediately. From somewhere over his left shoulder he heard Abe say, "Hellboy."

He twisted his head. To his surprise, Abe was standing, apparently untethered, on a circular platform of rock, etched with what appeared to be runic symbols. Liz was standing on a similar rock platform beside him—but curiously she appeared to be asleep on her feet, her arms hanging limply, her head drooping forward so that her hair formed a curtain over her face.

"Hey, buddy," Hellboy said, his voice echoing across the cavern, bouncing back from the rock walls, "what's happening?"

Abe glanced down at the platform he was standing on. "We seem to have been restrained by psychic bonds of some sort."

Hellboy looked down at his hands and feet, and was surprised to discover that he wasn't chained, after all. Like Abe, he was simply standing on a flat, raised stone into which a complex pattern of symbols had been carved.

In some ways this was even *worse* than being chained. This was as if someone was trying to make him look stupid. Grunting with effort, he tried to lift a leg, and found that it was impossible. He clenched his stone fist, flexed his muscles, and once again attempted to move his arm. But although he could see the bicep bulging and feel the ache of his straining sinews, he couldn't shift the limb even a fraction of an inch.

"*Dammit!*" he roared, his voice once again echoing around the cavern.

"Don't waste your energy," Abe said. "We're not going anywhere."

Hellboy took a deep breath and had a good look around. The cavern was dominated by a jagged spar of rock, which jutted up from the center of the stone floor. The spar was maybe ten feet wide and thirty feet high and surrounded by an intricate pattern of occult symbols. The now-familiar eye symbol had been carved into the base of the spar itself.

Beyond the spar, set into the circular wall at regular intervals, were a number of arched openings, through which only darkness could be seen. The cavern itself was lit by myriad candles, each one as long and thick as a child's arm. Some of the candles were set into sconces attached to the wall, whereas others were arranged at various points around the chamber, jutting from copper-colored candlesticks, each the height of a tall man. A thin breeze ran through the cavern, causing the flames to flicker, shadows to loom and dwindle in the hollows of the uneven wall.

"I guess that must be the center of operations," Hellboy said, nodding at the spar.

"The lodestone," said Abe.

"Was there anything in Kate's notes about it?"

"Only in a roundabout way. Remember the theory of London being a kind of occult grid, with certain buildings positioned where the grid lines cross?"

Hellboy nodded.

"Well, Kate found various references to a lodestone—a kind of central axis point, which the energy released via the campaign of occult placement would be fed into. She didn't find any hard evidence to support the theory that the lodestone existed, but all the references to it said more or less the same thing—one, that the main mass of the lodestone was beneath the surface of the earth, and two, that it acted as a . . . a storage battery for the energy, which would then be used to fully open the Eye after the final sacrifice."

"Final sacrifice," Hellboy muttered. "I don't like the sound of that." He was thoughtful for a moment, then he said, "So that thing there is pretty much just a gigantic squirt gun, sucking up all the bad juju and then spraying it out." He was silent for a moment. "So what do you reckon would happen if we broke the squirt gun?"

Abe shrugged as best he could. "My guess is the energy would still erupt outwards and cause just as much devastation. The only difference would be that the All-Seeing Eye wouldn't be able to use it and direct it. It would be out of their control."

"But a mad dog is still a mad dog, whether it's on a leash or not," said Hellboy.

Abe nodded.

"In that case I guess we have to cut off the supply at its source?" Hellboy said.

"I guess," said Abe.

"And how do you reckon we do that?"

"I don't have a clue," Abe admitted.

There was a groan from Liz. Slowly she raised her head, her hair falling back from her face. She rotated her jaw, as if to check it was still in place, and murmured, "Must have been a hell of a party." Then she opened her eyes and looked blearily around. "Oh shit."

They quickly filled her in on what little they knew, and on what they had guessed from their surroundings.

As if a door had opened somewhere, the candle flames suddenly flapped like tiny luminous flags, causing shadows to balloon and shrink in the erratic light. Instinctively all three looked towards the arched openings beyond the lodestone. Sure enough, after a few moments, people began to file silently into the cavern, and to take up what appeared to be appointed positions around the stone itself. Apart from one very obvious characteristic, there appeared to be no common link between them. They were of different races, of both sexes, and looking around, Hellboy calculated the age range to be from around twenty to maybe eighty. Perhaps most incongruous was the fact that the people were dressed in their everyday clothes—some were in suits and ties, while others wore jeans or skirts, T-shirts or dresses, sandals, shoes, or sneakers.

The only characteristic which *did* link the people was that, irrespective of sex, age, or ethnicity, they had each shaved their head, and by doing so had revealed that they all possessed a tattoo on their crown, which depicted the now-familiar symbol of the All-Seeing Eye.

Hellboy watched the people, maybe forty or fifty of them, file into the chamber and gather around the lodestone. Not a single one spoke; not a single one caught his eye, or even so much as glanced in his direction.

He cleared his throat, and said loudly, "So the floor show's about to start? About time. I hope there's a comedian. I always like a good comedian."

He was studiously ignored. He breathed a deep, theatrical sigh.

"I gotta tell you, guys," he continued, "that bald head/tattoo combination is *not* a good look. There are so many of you that just don't carry it off. Especially you, madam, in the blue dress."

Hellboy didn't expect to achieve much with his banter. He was simply testing the ground, searching for a chink, a possible opening. But if he couldn't find one, he'd simply settle for making a few of these misguided idiots feel stupid or uncomfortable—or even annoyed at the fact that he was undermining their vile and pompous ceremony.

He had to admit, though, that they were a well-trained bunch. No one batted an eyelid. He had expected the odd glare, or at least a frown or two, but they behaved as if he, Abe, and Liz were not even there. He gave another experimental tug on his invisible bonds, but they were immovable. He racked his brains, trying to work out how he could put a stop to what was about to happen. There must be *something* he could do.

The acolytes had taken their places around the lodestone now, and were peering up at it, silent, motionless, expectant.

"What're you expecting it to do, tell you the meaning of life?" he growled. " 'Cause if you are, then I gotta tell ya, that *so* ain't gonna happen. I've met hundreds of deluded freaks in my time. Thousands, even. And you know what? You people have all got one thing in common. You go away disappointed in the end."

He looked up, sensing further movement around one of the arches—a shifting in the darkness, the impression of someone or something approaching. Next moment he hissed in a breath, his skin tightening with anxiety. Two guys, each sporting the characteristic shaven head and tattoo, had appeared, and between them they were carrying a wooden chair, to which was tied the helpless body of Cassie.

Cassie was gagged, blindfolded, and clearly terrified. Her head was jerking from side to side, as if she anticipated an attack at any moment. Tears had leaked from beneath her blindfold and formed clean tracks down her grimy cheeks. Her muffled whimpers echoed around the cavern walls.

Although he couldn't rescue her, Hellboy knew that at least he could reassure her. "Cassie," he called, "it's me, Hellboy. I've got Abe and Liz with me, so you're not on your own. Thing is, we're prisoners too, so there's not a whole lot we can do just now. But I promise you, first chance I get I'm gonna get you out of here. Understand?"

As soon as Hellboy had started talking, Cassie had become very still. Now she nodded eagerly, and Hellboy was pleased to see the tension go out of her body a little. He only hoped he could follow up on his promise. It was fine to *tell* someone you were going to help them, but it was another to actually do it.

He opened his mouth to speak to her again, but at that moment a man in a gray suit entered the chamber. Like the other acolytes, he had a smoothly shaven head and an eye symbol tattooed on his crown. But it wasn't this which shocked Hellboy into silence, and which caused Liz to gasp as if she had been punched in the stomach.

The new arrival walked over to Hellboy, looked up at him, and smiled. Then he looked over at Liz and Abe and smiled at them, too.

"Surprised to see me?" he asked.

"Nah," said Hellboy dismissively, "always thought you were a creep."

The man in the gray suit was Richard Varley.

☠ CHAPTER 15

Varley laughed. With his shaven head, gray suit, and self-possessed manner, he seemed a different person from the friendly young academic who had befriended them on their arrival in England.

"Is that right?" he said. "Still managed to wind the lot of you round my little finger, though, didn't I? And you know what? It was *so* easy."

Hellboy glanced over his shoulder at Liz. Sounding bored, he said, "Oh, this is the part where he gloats for a while. Just in case I nod off, give me a shout when he's finished, willya?"

"Sure thing," said Liz. She was seething inside, furious that she had spent so much time with Richard without once suspecting that he was responsible for the terror and mayhem they had come here to try to prevent. However, she was damned if she was going to give him the satisfaction of seeing how upset she was. And so she looked him in the eye and snorted, as if she could barely contain her laughter. "You know, Richard, you look like a real dick with that tattoo on your head. If you were gonna become the deranged leader of a crazy cult, couldn't you at least have chosen one that was less dorky?"

Varley looked at her pityingly. "Is that the best you can do, Liz? Make stupid jokes while your world ends?"

Liz shrugged as well as she was able. "Okay then, let's get serious. Tell me about the tattoos. Why the top of the head? Why not somewhere less conspicuous? On the ankle, maybe? Or the left butt cheek?"

THE ALL-SEEING EYE 271

Varley shook his head. "You people really are pathetic."

Hellboy's mind was racing. They were in a perilous situation here, and if he didn't come up with some way to stop what was happening—and soon—then not only he and his friends, but also the city of London and its ten million inhabitants, were going to be well and truly screwed. Like Liz, however, he was determined not to show how rattled he was, and how helpless he felt.

"*We're* pathetic?" he sneered at Varley. "You should take a good look at yourself, buddy! I mean, what do you hope to achieve here, huh? So you're gonna open the Eye and end the world? Well, whoopee-doo! That'll be a fun day out for everyone! And what do you think's gonna happen to *you* when all hell breaks loose? You think the demons and monsters and boogeymen are gonna shake your hand and carry you around the streets and make you their little monkey king?"

Varley scoffed. "You know so little."

"I might not know much," Hellboy said, "but compared to you I'm the all-time *Jeopardy!* champion. I've been around a long time, saved the world once or twice, and seen a whole lot of tin-pot cults like this one come and go. And if there's one thing I've learned over the years, it's that regular folk and denizens of hell . . . well, they just don't mix. See, you might think you *like* the idea of ripping this imperfect world apart and starting all over again, or even of being some kinda ruler over chaos, but when it comes right down to it, it just ain't practical. The big bugaboos down there don't give a spit about you. You're just a means to an end for them. Soon as you open the box, they'll be out of there like an express train, and they'll mow you down soon as look at you. So my advice is this: pack up, go home, grow some hair. Otherwise—and you mark my words—you'll be opening up a whole world of hurt. Not for the people out there, but for yourselves. Believe me, I *know*."

This was a long speech for Hellboy, and the echoes of his voice rang out around the cavern. Varley looked at him as though he were

something curious and strange and new. Then he turned to his acolytes and raised his arms.

"The last of the stolen souls have been accepted by the Infinite," he cried. "The twelve great Locks of London have been
breached, and soon the Eye will open once more, bringing with it a
glorious new dominion. Father will turn against son, friend against
friend, neighbor against neighbor. We, my children, are the openers
of the way. We will walk in the chaos. We will stand at the doorway
between the two worlds, and neither shall exist without us. Soon
all states, all realities, will be ours to command. We are the key. We
shall become all powerful."

"Yeah," said Hellboy dryly, cutting in on his words, "that's what
they all say."

Abe looked almost sad. "You're an intelligent man, Richard.
Don't you realize how empty those words sound? They're an en-
ticement, that's all. They don't *mean* anything."

"Abe's right," Liz shouted. "If you know what's good for you,
Richard, stop this now. You're nothing but a little kid who's been
offered candy by a stranger. The car door's open and the engine's
running, but you don't have to get in. There's still time to turn
around and go home."

Varley spun and looked at each of them, his eyes blank, face
expressionless. He fixed on Hellboy, and his lips curled back in a
clench-toothed grin.

"When the Eye opens, I'm going to make you my slave," he
said. "You'll follow me around like a little dog and do exactly as I
tell you. These other two are nothing. I'll leave them here to rot in
the darkness."

Liz glared at him. She was gripped by fury and desperation, but
again she tried not to show it. In a clipped voice she said, "That's
not gonna happen, Richard. We're not gonna *let* that happen."

"You have no choice," Richard said blithely. He turned his back
on them and walked unhurriedly towards the lodestone, a couple of

his followers moving aside to let him through the wide circle they had formed around it. Directly in front of the stone, a few inches higher than the rock floor, was a circular platform, similar to the ones on which Hellboy, Abe, and Liz were standing. Cassie's chair had been set down on the platform. As she heard Varley's footsteps tapping across the stone towards her, she hunched up her shoulders and drew back, like a turtle attempting to retreat into its shell.

Varley came to a halt just in front of Cassie, looking down at her. He stood there for perhaps five seconds, and then slowly he raised his right arm, holding his hand out to his side. Immediately a stocky man stepped forward out of the circle, reaching into his black jacket as he did so. He drew a cleaver from an inner pocket, came forward, and placed it in Varley's outstretched hand. Then he walked calmly back to rejoin the circle.

The blade of the cleaver flashed yellow in the candlelight. Gritting his teeth, Hellboy began to struggle against his invisible bonds once more, his movements more frantic now, shoulder muscles bulging beneath his duster, the tendons in his neck standing out like cables under his skin.

"Don't touch her, Varley!" he bellowed. "If you hurt her, I swear I'll kill you."

Varley ignored him. Cassie was whimpering again now, sensing that something terrible was about to happen. Savoring the moment, Varley raised the cleaver above his head.

"Accept this final sacrifice!" he bellowed.

"*Richard, no!*" Liz screamed.

"*Varley!*" roared Hellboy.

The cleaver flashed down.

Cassie's blood sprayed across the stone.

☠ CHAPTER 16

"*No!*" howled Hellboy, the word booming around the cavern, chasing echoes of itself. He continued to strain against his bonds, but it was already too late. Though still tethered, Cassie's body was jerking so violently as the lifeblood jetted out of her that the chair was jumping and scraping on the stone platform. The savage blow from the cleaver had not only slashed open her throat, it had almost severed her head. Blood had erupted from her jugular in an arterial spray, most of it spattering onto the lodestone and running down over the eye symbol. Some of the blood had arced over the acolytes gathered in a circle around the stone, but not one of them had broken rank, not even when blood had rained down on their shaven heads and their shoulders, staining their clothes.

Varley stood facing the stone, his hands raised as if in triumph. Blood was running down the blade and handle of the cleaver, and onto the sleeve of his expensive gray suit, but he didn't seem to care. Enraptured, he turned and looked into Hellboy's anguished face, his eyes shining with a fanatical zeal.

"The Eye opens," he breathed.

"I'm going to kill you," Hellboy muttered, and the cold intent in his voice made even Abe shiver. "Whatever it takes, Varley, I am going to take you apart piece by piece."

This time, however, Varley didn't even seem to hear him. He was in a world of his own. He turned back to his acolytes.

"Prepare yourselves, brothers and sisters," he cried. "Prepare yourselves to accept the infinite!"

The acolytes leaned forward, as if bowing to him. Hellboy, too, hung his head, though for entirely different reasons. At that moment he felt sickened, wretched, exhausted. He remembered the promise he had made to Cassie just minutes before, how he had told her he would get her out of here. He remembered meeting her that morning, the bloom of life in her cheeks, the flash of intelligence and humor in her green eyes. He remembered how Luigi, owner of the Bagel Palace, had told her that she was beautiful, that she lit up his life like a lantern.

He raised his head, which felt heavy as an anvil, and glanced over his shoulder. Liz looked stricken, her face deathly pale.

"Why didn't you burn him?" Hellboy said hoarsely. "Why didn't you roast the bastard?"

Liz's horrified gaze flickered over to him. She shook her head. Her mouth moved silently for a moment, trying to form words, before she spoke.

"I couldn't," she all but sobbed. "I tried, HB, I really did, but . . . I just couldn't. This damn spell . . ."

"Look at the lodestone," said Abe.

Hellboy forced himself to turn back. At first he could see nothing but Cassie's mutilated body, and then he saw that the eye symbol carved into the stone was beginning to glow with a pearly, iridescent light. Even as he watched, the light grew brighter; it seemed alive somehow, sinuous and snakelike.

Varley laughed and threw the cleaver almost carelessly to one side, not even bothering to look as it skidded across the stone with a metallic clatter. Just as carelessly he dragged Cassie's chair from the front of the stone and shoved it aside. Hellboy clenched his teeth as the chair toppled over, as her head smashed against the ground. He knew she was dead, that nothing could hurt her now, but the callousness of Varley's action, the way he treated her as if she were nothing but garbage that was in his way, caused the blood to boil in his veins.

The eye symbol was now almost too bright to look at. The light was radiating outwards, strands of it curling around the chamber, probing and exploring, as if searching for something. It crawled and looped around the acolytes, who shuddered and jerked at its touch. It was as if the multiple light strands were ropes of living electricity, delivering shock after stinging shock.

Hellboy watched as the light slithered over the face of a pretty girl about Cassie's age. The girl's eyes were full of pain and her mouth was open in a cry she couldn't expel. Her body was going into spasm, alternately rigid, then slack. It made him think of a fish in a net, desperate to break free, but barely able to move. He felt no sympathy for her. As far as he was concerned, these people deserved whatever was coming to them. The light prodded at the girl's eyes, making her gasp in agony, and then it climbed higher, across her forehead, over her scalp.

Finally it found the eye tattoo, and all at once it seemed to come alive. It reminded Hellboy of someone who has been blundering about in a dark room suddenly finding the light switch. It latched onto the tattoo and appeared to be instantly absorbed into it, causing the symbol to blaze as brightly as the one on the lodestone. At this new violation, the girl's eyes stretched wide and her mouth opened in a soundless scream. Her body jerked violently, like a puppet.

The rope of light that had clamped itself to the girl's head now seemed to send out a pulse, a signal. As if a nest of sleepy vipers had suddenly become aware of the potential victims in their midst, the light strands rose up en masse. They hovered for a moment, and then swooped down, striking at the acolytes, clamping themselves to the tattoos on their shaven heads.

The acolytes writhed and twisted, but to no avail. Some managed to scream or whimper or make strangled choking sounds,

THE ALL-SEEING EYE 277

though most were clearly beyond that, their vocal cords frozen with the excruciating torment they were being forced to endure.

Varley seemed unconcerned by the suffering of his followers. "Accept the infinite, brothers and sisters," he called, his voice ricocheting around the chamber.

"It's killing them, you moron," Hellboy snarled. "Can't you see that?"

Still Varley ignored him. He stood in front of the lodestone, in a pool of Cassie's blood, hands extended as if in welcome, smiling slightly. He looked utterly relaxed, more than ready to embrace the power that was causing his followers such distress.

And then, as if at some unspoken command, the tendrils of light suddenly and simultaneously shot inwards, engulfing Varley's body in a blazing sphere of effulgence. The tendrils were almost as thin and straight as laser beams, though they more closely resembled the spokes of a wheel with Varley at its hub. The self-styled sangoma of the All-Seeing Eye stood with his arms upraised, a man made of fire and light. He was grinning widely, bathing in the radiance.

His triumph did not last long.

Many of his followers were on their knees now, or had simply collapsed altogether, their bodies convulsing. For perhaps fifteen seconds Varley continued to grin as he bathed in the light, his eyes half closed, like someone luxuriating beneath a long, hot shower.

Then Liz said, "Jeez, look at their heads." But Hellboy had already seen what was happening. The heads of the acolytes were swelling like balloons. Some were even beginning to split, leaking blood and fluid.

Suddenly the skull of a large black woman in a floral-print dress erupted outwards, as if a bomb had gone off in her cranium. Splinters of bone and lumps of brain matter spattered across the floor. The instant it happened the thread of light sprang from the dead woman like a length of released elastic and added itself to the light massing around Varley.

Within seconds more of the acolytes were dead, their brains and skulls simply bursting, unable to withstand the pressure of the energy that was consuming them. Soon the stone floor of the cavern was littered with corpses and awash with blood. Each time an acolyte died, the attendant thread of light snapped away from the lifeless body like a vacating parasite and relocated to the ever-brightening nimbus enveloping Varley.

Indeed, the light surrounding the leader of the All-Seeing Eye had now intensified to such an extent that he had become little more than a vague fiery outline in its center. Even so, Hellboy could see enough to tell that Varley was no longer smiling. Instead his face looked haggard, his mouth yawning open in a silent, agonized scream. His hands were no longer raised, but moving like those of a man underwater, trying to fend off an attack from a voracious marine predator.

"No," he moaned suddenly, his head thrashing from side to side, and even in that single word Hellboy could hear the terrible strain he was under. "No, I . . . control you . . . I control . . ."

All at once Varley's body went rigid. His head snapped back, as if he had been punched on the jaw.

"I think it's showing him who's boss," Liz said grimly.

"And I think that now might be a good time to say I told you so," Hellboy rumbled.

"Far be it from me to sound a note of false hope here, guys," said Liz, "but I think I can move a little."

Abe nodded. "Me too. The holding charm is breaking down."

In front of them, Varley was not merely dying, but diminishing, his body fragmenting as the light picked it apart. He did not scream in pain as he died, or rant in anger, or beg for mercy; neither did he twist or writhe or struggle. Instead he went quietly, seeming simply to let go, to fade away. Hellboy was not sorry that the man who had slaughtered Cassie was dead, but he felt cheated that he himself had had no hand in it.

"I know what you're thinking," Abe said.

Hellboy scowled. "Is that so?"

Abe said softly, "If you'd have killed him, Hellboy, you'd never have been able to live with yourself."

"You must think I'm a better guy than I am," Hellboy muttered.

Abe shook his head. "I don't think so," he said simply.

There was hardly anything left of Varley now. He had been reduced to an indistinct core of darkness in the midst of the blazing ball of energy. As the three of them watched, even that was consumed, until there was nothing left but light, which began to swirl and writhe and probe around the cavern once more, restless and without direction.

Hellboy found he was finally able to step down off the stone platform. As the feeling flooded back into his body, he hunched his stiff shoulders and stamped his hoofed feet on the ground.

Liz came up beside him and touched him gently on the arm. "Sorry about Cassie," she said.

"Yeah," said Hellboy gruffly, "me too."

"So . . . what happens now?"

Hellboy looked at the light swirling around the chamber like a mass of tangled ghosts. "Anyone got a big net?"

"Yeah, I thought this stuff'd be . . . I dunno . . . more impressive somehow," said Liz. "I thought it would erupt out of the earth like molten lava or something."

"I think what we're seeing here is just a drop in the ocean," Abe said. "The lodestone is only a *tap* for the mains. Once the tap has been turned on . . ." his voice trailed off.

Liz sighed. "Yeah, I guess I kinda knew that." She pointed upwards. "The faucets are all up there, right? All those little breaches we saw this afternoon? I guess they're going to widen, aren't they?"

Abe nodded. " 'Fraid so."

Liz moved towards the lodestone, carefully stepping over the strewn bodies of the acolytes, avoiding the pools of blood and clots of brain matter.

"So how do we turn the tap off?" she asked.

"I don't know if we can," said Abe.

As the two of them examined the lodestone, Hellboy stayed where he was, peering up at the still-swirling light suspiciously. He had the feeling it was circling him like a shark, sizing him up. He watched as it coagulated in one area, close to the ceiling. After a moment it extended a tentative tendril in his direction.

"Er . . . guys," he said.

Before he could say anything else, the light swooped down at him. Hellboy swore as it coiled around his body, burning like acid through his physical and mental defenses. He felt it pouring into his mind, overhauling his thoughts. The sheer physical intensity of the assault was so immense that he could easily comprehend how the less-robust bodies of the acolytes had simply ruptured under the pressure.

Even Hellboy was not sure he had ever felt pain *quite* like this. It was crippling, breath snatching, all encompassing. It was like having steel hooks embedded in his brain, like liquid fire pouring through his veins. It was only sheer force of will that stopped his legs from buckling beneath him, that prevented him from retreating to a tiny, dark place within himself and succumbing instantly. He gritted his teeth and roared and fought back and thought about Cassie, who had died in order that this abomination could be released into the world.

But, hard as he fought, Hellboy knew deep down that it would not be enough. The light was vast and ancient and far more powerful than he was. His only faint chance of defeating it was to attack it at its source—to switch off the tap, as Abe had said.

But how?

Liz floated into his field of vision. Instantly Hellboy felt the impulses and urges of the thing inside him, felt its desire to hurt her, to possess her, to feed on her suffering, to drain her dry.

"*Go!*" he roared, his voice already roughened by the light's influence. "*You and Abe go now, before I . . . before it makes me . . . hurt you . . .*"

"We're not leaving you," Liz said.

"*GO!*" Hellboy bellowed at her.

He waved his massive right hand in a gesture of dismissal. Through the cracks and grooves in the red stone he saw the swirling, fiery light pouring out of him. And all at once, as though for a split second he had glimpsed the heart of the light itself, he knew what he had to do.

He lurched up to the lodestone, forcing himself to plant one hoof in front of the other. With each step, he felt the light trying to drag him back, trying to gain mastery over the mental impulses that powered his body.

Eventually, however, he was standing on the spot where Varley had been devoured just minutes before. Gathering his resources, forcing his body to move in the way *he* wanted it to move, he drew back the clenched fist of his stone hand, and then pistoned it forward, as hard as he could, into the floor.

The sharp, almost musical clash of rock against rock reverberated around the cavern. Fighting every inch of the way against the force that was trying to subsume his mind, he drew back his fist and smashed it into the floor a second time.

This time the rock gave a little where his fist impacted with it, and a thread of a crack appeared. Hellboy punched again, and the crack widened and spread; blood began to run down into it.

He hit the floor a fourth time, and on this occasion his fist smashed right through, encountering nothing on the other side but a cold subterranean breeze. As he drew back his hand for another punch, a sizable plug of rock on the edge of the small hole broke loose, and with a grating squeal it fell downwards, leaving Hellboy peering into a jagged triangle of darkness.

Vaguely he heard Liz's voice once more. It sounded like a faint radio signal from some unimaginably distant land, reaching him through a furious swarm of static.

"Oh my God, Abe, look," she was shouting. "Look at what he's doing!" He sensed her coming closer, yelling at him, though even now she still seemed a long way away.

"Stop, HB! If you can hear me, *stop this right now!* This floor isn't solid. It's like a . . . a crust, or a bridge, or something. If you weaken it any more, it'll collapse, and we'll all fall. We'll all *die. Do you understand?*"

Hellboy *did* understand. Despite appearances to the contrary, he knew exactly what he was doing. He dragged his head up, aware that the light was pouring like fire out of his mouth and eyes, that to her he must look utterly possessed.

"*Go!*" he roared again. His voice emerged as a gurgling, tortured parody of itself, but he hoped she would realize that the words were still his. "*You and Abe . . . get out of here . . . NOW!*"

Through his burning, swimming vision, he saw her staring at him, anguished and uncertain. Then Abe appeared by her side and took her arm. "Come on," Hellboy heard him say. "Let's do as he says."

Liz did not cry often, but Hellboy could see she was fighting back tears. "But we can't just leave him," she wailed. "He doesn't know what he's doing."

Abe nodded. "I think he does. I think he's still in there somewhere, and I think he's doing the only thing he can."

Liz looked ready to protest further, but she had been in enough desperate situations with him and Abe to know that the one thing you *didn't* do when the shit hit the fan was stand there arguing. So instead she simply glared at Hellboy, and shouted angrily, "Don't you dare die, you big idiot!"

Then she and Abe were gone. One minute there, the next not, as if they had simply disappeared.

Hellboy returned to his task. Remorselessly he drew back his stone fist and pummeled the floor a fifth time, and then a sixth. More rock broke away and fell into the chasm. The darkness within the widening hole was so impenetrable that if it hadn't been for the stagnant flow of air gouting up like a foul exhalation of long-held breath, Hellboy might have believed it was nothingness.

He hit the floor again. Again. Under constant siege from the light, he felt himself diminishing with each blow, reduced to a tiny knot of resistance. He was operating almost on instinct now. He hit the floor again. Again. Again. More cracks appeared, zigzagging across the floor. More rubble broke away and toppled into the depthless dark. Just another few blows, he thought, and the hole would be wide enough to accommodate his massive body. Trying to ignore the burning agony of the light scrabbling frantically at his thoughts, he pulled back his fist and brought it smashing down once more.

With shocking suddenness the floor gave way beneath him.

Spider-webbed with cracks, all at once it simply caved in with a great rumbling crash, and a split second later Hellboy was falling into darkness. His body twisted and turned as he fell, a red speck among the rain of tumbling rock and human cadavers. With his extra weight, he quickly outpaced the corpses of the acolytes, though he couldn't outpace the larger chunks of rock, many of which collided with his spinning body on the way down, bouncing off his head, his shoulders, his back.

He fell for a long time—far longer than he'd ever fallen before. He didn't exactly feel scared as he tumbled through the darkness, though he did feel apprehensive. Tough as he was, Hellboy didn't *enjoy* pain, and landing after a long fall was never much fun. Plus he knew that if he didn't manage to get out of the way almost as soon as he hit bottom, he would quickly find himself caught in a very nasty downpour of rocks and human remains.

Although this was not the best situation in which he had ever found himself, at least there was *one* positive aspect to Hellboy's descent. As soon as the floor had given way, he had felt the light sliding out of him, vacating his body. Maybe it was reluctant to return to the darkness in which it had been trapped for so long, or maybe it had simply given him up for dead as soon as he had started to fall. Either way, Hellboy was grateful that the light had decided he would no longer make a suitable host. At least it would be one less battle to fight.

His duster billowed around him as he plummeted downwards, falling end over end with no immediate prospect of landing. Sharp-edged boulders slammed into him. He was just wondering whether Liz and Abe had gotten out okay, and whether they were having an even tougher time up top than he was down here, when the ground rushed up to meet him.

He didn't see it, of course, or even sense that it was coming. One second he was simply falling through the air and the next he wasn't. As expected, the impact was not pleasant.

"Aw, crap," he moaned. He was hurting all over. Feeling as though he had just been in a weeklong fistfight with an opponent as tough as he was, he forced himself to stand and broke into a staggering run. He had no destination in mind, or even any idea of what lay ahead of him. His main priority was simply to get out of the way of all the stuff that, sooner or later, would be falling to earth in his wake.

Some of the heavier rocks were already landing around him, hitting the ground hard enough to partially bury themselves. For maybe ten seconds he heard big chunks of rock landing behind and around and even in front of him. And then, in addition to the rocks, he heard softer things beginning to land, each one making a sound like a vast rubbery bag of liquid bursting open as it hit the ground. Yet although he was splashed a couple of times, it seemed that *someone* at least was smiling on him tonight, because within a few seconds Hellboy was out of the danger zone, having been struck by nothing worse than a few fist-sized chunks of falling debris.

He stopped, listening to the pattering sounds of the stuff still falling behind him, and leaned forward, hands on knees, to take a breather. He couldn't pinpoint a single part of his body, either inside or out, that was currently without pain. Man, this had been a bruising assignment. Not that he was complaining. He might bitch about the bumps and bruises occasionally—and was frequently ribbed by Liz and Abe for doing so—but he never let them slow him down. He had never encountered a pain yet that stopped him from doing his job.

Eventually he straightened up, wincing, and patted the pouch on his belt which contained his torch. He half expected to hear the loose jangle of shattered metal and plastic, but to his surprise it seemed okay. He unclipped the pouch, drew the torch out, and thumbed the switch. Nothing happened. "Crap," he murmured, and gave the torch an experimental shake—and suddenly a bright beam of light flared from it, illuminating the area around him.

Hellboy flashed the torch in every direction, getting his bearings. He didn't linger on what was behind him; the mass of pulverized corpses was not pretty. With no ceiling above him, and whatever walls might exist to his left and right beyond the range of the beam, he could almost have believed he was outside. It was only the close air and the dank, earthy smell that ruined the illusion that he was standing on a huge plain or in a vast desert beneath a starless sky, with nothing to see but the base of a colossal mountain some twenty or thirty meters ahead of him.

He wondered briefly whether he had fallen through some transdimensional gateway or whether this was simply some vast cavern, miles and miles beneath the streets of London, far below the tube tunnels and the bomb shelters. Then he pushed the thought aside, thinking that it didn't much matter either way, and walked across to the mountain. He reached out and placed the palm of his stone hand on its bare vertical surface. It was cold, almost freezing to the touch. He looked left and right, wondering how long it would take him to walk all the way round. Considering the distance he had fallen, he guessed it would take hours, maybe days. The circumference must stretch for so many miles that he probably wouldn't even get the sense he was walking in a circle.

Hellboy supposed that the peak—the lodestone—must jut out at an oblique angle, otherwise when he had fallen he would surely have bounced off the sides of the mountain as it widened further down. He knew that the source of the energy was down here, that the true Eye from which all things flowed was somewhere in this vicinity. He had gleaned this from the energy itself, when it had tried, and almost succeeded, in subjugating him. When it had touched his mind—or rather, when it had torn into his mind, trying to strip his thoughts away—it had been unable to avoid unwittingly revealing a little of itself, a tantalizing glimpse of its origins, its nature, its unceasing and voracious hunger.

He closed his eyes and placed his stone hand on the rock face once more, trying to tap back into the burning memory of the moment when the energy had touched his mind and briefly revealed itself to him. Abe would have approved, he thought wryly. His friend was always encouraging him to get more in touch with his spiritual side.

Deep in his mind, lodged there like stubborn shreds of meat jammed between his back teeth, Hellboy was aware of a confusing jumble of images. He went deeper, down to where the pain was. He saw something blue—an egg, a crystal . . . *an eye!* And he had the sense of a journey, of being released from the eye, of soaring up through the empty darkness and into a world full of busy thoughts, raw emotions, the juicy and delicious pulse of life . . .

When he came to, his head spinning, he was walking around the base of the mountain. It was slightly disconcerting at first. He felt like a puppet, in thrall to thoughts that were not his own.

But then he realized he was simply following the energy to its heart, that he was being drawn to the source of the entity that had tried to possess him. It was an instinctive thing, his body merely obeying the instructions of his subconscious mind. And so he kept going, through the silence, and the heavy, dank darkness, his torch beam lighting the way.

He had been walking for maybe fifteen minutes when he came across the door. It was simply carved into the side of the mountain, an arch whose apex was twice the height that he was. The now-familiar sign of the eye had been gouged into the rock. There was no handle, no bell push, nothing. Hellboy gave the door an experimental shove. It seemed immovable, almost as if it had been drawn onto the rock rather than cut from it. He put his shoulder to it and pushed harder. It didn't budge.

"Open sesame?" he muttered hopefully, then he banged on the door, the clash of rock on rock spiraling up through the blackness. Finally he growled, "Aw, to hell with this," and drawing back his stone fist once again he slammed it directly into the center of the eye.

Most of the symbol imploded in a powdery mass of rubble. Cracks zigzagged out from it in all directions. Hellboy clenched his jaw and kept on punching, and although the muscles at the top of his right arm and across his shoulders hurt like hell, he didn't stop until he had punched out a hole large enough for him to step through.

Dust sifted down through the beam of his torch as he looked around. He was in a tunnel, high and wide enough to drive a tank through. The walls of the tunnel were not smooth, and the ceiling was jagged, uneven. He shone his torch ahead, but darkness swallowed the beam with no end of the tunnel in sight.

He began to walk. His surroundings didn't change much. He tramped confidently, unerringly, through a whole maze of tunnels, sometimes turning right, sometimes left, sometimes taking the tunnel that sloped downwards, and sometimes the one that required him to climb a slight incline before it leveled out.

Some of the tunnels had water dripping from the ceiling or trickling down the walls, but most were dry. Occasionally the tunnels would widen out before narrowing again, but never did they become any narrower or lower than the one he had started out from.

After about half an hour the batteries in Hellboy's torch started to fade, so he replaced them. It always bugged him in movies when FBI agents were plunged into darkness because their torch batteries had died on them. In real life, properly trained agents always carried spares; stuff like this was never left to chance.

By the time he came across the second door he knew he had traveled deep into the heart of the mountain. He knew too that if the energy had not touched his mind just for that split second he would never have found this place.

The second door was similar to the first—maybe not quite as high and wide, but pretty much the same shape, and once again bearing the telltale eye symbol. Switching the torch from his right hand to his left, Hellboy didn't even bother with the preliminaries this time. Ignoring the stiffening pain in his joints and muscles, he began to punch with just as much gusto and intent as ever. As before, the door cracked and crumbled and eventually caved in beneath his assault. Wafting stone dust out of his way, Hellboy stepped through the gap.

He found himself in a vast space, a natural cathedral. Stalactites and stalagmites, both hundreds of feet in length, had stretched to join in the middle, forming colossal pillars. The walls glittered with phosphorescence, illuminating the chamber to such an extent that Hellboy was able to put his torch away. Somewhere ahead of him, in the gloom and the shadows, something was glowing with a soft blue light.

He moved forward, the clack of his hooves echoing around him. As he neared the blue glow, the shadows seemed to recede, like a series of tattered veils drawing back to reveal the scene ahead.

The blue glow was coming from a huge crystal that was set into the forehead of a black statue standing in the center of the cavern. The statue was maybe thirty feet tall, and looked like a mummified corpse made massive and twisted by layer upon accumulated layer of glistening, coal-colored rock. The thing's face was skeletal, its mouth, full of jutting black teeth, yawning open in an endless, silent scream. Its third, glowing eye (*the Devil's Eye*, he remembered Abe saying over lunch at the Three Cups) was in marked contrast to the two beneath it, which were shriveled in deep sockets. Bulging growths of rock on the statue's limbs and torso made it seem malformed, elephantine. Corkscrewing stalagmites of rock stuck up from its misshapen head like a pair of strange, crooked horns.

Hellboy approached the statue slowly, wary of traps. "Well, aren't you a handsome devil?" he murmured softly.

It was only then he noticed the figures that were flanking the statue. Like their leader, they were black and misshapen, and the reason he had not noticed them immediately was because each was in a crouching position, and at first glance had resembled nothing but a massed formation of glittering black rocks. Now, Hellboy realized he had seen one of these creatures before. A few days ago, in the tunnels of the London Underground. And that one had been very much alive!

When the B.P.R.D. team had gone down into the tunnels to talk to the creature after Hellboy's initial contact with it, they had not been able to find it. The assumption had been that it had returned to whatever realm it had appeared from. Hellboy now recalled what the creature had said to him, though. It had said that it had been human once. It had said that "they" had looked into the Eye and slept. Hellboy looked around at the ranks of glittering black statues and could only wonder what decadeslong dreams the original members of the All-Seeing Eye had had.

He turned his attention back to the leader, to the vast creature bearing the Devil's Eye itself. He remembered what Abe had told him about the founder of the All-Seeing Eye, Maximus Leith—about how he had mysteriously disappeared one day, leaving all his worldly possessions behind.

"Well, I guess the cops can finally call off the search, huh, Maximus?" he said softly.

He stepped forward, clenching his stone fist . . . but suddenly he remembered something else Abe had said during that interrupted lunch in the Three Cups. He had said, "If you fall into the Devil's Eye, you become his forever." Well, Hellboy *had* fallen, but he doubted whether the words had been meant so literally. Leith and his followers had fallen too, but they had fallen in a different way—by looking *into* the Eye, by opening themselves up to it mentally and physically.

Hellboy scowled. He was itching to smash the Eye, to drive his fist right into the center of the damn thing, but all at once it occurred to him that maybe that was exactly what it *wanted* him to do. And that maybe it wouldn't therefore be such a good idea to bring the Eye and the so-called Hand of Doom together.

With a reluctant sigh, he looked around for a suitable rock with which to do the job. He spotted one behind him, a few meters away, and clomped over to pick it up. It was about the size of his head, and although it wasn't particularly heavy, it was an awkward-enough shape that he had to use both hands. He bent down with a groan, his muscles aching, lifted the rock, straightened, turned.

"Oh, crap," he said wearily.

The black stone figures were slowly unfurling. They made a sound as they did so, their joints squeaking and clicking, as if they hadn't been used in a long time. Their mostly empty eye sockets were now lambent with the same iridescent light that had almost overwhelmed Hellboy. Dropping the rock, Hellboy spread his hands.

"Come on, guys, I'm sure we can talk about this," he said.

They came for him, grinding and creaking, slowly at first but moving more easily with each step. Knowing he had no choice,

Hellboy stomped forward to meet them. He had fought big guys before, and knew that he could punch a lot harder than most of them. Problem here, though, was sheer weight of numbers. Lumbering brutes though they were, there was no way of dodging all the sledgehammer blows that he felt sure Leith's followers would throw in his direction.

As soon as the stone giants came within range, Hellboy started swinging. He took a few of them out—he drove his fist right through the chest of one, shattering the creature's ossified heart, and smashed the jaw clean off another—but the rest surrounded him like a gang in a schoolyard and methodically began to pummel his already tenderized body.

He fought bravely, but little by little the guardians bore him down. He took blow after blow, and eventually his legs buckled under the incessant barrage and he hit the deck. Even then, however, he continued to fight. As the guardians crowded round him, he struck out at the forest of legs, attempting to break kneecaps, splinter shin bones. But as the blows continued to rain down on his head and shoulders, his thoughts began to swim. He tried to concentrate on what mattered—avenging Cassie, saving the world—but at last a particularly savage blow caught him behind the ear and he slumped forward onto his hands and knees. He roared his defiance, but it was not enough to prevent his arms giving way, his face hitting the rock floor.

He thought again of Liz, of Abe, of Cassie. He thought of all the people he was letting down. He couldn't lose now. He *couldn't*. But even as that thought burned fiercely inside him, he was aware of consciousness slipping away, of everything going black . . .

And then suddenly he realized that the blows *had* stopped. He blinked as consciousness slowly returned. Yes, it was true. The blows really had stopped. And yet somewhere he could still hear the fight continuing, could still hear the clash of blows, the sharp crunch of rock on rock.

With an enormous effort he raised his head. It felt massive and misshapen, and far too heavy for his neck muscles. He looked around, but at first he could see nothing except a confused shimmer; the vague impression of massive black shapes moving in front of him; a wavering light, like a blue ghost in the darkness.

He focused on the ghost, and little by little the glow from it seemed to expand, to illuminate and clarify its surroundings. He realized that the "ghost" was in fact the Devil's Eye, which blazed in the center of Leith's forehead. But what was astonishing was not that Leith had creaked into life like his followers, but that he was currently caroming his way through them, shattering heads and crushing limbs, sending huge black bodies careering and collapsing this way and that.

He had help too. Another of the rock creatures was standing shoulder to shoulder with Leith, battling his fellow guardians. Hellboy peered hard at the creature. Was it the same one he had spoken to in the tube tunnel, the one that had first told him about the All-Seeing Eye? He wasn't absolutely certain, but he thought that perhaps it was.

Through sheer force of will, his teeth clenched against the pain, Hellboy pushed himself first into a sitting position, and then into a standing one. He swayed a moment, his vision blurring. He might hurt more than he could remember hurting before, but as long as he could stand and move and punch, he would do whatever he could to carry out his mission. And so he let out a battle cry that seemed—temporarily, at least—to make the pain and stiffness flow out of his limbs, and he plunged into the fray once more, his stone fist pistoning forward, smashing into black rock that had once been sinew and flesh.

Side by side, Hellboy, Leith, and the tube creature battered their opponents to defeat. They made a good team, Leith and his acolyte providing the brawn, Hellboy moving in to finish off combatants that were already reeling from his unlikely partners' demolition-ball blows. Though Hellboy was quick and lithe compared to his opponents, he was aware that he was operating purely on adrenaline. Tough as he was, if he came out of this one alive he doubted he'd be able to move for at least a week afterwards.

What quickly became apparent was that the stone figures were reluctant to fight their leader with the same relentless force that they had defended the Eye against Hellboy. Evidently they were torn between defending themselves against an outright aggressor and protecting the very artifact that had imprisoned them. As a consequence, Hellboy, Leith, and the tube creature were able to press home their advantage, to cut a swathe through the guardians. Hellboy might almost have felt sorry for his opponents if they hadn't already inflicted so much pain on him, and if there hadn't been so much at stake.

Although the guardians were reluctant to inflict damage on their leader, the same could not be said of their fellow guardian, who had briefly found himself back in the world from which he had been plucked a century before, and who as a result of that had perhaps rediscovered a little of his humanity. Peripherally Hellboy was aware of the tube creature suddenly crashing to the ground under a rain of blows, and of subsequently being smashed into fragments until he stopped moving. He silently wished his fallen comrade farewell even as he himself continued to wade forward, following up the groundwork established by Leith. Using this tactic, Hellboy and Leith slowly, methodically overcame their opponents, the massive stone figures falling away until finally Hellboy and his unlikely ally were the only ones left standing.

In the sudden silence that marked the aftermath of battle, Hellboy looked round at the fallen enemy, their broken bodies strewn across the floor of the chamber. It was only now that he had a chance to wonder why Leith had helped him, and what would happen next. Because despite their alliance, Hellboy's objective had not changed—he was still determined to smash the Eye and destroy the energy that even now could be tearing London apart.

He stepped back from Leith, and once again looked into the tortured, skeletal face. As his eyes met the shriveled eyes of the creature, he grunted in surprise. Just for a moment something had leaped across the mental divide between Hellboy and the massive stone figure. Like an intense but fleeting flash of light, Hellboy had the distinct sensation of a mind trying to communicate, of a soul touching his. He saw a confused jumble of faces in his mind's eye, some of which he recognized from grainy, photocopied mug shots that had been attached to the forensic reports of the murder victims. Then one particular face rose to the fore—green eyed and beautiful—and a voice softly spoke his name. He blinked and stared up into the unmoving face more avidly. The blue light in the Devil's Eye swirled like luminous mist.

"Cassie?" Hellboy murmured. "Is that you in there?"

The Leith creature didn't speak, but slowly it raised a hand in an oddly touching gesture of supplication. Hellboy hesitated a moment, then he took the hand in his own.

And suddenly he knew it was true. Unwillingly, Cassie and the others had given their blood, their lives, to open the Eye. Yet, it seemed that although the Eye had consumed their lives, it had not consumed their souls. Somehow Cassie's spirit, young and fresh and full of rage and goodness, had joined with the other souls trapped within the lodestone and had used the channels created by the final sacrifice to flood into Leith and overwhelm him. Or perhaps Leith himself, resentful of being betrayed and trapped, or weary and wanting nothing but release, had drawn Cassie and the others to him, opened himself up to them willingly.

All at once the massive, twisted shape that had once been Maximus Leith slipped its hand from his and crashed down onto its knees. Hellboy jumped back, thinking it was about to topple forward and crush him, but it remained on its knees, head bowed, as if in an attitude of prayer.

At first Hellboy thought that it was slipping back into its de-cadeslong sleep, that the spirits of Cassie and the others were vacating it or perhaps losing their influence over the vast stone body. But then he realized that in fact Leith or whoever inhabited him was simply offering himself—or more specifically, it was offering Hellboy the Eye, to do with as he wished.

Hellboy had no idea what would happen to Cassie and the others if he destroyed the Eye, but he knew he had no choice. He looked down at the floor, saw a curled fist that had been smashed clean off the wrist of one of the stone guardians, and picked it up, hefting it in his hand. It was heavy, and it would make a decent bludgeon. The Leith creature was still motionless, but the blue lights within the Devil's Eye were flickering madly, as if anticipating its fate. Hellboy drew back his arm and swung the stone fist right into the center of the Eye.

The Eye exploded with an eruption of blue-white energy, which blew Hellboy off his feet and halfway across the chamber. *Here we go again*, he thought, as he hurtled backwards through the air. Then he landed, crashing down onto hard, jagged rocks, and the world grayed out for a while.

He came to a couple of minutes later, groaning and shaking his head. Was it *really* possible to add any more pain to that which he'd already accumulated? Not for the first time that day, he staggered to his feet and stood swaying for a moment. When the walls stopped spinning, he looked across to where the Leith creature had fallen.

It too had been blown backwards when the Eye had been destroyed, and was now lying on its back, twisted and broken, some distance away. Most of the top of its head had shattered into fragments when the Eye had exploded, but despite this it was still moving feebly, like a beached fish in its last stages of suffocation.

Hellboy limped across to it and dropped to his knees. He looked into its dead eyes once again, but there was no flash of recognition now, no indication as to whether Cassie still inhabited the twisted, crystalline form. All the same, Hellboy shuffled forward and gently lifted the shattered head into his lap.

"I'm sorry," he mumbled simply.

In the cold gloom of the underground cavern, he sat with her a while, silent and alone.

EPILOGUE

"So all this muti stuff was just a red herring, then?" Liz said.

Abe shook his head. "Not at all. It was just Richard's area of expertise, which he adapted to open the Eye. I guess he stumbled across references to the Eye through his research, and found out that London had been built on a vast reservoir of energy which he thought was his for the taking."

"Energy that was already leaking through the cracks," said Liz.

"Yes, and which he was able to use to a limited degree."

"Like in Olusanya's flat, you mean? He was pretending to be scared when all that stuff was flying at me, but it was him all along, wasn't it?"

Abe nodded.

Liz looked disgusted. "That creep. I hate the fact that I didn't see through the guy. I hate the fact that I even *liked* him."

"We all did," Abe said. "You shouldn't blame yourself."

"I still should've seen it."

Liz walked across the hotel room and looked broodingly out of the window. Two days on from the chaos, and superficially London hardly seemed affected by what had happened.

"I'm not sure Hellboy ever liked him that much," she murmured.

"Hellboy never likes *anybody* that much," Abe said with just the barest suggestion of humor.

A tiny smile flickered across Liz's face. "That's what makes him such a good judge of character."

There was a short pause, then Abe asked, "How *is* Hellboy? Have you spoken to him this morning?"

"Only through the door. He grunted at me a couple times."

Abe nodded. Since Hellboy had emerged in a shocking state yesterday, having apparently spent the past twenty-four hours climbing an underground mountain several miles high, the two of them had had only a sketchy account of what had happened down in the bowels of the earth. All they knew for sure was that it had involved both Cassie and Maximus Leith, and that it had effectively killed the Eye energy stone dead.

When Abe and Liz had fled the house in Ranskill Gardens the night before last, the consequences of the final ceremony were already starting to be felt throughout London. The "eyes" which had opened up earlier that day had quickly begun to proliferate and widen, to run one into another, as the malign energy had poured through them. Within an hour, people affected by the energy had started to flood from the buildings in which they had earlier taken refuge and rampage through the streets, tearing frenziedly at each other like wild animals. Cars had been wrecked, buildings had been set on fire, and police and army personnel, who had been similarly affected, had added to the carnage by firing their weapons gleefully and indiscriminately into the crazed mob.

Casualties had been high. Even now, bodies were still being cleared from the streets and carried from houses and municipal buildings. It was thought that the death toll from the two hours of chaos that had swept through the city would eventually number in the thousands, and that criminal damage to property would run to millions of pounds.

"You knew Hellboy would come through for us, didn't you?" Liz said.

"I didn't know, but I hoped," Abe replied.

"And what if he hadn't stopped it? What would you have done then?"

"I would have done exactly the same as you."

"Which is?"

"Whatever was necessary."

Liz saw a black cab drive past the front of the hotel, a child walking hand in hand with its mother on the far side of the street. London had been devastated but life went on. What was it the Brits called it? The Dunkirk spirit.

There was a rap on the door. Not timid but respectful, mindful of the fact that the occupant might be sleeping. Liz expected it to be a hotel employee—one of the handful who had been fit enough, or desperate enough for money, to come back to work so soon after the terrible events of Wednesday night, when a pitched battle in the foyer had left five people dead and a dozen hospitalized—to let them know that their car was here to take them to the airport.

But then a voice, low and weary, said, "Guys?"

Liz ran across the room and yanked the door open almost hard enough to give herself whiplash.

"HB!" she cried.

He appeared a little taken aback by the enthusiasm of her greeting. There was a moment of uncharacteristically awkward silence, and then he muttered, "Mind if I come in?"

"Do you really need to ask?" said Liz, and dragged the door open wider, flattening herself against the wall to give him room to pass.

He ducked under the lintel and entered. He'd been in his room for the best part of the last twelve hours. Liz had assumed he was sleeping, but he might just have been brooding on events, running them over and over in his head. He still *looked* utterly beat, that was for sure. His shoulders were slumped, his lantern-jawed face was drawn, and every visible part of him aside from his stone hand was covered in cuts and bruises, bumps and lumps. He looked, in short, like a heavyweight boxer after a particularly bad mauling. The bridge of his nose was one huge scab and his left eye was a yellow slit within a swollen pouch of blackened flesh.

"How you guys doing?" he asked, looking around. "All packed up, I see."

Liz nodded. "How about you? Don't tell me you need me to close your suitcase again?"

He smiled a little at that. "Actually, that's what I wanted to talk to you about."

His words gave Liz a sudden hollow feeling in her stomach. "Oh?"

"Yeah, I . . . er . . . I think I'm gonna duck out for a while. Take a break."

"You mean you're not coming back with us?" Liz said, trying not to sound disappointed.

"Not just yet. I'll get a later flight. Coupla weeks, maybe."

"Where will you go?" Liz asked.

"Somewhere peaceful. The Cotswolds, maybe. I got friends there."

"The Finches?"

He nodded.

Liz put a hand on his arm. "We'll miss you," she said.

Hellboy looked embarrassed, awkward. "Yeah."

Abe had sat through the exchange silently. Now he said, "I think it's a good idea. Do you want us to let Tom know where you are?"

"Uh-uh," Hellboy said, shaking his head. "In fact . . ." He delved into the pocket of his duster and pulled out his satellite phone. "Take this back for me, willya?"

Liz took it off him almost reluctantly. "You won't stay away long, I hope."

Hellboy chuckled. "Nah, just when you least expect it, I'll turn up again like the proverbial bad penny. Always have, always will."

Then the laughter faded. His voice became gruff, somber.

"After all," he added, "what else can I do?"

MARK MORRIS became a full-time writer in 1988 on the Enterprise Allowance Scheme, and a year later saw the release of his first novel, *Toady*. He has since published a further thirteen novels, among which are *Stitch*, *The Immaculate*, *The Secret of Anatomy*, *Mr Bad Face*, *Fiddleback*, and *Nowhere Near an Angel*. His short stories, novellas, articles, and reviews have appeared in a wide variety of anthologies and magazines, and he is editor of the highly acclaimed *Cinema Macabre*, a book of fifty horror movie essays by genre luminaries, for which he won the 2007 British Fantasy Award. His latest novels are *Doctor Who: Forever Autumn*, which was voted best Doctor Who book of 2007 by readers of *Doctor Who magazine*, and *The Deluge*, published by Leisure Books in the U.S. Forthcoming work includes a novella entitled *It Sustains* and another book in the immensely popular Doctor Who series, *Ghosts of India*.

A new novel by the author
of *The Midnight Road*

EMERALD HELL
TOM PICCIRILLI

Hellboy created by Mike Mignola

Hellboy comes to the crossroads in Enigma, Georgia, a small town
plagued by strange occurences. Sent to keep an eye on Sarah Nail, a
young girl hiding from the curse of her family, Hellboy becomes en-
tangled in the blood debt of an evil mystical preacher, Brother Jester.
Stuck between human malice and the mysteries of the occult, Hellboy comes up against an intrigue of ghosts, demon trees, talking bull-
frogs, and a race of lost mutant children. Acclaimed horror author Tom
Piccirilli creates a thrilling new Hellboy tale that will chill the blood!

ISBN 978-1-59582-141-6 | $12.95